Rubicon Harvest

C. W. Kesting

Rubicon Harvest

Jon slowly turned to meet Lilly's gaze, then allowed his chin to sag heavily to his chest. He sighed deeply and shook his head while whispering, "I'm just not convinced that it's right. What if this were all meant to be? Part of some grand cosmic plan, and not to be messed with? Who am I to alter that? Who are you to decide how destiny should be played out?" He raised his tired face to her, imploring her with an exhausted gaze.

Lilly slowly shook her head and crossed her arms in front of her chest. "It's not about metaphysics and karma, you know that, Jon. We were meant to evolve, whether through natural selection or technological advances. How can we not offer a cure for a condition that would otherwise limit the way a fellow human being lives their life? How can we ignore obvious improvements in the way we experience our world?" She paused waiting for an adamant retort or emotional argument.

What They Are Saying About

Rubicon Harvest

Technology and medical research continue to take us far beyond what we have known. *Rubicon Harvest* by C. W. Kesting carries the reader even further; step by thrilling step. A strong premise captures readers; interesting characters and the stark issues underlying society draw you further into this world. You'll laugh, cry, cheer and curse, coming away subtly educated. And more importantly... you will be entertained!

—**lizzie starr*
~romance with a sparkling twist~

Chilling and intense, Kesting's *Rubicon Harvest* takes you to a time and place none of us really want to go... yet it's just around the corner. Strong descriptions and dialog lock you into the story and compel you along its dark journey into a society that seems all too real and inevitable, but shines here and there with the bright human qualities that flash hope and salvation against the architects of despair and destruction.

—G. David Clark
Sunset Dancer

Rubicon Harvest

C. W. Kesting

A Wings ePress, Inc.

General Fiction Novel

Wings ePress, Inc.

Edited by: Elizabeth Struble
Copy Edited by: Christie Kraemer
Senior Editor: Leslie Hodges
Managing Editor: Karen Babcock
Executive Editor: Lorraine Stephens
Cover Artist: Richard Stroud

All rights reserved

Wings ePress Books
http://www.wingsepress.com

Copyright © 2008 by Christopher Kesting
ISBN 918-1-59705-650-2

Published In the United States Of America

Wings ePress Inc.
3000 N. Rock Road
Newton, KS 67114

Dedication

Rubicon Harvest is dedicated to the undiscovered authors of tomorrow's stories.

A memory is what is left when something happens and does not completely unhappen.

—Edward de Bono

What does a fish know about the water in which it swims most of its life?

—Albert Einstein

Prologue

"Do you understand?"

The question resonated in his mind. The voice strange and electronically altered.

He remembers feeling himself nod in the affirmative, mentally detached, yet physically unhesitant as a silent scream of emotional defiance rose from deep within.

"I'd like you to verbalize your understanding for the record," the synthesized voice had commanded, reverberant in his head.

He felt his lips part as an involuntary response swelled in his throat and then fell out of his mouth entirely beyond his physical control.

"I will retire all active players present at the meeting," he had said. "Upon completion of this, I will immediately remove the component from operational status."

As he heard the words, the sound of his own voice had horrified him—familiar yet alien—chilling his blood. Another wave of fearful reluctance swept up from the depths of his soul then faded—a final smoldering ember of self-control.

What he *was* is now completely detached and isolated from what he has *become,* both physically and conceptually. His mind has lost ground to the invading presence in his head, stripped of the will to resist. His body is now a mere shell—an organic vehicle.

He remembers; even though They insist that after the Change memories are impossible. They are extremely intelligent, perhaps even geniuses, and he certainly gives Them credit where credit is due. But in this, They are wrong.

Memories echo.

They are seemingly much more than the electrochemical etchings imprinted upon the fleshy folds of the physical brain. There is substance and energy within them, and on some quantum level, he instinctively senses this as a universal truth as naturally as he experiences his own effortless heartbeat.

He would've liked to share this with Them as it might aid in the advancement of Their theories, correct Their misconceptions.

But he is unable. He has no control over his physical manifestation. His body had ceased being *his* soon after he awoke.

Now he sits and stares in reticent awe upon the fresh corpses, retired by his own hand in a flash of lightning quick precision. The remaining extracorporeal segment of his awareness wails in moral agony at the sight of the carnage, heavy with regret and suffocating in guilt.

Yet, his physical self simply sits, methodically preparing for the next step in the completion of the ordered task.

He has become a tool—an unwilling albeit effective and reliable instrument.

Upon completion of this, you will remove the component from operational status.

That directive echoes from the deeper levels of his memory, and though he realizes the implications of this single act; he cannot accept his inability to stop it.

Completely free from conscious control, he watches his hand as it deftly spins the ancient revolver, inverts it and raises it to his eye for a quick inspection of the cylinder. Light wisps of acrid smoke curl from the breach. Each of the six chambers holds a round—shiny brass casings—half of which are dimpled in the middle from the impact of the fallen hammer on the firing pin. The blued steel of the muzzle is still warm from the previous firings.

As he brings the weapon to bear upon its final target, the echo of his terminal directive lingers in the shadows of his fading memory:

...you will remove the component from operational status.

His physical body prepares to execute as he entertains one last cogent thought that could be considered wholly, and independently, his own:

Though, indeed, I still am; where will I go from here?

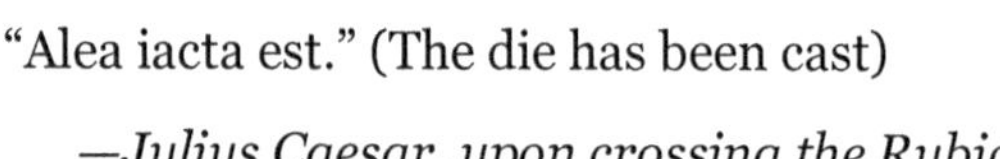

"Alea iacta est." (The die has been cast)

—*Julius Caesar, upon crossing the Rubicon*

One

Corpus Delicti

"Damn it!" He mumbled to himself as he reached for the thin vibrating object tucked tightly into his fabric belt.

Jon Webb shook his head, exhausted, as he strode past the reception kiosk of Corporate Campus security; oblivious to the curious glances as he read the incoming text page on his Penguin Personal Digital Device. The luminous screen of the PDD cast his face in eerie green phosphorescence. As he scanned the scrolling message his eyes widened, the moist curves of each globe reflecting the electric green glow from the flat LCD screen.

He sighed and let the PDD fall away from his hand. An invisible magnetic tether snared the small device in free fall, automatically pulled it back toward Jon's waist and resecured it firmly to his belt.

He turned and strode back toward the main bank of OmniVators. His thick fingers absently tapped the lightweight cover of the PDD affixed to his magnetic belt next to the plasma Fasor and the sleek, well-concealed 15mm Heston automag. He nonchalantly adjusted the crease in his vest and smoothed his dark uniform mock turtleneck while speaking in clipped phrases to the voice command module embedded in the smooth steel of the 'vator's twin control panels.

"Webb, Jon. Security. Novus Mordi one-five-six. Outbound request."

"Jonathan Webb," responded a pleasant, mechanical female voice. "Security director. Confirmed. Destination, please?"

"Delta Wing, fourth floor. Development and Engineering. Main Conference and Briefing." Paul MacDonald had now triple paged him, and for a man as measured and precise as MacDonald, that was twice too many. One did not ascend the biotech corporate ladder as rapidly as he by overreacting. Paul MacDonald had earned his rightful place beside Barrett Lacombe as Phoenix-Lamneth's second in charge through meticulous study, ruthless politics and a detail-oriented execution of action plans. He did not need to repeat himself.

As he waited for the 'vators arrival, Jon allowed his gaze to wander over the cavernous mezzanine of the Phoenix-Lamneth campus.

Rich dark hardwoods and glittering steel adorned Barrett Lacombe's kingdom. Smoked glass walls curved gently upward to merge with the grand four-story high ceilings draped in a plethora of synthetically fortified flora. Thick ropes of flowering ivy, heavily veined palm fronds and vibrant ferns swayed in the high currents of recirculated air. Throughout the spacious atrium, majestic stone and wooden pillars rose out of the polished marble floor, topped with glittering golden orbs.

"Hey, Jonno! Man, I thought I missed you. What's up?" A breathless voice approached from behind. The man exaggerated his exertion as if he had just run miles to get there.

"You're late," Jon snapped looking at the LCD screen mounted in front of him. His name, ID number and destination were displayed in cool blue against soft vanilla white.

He spoke sharply to the 'vators controls as he amended his request. "Add Donovan, Maxwell. Security. Novus Agus two-three-three. Override authority. Accompany by proximity."

"Maxwell Donovan. Security agent. Probationary. Confirmed. Please maintain one-hundred percent proximity," responded the female command.

"Gotta keep the new guy on a short leash, huh?" Max quipped referring to the computer's request for him to be chaperoned.

Jon gave the younger man a short, impatient glare then stepped through the smooth alloy portal when it silently snapped open. Max followed hesitantly taking up a position close to Jon's side despite the spacious interior of the cab.

Jon abruptly glanced at Max as the younger man sidled up close to him.

"What?" Max exclaimed defensively. "She wanted you to keep proximity. I'm just playing by the rules."

Jon simply glared, narrowing his sharp dark eyes.

Max got the hint and took two steps to his left as the portal whispered sharply closed. Shaking his head he mumbled, "Jesus—"

"Destination, Delta wing, fourth floor," instructed the soft and hidden female voice. "Confirm and execute."

"Execute." Jon sighed.

"Look, Jonny. I just want to try and get—"

"It's Jon. Not Jonny, Jock or any of those other fraternity buddy handles. Okay?" Jon snapped. "While we are on duty, I am not your best friend. I am your boss. I'm responsible for all of the security issues within this one hundred-fifty-acre campus. You are only one of hundreds of employees that I need to keep tabs on," Jon asserted.

His tone softened a bit when he realized his quick temper had once again flared.

"Look, I'm trying to do the job without allowing too much physical or emotional harm to come to either of us," he continued. "I choose to keep my professional distance while exercising my authority. It will work better that way. That being said, I'll be candid with you," he sighed.

"I'm impressed by your progress and believe you're evolving into one hell of a fine security officer. You need to work on your management skills, stop being a buddy to your subordinates and start making more on-the-spot corrections. Being well liked does not garner respect. Lead by example and you'll go far."

Jon turned slightly to catch and hold Max's eyes with his own hard gaze. "You do your job well and ensure that you don't make either one of us regret that I gave you this opportunity. Are we clear?"

"Christ, Jon. I just wanted to apologize for being late and try and clear the air between us. Look, I'm not going to stop trying to talk to you like a human. You choose to be the stoic, uptight asshole perfectionist and silent genius if you want. I ain't buying it." He paused and smiled. "At least not the genius part."

The OmniVator shifted ever so slightly as it traversed the horizontal plane of its vertical ascent and began moving laterally. The LCD on the wall in front of them displayed their position relative to rest of the sprawling Phoenix-Lamneth campus along with the elapsed time of their journey.

Jon's rigid face finally cracked, the corner of his mouth turned up into a smirk.

"Apology accepted," he said casually.

Max shook his head again and sighed. "So, what's the deal? I'm supposed to be heading home to a shot and a shower."

"Don't know. Just got a triple page from Paul MacDonald. A Priority Black, which means that only he knows. And, of course, Lacombe. Your presence as last night's supervisor was specifically requested."

"By name?" Max asked, surprised.

Jon frowned at the younger man and his wild unkempt dark hair that was the style. Max looked much younger than his actual thirty-five years. Untested confidence flashed under every wry smile, sparks of wit and innocent mischief etched the surface of his deep blue eyes. Max was a handsome, confident young man, but at this moment he appeared fragile and weak in the dim light of the 'vator. He appeared spooked and concerned—a look Jon hadn't seen from the man in many years. It worried him.

"Do you believe that the office of the CEO actually knows you even exist?" Jon asked him honestly.

"God, I hope to hell not." Max smiled wanly.

Jon felt a sudden twinge of compassion for his longtime friend. Max had only been on the job three months, brought in by Jon himself after assisting the younger man in wrestling some personal demons back into their closet. Max's fall from grace came on the heels of Jon's own dance with personal turmoil, and throughout their fifteen-year history, the two men had always been there for one another.

"Hey, relax. I'm sure this is just about that big brief coming up. If anything were truly amiss, with you or your performance, P-Mac would just let me handle it. And I haven't heard anything detrimental." Jon eyed Max carefully. "Is there any reason I should be concerned, Max?"

"Absolutely not," Max blurted out trying not to sound defensive.

"Now is the time. Be smart and tell me if there is."

Max looked directly into Jon's eyes, the young confidence flooding back into his smooth face. Max seemed to know that his old friend was asking an unspoken question: *Are you still clean?*

"Nothing to tell, boss. Last night was slow and quiet."

"Then you have nothing to worry about." Jon eased his hands into the pockets of his crisp dark cargo pants and sighed as he stared through the brushed steel of the 'vators interior walls.

The OmniVator hummed to its programmed stop and engaged the arrival station with a soft click. The portal whispered open as the soft feminine voice welcomed them to their destination.

~ * ~

They walked down the curving hallway; past brushed silver doors with granite and marble-cased doorways and small alcoves of mahogany and oak sitting benches. An occasional flat screen display illuminated the corridor with simple prints of landscapes, seascapes and skylines.

The hallway eventually opened into a spacious reception area with a modest streamlined wraparound workstation. It was presently deserted. Jon moved to the inside of the desk and activated the slim computer. It routinely asked for a password and codon. Jon attempted his verbal identification cue and standard security override codon without success. The screen remained locked.

"Well, at least all the reconfigs are still in order. I rejuiced this sector myself yesterday in prep for the brief. MacDonald has claimed an official Priority Black. It's all locked down," Jon explained.

"Gentleman," a distant, tinny voice emanated from a hidden speaker. "If you could please join us in the lounge, down Apple Hall."

The corridors in the Development and Engineering wing were all named after historical pioneers in the technology game, a kind of homage to the groundbreakers and risk takers of the past. Gates Hall, Yuegisto Hall, Mendel Hall, Sakamoto Hall and twenty others spiraled off from the main hub of the D and E reception area like great spokes in a wheel. Each corridor led to labs, offices and information vaults, all unique to the various technological disciplines that grew out of the fertile soil of Phoenix-Lamneth Corporation.

Jon and Max approached the threshold of Apple Hall, sealed by a heavy steel-reinforced oak door securely locked by four independently automated sliding bolts, each about two feet in length and nearly three inches in diameter. The bolts firmly engaged the stone and steel jamb of the doorway. A small octagonal panel embedded to the right of the door one and a half meters off the floor contained the whole of the security measures.

Jon activated the panel by pressing a pressure sensitive strip just below the frame. A small drawer rotated outward and angled slightly down, revealing a smooth number pad containing all ten digits arranged in random fashion. The holographically projected positions of the numbered touch pads changed randomly with each user. Jon entered his personal code and waited. Seconds later a thin, clear flat plate slid horizontally out of the lower half of the panel and a small drawer popped open to the right. Jon withdrew a small clear mouthpiece from the drawer and placed it in his mouth, leaving a small clear tube dangling from the front. He inserted the tube into a small oval opening in the upper portion of the panel, placed his hands palms down on the flat plate, took a deep breath and exhaled gently and evenly. Condensation formed in the tube and the glass plate glowed brilliantly, illuminating his hands from below.

Jon held this position for a few seconds as a thin slot opened in the panel at approximately eye level. A narrow arc of shiny metal rotated out toward Jon's forehead, which he leaned into until the strip of metal wrapped snugly across his brow. He looked directly into the open slot as a dim orange laser traced a thin vertical line across his face. After a second or two of humming, two distinct clicks reverberated through the machinery.

Two of the four bolts in the door rotated evenly one complete revolution; there was a pause and then the remaining two bolts rotated as well. They did not retract, but remained engaged in the thick wall.

"What, it didn't like you?" Max asked awed equally by the complexity and the paranoia.

"No, it was programmed for two entrants, not just one. They're expecting us both. You need to be scanned. You're not cleared for this area. No one is, in fact, unless I juice them in. Of course, MacDonald, Lacombe and the D&E guys have their own access," Jon explained.

"So—"

"So, step to the plate and blow some DNA into the brain box." Jon gestured with his hand for Max to do just that.

Max grabbed a second disposable mouthpiece, raised his eyebrows at Jon and shrugged. He placed the plastic in his mouth, secured the tube with his teeth and pushed the free end into the hole as Jon did. He then cautiously laid his hands palms down on the flat glass. He began to take a deep breath when Jon stopped him with a hand on his shoulder.

"Wait a sec. It needs to *not* recognize you. It will then ask for a one time authorization which I can input."

The LCD screen glowed dull white and then queued up an inquiry in five different languages. The same phrase appeared in sharp green-blue font, written in English, Spanish, Japanese, Arabic and French: *Unknown subject. Request authority override and verification. Enter codon for initialization.*

Jon reached for the numbered keypad and began typing numbers. As each number was entered, a slight flicker flashed across the smooth holographic touch pad and the numbers randomly scrambled.

"Keeps unauthorized entrants like yourself from memorizing the pattern of the inputted numbers," Jon explained.

Max quickly looked down and realized that from this angle he couldn't even see the actual digits displayed; they were a translucent blur no matter how hard he strained to get a glimpse. No chance to memorize the numbers themselves either. Max nodded, clearly impressed.

"Okay, you're ready. Just exhale slow and even and keep your palms flat. The plate gets real warm, real quick," Jon advised.

"These new multifactorial biometric scanners have revolutionized access security," Jon said. "Core DNA and enzymatic samples from exhaled moisture, bilateral palmar printing, body temperature validation, and of course, retinal scan." The orange laser stroked across Max's face.

"Gone are the days of faking prints from latex peals or trying to pass off sampled saliva. With the simultaneous scan and thermal verification, it's nearly impossible to fake it. If all the data doesn't come from the same living source, it's over. One hundred joules of plasma at thirty hertz zaps you into helpless Jell-O, you fall to the floor and we come and scoop you up," Jon explained.

The display flashed clear and then in multiple languages: *Expressed entry granted for subject Donovan, Maxwell, in proximity with Webb, Jonathan. Period of approval - two hours.*

The security panel closed silently and a small square tray and opening presented itself at the base of the wall to the right of the door. Jon dropped his plastic mouthpiece onto the tray, as did Max. A soft whirring sound emanated from the opening as the tray retracted.

"Incinerator," Jon indicated with a wave of his hand. "Door won't open until we've destroyed the mouthpieces."

On cue, the steel bolts smoothly slid from the socket in the jamb and the door silently swung open.

"After you, sergeant." Jon followed Max through the door.

~ * ~

The two men walked down the wide carpeted corridor toward a large tinted glass wall. As they drew within a few feet, the smooth surface of the glass creased and swung open toward them. A man in a dark gray suit stepped out from behind.

Paul MacDonald stood over six feet, with the athletic build of a lean wide receiver, his face a stern and chiseled bust of confidence and success framed by perfectly sculpted raven black hair. He seemed to hover purposefully rather than stand, poised to strike with deliberate deadliness.

He gracefully swept his right hand out and then back toward his broad chest, a gesture meant to summon the two security men forward without delay. His two middle fingers were adorned with large, masculine gold rings that glimmered with prismatic and ornate gems. His metallic gray eyes bore into Jon and Max never once blinking or wavering.

The men approached and MacDonald smoothly tossed the glass door the rest of the way open with a strong and sure flick of his wrist as he edged slightly out the way. They passed the silent centurion as his eyes followed their every step. Max held his hand out to MacDonald.

"Max Donovan," he introduced himself.

MacDonald simply stared at the younger man's smiling face. His steely eyes flicked down at the extended hand for just a fraction of a moment then returned to Max's puzzled eyes. MacDonald shook his square head once to the side, almost imperceptibly, and never made a move to shake the offered hand.

"Mr. Webb, would you please accompany Mr. Donovan to the table and take up positions on either side of the recorder while facing the detective," MacDonald commanded in a deep and stern voice.

Max and Jon briefly glanced at one another and then cautiously moved toward the long, smoked glass table. They each took a black metal swivel chair flanking either side of a flat silver box situated in the middle of the table. Opposite them sat a quiet, yet watchful man. He allowed a soft and welcoming smile to cross his narrow and angular face. His eyes were mellow and sleepy, set closely astride a straight and cutting nose. He ran thin fingers through his long, dark hair, smoothly feathering the wavy strands from his brow.

"Gentlemen," the man leaned across the table and greeted them each with a sweeping handshake. "I'm Detective Gionetti, Western Federal Homicide, LA County division."

His eyes softened sympathetically, almost sadly, as he embraced each of the men's hands in a firm and commanding shake. He held each of their gazes an equal amount of time, then glanced toward MacDonald, yet still directed his comment to the two seated men.

"By the looks on your faces, I'd say this is probably the first time you gentlemen have been made aware that there exists a situation that requires my services?" Gionetti let his disapproving gaze linger on the stalking figure of MacDonald.

MacDonald returned Gionetti's barbed comment and stare with a stern, forceful tilt of his chiseled head and a slight sneer as he replied defensively. "This has been a Priority Black situation that requires the most severe and stringent discretion. Mr. Webb is our interim Chief of Security and Mr. Donovan there," he nodded toward the man, "was the security house supervisor on last evening's shift. They're the only Security personnel who need to be involved at this juncture and were to be notified at the appropriate time, only after the discovery had been contained—"

"And that time is now, Detective," a stern voice interrupted MacDonald from the open doorway.

A small, soft, tired man shuffled into the room from behind MacDonald and leaned against the mirrored wall directly opposite the men seated at the table.

"So if you would, please begin your inquiries and get me some damned answers." Barrett Lacombe's already thin voice faded as he let his gaze drift up to the ceiling. The chief executive sighed deeply and then leveled his tiny black eyes at Gionetti, arching his eyebrows to pose either a question or administer a threat.

Detective Gionetti had turned around in his chair, his arm resting on the curved back, and he now met Lacombe's gaze with wide and curious eyes. He paused a moment, on the verge of saying something in recovery, thought better of it and swiveled back toward the seated security agents. "Of course," Gionetti said. "We should begin."

He noted the puzzled looks on the faces of the men before him. He dug into the deep pocket of his long leather overcoat draped over the chair to his right and withdrew a thin silver remote control.

"Gentlemen, I am here to investigate the violent slayings of four Phoenix-Lamneth employees."

He pointed the remote at the flat, steel box lying in the center of the table. It softly whirred to life as the top wound up and out like fabric accordion springs, thinning as it grew to eye level with the seated men. A bluish-orange plane of coherent light flashed from the top of the alloy cone in a sharp snap. The thin fan of light swept in the horizontal plane three hundred-sixty degrees before locating and then oscillating between the two security officers.

The sliver-thin vector of light thrummed with subaudible harmonics as it collected visual and audio data, detected micro changes in surface temperature of the skin as capillaries either flushed or drained, sensed nano-unit changes in intraocular pressure within the globe of the eye and evaluated heart rate and respiratory quality for subtle alterations, all in an effort to ascertain the truthfulness of responses from interviewees.

Successful results with the PALM, or Physiologic Analytical Logic Matrix, required the skillful employment of carefully crafted questions and the utilization of psychological nuances by a masterful interviewer.

Detective Salvatore Gionetti had chosen to go with a straight, undiluted approach with the two security officers and it was clear that his blunt delivery of the news of the murders and the intimidating presence of the PALM recorder had the desired effect on the two security officers.

At first, Jon and Max just stared at one another, then scanned the room for confirmation from the other men. MacDonald stood with his feet shoulder-width apart and arms tightly crossed. His unblinking eyes darted between Jon and Max. He said nothing.

Lacombe remained leaning against the glass wall, his arms loosely draped behind his back, his face tilted upward with his eyes closed. He also said nothing.

"Who—how—" was all that Max could manage before Gionetti continued.

"Sometime last evening. We'll have a narrower window after the post mortem is complete, but it looks to be sometime just before midnight. Four Phoenix Lamneth employees were executed within these walls."

Jon immediately looked around, wide-eyed and disbelieving.

"Oh no, not this exact room," Gionetti explained reading the man's surprise. "But in this wing of the building. Well within the ironclad security around us. We'll take a walk down to the scene shortly. I really wanted to establish some ground work, get a foundation established and kind of ease into this with you."

Gionetti paused a moment to allow the initial shock pass and the dust to settle. He glanced over his shoulder to see Barrett Lacombe slowly massaging the bridge of his nose between his thumb and forefinger. The man's eyes were clenched and he seemed to be holding his breath. He looked as if he had slept in his eight thousand dollar suit.

It was only then that Gionetti noticed the man's shoes. The most powerful man in the Western half of the continent and the grandfather of twenty-first century biomedical technology was wearing leather moccasin-style slippers, well worn and untied.

Gionetti felt a mix of pity and sympathy for the man. Despite Lacombe's lofty perch atop the corporate universe, he was globally well liked by the public, and if not envied, at least respected by his peers and competitors, of which there were few. This tragedy had obviously exhausted him.

Gionetti turned back to the seated men. They stared back hungry for explanation. Their eyes searched for understanding and clarification.

He forged on.

"I gotta tell you, though, with all of this high-speed technology and wizardry around us..." He swept both arms back with dramatic flair. "I'm a little baffled as to how anyone could enter this facility with *any* sort of weapon, especially an obsolete firearm, access what is essentially a vault—undetected—and kill four highly regarded scientists at point blank range with head shots in close quarters and then slip out. Again, undetected." He raised a questioning eyebrow at the security men.

At the mention of the four victims, Lacombe caught his breath and moaned, shifting his weight from shoulder to hip as he remained against the wall.

Jon looked blankly at his hands, idle and folded loosely on the table. He wished for a glass of something to drink—water, or even better, the smoky sourness of a tight bourbon. He felt as if he should say something—anything—yet, he fought the urge.

It was obvious that Gionetti was skillful at playing the interview game; waiting for information to be freely volunteered; leaving silent, open spaces between shocking bits of facts, baiting the interviewee to nip at the hook and roll over to reveal a weakness. Jon was familiar with the tactic and held his ground. This was one huge revelation, and he was sure there was more to come.

Max, however, was less experienced and squirmed next to him, restless and wanting to speak, to act. Jon sensed that he was going to give in to the urge to do something, and before he could intervene, Max began stammering, "How could this be? I mean, it's impossible. Last night was quiet. I would've been alerted to any breach. This is crazy. I—"

"Enough, you fucking asshole!" MacDonald erupted. "This had to be an inside job, and if you're not directly responsible, then you're somehow involved!" Paul MacDonald glared at the stunned man defying him to defend himself.

Gionetti cringed at the verbal explosion, immediately swung toward the enraged executive and stifled him with a single look. MacDonald blinked and cocked his head to the side as if to say *What? What did you expect from him, a confession?*

Gionetti had clearly lost the advantage and was about to work out a recovery strategy when MacDonald suddenly flared back up and began to berate the two seated men.

"And you, Webb. Do you have anything to add? This shit bag is your responsibility! And now you—No, we—have four fucking bodies on our hands. Just what in the—"

"Paul," Barrett Lacombe calmly asserted. "Paul, that's quite enough." He glanced over at his assistant with the impatient yet sympathetic look of a master remorseful over his dog's behavior but realizing that it's much too late to retrain.

"Detective Gionetti, please continue," Lacombe said calmly. Then he addressed Webb and Donovan. "Gentlemen, no one has been formally charged with anything, and though the circumstances are quite bizarre and, to be brutally honest, suspicions are understandably high, we all want to do the right thing and get to the bottom of this tragedy." Lacombe glanced tiredly at Gionetti. The detective took his cue and immediately regained control of the situation.

"Look," he began, "I need to establish a timeline for last evening's security personnel—essentially where was everyone, and how did this go undetected. We have a serious and delicate situation here." Gionetti glanced around at the two executives standing just behind him.

"I thought that we might as well go down to the scene and begin there," Gionetti suggested.

Against Lacombe and MacDonald's wishes, Gionetti was planning to show the murder scene to the men. Usual protocol required strict isolation of any murder scene, to facilitate collection of uncontaminated evidence and complete examination of the bodies. However, this situation was other than usual.

The executives of Phoenix-Lamneth seemed convinced of inside involvement, and in light of the high security measures necessary to access the areas within the corporation, the suspect pool dramatically narrowed to those with immediate access.

Gionetti seemed inclined to agree with the head executives and was assuming a huge risk in potentially contaminating the crime scene. Apparently, his instincts told him there could be some beneficial gain from their visceral reactions to the carnage down the hall.

Gionetti rose to his feet and clasped his hands together, gazing first at Barrett Lacombe, then MacDonald. Lacombe glanced at the floor and audibly sighed while MacDonald continued to glare at the seated security officers. Gionetti addressed Webb and Donovan as he turned to the glass door.

"Gentlemen, if would please join us." He paused and allowed Paul MacDonald to lead the way.

Webb and Donovan had risen and walked somberly out of the conference room behind the VP, followed closely by Lacombe with Gionetti bringing up the rear.

The hall was carpeted in light tan and green Berber splashed with interlacing patterns of swirls and spirals. The firm surface muffled their footfalls as the group stepped down the corridor past evenly spaced mirrored doors and handsomely crafted dark wood walls. Twenty meters ahead at the intersection of a second corridor, two thick, frosted glass double doors lay waiting, partially open. Bright fluorescent light spilled out from the interior of the room, casting a slanted angle of pearly whiteness across the patterned carpet.

MacDonald stopped short of the threshold, stepping aside and reluctantly deferring control of the situation to the detective. Gionetti stepped to the front, casually inserting himself between MacDonald and the two security officers. He turned toward the group and caught Lacombe rubbing the palms of his hands into his eyes, attempting to massage away the exhaustion and tension. Gionetti passed out thin, nonlatex gloves to the men.

The inspector back stepped into the room as he absently pulled on his own pair of gloves, signaling for the men to follow. He studied Webb and Donovan as they entered. The detective spoke as the two men took in the scene before them.

"As you can see, we have four dead bodies. Shot at point blank range. What you see now is exactly how the scene was discovered by Mr. MacDonald at 5:45 this morning." The detective allowed the scene to speak for itself. His eyes never left the faces of the two security men.

At the center of the room, four steel-framed, leather upholstered chairs were situated evenly about a large square glass and steel table. A body occupied each chair, three of which appeared to have placed their heads down on the cool thick glass surface of the table for a quick nap, the peaceful suggestion of which was betrayed by the congealed puddles of blood that all but completely covered the surface of the table.

Thick, irregular clots of hair, bone and grayish-white brain matter lay embedded throughout the blood slick. The surface of the coagulated blood had actually become wrinkled, as if a large quantity of scarlet pudding was left to mature on a counter top, its fibrous skin growing thick over the hours. A quantity of the dark fluid had dripped over one edge of the table and collected in a thick, sticky puddle soaking the carpet a rich burgundy. Small tendrils of the bloody gel had clotted in mid-drip, like bitter black frosting on a macabre cake.

The fourth body was also seated, facing the doorway; however, the chair was pushed away from the table. He slumped awkwardly in the chair, his head hung low, chin against his chest. Precious blood from a head wound had pumped not onto the glass surface of the table to mingle with that of his colleagues, but rather had flowed freely down his torso, pooled in his lap and spilled across his thighs, soaking the leather seat and the carpet beneath.

His arms hung limply at the sides, the cuffs of his suit jacket filled with clotted purple fluid. The wall behind him was flecked and streaked with fan sprays of blood, as if some winged creature—perhaps a fallen, angry angel—had left its photographic shadow emblazoned on the smooth cream-colored plastic surface.

All four of the bodies were dressed in fine professional attire. The three men wore charcoal or gray suits with sensible yet attractive shoes, while the female was in a sheer blouse, modest navy skirt and low heels. Their carefully chosen wardrobes now forever stained with liters of thick, spoiling blood.

Only three of the four bodies around the table wore thin white lab coats over their clothes, unbuttoned and spread open beneath their slumped forms. A small plastic rectangular badge was clipped to each of the exposed lapels of the white clinical jackets. Upon each badge, the holographic logo of Phoenix-Lamneth Corporation glinted and wavered in the fluorescent lighting: A golden, gothic bird ascending through a blazing inferno of flames that engulfed a green and blue sphere; superimposed over a silhouette of a nondescript man and woman reaching earnestly toward an elaborate streaming fountain. The laser inscribed holographic images alternated in clarity and detail as the angle of view changed.

A pair of thin, wire-framed eyeglasses laid to the side of the female's head, frozen in the gelled glop, the lenses smeared and dark.

The scene was violent and complete. The air held the rich tang of acidic copper that overpowered an underlying hint of something almost sweet, but not quite.

Max Donovan remained frozen at the entrance to the boardroom, his hand slowly working at his lips, twisting and pulling as he took in the grisly scene. Paul MacDonald silently eased up behind him and whispered in his ear, causing him to jump.

"Think we'll find any prints in all that mess? Or DNA?" Max flinched, but never took his eyes off the bodies. Paul pulled back and softly clicked his tongue a few times, drawing a quick and scolding glance from Lacombe.

Jon Webb had carefully moved into the room and was slowly circling the table, watching his footing to ensure he avoided the spilled pools of gore. His face remained unbroken with reaction, almost stoic. His eyes darted over the horror as he appeared to file and categorize each detail. Gionetti noticed the man's approach and tact as one of experience and design.

Sal Gionetti pulled his Personal Digital Data device from his belt and began tapping out instructions, and after a few seconds began to read from the small screen's display.

"According to the security entry logs, each of the victims clocked through the main threshold here in D and E between 23:45 and 23:55. It would appear that they were having some sort of late night meeting." Sal glanced over at Lacombe and MacDonald. "Perhaps we'll know more once the ID's are finalized," he continued.

"I guess I'd like to know a little bit about the status of the security at that time." The detective gazed directly at Max Donovan, who was still wide-eyed from the scene before him.

Jon Webb continued his quiet perusal of the room.

"Mr. Donovan," Gionetti repeated, "As the security officer on duty last night, could you enlighten us? Where were you at that time?"

Max blinked twice, as if to clear his vision and cocked his head to the side. He glanced toward Webb for guidance, but Jon was inspecting the wall behind the fourth victim—the man who was seated away from the table. The body without a lab coat.

MacDonald jabbed Max in the small of the back and snarled between clenched teeth, "Answer the man, asshole!" Then he spoke louder as he noticed Webb crouching behind the fourth body.

"Hey! Webb! What the fuck are you doing? Get away from there! Get your ass back over here!" Then, to detective Gionetti, he said, "Should he be back there? I mean, this is a crime scene, for Christ's sake. What if something gets fucked up? Contaminated?"

Then Paul turned to Lacombe. "Shit, I knew this was a bad idea. I mean—"

"Mr. Webb, please, he's right," Gionetti expressed. "Would you please come away from there? I think we've seen enough here."

Jon rose slowly, still intently studying the lower half of the wall behind the coatless victim. As he turned to leave, his gaze fell on the body itself, inspecting, almost searching. Reluctantly, he joined the men at the door.

The detective turned to Lacombe, ignoring MacDonald for the moment.

"Sir, we should probably return to the conference room and record our formal statements. I have what I had hoped for from here. The Forensics team will finish processing the scene and remove the materials accordingly. I see no need for your continued presence at this time. Unless, of course, you prefer to stay."

Lacombe nodded gently and looked at MacDonald. "No, detective. We'll leave you to complete the interviews. Paul, I'll need you. After you escort these gentlemen back to the conference room."

With that, Barrett Lacombe turned on his heels and strode rapidly down the hall, hands deep in the pockets of his baggy trousers.

MacDonald turned to allow the men to exit the room and followed as they marched slowly back to the interview room.

Two

Jon's head swam in a gossamer fog after meeting with the investigating detective. Since the revelation of the murders and seeing the bodies, he had been acting on survival instinct alone. It was only now, as the 'vator doors whispered open to allow the passengers exit that he began to feel somewhat grounded.

Men and women of varying size and ethnicity swam around him as they exited the 'vator, melting into the mass of bodies that moved forward to enter the conveyance. The tide of bodies, clothed in gray and beige work tunics, business suits and modest casual attire ebbed out ahead of him, slowly thinning as the gel of humanity spread across the marbled floor of the mezzanine.

Jon allowed the current to carry him to the right, toward the information kiosk embedded at the base of a tall ivory marble column.

He had experienced a silent epiphany while riding the 'vator down and now sensed that he might find what he was looking for there.

As he approached the wraparound counter of dark wood and stone, he locked eyes with the attendant manning the information station. She was young and dark, with a friendly and professional manner. Her smile announced that she was excellent at public service, and that if she couldn't answer your question then she wouldn't rest until she found someone who could. Jon hoped for his sake that this were true.

He drew close to the counter as the young girl adjusted her position and readied herself to be of assistance with a firming of her face and a gentle squaring of her shoulders.

Then, as suddenly as it struck, the flimsy intuition that presented itself moments ago in what appeared to be a solid epiphany began to fade, receding into the foggy shadows of his rattled mind. He was slowly losing grasp of the idea, desperately in need for that single bit of fact that would cement the whim into a solid nugget, subject to immediate recall as easily as one's own name. He felt as if he were suddenly and unexpectedly shaken from a deep and vivid dream whose details were slowly fading, yet the emotional effects still resonated.

The girl behind the counter proffered a winning smile and addressed Jon. "Good morning, sir. How can I help you?"

Jon pulled short of the counter by four feet and glanced to either side of the enclosure.

Multiple flat Holo screens covered the walls on both sides, displaying campus directories, real time news reports, three dimensional interactive maps, market tickers and a variety of corporate advertisements. He mentally struggled to regain the tenuous hold on the thought that brought him here, but was loosing in the effort.

Shit! What was that thought, something about… what, food? No. Drink—or maybe a party. Damn, it was so simple, and yet so vague.

"Sir, is there something—" she repeated.

"Mr. Webb!" a voice echoed through the lobby. "Jonathan Webb!" Jon turned, startled. The ghost thought vanished completely.

The young girl frowned slightly and was about to repeat her inquiry when Jon addressed her absently. "Thanks. No, I got it."

He scanned the crowd for the source of the call as a gentle tug at his elbow stunned him. He turned quickly with his hands raised in a defensive posture.

"Whoa! Easy big fella." Detective Gionetti stood there with his hands partly raised in mock surrender. "Sorry to spook you; I just didn't want to lose you in this crowd." He smiled, soft and genuine, as he swept his gaze across the open expanse of the lobby. "God, this place is huge. I never cease to be amazed at the grand spectacle of it all." Gionetti shook his head slowly, still smiling. "I definitely ended up in the wrong line of work. Should have studied more at the University."

Jon cocked his head to the side and contemplated a selection of responses. He was to be cautious around the inspector. Despite his amiable approach and casual banter, a detective never quit working. He was still fishing and wasn't going to go away.

Gionetti's face cracked instantly and his poise stiffened as he sighed heavily and met Jon's direct stare.

"Okay, so I guess I shouldn't waste the 'good ole buddy' routine on the likes of you, huh?" Gionetti offered. "You're not likely to buy that box of shit anyway, are you"? Gionetti smiled again and let a small satisfying breath whisper past his thin lips. "Look, Webb. Let me buy you a coffee and you and I can have a little talk. As a professional courtesy from one detective to another. What do you say?"

Jon hesitated and was about to form a polite response in the negative when Gionetti reached out and took a non-threatening, yet firm grasp of his elbow. Their eyes met and Jon suddenly felt lost again in a haze of confusion and uncertainty.

"One coffee, we sit and have a short and comfortable talk. We both may learn a little something." Gionetti smiled again, this time confident and assured.

~ * ~

They brought their tall thermal coffee containers through the crowd and found a small glass table near the fountain at the center of the courtyard. The sun baked the interior of the enclosed atrium in a blanket of radiance that refracted through the thick glass dome in a hazy prismatic display. Despite the frigid temperature outside, the air within the atrium was warm and humid, a vestige reminder of temperate California winters recently passed.

Jon and the detective sat across from one another silently sipping their beverages, each casually eyeing the crowd. After a few moments, Gionetti broke the silence.

"So, you were a New England Trans-county ID before the Fed assumed control?"

Somewhat stunned at first, Jon was silent. Then, realizing that the inspector had clearly done his homework, he nodded in resignation.

Before his current tenure as security chief, he had spent eight years on the New England and Boston Counties Inspector Detective Special Unit: A crack team of low profile, field expedient detectives who took on the tough, cold homicide cases that had plagued the East Coast during the turbulent post war decade. Most of the cases they worked back then involved high-profile community and governmental leaders—corporate and academic executives, senatorial assistants, political lobbyist—all either murdered or abducted by extreme activists during the era of special congressional hearings simply known as The Great Debates.

"Crazy fucking times, I guess," Gionetti added. "I was in China then, with the EuroCom STR. The First of the Seventh, cleaning up after the WEC rolled through." He sighed and looked vaguely distant. "Now that was some bizarre shit…" He shook his head and took a slow, careful sip of coffee. Jon eyed the man questioningly.

The First of the Seventh European Command Special Tactics and Reconnaissance (STaR), or Black Hands, were an elite covert special operations military unit put together during the aftermath of the invasions into Saudi Arabia to address the issue of reintegrating plausible governments within those countries ultimately conquered by the U.S. and European-led World Economic Coalition.

As a collection of the finest military operatives from all branches of the Armed Forces, the Black Hands ensured political and economical stability through the employment of extreme measures from within countries under reconstruction. Their tactics usually involved locating and eliminating rebel and terrorist opposition and extracting information from insurgents by less than gentle means.

Jon Webb was, himself, an ex-soldier having served a six-year stint as an Army Ranger before getting put out on a bogus and crafty medical discharge. He spent three of those years in the sand fighting next to Marines and British soldiers during the Arabian Wars, and while in Saudi, he had witnessed the Black Hands exercise their craft on the remaining ruling families of the region.

In less than one month, all of the remaining Saudi royalty were thoroughly expunged. High echelon relations with every extreme terrorist cell throughout Asia and Europe—large or small, Muslim or Irish Catholic—were exposed by name and location, and every dollar of terrorist funding seized and traced to its source.

The Black Hands achieved in three weeks what western democracy had struggled vainly with for over twenty years. And they didn't lose a single man in the process.

Jon took a long sip from his coffee and raised an eyebrow at the detective. The inspector noticed this and chuckled softly as he shook his head.

"Ah, a Doubting Thomas in the crowd. No matter. You'll believe what you want, regardless. I just thought you'd like to know that we do have something in common. I've nothing to gain from exaggeration or elaboration. After all, I'm not the one suddenly finding myself on administrative probation, curfew, and quite honestly; at the top of a very short list of suspects tagged for a high profile multiple murder."

With that, Jon stiffened and, for the first time in a long time, felt white-hot rage well up from deep within his bowels.

There it was now—out in the open. He was formally considered a suspect in the case. He glared at the detective and for a brief moment his mind flashed red with violent intent. He envisioned smashing the smaller man's face down on the table with one quick shot to the back of the head; ramming splintered fragments of his nose into the soft brain tissue behind his narrow eyes.

The instant passed as quickly as it appeared, and Jon flared his nostrils with a deep and controlled inhale. All the while Gionetti kept his gentle and sleepy gaze distant and slightly away from Jon's direct stare.

Now the detective turned purposefully toward the larger man, focused his light green eyes on Jon's stern, yet trembling features.

"If you pause for just a moment and consider the implications of any action you may take from this point on," the detective began, "you would have to agree that if there ever was a time when the phrase 'discretion is the better part of valor' applied... this would most certainly be that time." Gionetti allowed his statement to gain potency within the silence that followed.

Then he added, "Of course, it's early in the investigation, and we obviously don't have enough to formally pursue anyone. You are only one of many whom I'd like to question, but frankly, I want to begin with you. I think you have some definite ideas about this situation and I'd like to hear what they are."

Gionetti leaned toward Webb and eyed him knowingly. "I watched you case that room like a seasoned investigator."

Gionetti's facial features softened and the friendly, sleepy countenance reappeared. "So, as the Director of Security for Phoenix-Lamneth Corporation, what are your thoughts on how all of this could've happened?" He fell back into his chair and crossed his arms

"Interim Director," Jon replied quietly.

"Hmm?" Gionetti leaned forward. It was the first time Webb had spoken this morning aside from his recorded testimony, and Gionetti was again surprised by the gentle baritone.

"I was brought in as interim chief nearly two months ago. The old guy was being groomed for a new position up in one of the exec's offices. Serving coffee and kowtowing to the circus of suits, or something," Jon replied.

Gionetti nodded empathetically at the blue-collar barb.

"So, I'm acting chief until they find a permanent replacement." Jon rubbed the back of his neck.

"They ever offer the position to you? Permanently, I mean," Gionetti asked.

"Never really came up. Not sure that I'd want it. Not very stimulating. Way too much like the Army." Jon hesitated and then added, "Actually kinda boring. Until today."

"Yeah, until today," Gionetti echoed. "So, about today—or last night, actually. Your thoughts?" Gionetti narrowed his eyes to give the impression that whatever Webb had to say next was the most important thing he had to listen to.

"I don't know. I mean, with the way it looks; yeah, I gotta think inside job. But I just can't get my mind around that right now. It's hard to figure why those four particular people were whacked."

"So you buy the execution angle?" Gionetti looked slightly surprised.

"Yeah, I guess. Why? You think otherwise?" Jon asked.

"No. I mean, I don't think it was a suicide pact or anything. We'll know more when the PM is complete." Gionetti dismissed the line of inquiry and changed tack, but Jon made a mental note of the inspector's hesitant eyes and small twitch at the corner of his mouth.

"What can you tell me about the security measures in place last night?"

"Standard stuff you passed through going in and coming out. A whole array of biometrics designed with little to no margin of error. I've rarely seen false negatives, and almost never seen a false positive," Webb declared.

"So, nearly impossible to fake an ID or fool the system into unauthorized entry?" Gionetti asked.

"Yeah. Again, I guess you're looking at only people with access," Jon stated somberly.

"Which is a fairly small pool of people, am I right? MacDonald tells me that aside from himself and Lacombe, the possibilities are nine, including you, Donovan, and the four victims. The remaining three are maintenance engineers with temporary access to that wing of the facility for the purpose of repairing some plumbing in the reception area lavatories," Gionetti announced. "And my understanding is that those guys could not get past the main reception area and into the more secure areas."

"So you're back to me and Donovan," Jon expressed with a frustrated sigh.

"Well, MacDonald and Lacombe, too," Gionetti added.

Jon was surprised to hear the detective verbalize the names of the chief executives, but was glad to see that Gionetti had not simply ruled them out either. Suddenly a thought occurred to him.

"So why haven't you even asked me for an alibi? Demanded corroboration? I mean, as you said, I'm at the top of a very short list." Jon looked questioningly at the man.

"Why bother? You could lie, and then I'd find out later and get all confused with why you would lie in the first place and further incriminate yourself. Or you could tell the truth, and it wouldn't matter anyway if I liked you for the murders and had a hard-on for pinning you with the crime.

"Bottom line is that most people lie when asked to account for their time and activities. I don't know why. Perhaps they don't want to get busted for being involved in something else, totally unrelated to the incident in question. They're having an affair and don't want the clandestine rendezvous to come out, or they lied to the boss about being sick to get an extra day or two of weekend.

"I think most people just lie out of habit. I think it's human nature to be suspicious of ourselves without any reason. Self-aware paranoia." Gionetti paused and took a sip from his cup. "Besides, I'll find all of that out routinely and without internal bias. It's the liquid-digital age, my friend. And with optical processing, I can find out what DVD you rented twelve years ago if I was so inclined," Gionetti finished rather matter-of-factly.

Jon knew the man had a point. With the perfection and ultimate worldwide availability of the optical computer chip, digital data processing had made a literal quantum leap almost overnight.

Nine years ago, a small Canadian pharmaceutical company—North American Apothecary—had been struggling to meet the explosive demand of providing affordable Canadian manufactured medications to the United States in the wake of the newly passed North American Pharmaceutical Reform legislation and had merged with an even smaller upstart data consultation group in the hope of finding a way to streamline logistics and improve distribution to the lower portion of the continent.

This small data processing research group, Polar Innovations, had been quietly on the brink of a phenomenal discovery, and with the astronomical funding generated by the open traffic of therapeutic drugs to the U.S., they were able to hire a group of five extraordinary young physicists right out from under the noses of the top leaders in the American technology community.

Nearly half a century in the making, but now with unlimited and uninterrupted resources, these brilliant young scientists were able to solve the optical processing problem in less than four years.

Born just less than a decade ago under the nearly frozen tundra of the Canadian wilderness, a synthetic crystalline matrix had been married with pure argon gas to create the first significant optical processing circuit: a logic engine that processed and analyzed data thousands of times faster than the fastest processor chips of the day.

Within months of the discovery, methods of mass-producing smaller, faster chips were perfected and less than eighteen months after that first circuit was fired, Polar Innovations went public. Traditional computer technology was instantly obsolete and the new standard in technology had forced the world into an overnight evolution.

"So, what now?" Jon asked folding his hands around his coffee.

"I wait for the post-mortem on the bodies, gather what data I requested from your bosses and put together a case." Gionetti glanced past Webb. "It's not like any of you guys are going to run. I mean where would you go?"

Jon was a little taken back by the inspector's casual approach. The man had been open about his suspicions without being accusatory and freely disclosed facts about an ongoing investigation, all behaviors that ran contrary to usual homicide investigation protocol.

However, Jon sensed a distinct method to Gionetti's mechanics and was beginning to admire the original tactics. After all, the case was fairly self-contained. All that was needed was the proverbial smoking gun, and that usually came in the form of forensic minutiae from the post-mortem and scene scrub. In Jon's prior experience, DNA and other signature evidence always illuminated even the darkest of mysterious cases.

The smoking gun.

There was that familiar sense of epiphany again, teasing Jon with clarity and revelation, like a fleeting glimpse of something extraordinary out of the corner of one's eye. He concentrated on letting the shadowy thought coalesce into solid meaning, but...

It faded into the blackness of his exhausted mind.

Jon finished his coffee in a deep gulp and raised his eyebrows toward the detective, as if to say *Well, it's been a treat, but I got a thing.*

"I guess I should let you get going," Gionetti exclaimed with a shrug and a sigh. "Where will you be spending your time for now? If I need to get a hold of you, that is."

"You have my home numbers in my file, I'm sure. I usually only step out for a bite to eat or to pick up the groceries," Jon replied.

"Or to visit your family, right?"

Then Gionetti cautiously added, almost in a whisper. "I'm truly sorry about that. MacDonald gave me everything on you and Donovan. I read about the attack. I don't mean any disrespect."

Jon bristled momentarily, stiffened and then caught the sincere gaze of the inspector's green eyes. He softened a bit and nodded almost imperceptibly.

He stood and tossed his coffee container into the rectangular opening of a trash incinerator. Instantly, another flash of potential realization swept through his mind; like a tingle of déjà vu.

The incinerator.

Jon hadn't experienced this many tickles of bothersome fleeting notions since his wife's attack. He knew from experience never to ignore them once they began, as they often led him to the truth.

He offered his hand to the detective and moved to leave, trying to mentally shake the confusion left by the lingering dust of the nagging flashes of insight.

"Detective Gionetti." Jon nodded farewell as the detective rose.

"Sal," the man offered. "Short for Salvatore. Fourth generation Chicago Italian. Southwest side." He smiled and shook Webb's hand.

Webb smiled back loosely and then dropped the man's hand. As he turned, he paused and spoke without facing the inspector. "Detective—"

"It's Sal, please."

"Were all four of the bodies positively ID'ed?"

Sal Gionetti frowned at the man's broad back and hesitated before answering. "Why?"

"If so, by whom?"

"Again, why do you ask?" Gionetti was curious. "Those names won't be released, nor will any facts involving this case. Are we clear on that, Webb? This situation has a corporate level gag order on it from echelons above even me."

Jon sighed. His heavy shoulders rose and the muscles of his back flexed beneath the fabric of the heavy uniform. Gionetti just now realized how large and athletic the man was. Jon Webb was a physical presence.

"They were identified by whom?" Jon quietly repeated the inquiry, "MacDonald or Lacombe?"

Gionetti hesitated and then, almost on a whim, just to play along because he suspected something of value was transpiring, he answered, "MacDonald ID'ed the bodies and Lacombe verified."

"Scene integrity remained intact?" Jon asked.

"Now you insult me by questioning my scene sterility? How long has it been since you worked a wet case, Webb? You're out of the game now. Don't go playing some kind hero PI on me!" Gionetti was getting pissed and seemed to suddenly regret opening the envelope of confidence for Webb.

Jon slowly turned around to face the detective. He stood a foot taller with nearly forty-five kilograms to his favor. Webb slipped his arms into his heavy wool overcoat as he gazed at the detective. He buttoned the bottom three buttons as he spoke methodically and in careful measure. "Only three of the bodies had identification badges pinned to their jackets, and I didn't see a fourth badge lying about."

Gionetti stared, mouth agape, trying to process any significance to this revelation. "So," he began, "the killer swiped the badge to facilitate his exit and..." He trailed off as the logic of the circumstances settled in. His eyes shifted to the side in brief consideration and then locked back with Jon Webb's dark glare.

Jon nodded slowly as he recognized the realization in Gionetti's eyes. "Nobody clocked out, did they detective? The fourth badge is missing and I don't think that's an accident." Jon cocked his head slightly and leaned forward to whisper directly to the inspector, "So why take it?"

Detective Gionetti arched his eyebrows in consideration, about to add a suggestion as Jon Webb spun on his heels and strode away in long, heavy strides.

As he walked away, he tossed a half glance over his left shoulder back toward the standing detective. In the authoritative tone of a professor revealing the solution to a problematic theorem, he concluded the conversation.

"Unless, Detective Gionetti, somebody is trying to conceal the identity of the fourth body."

Gionetti watched as the tall security agent melted into the undulating crowd.

Three

The Rainey Clinic was situated at the end of a long and winding brick paved approach ending in a grand circle drive that wound around a gothic Romanesque white marble fountain, complete with naked cherubs frozen in dance among stone carved swans and unicorns. In the summer, lush moss and ivy clung to the rim of the fountain's main bowl and the mist from the multiple sprays hung just above the foliage. On sunny days one could be sure to see a number of miniature rainbows hovering over the fountain's characters.

However, now, in the chill of California's new winter climate, frost clung to the cherubs' chins like crystalline beards and dingy orange and brown leaves clotted the fountain's chipped and flaking bowl.

In contrast to the fountain's call back to antiquity, the Clinic's main entrance was more neo-classic, almost European with its wide expansive windows and dark oak lattices, tall arched wooden doors and sloping cedar gables. Rich, cultured stone decked the facade and limestone wedges tied in the corners.

Jonathan Webb parked his small, leased car in the only available slot on the side of the building's wraparound front porch. He emerged from the vehicle and squinted back down the approach drive, expecting to see the tail vehicle that had followed him from the city. No car presented and after a few moments, Jon stepped out of the shadows cast by the tall ash and evergreens and into the sunlight. He slipped on a pair of sunglasses to shield his eyes from the glare and steeled himself for the visit as he walked toward the front entrance of the Rainey Clinic for Neurologic Rehabilitation.

As he stepped on to the limestone porch and past the large potted ferns, he again marveled at the natural beauty of the clinic. *Sarah would have called it "ski-lodge chic".* Then she would have gone on about how with some creative and thrifty purchases and only a few weekends worth of Jon's labor they could transform their smallish ranch-style home into an alpine retreat that would rival the real thing. She was good with things like that, and even though she would rope him into taking on projects far beyond his capabilities, together they would figure it out and end up appreciating a finished result that he gratefully had to admit was appealing.

Jon turned the thick glass doorknob, pulled open the heavy wooden door and stepped into the shadows of the foyer. Immediately to the left was a recessed reception desk manned by a pleasant man in casual attire with a wireless comlink in his ear. Jon approached and swiped off his shades.

"Hi," he smiled weakly. "I'm Jon Webb, for Sarah and Matthew".

"Of course, Mr. Webb, please log in and I'll have an escort up momentarily."

The man immediately busied himself with some unseen task at a hidden keyboard as Jon turned toward a waist high marble podium set into the richly stained cherrywood wall. He placed both hands palm down on the smooth glass of the print reader and then stepped away once the unit chimed its soft musical tone. He turned back toward the receptionist as the man handed him a thin plastic badge affixed with a small metal clasp.

"Your ID badge, Mr. Webb. Please don't lose it or remove it from the premises."

Jon accepted the badge and nodded weakly. He left the reception counter just as a wood and glass door silently opened across the foyer. A young woman in soft peach colored scrubs greeted him, holding the door open with her shoulder.

"Good to see you, Mr. Webb. How are things?"

"Not too bad, Lilly. Thanks." He allowed the small talk to continue as they traveled down the short corridor and descended two flights of stairs.

Out of courtesy and habit, he responded to her polite inquiries softly and nodded when it seemed appropriate during her cordial banter, though he processed and retained nothing of their exchange. As was custom by this time in the journey, he operated purely on memory and primitive instinct, automatic and void of purpose.

"Mr. Webb?" Lilly's voice held concern, breaking through to the distant responsive portion of his self. He glanced at the young woman as if just waking from a nap.

"I was going to suggest that we visit Matthew first today. It's a good time right now, as he just finished in the crafts room and may be more responsive. He really is making some important and exciting strides." She paused, anticipating Jon's negative reaction to the suggestion.

He was usually adamant about spending time with Sarah first and then visiting with his son. This time, however, he merely whispered an almost inaudible, "Fine." His eyes remained somewhat distant and clouded.

Lilly placed a warm hand on his arm and smiled gently.

"Is everything all right, Mr. Webb? We can still go to Sarah first if you like. I just thought you might like to try interacting with Matthew when he's at his most approachable."

Jon blinked back a few spasms of moisture in his eyes and shook his head. He reached over and held Lilly's small hand in his own as he smiled quickly, swallowed back a sob and nodded for her to proceed forward.

Lilly squeezed his hand, let it linger a moment and then led him down the hall.

The staff at the Rainey Clinic always seemed to be acutely cognizant of each client's emotional needs. They had known Jon perhaps the best because he had been coming the longest of any. His wife Sarah and son Matthew had been placed there just over three years ago, but for entirely different reasons.

In addition to providing state-of-the-art, long-term care for the infirmed, Rainey Clinic was the leading research facility in rehabilitation and recovery of patients suffering from acute neurological injuries. Specializing in people victimized from a vast array of neurological insults, the Clinic employed leading-edge technology in the fields of microprocessor physiokinesis, micro electrical ablation and ribosomal override, therapeutic nuclear cloning and stem cell implantation.

The results achieved over the past decade in treating and curing diseases like Parkinson's and ALS had been heralded as modern miracles whose inspirations had carried over into the medical research venue in efforts to treat and ultimately cure disease processes like diabetes, some forms of cancer and even blindness and deafness.

The advent of the optical digital processing chip and the breakthroughs made in stem cell therapies, along with the removal of restrictive legislation, allowed for the privatization and commercialization of technology and innovation on such a global scale that significant and meaningful advancements were made almost weekly.

Lilly and Jon came to a double wooden door with frosted glass windows and a hand print reader. Lilly spoke into the small voice-recognition screen-mesh imbedded in the wall and placed her hands palms down on the reader. A soft musical tone followed by a metallic click signaled the unlocking of the doors. They proceeded through, Jon holding the door for the lady.

Lilly went directly to the nurses' station, retrieved a small disc and slid it into the slim black reader dangling from a cord around her waist. Immediately, the LCD screen of the slim device glowed with a mellow green and flickered as a number of brightly colored desktop icons popped up in a random spread display. She touched one of the icons and scanned the contents of the requested file quickly.

"Matthew has really been progressing well," Lilly began as if she were reporting to the medical board during grand rounds. "He seems to be showing interest in more diverse activities than before. He doesn't lock into one repetitive behavior as much as he used to.

"This is just my personal impression," she continued. "But I think that if you were to reconsider allowing a mapscan and matrix diagnostic, we might be able to definitively locate one or more foci for possible therapy. It really wouldn't cost much for the initial architecture, and of course, it's all painless for Matthew." Lilly spoke as they walked, her finger nimbly flicking the laser-stylus across the flat screen, touching various icons on her Polar Innovations Penguin PDD.

She glanced up at Jon and then paused in her stride. Jon instinctively halted his step as well and met her gaze. He smiled lightly and gently shook his head. She dropped her eyes shamefully and stammered.

"I'm sorry. Of course, I know your position, and it isn't going to change. I guess I'm just the consummate clinician. I just see so much success with our other clients and to deprive Matthew of enjoying his full potential... well, it frankly frustrates and saddens me. I'm sorry, Mr. Webb, but I do work with Matthew every day, and—"

"Lilly, relax. I appreciate your concern and I do listen to your opinions. You make a valid argument and I appreciate your candor. It's just not the right decision for me. I know that it's hard for you to accept or to understand, but for now please let the lobby for my approval stop," Jon calmly pleaded with the young doctor.

Lilly sighed and shook her head at first, then nodded in understanding and inhaled deeply gathering her composure and professionalism. She looked up at Jon, smiled weakly and reached to guide him by the elbow.

"Let's go see your son."

~ * ~

As they walked down the sterile hallway of robin's-egg blue laminate walls and black marble floors, Jon Webb allowed his mind to drift back to a time before the Rainey Clinic and its well-meaning, though ultimately self serving, staff of techno wizards; a time when he knew nothing of transnuclear cloning and stem cell implantation; and the concept of optical processing arrays and cerebral cortex mapping were fanciful whims of futuristic novels.

He daydreamed of lazy afternoons on the lake with Sarah and a cooler full of cold beer in a rented pontoon boat, drifting with the gentle but steady summer breeze, both of them barefoot and clad in only half of their clothes as they dozed against each other in a post coital haze. Sarah would eventually break the warm silence with a comment about the clouds swimming lazily overhead or to offer her latest suggestion on how to decorate the guest room of the lakeside cabin.

During those rare and treasured times, he never felt more at peace and so far away from the memories of the war torn cities of his military service or the political carnival and public carnage of the homicide investigations. Sarah was pure, unrefined innocence and feminine strength. She reduced him to welcomed mortality and cultivated in him a sense of pride and honest ambition. Without her constant visceral influence, Jon would have continued to spin into the abyss of an alpha male dominated existence complete with substance abuse and splintered social schizophrenia.

She not only grounded him in humanity, but transplanted herself within his soul.

Then after two years of blissful marriage and some effort, Sarah became pregnant. Jon knew from the moment she broke the news on their way to the cabin for a long weekend that his world would be forever changed.

He never dreamed that the excitement of anticipation would metastasize into the cancer of despair that passed for his present state of existence.

Lilly led Jon through another pair of heavy wood and frosted glass doors and up to a long smoky window. As they approached, the glass lost its smoky appearance as the polarized sheets of crystal shifted to accommodate an automatic change in lighting from within the room on the other side. Jon gazed apprehensively through the glass and stared unblinking as his emotions raced to catch up with what his eyes revealed.

Soft, thick tears welled in the corners of his dark green eyes and he willed them not to fall. He drew a deep breath and allowed an involuntary smile to escape from the depths of his resolve and spread across his face.

Beyond the polarized one-way glass of the observation room, his four-year-old son, Matthew, played quietly at a low table with another little girl of about the same age. They were each making platefuls of plastic toy foods and then sharing them with one another.

Matthew had just slid a purple plastic plate in front of the girl, loaded with what looked to be fake cauliflower, a chicken leg, a small can of soup and a flat, stiff pancake complete with molded plastic whipped cream topped with a bright red cherry, which she gracefully accepted. She returned the gesture by offering a small basket of plastic french fries and a realistic and surprisingly appetizing banana split boat. Matthew smiled his usual wide and animated grin while clapping his hands excitedly. Jon simply watched in awe and sadness as the love he felt for the boy drowned him.

Matthew had been born at the Rainey Clinic, delivered by Cesarean section from a comatose mother who, to this day, lay just one floor above in a catatonic sleep. He had never left the grounds and never known his parents. It was debated by some clinicians that Matthew didn't even understand the concept of parents or siblings and therefore would only be confused by introducing the idea and forcing the relationship.

Webb was known to his son only as Jon, a friend who visits from time to time and tells wonderful stories. The staff at Rainey felt it best to begin the relationship between the young boy and his father in a casual, noncommittal manner and avoid the daunting task of trying to explain the true situation to Matthew before he was ready to process it.

After The Incident—as it had come to be referred—and his wife's subsequent demise, Jonathan Webb found himself plunging headlong into self-destruction, sucked into a vortex of obsessive rage and blind revenge, fueled by demons both past and present.

Jon had brought his vegetative wife to the West Coast clinic from Massachusetts Global on advice from a friend, when he was still open to suggestion and before he fully decompensated. He had kept constant vigil over Sarah's beaten and broken body, bathing and dressing her with all the gentleness afforded a newborn, carefully redressing her wounds and thoughtfully selecting the colors and styles of her sleepwear.

Obviously, the fetal Matthew had survived the graphic ordeal that had laid his mother to waste and stole his father's soul; and when it was decided that Matthew should be brought into this world, Jon stood at Sarah's head and whispered into her ear through the entire operation. Once the umbilical cord had been clamped and cut, and the pediatrician was comfortable with status of the newborn, Jonathan Webb held his boy swaddled in warm soft blankets. He never took his eyes off Matthew's fresh and wrinkled face and he never let loose of Sarah's limp hand.

Jon stayed for one more night after the evening of Matthew's birth. He had held his son and caressed his wife's brow. He played with the baby's fisted hand, splaying out the tiny fingers and letting them grasp his thumb. He kissed his wife's face constantly and traced her still features with his infant son's small fingers. He repeatedly unwrapped the blankets and inspected his son's body from head to toe.

They told him that they expected a certain degree of cerebral insult in Matthew resulting from the lack of oxygen Sarah endured during The Incident. He had learned that *in-utero* anoxia could lead to various degrees of brain damage, and was prepared for anything. But when he held his son, naïve hope had flourished; as he could see neither signs of obvious damage nor indication of deformity or malformation. Matthew looked absolutely perfect.

But Jon knew. He was consciously, albeit unwillingly, aware that it wouldn't be until later; during Matthew's development, that deficiencies would present themselves. For that moment he simply enjoyed the illusion of perfection and basked in the warm healing glow of denial.

Jon Webb disappeared for nearly two years after that night. A certified check arrived the first Monday of each month to cover the costs of Sarah and Matthew's care, the postmark always vague and distant. Few people had known of Jon's whereabouts during that time and even fewer knew of the events that transpired and what ultimately brought Webb back to his sleeping wife and growing son.

The staff at Rainey was skeptical at first about Jon's return, thinking he had slipped off the edge of the planet and fallen forever into a great emotional abyss. They were concerned for the safety of the patients and staff, and wanted to be assured that he was not a dangerous man still anguishing with hatred and dark thoughts. They also wanted to be assured that Jon's further presence would not have a negative effect on young Matthew.

Eventually, compassion and a healthy dose of pity won over cynicism and after many sessions with the Clinic's own psychiatric and psychological staff, Jon Webb was allowed to re-establish himself into the lives of his family. He proved to be a quiet, healing man with realistic expectations and a willingness to do whatever was necessary to prove his worth.

Now, for nearly two years he had returned at least three times during the week and on all weekends and holidays.

Although the Rainey Clinic still maintained legal custody of Matthew.

"Who's the girl?" Jonathan asked Lilly.

"That's Penny. Penelope. She's five, almost six. Been here about three weeks." Lilly paused, and then added, "She drowned at age two in a hot tub. Apparently her hair got caught in the filter and trapped her under the water long enough for her to arrest. She was pulled from the tub and immediately resuscitated but not before some cerebral insult could occur.

We've just recently allowed her to interact with the other children and it has been wonderful to watch how they imprint off one another."

Lilly turned to Jon as he stared through the glass at his son. She added, "We're hoping to map her soon."

Jon slowly turned to meet Lilly's gaze, then allowed his chin to sag heavily to his chest. He sighed deeply and shook his head while whispering, "I'm just not convinced that it's right. What if this were all meant to be? Part of some grand cosmic plan, and not to be messed with? Who am I to alter that? Who are you to decide how destiny should be played out?" He raised his tired face to her, imploring her with an exhausted gaze.

Lilly slowly shook her head and crossed her arms in front of her chest. "It's not about metaphysics and karma, you know that, Jon. We were meant to evolve, whether through natural selection or technological advances. How can we not offer a cure for a condition that would otherwise limit the way a fellow human being lives their life? How can we ignore obvious improvements in the way we experience our world?" She paused waiting for an adamant retort or emotional argument.

Instead, Jon just stood leaning against the glass window of the observation room with his head hung low and shoulders rolled forward in exhaustion. She reached out to touch an arm hanging limply at his side.

"When they first discovered the usefulness of penicillin," she continued, "people balked at the idea that some nasty mold grown for the sole purpose of curing certain infections was a positive step in the progress of mankind. Many important people viewed it as heresy, even evil. That we were toying with fabric of God's will. These were not religious zealots, but highly educated and influential members of society.

"Jon, these advances and scientific leaps of faith are as meant to be as was the tragedy that befell your family." Jon winced at the statement and looked up, wounded and defensive.

"I'm sorry, Jon," Lilly added tenderly. "Just don't let an opportunity for enhancing your son's life pass by without considering all of the views," she concluded with a distant smile and a patient gaze.

Jon sighed once again and looked back through the glass at his son. Matthew was now sitting alone wringing his hands as they lay in his lap. He gently rocked his upper body in casual circles looking about the room as if it were his first time there.

Penny was playing with large Leggo blocks on the floor in the far corner, methodically stacking only the blue pieces together. Both children were now oblivious to each other as they functioned in their separate universes.

Jon blinked repeatedly as if an eyelash were tickling his cornea, turned away from the window and began to walk slowly back toward the hallway leading out of the observation area. Lilly followed a few steps behind as she fished in her waist pack pouch for the keycard that would grant them access into the room itself; assuming that Jon intended to visit his boy.

"I want to see Sarah now," Jon stated quietly and without turning as he continued to slowly stride away from Lilly.

She stopped searching through the Velcro pocket for the keycard and looked up after the large man, somewhat stunned by his sudden change in demeanor. Lilly followed cautiously behind and answered softly, "Yeah, sure. I'll just call the unit so they'll be expecting us."

"I can manage alone. Thanks, Lilly. I'm sure that you have things you'd rather be doing," Jon responded solemnly.

He turned back to look upon her with a pensive and slightly bewildered gaze. The sudden change in Jon's manner and expressions seemed to confuse and frighten her, and she was instantly relieved that he suggested continuing without her.

"Okay." She managed a half smile and attempted to mask her relief. "I do have some matters to attend to." She hesitated and then added, "Look, Jon, I didn't mean to—"

He smiled back at her, suddenly genuine again and gentle as before.

Lilly broke off her thought and finished, "Just take care of yourself, Jon. I mean it. If not for you, then for Matthew's sake. You still have time to appeal the custody."

He nodded lightly and tossed her a wave that said both 'thank you' and 'I'm sorry' in the same gesture. He turned and walked toward the staircase. Lilly watched after him until he disappeared around the corner, then she reached for the phone and made the call.

~ * ~

It had been the damn blue Leggo blocks that triggered the explosion of images in his mind. He had been struggling in vain all day to wrestle the wispy tendrils of realization and revelation into a collection of coherent thoughts: First, upon seeing the bodies of the victims at Phoenix-Lamneth, then on the elevator ride down to the lobby and lastly during his coffee conversation with the detective.

Each episode brought delicate, tissue-thin thoughts to the frontier edge of his mind, teasing his consciousness with potential understanding, but eluding full comprehension like a distantly remembered dream seeming familiar only by recognizing its reoccurrence, yet not quite grasping its true substance.

In a past life, before The Incident, he had been accustomed to experiencing these moments of transient clarity. When he became mired in an investigation that seemed to offer no open angle from which to work a solution, he would find himself wandering aimlessly through a busy street market or fruitlessly doodling on the cover of a case file when a sudden and unexpected epiphany would strike him like a bolt of electricity from an open circuit seeking ground.

In an instant, all of the random and agonizingly familiar bits of information and images would coalesce and for a single clear moment, blaze a detailed portrait across the fabric of his mind—an acid etched negative of the universe frozen in one particular moment. The details required to answer the painfully unanswerable questions would, at once, clarify themselves out of the frothy jumble of ambient sensory input.

Some called it a sixth sense or even rudimentary clairvoyance. Jon simply thought of it as a state of heightened awareness brought about by intense concentration and emotional stress. Whatever the reason or origin of this gift, he learned early in life to trust it instinctively. Once the revelations became coherent, he had little difficulty in piecing the whole together.

Now, as he walked the hallway toward his sleeping wife, he worked at mentally filing and cataloging the images and realizations that had washed over him moments ago outside the observation room.

Though rather vague and disconnected, these newly understood images seemed important to current affairs. The ideas that had nagged him earlier became slightly clearer, although each realization asked more new questions than it answered.

As Jon had watched the children through the glass, the stacked blue Leggos that Penny played with had begun to blur. The sharp plastic edges became hazy and smooth, the bright royal blue softened to a crystalline sky blue and the irregular stacks blended into graceful curving lines.

As his vision blurred from the tears in his eyes, his perception of the rigid plastic pieces melted into the remembered images of watery ice sculptures of dolphins and mermaids dancing across frozen waves.

He recalled now, quite clearly, that there had been a total of eight ice sculptures randomly located throughout that long forgotten banquet room, each a different theme, and accented by a wide variety of lighting and eclectic foliage. Clarity forced him to remember that those elegant figures were illuminated from below with soft blue lighting giving the translucent ice an appearance of internal luminescence.

It was the mythological quality of the sea creatures that captivated him the most as he worked the party room that long ago night. In his mind, he was back at that party, overdressed and sipping ice water trying to look as if he fit in and not like the covert security that he truly was.

Physically, he had remained rooted in the present, just outside of the glass enclosed observation room seemingly watching his son through the smoky glass with Dr. Lilly Bakersman standing next to him. Yet, far back in his consciousness, within the shadowy recesses of memory and hiding from accidental lucidity, he relived that very moment at the party over one year ago.

The stacked blue Leggos had triggered the memory of the ice sculptures and, in turn, shuttled him back to the exact moment in his past when he had first met the man that he temporarily replaced as Chief of Security and the guest of honor for that evening's festivities.

The man whom Jon saw again this morning, quite unexpectedly, with the back of his head blown off.

The man without a security photo badge clipped to his jacket.

For the moment, Webb paused the mental video and indexed the moment for later reference. Now that he had complete recollection, he would never forget. Instead, he began preparing himself for the next step.

He had one more visit to make.

Four

Jon approached the extended care wing of the Rainey Clinic with a dark and heavy heart. Waves of regret and guilt began to wash over him with each step, ebbing and swirling around his bowels like thick, warm oil. Every visit brought trepidation, and he never left without also leaving some small, vital piece of his soul behind.

He continued to visit Sarah long after they told him that it was unlikely she would ever regain consciousness. They, the staff psychologists, said that it was therapeutic for him to continue to visit at his own pace, whenever he liked and as often as he wished. At first, he deluded himself into thinking that he did it to be the good husband and to set an example; in a way prove that he was capable of doing good and caring things, perhaps to even win favor and make a case in regaining custody of Matthew.

But the truth was that Matthew was better off here than with him, and everyone knew it. As much as he loved his son and missed having him in his life each and every minute, there is no way that he could provide the amount and quality of care necessary and still maintain a financial foothold.

In fact, visiting Sarah was the single most painful task he ever had to endure. Perhaps that was why he did it, as a sort of self-imposed penance for all of his sins. He knew that was partly true.

However, the real truth was even more painful. He simply was not strong enough to go on alone. If the situation were reversed, as he wished were the case with every fiber of his will, he knew that Sarah would come to see him every day.

Yet, she would have also moved on, found a new love, a new life. She would have started over and lived life as she loved it. But, unlike him, she would be able to share it in a way that was unselfish and unboasting. She would revel in her lightness and share it with him as he lay in darkness. Sarah was capable of love that transcended definition.

He missed her.

He believed that she was strong enough to exist in any climate, including the icy solitude of catatonia. As long as he believed she still existed out there beyond her shell, he would continue to visit and attempt to get one last glimpse of her through the broken portal of her body.

"Ah, Mr. Webb," a young man's voice echoed through hidden speakers as he stood in front of the clear glass doors leading into the extended care unit. Webb smiled through the glass and craned his neck to get a view of the man with the familiar voice.

A thin man in dark blue scrubs popped up from behind a white encased computer terminal. He waved enthusiastically and smiled wide and welcoming.

"Hang on, let me buzz you in." The man in scrubs dropped back out of sight. A moment later the door buzzed and Jon tugged open one half of the heavy set of glass panels and walked through.

"Hey! This is a pleasant surprise. No phone call, so I wasn't expecting you," the man exclaimed, genuinely eager to see Jon. He glanced quickly over Jon's shoulder obviously expecting to see someone else following in his wake. "You alone today?"

"Yeah, I left Lilly down in Pediatrics. She had some important stuff to finish up. I told her I thought I could manage without the guided tour." Jon smiled.

The man in scrubs shook his head and clicked his tongue a few times wagging his finger punitively at Jon. "Shame on you, Captain Webb. You know the Director's rules regarding unsupervised visits and unescorted travels."

Jon shrugged and rolled his eyes, still smiling. The man in scrubs extended his hand and Jon accepted it firmly. They shook like old war buddies.

"Robert, always good to see you. How're things?" Jon asked.

"Not too bad, all things considered. You?"

"As well as can be expected."

The exchange was routine, well rehearsed and darkly tongue-in-cheek. They had greeted each other in the same fashion since the first night that Sarah arrived. Robert's first words to Jon on that night were: "Mr. Webb, there are twenty-six letters in the English language, and more than a bazillion ways to arrange and work them into words and phrases. I have yet to learn of the right combination of selected letters to adequately express all of the emotions that one feels at a time like this.

"So, I like to start off with something that's comfortable and easy, even mechanical and lacking in conviction. After awhile, if we use it enough it will take on its own special meaning for us."

Jon liked the man from that very moment.

"So, they moved you to days?" Jon inquired, realizing that it was far too early in the day for Robert's usual evening shift.

"Yeah, they have some new staff and want to rotate them onto nights for a few weeks. Get them oriented in case there needs to be coverage due to illness or vacation, that sort of thing. I was assured that it would be temporary. Hey, speaking of which, you're a little early yourself. What gives?"

Jon hesitated, thinking of the slain bodies in the boardroom, and then answered honestly, "Early day at the office. Some things came up, and I thought I'd try for a little clarity."

"By clarity, you don't mean self pity and emotional flagellation, do you?"

Robert knew Jon all too well, but respected the man enough not to push too hard—just hard enough to remind him that he cared.

Jon winced melodramatically at the comment and feigned being wounded, even grimacing with a "you got me" sneer. Robert shrugged and popped a snack chip from a plastic container into his mouth.

"Hey, man, it's your eternity. Spend it however you wish," Robert preached.

Jon's gaze drifted over the nurses' station to the bank of small flat screen monitors, each assigned to a specific patient's room. Three of the fifteen screens were illuminated by white, red, and yellow tracings coursing left to right across a field of bright blue. Numbers and characters flickered along the bottom and at the margins of each screen.

One of those outputs was Sarah, her mind expressing itself only through the myriad sharp spikes and dull troughs as her various brain waves etched across the LCD display each minute. Thin, asymmetrical waveforms pulsed continuously on all three screens, and Jon often found himself wondering if by studying them long enough you could identify a person merely by the wave patterns their brain activity generates. He tried to mentally guess which one was Sarah's.

"You're missing someone," Jon said. He suddenly realized that there were only three live screens when there were normally four patients on this unit, including his wife. He looked back to Robert with a degree of semi-concern.

"Yeah, Jeremy is no longer with us." Robert revealed this news almost matter-of-factly, as if the young man's departure really didn't bother him, but Jon suspected that it touched Robert deep beneath his tough exterior, and he gazed at the young nurse with faint suspicion.

"No, I mean they transferred him to the 'U'," Robert clarified. "Family couldn't afford to keep him here, not at the rate we constantly had to revamp his halo inputs and readjust his suspensors.

"Besides, I don't think his output impressed the head shop much. I'm sure it was a mutual, if not amiable, parting of ways."

Jon nodded empathetically, reflecting on his own financial concerns. His current budget was fixed and already stretched to the point of snapping, and in light of the recent developments at Phoenix-Lamneth, he was sincerely worried about continuing Sarah's stay at the Clinic.

He was running out of favors as it was, and the Clinic's executive board overlooked many of the limiting criteria in Sarah's case and allowed her to remain in the Protocol program where she would continue to receive the best of care available in addition to the exposure of new and innovative methods. These oversights, Jon knew, came more out of pity for his family and the tragedy than pure philanthropy.

Whatever the reason, Jon never gazed once into the mouth of the gift horse and remained appreciative for all the Clinic had done.

However, recently he felt as if he were being pressured to allow them to push Sarah's and Matthew's care into the realm of research and experimentation. He refused despite their assurances that at no time would any harm come to either Sarah or Matthew, and in fact, the Clinic's ultimate goal was to improve the quality of life for all of their clients.

But, it wasn't fear of potential physical or even emotional discomfort that concerned him, but rather a more philosophic—perhaps, even theological—component had begun to weave an intricate mesh of confusion within Jon's own personal existential beliefs.

So for now, he adamantly held his ground and endured the pressure of the unspoken marker held over his head.

Robert, however, played no part in the scientific tag team pressuring of Jon Webb. As the only male, Robert was one of four clinical nurses who cared for the patients in the extended care unit. All of the staff was highly trained and extremely proficient, but Jonathan preferred Robert to the rest, perhaps initially due to their shared gender, but ultimately because of their chemistry.

The fact of the matter was that, though they all cared well for the patients and families, the other three nurses, for lack of a better euphemism, toed the party line. With subtle yet persistent suggestions regarding Sarah's future care and allusions to potential changes, the nurses constantly, if not politely, chastised him with each visit. He was pleasantly surprised to see that Robert was unexpectedly on duty.

Robert eyed Jonathan knowingly and popped another chip into his mouth as he rose from the workstation and walked around the desk to a clean white cabinet. He opened a small door, reached in and gently withdrew something small enough to barely lie concealed in the palm of his hand.

He turned to face Jon, a proud and excited grin spread across his face.

"Know what this is?" he asked.

Jon slowly shook his head and shrugged.

"This is the latest and greatest in optical liquid interface technology."

With a flourish, Robert waved his free hand over his pronated closed fist; then, like a magician, supinated and opened his fingers. Lying on his now opened palm was a small and perfectly clear cube of approximately five centimeters. The ambient light of the room struck the smooth surfaces of the cube and refracted in an explosion of dazzling prisms, fanning off the crystalline surface in sharp and vibrant rays.

"It's called the Ice Cube, from Polar Innovations. And it will revolutionize multimedia data recording and storage," Robert testified, full of excitement.

He was a self-proclaimed techno geek and extremely proud of it.

"It goes into production next week and will hit the market Thanksgiving Day. This is a prototype that I happened across—the usual suspects were involved." He gave a conspiratorial wink.

Robert's fiancé was a design engineer for Polar Innovations and allowed her future husband to play with all of her new toys, providing he sign a nondisclosure agreement of sorts—a kind of techie prenuptial agreement.

"I tell you, Webb, this is exciting stuff. Your standard digital flat disks can hold what, eight hundred to a thousand megabytes. Been that way for decades. Even the top-end hyper polished disks can only hold five to eight thousand—compressed." Robert shook his head and continued. "But this? Man, they don't even know what the maximum capacity truly is. Depending on the type of digital data and how it's formatted, you can load hundreds of gigabytes into one cube.

"A three dimensional array of liquid optical matrices aligned with all of the planes that could possibly exist within a cube's finite space. It's 3D hyper cubed to the 'n'-th degree!"

"I'm happy for you both, really," Jon said with a wry smile.

Robert waved him off and sighed.

"Okay, okay. But you'll be impressed when you see the applications I've run with just one of these." Robert started toward one of the glass enclosed patient rooms.

It was Sarah's room.

Jon gasped with a start and went to grab Robert by the scrub shirt's short sleeve. Robert deftly turned and sidestepped the advancing man.

"Relax, big guy. Have I ever let you down? You need to trust me on this, okay?" Robert gave Jon a look of confidence and assurance that tentatively put to rest any reservations he was feeling.

Jon cocked his head to one side, almost pleadingly. Robert nodded slowly, just once and smiled.

"Jon, I did this for you and Sarah. I really think you'll appreciate what I've got in mind. Just follow me and keep your mind open."

Robert led him through the open sliding glass doors and into Sarah's room. Soft lighting concealed in the overhead ceiling panels intensified in a gentle crescendo from darkness to dawn as an automatic rheostat activated in response to their entry. The room was small and perfectly wedge shaped, tapering out from the central core of the nurses' station like a slice of pie. All of the rooms encircled the centralized area in the same manner to facilitate optimal observation of all patients from one position.

Sarah's room held only the necessary items required for her care, tactfully concealed in drawers and small cabinets recessed flush into the curving ivory walls. There were no windows to the outside, the only light being provided by the overhead panels. No cards or flowers sat upon bedside tables, for there weren't any tables.

There was no bed, either.

Sarah floated, supine, exactly one meter above the glittering metallic mesh of the floor. Suspended between ceiling and floor, she hovered like an ethereal spirit in a fantastic display of levitation straight out of some fabled magician's encore.

The initial sight of her floating in empty space like some illusionist's glittery assistant never failed to give Jon pause, as if she were empowered with unearthly, perhaps otherworldly, abilities and that levitation was just the beginning. He struggled not to think about the classically infamous horror movies in which young women were frequently possessed by legions of demons and forced to demonstrate extraordinary feats that defied the accepted laws of physics and contorted the natural limitations of the human anatomy.

Instead, he forced himself to try to view her suspended form as a slumbering heavenly messenger having just completed an extremely important and sacred mission, exhausted from her long journey and resting for a spell before ascending back through the clouds to return to Paradise.

He marveled at his recent ability and willingness, whether conscious or not, to resort to popular religious symbolism for comfort and grounding. A reckless pessimist and ambivalent agnostic before The Incident, Jon never really gave much thought to religion in specific or the metaphysical in general. He operated in an empiric and reactionary world, and his philosophical make-up did not allow for fanciful romps through the nebulous dimensions of ontology.

Of course, that changed after Sarah had entered his life, melted and remolded his heart and then was abruptly transformed into the floating specter before him.

In reality, Sarah defied the laws of gravity neither by wicked demonic intervention nor by the grace of Heavenly lightness. She was suspended within a powerful, yet delicately focused magnetic field generated by specialized units embedded in the floor and ceiling. Her body was buoyed by extremely lightweight and highly magnetic pins surgically implanted in the long bones of her limbs, her pelvis, scapulae and vertebrae. The ultra thin ferrous-alloy rods balanced themselves—and so the body part in which they reside—evenly between the opposing poles of the magnetic field.

The frequency and flux of the focused field could be precisely manipulated and adjusted for each rod independently, allowing the levitated body to be lowered, raised and even rotated three hundred-sixty degrees around the longitudinal axis, placing the patient supine, prone or in any degree of lateral lie that was required.

The Magneton Anatomical Suspension System (MASS) revolutionized long-term patient care by eliminating complications such as lethal infections arising from pressure sores acquired during the prolonged stasis of being bedridden and allowed for unlimited and uninhibited access to a patient for daily care and treatments.

Jon gazed upon Sarah's floating form, primly draped in lightweight golden linen. The slender fingers of her left hand hung limply from beneath the thin sheet, held along the side of her body by the magnetic pins anchored in her radius and humerus, the nails on each finger finely manicured and buffed to a smooth sheen.

In a distant and nearly forgotten world far outside of these walls and far from the invisible magnetic hammock in which she lay, she had taken pride in her appearance; and though she'd wore little makeup, she did obsess about her hands. They were always well scrubbed, yet soft and usually smelled faintly of melon. Except for the distinct creases lining her palms—those mystical impressions that prophesized ones longevity in life and love—and the faint folds over dainty knuckles, the skin of her hands was porcelain smooth and unblemished by the shadows of veins.

She had often said that if it were true that you could guess a person's occupation in life by the appearance of their hands, then she was going to make it difficult for even the most astute detective to ascertain the business at which her delicate hands toiled.

It was evident, as he looked down at his own scarred and crooked hands, that Jon carried on them too much of the oily past smeared with the grime of the present. However, no one would have ever guessed by examining her hands that Sarah wielded hammer and chisel against marble or that she carved intricate coils of ivy and braided scrolls into hickory fireplace mantles and grand cherrywood headboards.

She had been an extraordinary artist who preferred the tools of old world craftsmen to that of soft bristle brushes and pastel oils on clean canvasses.

For a moment, Jon allowed his skin to reminisce about the way it felt when her hands would caress and her fingers explore.

"It's really all about space, man." Robert's voice swam back into Jon's head from behind the incoherent fog of fading memories and melancholy. "With enough space, you can do anything."

Jon blinked rapidly and cleared his mind, refocusing on the present.

Sarah's linen draped form trembled slightly from Robert's quick movements as he worked on some obscure equipment laid out on a small workstation at her head.

Jon's angelic vision of his wife faded as he could now see the braided mass of thin silvery wires emerging from underneath the cloth skullcap covering her head.

The Halo not only monitored and recorded continuous brainwave activity, but also provided a vehicle for various input stimulations of Sarah's cerebral sensory regions. At certain times, small electrical impulses would stimulate areas of her brain responsible for taste, smell, sight and sound in hope to elicit a change in her resting EEG wave patterns and demonstrate some degree of cerebral responsiveness.

However, to this point, Sarah had shown little progress in helping the Clinic gather data to further their cause. Apart from the occasional flicker and oscillation of alpha and delta waves during random focused cerebral stimulations, much of Sarah's brain activity painted a quiet and nearly static picture.

"Jon." Robert turned to look squarely at the man.

In his hands, he held a thin book-sized box with a brushed black metallic finish. The Ice Cube was seated firmly into a recessed square opening in the center of the unit.

Robert continued, "I want you to keep an open mind and hear me out completely before reacting." He paused and waited for a sign of confirmation.

Jon nodded slowly and crossed his arms as he cocked his head to one side, eyes jumping between the young nurse and the slim box holding the Cube.

"I think I've come up with an idea that may enhance your ability to communicate with Sarah." Robert allowed a few seconds to pass, gathering his courage. "I know how you feel about further invasive steps and all of that. And I totally understand and even agree with you in principle, but like you, I also believe that her spirit—her soul—exists somewhere within her, trapped in that broken shell and frustrated." He looked solemnly at Jon Webb and searched for a hint of acknowledgment.

The man simply stared, still and unwavering.

Robert sighed and then proceeded. "You've been talking to her since day one, as have I. We play these old CD's and MP16's endlessly." He gestured toward the thin lightweight earphones gently looped around the soft exterior folds of Sarah's ears. Soft music whispered out of each in airy and nearly inaudible breaths.

"We even occasionally zap her with a few random volts of energy, and yet there has been no significant change in her EEG."

Jonathan grimaced sourly at the last statement and began to grow red in the face and down the neck. Small veins in his forehead began to throb.

"Don't get me wrong," Robert explained quickly. "We're operating without any knowledge of what she can or cannot experience. We are doing what we can, based entirely on faith, Jon. Faith that, somehow, she can hear us or even wants to hear us.

"But what if we're going about it all wrong? What if the accident, the assault, left her physiologically deaf? Or even more intriguing, psychologically deaf? What if she has shut down her external material senses and retreated to a deeper depth than we can possibly know?"

"These possibilities have already been discussed," Jon replied bitterly between nearly gritted teeth. "What are you suggesting? That I should give up the only thing that I have left to keep me connected? Is that what you're implying? Please say that you haven't joined their team and are pushing me away. Please tell me that isn't the case, Robert!"

"God, no!" Robert physically recoiled in shock and surprise. "Jon, no. I love you guys, and I believe what you believe. I'm not suggesting anything of the sort."

Robert blinked regaining his focus. "What I want to offer you is a chance to improve the odds of her hearing you." He held up the Cube, loaded into the slender black box.

"I think this may hold the key to opening Sarah's mind to you." Robert smiled with tender compassion and conviction.

The Cube tossed faint rainbow prisms across the room as Robert moved toward Jon and held out the device. Jon simply looked down numbly at the box and shook his head.

"Jon, the Ice Cube holds the answer to the problem of providing enough digital space to setup an input matrix of streaming digital data and then code it for translation at the visual cortex." He waited for Jon to look up and make eye contact. When he did, the beginnings of tears were struggling at the corners of Webb's eyes.

"This means that you can record a visual message and transmit it directly to Sarah's consciousness," Robert said softly.

"How, Robert? More surgery, more tomographic mapping and sterotaxic probing? And then we aren't even sure of the exact target area?" Jon asked rhetorically. "No, Robert. Not ever again."

"Jon, no! Absolutely not! The hardwiring is already there. The Halo has already mapped out the entire visual cortex for us. The pathway already exists. We just have to change the programming language." Robert hesitated and then continued. "I can prove it, Jon."

Jon Webb gazed questioning at the younger man, confused and angered by his assertions. He raised an eyebrow, almost as a threat.

"I confess that I did one little test run without your knowledge or approval, and you can kick my ass for that later if you wish. I suppose that I'll deserve it. But wait and see for yourself." Robert cringed away from the larger man and set the box on the flat worktable at Sarah's head, taking another quick defensive glance toward Jon, half expecting him to pounce.

Jon did not move, however, but remained grounded at the side of his floating wife. His hand instinctively rose to caress her arm. His eyes, though, never left Robert's face. Robert took the silent stillness as a cue and proceeded quickly with his planned demonstration before he lost the opportunity.

"I've reprogrammed the Halo for interface with my Cube reader here, and have bypassed the mainframe's recorders."

The Clinic's computer system was so elaborately integrated that every second of every patient's monitor was recorded, analyzed and processed. Each significant change and event was indexed and tagged, then presented in a summarization report each shift. Nothing could be missed, even if initially overlooked by the human staff.

"I'll run a prerecorded loop of EEG waveforms and vitals through a secondary feed that I constructed. The system will never recognize the redundancy. It's an inbred fault of the parallel analyzers."

Robert quickly worked at the tiny keypad of a Penguin PDD he produced from his scrubs waist pouch. As he tied in small cables from his PDD, the Cube reader and Sarah's Halo, his fingers blurred with deftness and precision. When he paused to look up at Jonathan, he blinked a few times and offered a crooked half smile.

"Again, man, I'm sorry, but I had to know before I laid it all out for you." He shrugged and turned the PDD so that Jon could see the small green LCD screen.

"I'll send her a single, concise image, repeating about three times a second for five seconds. Watch the waveforms." Robert pressed an icon on the screen and three distinct EEG tracings began to etch across the luminescent field from left to right. The tracings mirrored those on the screen mounted above Sarah's levitating body. Robert then activated the Cube reader, which operated silently.

Suddenly, on the PDD's small display, there was a flickering of first one, and then all of the waves. The peaks were momentarily sharper, the troughs more jagged and the overall flow of the tracings appeared disrupted, almost interfered with. Gradually, each tracing subsided into their previous innocuous states.

The tracings on the screen above Sarah and outside at the nurses' station remained unchanged throughout the exercise due to Robert's successful bypass of the Clinic's mainframe.

Robert clapped his hands together once, bit his lower lip and looked to Jon for a reaction. He received none. Webb remained still, his gaze drifting from the small PDD screen to his wife's frozen face.

"Yeah, okay. Not very impressive at first, I know. But check this out," Robert exclaimed, barely concealing his pride. Jon glared at him as if to say *Oh God, there's more?*

"Watch the screen again," Robert commanded.

The small PDD screen now split. The left half remained busy with the task of recording Sarah's EEG while the right half refreshed with a pure white background and a still image of the lower half of a man's face, the top margin of the scene sliced across the bridge of the nose just below the level of the eyes.

The man's face appeared young and cleanly shaven. Suddenly, the image came to life. The man's lips parted in a slight smile and then gently opened as a perfect dew covered fruit was raised to the mouth. Straight, bleached white teeth took a modest bite of what appeared to be a peach and began to chew in closed mouth delight. A smile touched the corners of the mouth as the video abruptly stopped, frozen in mid-mastication.

Jon looked to Robert with questioning eyes and a wrinkled brow.

"That's the image I've produced. Something that was easy and familiar, yet would provoke an emotional response. I just thought fresh fruit might trigger something—I don't know—innocent and enjoyable," Robert explained.

"Now, watch and listen." Robert again keyed several icons, and then adjusted the bright flat screen for Jon to observe. The image of the mouth came up, frozen at the beginning of the clip. The EEG continued across the left half of the small display. This time when the video clip began, an audio track narrated the scene in a voice both neutral and eloquent, almost professional.

In a soft, slightly baritone timbre, the voice simply said, "Jon takes a bite of the peach."

Jon flinched at the mention of his name and quickly glanced at Robert, who was smiling and watching Jon's reaction with great amusement and obvious pride.

Suddenly, out of the corner of his eye, Jon noticed the left half of the PDD screen. The waveforms were alive with energetic dances, bounding like threads of fine silk tied to a fan blowing on a summer day. The luminescent tracings seemed to be stretching long unused limbs, quivering in the throes of bioelectric ecstasy.

Jon gazed up at the wall-mounted screen above Sarah's hovering form. The EEG tracings depicted there remained unchanged from their previous sleepy state, and thanks to the prerecorded loop, no one but Robert and Jon were witness to the phenomenon.

Jon's wide-eyed gaze dropped to the small LCD as the video clip continued to run with its soft narration emanating from both the PDD speakers and the small earphones around Sarah's ears. He glanced from his wife's statue-still face to the rapidly weaving EEG and back again. He licked his lips and formed cautious words with a dry mouth.

"Is this real? Are these her responses—to that?" Jon asked, wanting to believe, afraid to commit.

"Yes, Jon. They're real." Robert smiled as he spoke.

"The visual alone worked well. But when coupled with the audio and, I believe, the mention of you by name—well, look at the damn screen! She hears us, Jon. Not only that, I really think she understands. Go ahead, feel her pulse."

Jon reached for her thin wrist and felt the rapid, vibrant beat of her heart, bounding as if straining to be heard. Her normal heart rate was a steady sixty to sixty-five beats per minute and never changed, even during the routine invasive procedures of blood draws and the like. Now, it was nearly double that.

Jon's eyes teared as he lost the struggle to contain his composure. His shoulders convulsed as he wracked with sobs. He fumbled with her hand and dropped to his knees, pressing her palm against his face as he purged the torrent of emotions that had swelled within throughout the day.

Robert silently stood aside as Jon exorcised the pent-up demons of long held sadness and desperate hope. He didn't want to violate the sanctity of the private moment with an unintentional, yet voyeuristic presence, so he instead turned his focus on the EEG display of the PDD.

The vidclip had ended moments ago, yet unlike the first run, the EEG tracings remained acutely animated. Only after several minutes did they diminish, finally returning to their previous restful baseline.

Five

Detective Salvatore Gionetti stepped into the crowded office space only after invitation by the somber and obviously preoccupied man in purple scrubs.

The Coroner's Main Forensic Lab was a large, sterile example of breakthrough technology featuring all of the toys and mystery-solving tools afforded modern investigative pathology. Simple street detectives such as Gionetti were rarely allowed to set foot across the sacred threshold and into the realm of super science.

Instead, he was meeting with the Chief Medical Examiner in one of his satellite offices tucked discreetly out of the way at the end of a dark hall two floors below where all of the real action took place.

Sal couldn't help but think of Dorothy, the Tin Man and the others as they first took an audience with the Great and Powerful Oz, wondering what it might have felt like when they finally realized the true identity of the Wizard.

He smiled as he gazed upon the disheveled and gaunt man seated behind the desk before him. *Pay no attention to the man behind the curtain*, he thought wryly.

Sal continued to smile as he hooked the back of an ancient looking wooden chair, gently spun it around to face the desk and took a seat without a word.

The Medical Examiner never looked up from the yellowed and crinkled files. He absently fingered a nub of pencil wedged behind his floppy, hairy ear as if he forgot he placed it there earlier and just now realized his absent mindedness. His thin and veiny fingers were discolored from tobacco stains; or, perhaps something more visceral about which Gionetti chose not to speculate.

"So, detective," the older man began. "What is it that interests you this afternoon?"

"The four bodies from Phoenix-Lamneth."

"Ah, the quadruple assassination."

Now the doctor looked up with faded rheumy eyes. His face glistened with a sheen of stale oil, almost greasy. He breathed through an open mouth that revealed far too many crooked and rotting teeth, bruised yellow and black. His thick, cracked tongue brush-licked his thin cyanotic upper lip, leaving no trace of moisture.

Sal Gionetti smiled thinly, nodded and then gently spread open his hands as they lay across his lap in polite response, all the while bristling internally at the doctor's off-handed assumption of premeditated assassination. He simply waited for the doctor to continue.

"Yes, a nasty piece of work there," the doctor said. "Though you really didn't need me or my extremely overworked staff, for that matter, to give you a conclusive cause of death, now, did you?" The doctor arched his eyebrows, pursed his lips and tossed him a disappointed sideways glance.

Gionetti continued to smile politely as he literally, and carefully, began to bite the back of his tongue. He had never dealt directly with the Chief Medical Examiner before and wasn't relishing any continued or future contact. Most of his relationships within the ME's office were with the staff examiners and their assistants; all of whom were professional, polite and even colorful, if not touched with a harmless, albeit morbid sense of humor.

Apparently, this case was high profile enough to require the Wizard himself to come out from behind the curtain to dazzle the meek inhabitants of Oz with his expertise.

Blinking rapidly, as if a speck of dust had suddenly landed in his eye, the doctor shifted his gaze back to the pile of seemingly disorganized files and sighed, shaking his head as he mumbled incomprehensibly. Sal assumed he was searching for the appropriate files and was hoping for a quick resolution to their meeting when a young woman rapped twice on a bookshelf with her knuckles as she stepped through the door at the back of the office and into the dim shambles.

She was also dressed in purple scrubs and carried a neatly packaged blue binder under her arm. The doctor ignored her entrance and without looking up at her or Sal motioned for the documents to be handed over to Gionetti. Sal accepted the file folder with a nod and soft, "Thank you."

Strange, Sal thought. *I hadn't even asked for the file, yet.*

The young woman held Gionetti's gaze for the briefest of seconds, and then let her eyes drop to the blue folder while she reluctantly, almost remorsefully, allowed her hand to fall away as Sal received the binder. He narrowed his eyes at her, posing an unspoken question that she rebuked quickly with a slight jerk of her head toward the Chief ME.

"Dr. Palmerson is ready for the review, sir," she spoke to the haggard man hunched over the debris strewn desk. "Shall I wait for you or go on ahead?" Her eyes fought the urge to glance over at Gionetti.

Curious, Sal thought.

"No, Tabby, go on ahead. I'll be there shortly. I can't find that blasted dictation from last time." The doctor continued to mumble as he struggled with the weight of the tangled papers. The woman moved to the doorway from which she entered and paused just outside of the office. Her back remained turned toward the interior of the office, but the poise of her head said she was intently listening. She was stalling to eavesdrop and Gionetti kept her keenly within his peripheral vision. He cleared his throat and thanked the doctor cordially while eyeing the woman outside of the doorway.

The frustrated doctor looked up at Gionetti with a gaze of surprise that the detective was still there.

"Yes, well, it's all there. Sorry for the hard copy. Going through a bit of reorganization within the data recording system and we obviously haven't had the time to formally transfer it holographically.

"Pretty cut and dry, though. Four lethal posterior headshots. Powder residue and flash burns verify the obviousness of close range. Who uses firearms anymore?" The doctor shook his head, referring to the use of outdated gunpowder-propellant cartridge-type projectiles.

Bullets.

"Nickel-jacketed shell casings from the looks of the mass spec. Four standard .38 caliber Trident slugs dug out from the interior walls of the room, complete with four hardy samples of brain matter that DNA-match with our victims. No question about the cause of death."

With that, Gionetti noticed the lingering woman visibly flinch and shrink closer to the doorjamb.

"Time frame?" asked the detective.

"I confidently put the time of death between 23:00 and 00:30," the doctor stated as if testifying before the Grand Jury. Then with a practiced air of boredom and impatience, he added, "Now, if you'll excuse me, I have a resident review to oversee and young, hopeful minds to enlighten."

"Of course, and thank you for your time." Gionetti quickly glanced toward the doorway. The woman was gone.

Sal rose and extended his hand to the doctor who reluctantly shook and then turned to leave.

"Ah, doctor?" Sal asked. The ME paused with his back to the detective then turned, visibly annoyed. "Yes, detective?"

"Just a quick question. Are you certain about that TOD? I mean, it seems like a fairly wide window."

The doctor raised his eyebrows and sighed, looking dismissively at Sal. "The majority of the brain tissue in all four samples was cauterized along the track of the bullet. The surrounding bulk of gray matter was jellified from the tumble of the slug and the sheer forces associated with violent encroachment into the cranial vault—the skull—making accurate cerebral death chronology by tissue analysis, which is our standard means of determining time-of-death, nearly impossible.

"So, based on what small, unadulterated samples we could, literally, scrape up and the results from the cardiac tissue analysis," he paused dramatically, and then added with mild arrogance, "Yes, I confidently put the time-of-death for all four victims between 23:00 and 00:30. That is the best I can do." He looked at Gionetti calmly, yet impatiently waiting for further discussion on what he deemed a moot subject.

"All right. Thank you, again, doctor—"

"You're welcome, detective. Good luck with your investigation." He turned and was out of the door before Sal could respond in kind.

Sal shook his head and chuckled as he strode out of the office and into the dim hall. *Odd bird,* he thought. *I never even got his name. And jellified? Was that even a word?*

Gionetti continued down the narrow, winding hall toward the old vertical elevators so common in buildings dated from the later part of the twentieth century. While he waited for the lift to arrive at his floor he took a quick glance at the inside cover page of the ME's report.

As he skimmed over the preliminary language and usual professional jargon, he noticed some loose sheets of thin paper folded between the interior pages of the report. He began fanning through the bound document to locate all of the loose pages when a small hand stayed his efforts with a firm grasp of his wrist. He snapped his head toward the owner of the hand, and startled, instinctively pulled the blue file folder closer to his body.

"Best to wait and look that over at home, with the doors locked," said the small woman from the ME's office.

"Tabby, is it?" asked Gionetti swallowing his surprise.

She smiled, half-heartedly. There was real fear just below the surface of her features. What usually passed for soft, even adolescently pudgy, was now taught and blanched with concern. The tension hardened her jaw line and stiffened her rounded cheeks. Her green eyes burned with jittery paranoia, darting from side to side without really moving. Her hand remained firmly on his wrist, tight and almost pleading.

The elevator chimed and the doors slowly retracted to the side. Sal glanced into the car to inspect for passengers. It was empty.

Her eyes never left his face as she spoke. "Flavham lied," she said sounding relieved to finally verbalize a long withheld breath. "I assisted him on the post mortems; if that's what you want to call them." Her eyes sifted through the shadows down the hall behind them. Sal said nothing, his open face encouraging her to continue.

She nodded at the blue binder. "That's the report, all right. The loose pages are my additions. I can't go into it now. Not here. Suffice to say that Dr. Flavham came out of nowhere two weeks ago as an interim replacement for Dr. Nichols, the actual Chief ME. He's supposed to be running things, but has just been going through the motions." Her eyes jumped from left to right.

"That is," she continued. "Until yesterday. He had refused to do any other routine PM's over the past two-and-a-half weeks; and now, suddenly, he has inserted himself as the ME on this particular case." She paused as the elevator doors began to slide shut. Sal caught them with an extended hand and looked back at Tabby with a confused furrowing of his brow.

"Well, he is the boss, and this is a relatively high profile case," Sal suggested baiting her for more.

"Interim ME. He's a temporary replacement, and as I said, came out of nowhere. I have yet to see any credentials, a CV, hell, the man has no skills from what I've witnessed!"

"He's *not* the ME?" Sal asked.

"You never actually met him?" She nodded in sudden understanding. "Dr. Nichols, I mean."

"I have to admit, no. I just assumed that cracked egg in there was him. I've always worked with the assistants or residents directly. And that was usually by voice or d-com. Rarely in person," Sal claimed.

She quickly glanced down the hall again, and then said, "Look, I need to get back before I'm missed, but we should meet later. Some place safe. I'll have more for you then." He nodded in quick agreement completely surprised by this sudden turn of events.

"Keystone—the club on Walthrop. You know of it?" she asked.

He raised his eyebrows. "Yeah, I know it."

Keystone was a hardcore, alternative lifestyles oasis, an anonymous haven for the well-to-do who didn't wish for it to be known with whom they were choosing to recreate. It was both expensive and elite.

She pursed her lips in a defensive pout, and then abruptly let it go. "22:00 tonight. Back bar by the aquarium. I'll find you," she ordered.

He nodded and then looked up and down the hall. They remained alone.

"Then who is he?" He nodded down the hall toward the ME's office.

"Flavham? Hell if I know. Nichols took an unexpected leave of absence two weeks ago for some family emergency. They brought in this clown to fill in. He's fucking worthless. I'm really not sure if he's even a forensic pathologist, much less a doctor." She sighed, slumped her shoulders and looked up at Sal.

She looked scared to death, but she continued, "Look, I'm relatively new here. Fresh out of residency, but I just can't believe what I'm seeing."

Sal frowned and then asked the question that troubled him most. "I never even asked him for the Phoenix file; yet you show on cue and hand it right over. How is that?"

Tabby shrugged and then whispered, "He said someone from Homicide would be by for the report and asked if I would prepare a hard copy."

"Why not digital?"

She shrugged again.

No digital record, no data trail, he concluded. *Therefore, Gionetti, my boy; no evidence.*

A door slammed down the hall, and she nearly jumped out of her skin. Sal reached reassuringly for her shoulder, but she instantly recoiled and turned away. As she walked briskly back down the hall, she glanced over her shoulder and quickly mouthed, "Tonight."

Gionetti nodded and watched her retreat. He then stepped into the elevator, allowing the doors to slide closed as he stared at the blue document binder clutched feverishly in his hand.

Curiouser and curiouser, Sal thought, with a wry nod to Lewis Carroll.

Six

Robert returned to the nurses' station with the slender black box carefully tucked under his arm; thin delicate wires trailing out from one tapered edge. He gently gathered the wires, quickly braided them into a tight coil and secreted the whole device under the white work surface of the desk as he spoke, "Now this is all preliminary, Jon.

"I mean, I haven't worked out all of the bugs. There is still a general language conflict with the initial burn and read primer, and translation algorithms are going to be a bitch to generate..."

His voice trailed off as Jon Webb sauntered behind him, approached the desk's edge and gazed at him beseechingly.

The man appeared as if he'd seen a ghost, his rough face softened by the conflicting emotions of elated excitement and fearful paranoia. He blinked twice to clear his eyes and took a deep breath as he raked his thick fingers through his close-cropped hair.

"Robert, can you really do it? Can what happened in there be the beginning of something..." He searched for the right choice of words.

"Phenomenal," Robert said. "Yes. I mean, I've already done it! Now it's a matter of making it meaningful.

"But it will take some time, and you need to think about what this means. For you and for Sarah. It could make things worse, you know."

Jon raised an eyebrow and frowned.

Robert elaborated. "Being able to communicate *to* her, but perhaps not *with* her. I just don't know if the networking will operate reciprocally. If I had to guess, I'd say that it might be impossible for her to respond in a meaningful way to any message you send. But there is no question that she receives and reacts. Whether or not we can interpret her responses remains unknown."

Robert shrugged and continued, "Man, I struggled with this for days after I thought it up. Should I go forward or not? Should I even mention it to you—hell, I guess in the end my ego made the decision for me.

"Of course, now I've crossed that ethical line. I can never go public with my work here without losing credibility."

"Or your job," Jon added wincing.

Robert gave a dismissive wave and grimaced. "Nah, fuck this place. They own all of the creative property coming out of here anyway. No, I think it might be time for me to invest in my own ideas. Branch out into the private sector. Nursing has begun to lose its appeal."

"I'd be sad to see you leave, but you're obviously wasting your talents." Jon crossed his arms and carefully chose his next words. "Robert, I'd like to see what we can do. Just once. I'd like to compose something for her. But I don't want to jeopardize you. This is dangerous territory with extreme consequences if we're caught."

"Webb, I've already considered that, and I wouldn't have exposed you to it if I didn't believe in it. I'm willing to take the risk. I will assume full responsibility." Robert smiled at Jon, and then eagerly typed in the last commands to withdraw his mainframe bypass and restore the centralized monitoring.

"You give some thought to what you'd like to say to your beautiful wife and how. I'll be ready whenever you are." He winked at Jon as he leaned back in his chair.

A soft musical tone chimed three times from within the desk's console. Jon quickly looked over the patient monitors expecting some flashing red warning or cautionary alert. But instead, Robert reluctantly leaned forward and activated a dark screen with the light touch of a finger. The screen came to life showing an elderly man with ivory hair and a crisp white clinical lab coat poised just outside of the unit's exterior doorway. He had just finished swiping his ID card and was awaiting approval and verification for entry.

The man glanced up at the camera and raised his eyebrows, his face otherwise stern and tight with visible arrogance.

Robert shook his head slowly and whispered, "Shit."

Jon cocked his head to one side. "What, what is it?" He moved closer to Robert and gazed over his shoulder at the monitor. Robert turned his head over his shoulder speaking to Jon in a frustrated sigh. "The Magnificent and Magical Merlin awaits."

Clearing his throat, Robert pressed the intercom button and spoke into the microphone with mock professionalism and feigned respect, "Afternoon, Dr. Matheson."

He released the mic button and turned to Jon. "You need to get out of here. He isn't here to compliment me on my dedicated service to the cause."

Jon faltered at the comment, swallowing hard. His eyes flicked toward Sarah's now darkened room and then back to Robert.

"No, no," Robert said reassuringly. "He couldn't possibly know anything about that. No, he's here to offer you the final ultimatum, I think. There's been a lot of talk lately, you know".

Jon nodded sadly.

"Just push yourself out. Say you got paged to work or something." Robert reached to press the door buzzer that would unlock the door and let the Associate Director of The Rainey Clinic inside.

He paused and glanced up at Jon offering a conspiratorial smile.

"You take some time, think about things, and I'll be in touch."

Jon dropped his hand to the young man's shoulder, gave a firm squeeze and returned the smile. "Thank you, Robert."

The door buzzed then clicked softly as Dr. Matheson entered the unit. He strode purposefully toward the nurses' station with choppy, pigeon-toed steps, his gait distinctively effeminate, his hips nearly swaying as he placed each foot directly in front of the other. His arms hung limply from his slumped shoulders, hands buried deep within the lab coat's side pockets.

He glanced about the unit, an obvious visual inspection. His head swiveled from side to side with the jerky movements of a bird surveying his roost. He came to rest at the front of the nurses' desk just as Jonathan was casually moving around the back and edging toward the exit trying to avoid making direct eye contact with the doctor.

The associate director rocked back on his heels and sucked his tongue pompously as he looked down on Robert who was completing some routine charting on the computer. Matheson made a soft clicking sound with his tongue as if to announce his arrival. It appeared as if he half-expected Robert to rise and acknowledge his presence.

Robert remained seated, however, and addressed him politely.

"Doctor Matheson, good to see you. I'll be with you in a moment." Robert continued with his deliberate keystrokes. The doctor glared at the subtle defiance appearing unsure how to respond.

Then he addressed Jonathan with a practiced empathetic smile, "Mr. Webb, so good to see you. I trust that your visit went well?"

Jon slowed his departure only slightly, enough to politely return the greeting.

"Yes, thank you. As usual, your staff has been extremely understanding and accommodating."

Robert tipped his head farther into his work as he tried to conceal the grin spreading across his face.

"Wonderful." Matheson paused, awkwardly searching for a suitable segue, visibly uncomfortable. "I actually just came from peds. Matthew is looking well. Dr. Bakersman assures me that everything is going fine. Bright boy, your son. Very special child. Handsome, too. Just a pleasure." Matheson's social ineptness only accentuated his caustic arrogance.

Jon merely smiled wanly at the comments giving the appearance of gracious acceptance.

"Thank you; he's certainly his mother's son," Jon offered suddenly feeling ashamed as if he were making an excuse. He cursed himself silently.

"Yes, indeed. And how is Sarah?" The question, obviously rhetorical, was directed more toward the nurse than the husband.

Robert quickly glanced to Jon for silent approval to answer; however, Jon was already formulating a response.

"As well as can be expected, considering," Jon offered, coolly clinical.

"Yes, well—" Matheson mumbled realizing how inane the inquiry sounded. He proceeded, though, onto the true nature of his visit. "Mr. Webb, if you have a moment, there is something I would like to discuss."

"Well, I do have to be going. I'm fairly late as it is."

"I'll accompany you. We can talk on the way out."

Jon nodded softly, once, and continued toward the exit as Matheson turned on his heels and raced to join him.

"Good afternoon, Robert," the doctor offered as he departed the unit and followed Jon through the open door.

Seven

As Gionetti exited the building, he tucked the blue file binder under the flap of his leather overcoat and turned his gaze skyward. The steel gray canopy of the late October afternoon was waxing over to the deep faded purple of early dusk, swollen with the promise of drizzle turning to fresh snow. A light, frozen mist spun down from above whirling in eddies from the heights and drawing wispy curtains of silvery cataract over the city.

He turned to assess the brick and stone exterior of the old building rising five stories above him into the autumn evening. The architecture reminded him of the many older buildings lining the crowded downtown streets of his hometown Chicago; the older store fronts of plate-glass and wrought iron, office and apartment buildings of flagstone and cinderblock alongside the modern monoliths of smoked glass and steel— never clashing, but co-existing in eclectic harmony. A virtual model of architectural symbiosis.

He turned back to the street and walked to the curb as a sleek ebony AirRide pulled silently to a hovering stop in front of him. The passenger door rotated open from the low frame, and he stooped to enter the vehicle. It rocked gently with his added weight buoyed on a cushion of air one meter above the concrete surface of the street. The door slid closed, and the vehicle glided forward with a whispered whine parting the dancing veil of icy mist and leaving a suspended wake of shimmering particles.

"How did it go, boss?" asked the driver.

Sal Gionetti shook his head and frowned. He sighed heavily and looked out of the side window through the wash of swirling moisture at the passing buildings—a solid wall of dull, dark brick and frosted glass broken only by the occasional empty intersections of cross streets. He longed for the sunshine and color of warm country summers.

Los Angeles was once a bright and busy circus teeming with characters and culture. Now, it echoed hollowly like a dusty old warehouse abandoned by restless tenants leaving fragments of memories and small, broken artifacts as the only evidence of productivity. The city ached palpably for enlightenment. He could feel the metropolis groan under the burdening weight of mankind's evolution.

They, as a species, were leaving behind far too much of the past, and in his opinion, the human race as a whole needed some closure.

"Sal?" the driver asked.

"Pete, this case is taking on a life of its own."

Silence filled the cab of the AirRide. The driver deftly negotiated a banking turn as the vehicle ascended into and gracefully fell out of the arc narrowly missing an abandoned tractor-trailer haunting the corner of a side street.

"Want to fill me in?" the driver suggested.

Sal tossed the blue binder onto the dashboard. Tiny frozen droplets of rain pelted the windshield and fractured on impact, fanning and crawling along the glass leaving jagged webs of water across the surface. Silhouettes of the writhing shadows wormed across the bright blue cover of the file folder as the limelight of occasional streetlights shone through the rain-streaked window. The driver activated the wiper and the windshield cleared with each passing sweep of the static arm.

The driver glanced at the file and then at Sal, raising one eyebrow inquisitively. His attention returned to the task of operating the vehicle when Sal spoke.

"Pete, we're playing a whole new game now, and I'm not even sure what the rules are."

Peterson shrugged and lightly shifted the vehicle laterally merging into the increasing flow of traffic. The sleet was solidifying into wet snow. Thin bands of white were pulled across the windshield by the wiper arm.

"Where to now?" Peterson asked.

"You're dropping me off in Beverly," Sal said.

He reached for the file folder, opened it and began to read.

Eight

"So, how are things over at Corporate Campus?" Matheson again attempted small talk as the two men walked the long curving corridors of the research facility.

"Business as usual," replied Jon without looking over at the doctor. "You mentioned that you had something you wanted to speak with me about. Is there a problem with Matthew?" Jon asked, cutting quickly to the chase, knowing full well that Sarah would be the topic of discussion.

"No, no. Matthew is doing quite well," Matheson replied dismissively. "Jon, as you know, our facility is focused on the task of opening the world's eyes to a whole new realm of medical care. We've willingly assumed the daunting task of removing the veil of doubt and fear from society's collective consciousness." The doctor smoothly shifted into solicitous lecture mode.

"No easy task, to be sure. However, over the past decade we have literally made quantum leaps forward in the field of neurological medicine. We have nearly eradicated Parkinson's and ALS with our stem cell technology, and may soon have a lock on cellular rehabilitation for stroke patients. These were once thought of as incurable, debilitating neurological disease states. But now, there is hope and a bright future for those unfortunate enough to become stricken." Matheson paused and slowed his step expecting some sort of awed response from Jon.

There was none. Jon continued his pace and the doctor was forced into a semi-jog to catch-up.

"Look, Jon—Mr. Webb, these successes are only possible through painstaking research and developmental applications. The Rainey Clinic has committed itself to that end. To achieve that, we must rely on—"

"Viable human subjects upon which you can implement your developmental applications. It's called experimentation, doctor, and I won't allow you to cut into my wife's head again. Or my son's, ever!" Jon stopped to face Matheson with a defiant stare.

The men had halted before a set a double glass doors opening into the lobby of the main reception area. Matheson gazed at his shoes and sighed heavily. "I understand your reluctance, in light of what you perceive as failures on our part."

"Perceive? *Perceive*?" Jon raised his voice in shock and anger. "There *were* failures on your part, you arrogant son-of-a-bitch!"

Matheson cringed at the verbal assault.

"I allowed the initial mapping and the placement of your HaloNet because you were confident—*confident*—that it would allow us to understand Sarah's physical responses and even lead to a method of meaningful communication.

"She was moving and responding to stimuli, Doctor Matheson! My wife could squeeze my hand when I held it and she wrinkled her brow when I kissed her."

"We can't be certain those actions were purposeful or meaningful," Matheson countered in defense. "That's why we insisted on the mapping and Halo."

"Exactly. I was content to believe that they *were* meaningful, but you planted that seed of doubt and offered me the Poison Apple. I selfishly took a bite. And now Sarah lies in a vegetative state. I don't even have what little there was to begin with. You speak of hope, yet you stole any shred of that away from me."

Matheson narrowed his eyes, tilted his gaze toward the taller man and with renewed strength, rallied his position.

"Look here, Mr. Webb. We explained the inherent risks of any invasive neurological procedure. We have been through this time and time again. I will not continue to apologize for our actions or our motivations. You were made fully aware of the potential outcomes, favorable or catastrophic. You consented and we gave our best efforts. The seizure was unpredictable, and quite honestly, probably would have occurred naturally regardless of our involvement."

He glared at Jon for a moment allowing the reality to settle in before continuing with a sigh. "The bottom line here, Jon, is that we can no longer justify Sarah's care without enrolling her in our Progressives. If you simply refuse to allow us further access, then we—you—need to make other arrangements for your wife's long-term care."

Jon simply stared at the man, fully anticipating this very moment, yet still treading in a thick pool of denial. Jon knew Matheson was right about his full consent, and that was the root of much of his guilt.

When they had first approached Jon with the idea of delving deeper into Sarah's mind to try and ascertain the meaningfulness of her physical responses, he was excited and hopeful. The staff assured him that the procedure of Halo placement and the initial cerebral mapping would be painless for Sarah.

However, there were still some risks involved.

Besides the obvious potential of infection associated with any invasive procedure, there was also a remote chance that the placement of the cerebral leads may cause changes or variations in her activity and responses. This, of course, was the whole idea—to illicit responses and then use them to map her neurologic network.

He had been told that her activity might improve or diminish, and that it was difficult to predict with any degree of accuracy how she would respond. Matheson himself reiterated that Sarah would never experience any discomfort and that in his experienced and professional opinion; she was an excellent candidate for this particular protocol.

Matheson had told Jon that he believed the HaloNet would offer hope in understanding Sarah's responses and bring actual, empirical meaning to the twitches and hand squeezes, and maybe even explain the occasional tearing and outbreaks of perspiration as something more than mere autonomic responses.

Jon had been awash with emotion in anticipation of some radical and wonderful revelation. Instead, two hours after her return from the completed and *successful* procedure Sarah had suffered an hour long, full-blown seizure that left her in a complete vegetative state. That was fourteen months ago, and Sarah had never shown the slightest sign of responsiveness.

Until today.

Matheson continued to look at Jon with a mix of exhausted sympathy and impatience. "Jon, it's time to move forward. There are some very good long-term care facilities in the metropolitan area. I'd be happy to make a few recommendations." He paused and then continued awkwardly, "As you know, we will remain legal custodians of Matthew until, well, whenever. And, of course, you are always encouraged to visit."

Jon narrowed his eyes, pursed his lips and shook his head slowly. "Thanks, that's big of you."

Matheson closed his eyes and spread his arms to his sides as he spoke. "Mr. Webb, don't continue to sour the sweetness of life with your vile bitterness. Frankly, it smacks of weakness and has little more effect on me than a mildly annoying cramp.

"You choose to continue to blame me, or technology, for your current state of sorrow. But remember, Jon…" He opened his eyes and looked coolly at Webb. "We didn't attack your wife four years ago.

"We've been there for you through it all. We brought Matthew into this world for you. We did our best to help you and Sarah. There is little more that we can do for you now. Help yourself, Mr. Webb. Move on."

Jon's eyes drifted to the ceiling as the doctor finished. Again, he knew Matheson was right, but to hear it from the pompous ass himself was too much to take on a day with as many emotional extremes as this one.

Jon turned to push through the glass doors, hesitated and then turned back to the doctor.

"All right, Matheson. Give me a few weeks. Say, after the holidays. I'll have arrangements made by then."

He would need time to work with Robert. He hoped that conceding now would take some focus off Sarah giving Robert the opportunity to fine-tune his new technology.

Matheson nodded with a weak and omniscient smile, as if to say, *Very well, then. It shall be done.*

Jon turned and pushed through the doors with nothing further to add.

Matheson's smile faded as he pulled a slim phone from his belt and placed a call. After a few seconds he spoke.

"Webb caved. No, not to Progressives. I told you he was adamant. Yes, relocation. A couple weeks. Plenty of time, I think. We'll start the prep work and have her ready in a day or two, as we agreed. Two thirds up front with the last third paid on demonstration—yes, and congratulations to you as well."

Nine

The Keystone was an orgy of green, blue, violet and red neon throbbing within a fog of multi-scented smoke. The club was large and labyrinth, with four huge bar stations and five elevated dance floors.

Like frantic wasps in a troubled hive, patrons swarmed within the maze of wide halls and large holographic screens that writhed with animated images. The thick atmosphere throbbed with deep, bass music as men and women in various stages of undress squirmed and slithered in erotic ritualistic dances reminiscent of ancient Roman ceremonies. Hidden apparatus over the dance floors sprayed brightly colored mist over the gyrating crowds, wetting loose garments of clothing, rendering them tissue thin and transparent, revealing much of the underlying anatomy.

Sal Gionetti pushed through the writhing masses, brushing against more moist body parts than he would have preferred. He worked toward the back bar, its massive aquarium looming high over the crowd. Small sharks and rays swam easily within their contained environment, seemingly oblivious to the sea of flesh below them or to the thunderous throb of electronic music throughout. As he wove through the tangle of limbs, he tried to ignore the surrounding depravity.

Wading through the debauchery, he passed a hallway that revealed what only could have been an orgy in the late stages of climax. The air reeked of spent Synth. Overt sex and drugs were common here among the patrons of the Keystone. That was the *motif*, as it were. Only the very wealthy and their invited guests were allowed to spend a night in Babylon; a five thousand International Credit cover charge ensured their discretion.

Sal had gained entry the old-fashioned way—with his badge. The owners never worried about police entanglements. Too many of the city's own finest frequented the catacombs of ill repute to allow for any legal discourse. They were allowed to operate business-as-usual provided they kept it elite and underground.

Sal approached the back bar under the aquarium and ordered a drink. Two women in lacy underwear and one shirtless young man immediately approached him, their eyes glazed by chemicals and the euphoric atmosphere.

"We're looking for a fourth. You interested?" asked one of the girls as she laid her hand on his. The other girl was nibbling at the man's bare chest while his eyes rolled back. He was humming some nursery rhyme that Sal recognized but couldn't place.

"No, thanks. I'm waiting for someone."

"Oh, aren't we always waiting, waiting and waiting. Why wait, when you can have the *now!*" The bare-chested man crooned as he ran his hands through the girl's hair. She moved her lips across his chest while he began to push her head down. She quickly, willingly dropped to her knees. The second girl shrugged and bent at the waist to join the other.

Sal grabbed his drink, tossed a bill at the bartender and moved along the bar away from the trio. A strong hand seized his wrist and nearly spun him around. He turned and glanced into a familiar pair of eyes.

"Tabby, thank God. I'm not sure I could handle another proposal." She eyed Sal up and down, taking a survey of his conservative wardrobe and cocked her head to the side. She smirked and then took his hand in hers. It was ice cold.

"Not to worry, detective. You're safe. I don't swing your way. Follow me, I've got a room."

She led him to the side of the monolithic aquarium, through a narrow corridor and into a stairwell lit by hidden black light. A small group of women were lounging about the stairs smoking and drinking in the dim purple glow.

They ascended two flights of stairs and came to a locked steel door. Tabby produced a key card and slid it through the reader. The door clicked and swung open, revealing a small cubical of a room, dimly lit and dank with smoke and musk.

Tabby led him by the hand to a small folded daybed against one wall where she directed him to sit. She then drifted toward the opposite wall as a tall, dark skinned figure emerged from the shadows, thin and graceful and draped in flowing ivory linen. The young woman's hair was rich auburn, long and spilling across her shoulders as she embraced Tabby and whispered in her ear, her eyes on Sal the entire time.

Tabby gently shook her head and kissed the girl on the forehead. The young woman slowly parted from Tabby, allowing her hands to linger a moment before withdrawing completely and retreating toward the door.

She continued to eye Gionetti as she sauntered past the daybed and opened the door, glancing back at Tabby with a slight pout on her small mouth.

"Thirty minutes, hon. Okay? That's all," Tabby assured her with a smile. "Maybe you can bring back a bottle of that vodka that I adore so much?"

The young woman nodded softly as she closed the door behind her, her eyes trailing down Sal's frame as the opening diminished. Sal had to admit, Tabby had taste. The young woman was breathtaking.

And also vaguely familiar.

Tabby approached the bed and sat on the corner opposite Gionetti. She played with her fingers in her lap as she began to talk, her gaze gradually meeting his as her confidence slowly strengthened.

"Thank you for meeting me here. I know it may be a little uncomfortable for you, but under the circumstances, I felt that this was the safest way to speak openly," she stated.

"No, not at all. I've been in far worse environments, believe me. I just feel as though I may be interrupting something. Your friend didn't seem pleased to leave us alone," Sal said.

"Carla can be jealous. She was actually disappointed that I didn't bring you along as a surprise treat." Tabby's voice softened with embarrassment. "She's been pressuring me into that for awhile. I'm just not ready to share." Tabby lit a cigarette and offered one to Sal. He politely shook his head.

"So, did you read the post mortem reports?" she asked.

"Yeah," he said raising his eyebrows, shrugging. "But you're going to have to dumb it down for me. I'm a little shaky on my laboratory interpretations. What is going on with this case?"

She took a long drag and spoke through a gray plume of sweet tobacco smoke. "Okay. Well, let's start at the beginning with Flavham," she began, tentatively at first, but then her narrative gained momentum.

"He shows up out of the blue one morning with news that Dr. Nichols, our Chief Medical Examiner, had to take some time off for a family emergency.

"Fine, no problem. It's business as usual around the lab. New residents stumbling over each other and the other four assistant ME's bickering about overtime and lunches."

"Now, aren't you a resident?" Sal asked.

"No, recent grad. Finished up at Cal and took this job five months ago. They were looking to bring the staff up to six full-time assistant ME's by Christmas. Right now, I'm number five."

Gionetti nodded, as she took another drag and blinked against the sharp smoke as it rose across her face.

"So, here's this Flavham guy. I'm new, so I wouldn't know him from Adam anyway. But none of the other ME's have heard of him either. The guy doesn't get involved in any of the cases, doesn't check up on us or offer any criticisms.

"I mean, it was like he was simply going through the motions. Yet, no one really batted an eye. We all kind of accepted the fact that he was just filling up a space until Nichols' return."

Sal waited as she lit a second cigarette off the first, and then stubbed out the butt under her heel.

"But now four bodies come in from Phoenix-Lamneth Corporate Campus, and suddenly he's super coroner. He insists on doing all four of the PM's himself and at first refuses any assistance.

"When he finally realizes the awesome task of going solo, he asks for me, specifically, to provide limited assistance. The other ME's offered to help lighten the load, but he refused and emphatically requested me, the most junior."

"You feel his request of you specifically was due to your junior status?" he asked.

"Absolutely. I think he figured that I'd be less likely to notice his incompetence and question his methods."

"Which you obviously did," Sal said.

Tabby nodded, looking around the room for something to focus on. She realized that she had been involuntarily hugging herself. She allowed her arms to fall back into her lap, the ash from the cigarette breaking off and tumbling onto the bed. She absently brushed at the flaky crumbs.

"It's difficult to get a decent job anywhere, and I've worked too damn hard and love what I do too damn much to fuck it up," she began. "And bringing this up could very well do just that."

She shook her head defiantly and continued, "But I can't, in good conscious, let this go without telling someone." Her eyes cautiously danced across Sal's quiet face, softly pleading for reassurance.

"What you've done and whatever you have to offer will be held in the strictest confidence, Tabby. I'll protect you as I would any informant."

She cringed at the word and worked her mouth into a sour frown as she digested that bitter reality.

"Great. Informant. Just what I was hoping for; a novel and grand stereotype. I even live the requisite deviant lifestyle defining that colorful character sketch," she said sarcastically as she gestured about the room.

Gionetti smiled warmly and shrugged. She half laughed, half sighed as she ran her fingers through her hair.

"Tabby, tell me about the post mortems. What's wrong with Flavham's report? What did you find?"

She looked directly at Gionetti and spoke the words clearly. "I think he was brought in to cover something up."

Gionetti bit the inside of his lip and allowed her time to explain.

"Four head shots. Four bodies. One scene," she said. "Looks exactly like what it was supposed to—a multiple assassination. But Flavham made the first and worst mistake in forensics; he assumed." She spoke with clinical confidence now, full of energy and emotion.

"Upon initial assessment, it's evident that the wounds are incompatible with life. These were fatal gunshot wounds; there is no doubt about it. But that's not necessarily what killed these people."

Gionetti eyed her questioningly, leaning back against the wall behind the bed.

"Flavham didn't even do a full craniotomy on any of the bodies."

Sal squinted at the term, its meaning temporarily eluding him. She nodded and explained. "Surgical removal of the scalp and skull, to visualize the contents of the cranium—the brain.

"Now granted, some of the heads were a mess, but it's still SOP to do a complete cranial dissection. Flavham just poked around the entry and exit wounds, hemmed and hawed a little and then moved on. When he saw me preparing for a crani on the first body he just looked at me all condescending like and shook his head, saying 'that's okay, dear, I think it's pretty evident what did these poor bastards in. No need to accentuate the obvious'." She shook her head and sighed.

"But, he told me—and his written report supports—that he dissected down and through the bullet tracks of all four patients, and that the brain tissue was in such a state that accurate cellular time-of-death would be nearly impossible. Now you're saying that he lied. That he falsified his report?" Sal asked.

Tabby nodded. "It gets worse. He didn't even run any of the labs for which he reports values. I drew the blood and tissue samples, but he never ran the tests." She raised her eyebrows for effect and tapped another cigarette from the crumpled box.

"So, not a single test was run on any of the samples taken from the bodies?" Sal asked, disbelievingly.

"I didn't say that the tests were never run, just that *he* didn't run them. He made up values to fit his report." She lit her cigarette and inhaled heavily. She spoke again with a long and throaty exhale of sweet smoke.

"I ran serum assays and full toxicology screens on all four of the bodies. Unfortunately, I was only able to do full cranial dissections on two of the four without raising his suspicion. The labs and findings from my assessments are contained in the handwritten addendum you received with his bogus report." She eyed him through the smoky haze drifting between them.

"Detective, according to my assessments, those people died before they were shot, or were well on their way. However, the toxicology screens came up clean; meaning no known poison or toxin was used. Which brings me to succinic acid and choline."

Gionetti cocked his head and responded carefully.

"Yes, I remember seeing those results. You highlighted them in red. What are they?"

"Metabolites of succinylmonocholine," she began. "There's a powerful paralytic drug commonly used during anesthesia called succinylcholine. It can completely paralyze someone in seconds when administered either intravenously or intramuscularly. It competes with naturally occurring neuromuscular chemical messengers in the body, binding at the junctions of the muscles and the nerves and essentially paralyzes the entire body for several minutes.

"The drug is rapidly metabolized by plasma enzymes in the blood and is quickly broken down into its constituent molecules. Ironically, succinylcholine is essentially made up of two molecules of acetylcholine, a naturally occurring chemical in the body. When the drug disassociates, it basically resembles acetylcholine.

"Therefore, detection is tricky, but not impossible, especially if you know to look for the end metabolites of succinylmonocholine—succinic acid and choline. A routine post mortem would not automatically scan for that."

"But you did. Why? What made you think of this drug?" Sal asked.

"Because the cardiac panel, which *is* part of the routine PM labs, showed critically elevated cardiac enzymes in three of the four victims. I also assayed cardiac tissue harvested from all four of the victims. These folks suffered severe coronary crisis resulting in massive MI's—heart attacks. They were dead or nearly dead before they were shot."

"How can you know that?"

"A head shot like the one they received results in instant death. Complete shut down of all organ systems. There's nothing left to run the machinery. Even though the heart may beat a few times after the injury, due to its own intrinsic pacemaker cells, the central neuronal intervention is completely severed. The heart stops beating, and then the tissues die along with everything else.

"The cardiac enzymes on labs will not be as elevated as with a full blown MI, and the cardiac tissue, upon gross and histological examination, appears far different than that from a heart that was starved for oxygen.

"When the heart is deprived of oxygen, as in a suffocation, it will work and struggle for its survival. There's a great deal of pain and suffering. There are obvious scars.

"It appeared obvious to me that the odds of three people simultaneously suffering a natural coronary event were astronomical. I sensed they were all forced to suffer some sort of oxygen deprivation."

"So, you immediately thought of paralyzing agents?"

"No, not immediately. But once you figure the logistics of trying to simultaneously asphyxiate three awake, otherwise healthy adults, without any physical signs of manual strangulation; well, the options sort of narrow down.

"Besides, I did a year of anesthesia as an intern before I committed to pathology. Succinylcholine fit the bill. So I tested for it and, voilá." She blinked twice and sniffed before releasing a shaky sigh.

"These people were executed, and made to suffer an agonizing death," she stated coolly.

"Wait. You said only three of the four suffered heart attacks prior to the headshots. What of the fourth?" Gionetti asked.

Tabby smiled and winked at the detective.

"Ah, good. I was wondering if you'd pick up on that. *That* guy died from his head wound, pure and simple. His cardiac workup was consistent with instantaneous brain death. And there was no trace of succinylmonocholine. He was spared death by paralysis, which reinforces my hypothesis."

"Why would someone put bullets through the brains of victims already dead from a nearly undetectable drug? Why go through all the extra trouble? What could it possibly gain?" he asked bewildered and stunned by the recent developments.

"Other than to make it look like obvious gunshot execution or to make some kind of statement, I don't know. That's for you to find out." Tabby exhaled a lazy cloud of blue-gray smoke.

Gionetti chewed the inside of his cheek contemplating the newly discovered facts of the case. He stared at the ceiling as he reclined against the cold stonewall of the dusky chamber.

"It seems like overkill," he finally exclaimed. "Pardon the pun."

"Yes, I agree. The whole point of using an undetectable, or hard to detect drug is to mask the murders as natural deaths. Putting a bullet in their heads was deliberate. Someone wanted you to think it was the primary modus operandi. I believe Flavham is somehow part of it, brought in to cement the illusion," she added.

"And in your opinion, this drug succinylcholine, would alone do the trick?" he asked.

"Absolutely," she responded nodding emphatically. "There would be no need to shoot them after injection. Unless the murderers were uncertain of the potential of the drug and wanted to be sure. But again, why go to the effort of utilizing it if you weren't confident of its success?"

"Then why not shoot them outright? Why go to the trouble of injecting them?" he asked himself aloud as much as addressing her. "And what about this fourth victim? When and why was he simply shot and spared the injection?"

Tabby slowly took a drag off her cigarette shaking her head numbly. Her eyes were glazed from the smoke, fixed in distant thought.

"Because it was a controlled kill," he slowly, quietly answered himself. "The scene was clean, Tabby. No signs of a struggle. No prints apart from the victims. Their bodies were casually situated around the table without any evidence that they were moved or positioned. They were killed as they sat calmly around the table."

Sal suddenly realized that in his attempt to work out the mystery he had just disclosed vital facts about the crime scene to an outside source. He just violated a golden rule in investigative work. He leaked details. Under the circumstances, however, he felt the transgression to be of minor consequence. The case had taken an abrupt and disturbing turn.

He continued to voice his thoughts, staring into the darkness of the room.

"If the fourth guy was shot first, then the others would have panicked. There would have been some sort of struggle, some excitement. Attempts to exit the room, subdue the perp, some sort of commotion. Yet, apparently they sat there and..."

He paused. His eyes widened as he processed his next thought. "You said *murderers*. Plural. Why?" He suddenly leaned toward her, anxious and aggressive.

"What?"

"Just a minute ago. You said 'the murderers', as if you assume there was more than one perpetrator."

Tabby blinked and then answered. "Based on what you've told me about the crime scene, it appears that the victims were more than likely subdued by some threat great enough to render them helpless. Held at gunpoint, or needle point, as the case may be.

"Otherwise, as you've said, there would have been some sort of commotion. A struggle or panic. It seems logical that it would take more than one individual to keep four people rooted in their seats. I just assumed—"

"Unless they knew the killer" he countered. Tabby considered this as she stubbed out the butt of her cigarette. She exhaled the last plume of smoke with a heavy sigh.

"Could one person effectively inject three people, nearly simultaneously, without them knowing it?" he asked almost breathless.

"Well, whether they realized they were just injected or not is a moot point. The effects of the drug after an intramuscular injection would occur within a minute. Depending on the injection site and the size of the device, it may only feel like a small pinch or insect bite. I suppose..." She trailed off considering possibilities.

Sal narrowed his eyes at her allowing her time to think through her response. She suddenly shook her head and frowned.

"No, I really doubt that you could smoothly deliver the requisite dose of succs to three separate individuals within seconds of each other. I mean, the amount of drug necessary to achieve effective paralysis in one adult, via IM injection, is about seven to ten cc's. That would mean a total of at least twenty-five to thirty cc's of drug concealed and delivered in secret. I don't know." She again shook her head doubtfully.

"What about super-concentrated preparations of the drug? That would allow for less actual volume. And believe me, delivery systems have evolved with advancements in nanotechnology. I've seen single filament threads of highly conductive metal, no thicker than a hair, deliver lethal doses of electric current from across a room." Sal offered his expertise somberly, yet assuredly.

Tabby eyed him curiously.

"I guess I have much yet to learn in forensics," she admitted. Then continued with renewed optimism. "I suppose if the drug were to be concentrated, and somehow delivered covertly, sure, there's a possibility that one person could carry out the task. But how?" she wondered aloud as Sal suddenly extended his hand as if to offer a greeting handshake. Tabby instinctively reached for his hand, then caught herself with a gasp of realization.

Sal frowned wanly and nodded.

"A simple handshake, firm enough to distract from a lightning quick needle stick into the flesh of the palm," he suggested. "They knew this guy. And I'll bet if you inspect the palms of their hands, you'll find evidence of injection."

Tabby's mouth remained agape as she examined the palm of her hand.

"Of course, that still leaves our fourth victim." Sal sighed and again leaned back into the wall. He stretched out his legs and turned away from Tabby looking for inspiration among the shadows of the darkened room.

"My instinct says that he was shot after the fact, perhaps forced to watch the others suffer," Sal suggested with an exhausted sigh. "Maybe to extract some information, I don't know."

"Well, if he witnessed their deaths by succs paralysis, he saw a very disturbing sight. They would have fasciculated violently. Each and every muscle would have rapidly contracted, and then relaxed as the drug saturated their neuromuscular junctions. Within seconds their bodies would go completely limp, and then, well..."

"Yeah, not pretty, I guess," he offered. Tabby shook her head slowly. They both sat silently digesting their conversation. Tabby began to look nervous and shifted her gaze from the door to Sal, and then back to her supinated hands.

"Detective," she finally broke the brief silence. "What makes you so sure that this was the work of a single individual? I mean, generally, the simplest explanation is usually the correct explanation. The theory of a single perpetrator just requires the acceptance of too many far-fetched assumptions. It's possible, but certainly not probable."

"Really nothing more than a hunch, Tabby," he replied. He wasn't going to involve the young doctor any more than she had already involved herself, and to reveal what he earlier believed to be coincidence as corroborating fact was to jeopardize the investigation. Tabby knew more than she needed and could be in danger if it were known what she just shared with Sal. Besides, what scared Sal the most was that he believed her every word.

He suddenly slapped his thighs and moved to get up. He had his focus earlier, but now things were starting to fall apart. He felt that he had a firm handle on a seemingly straight-forward case, and before his encounter with Tabby, believed that he would have a prime suspect in easy custody by morning.

However, the dynamics had changed. He still had a prime suspect, but now his doubts were growing and even more questions were raised by the evidence provided by Tabby.

She looked up at Gionetti as he rose, and for the second time that evening appeared frightened and lost. Sal smiled and winked reassuringly. She returned the smile, though weakly and without conviction.

"You did good tonight, Tabby. Don't doubt that for a second."

She shrugged, not in modesty, but rather uncertainty. Her gaze dropped to the floor.

"I do think that you should remain underground for awhile," he suggested looking around the room. "It's Thursday. Take tomorrow off and stay low for the weekend. Keep yourself concealed, just as a precaution. Do you have a place to go? Somewhere I can reach you?" he asked.

She nodded and shrugged again. "I'm sure that I can stay with Carla. She has a place at the beach, though I don't want to involve her. Or put her in danger either." Tabby gazed up at the detective seeming to implore him for strength and guaranteed assurances.

"Go with Carla. Give me a number, and I'll contact you when I have something concrete. You'll both be safe if you stay low and avoid me. And don't go back into work, not yet. Make some excuse." With a reluctant nod, she gave him a digital contact and he committed it to memory.

As he prepared to leave, he offered a departing handshake. She simply stared at his extended hand, looked into his eyes and they both shared a nervous laugh.

Ten

The ambient glow of wintry dusk barely illuminated the interior of the vehicle despite the almost phosphorescent quality of the thickening snowfall outside. Peterson held his paperback novel at an angle to the side window in an effort to continue to read as nightfall pressed onto the darkening street. He resisted the urge to flick on the interior reading light so as not to draw attention to himself or the sleek black Boeing AirRide.

Suddenly, the block danced with quivering shadows cast by the stuttering ignition of halogen-vapor street lamps as they fired to life, triggered by some unseen timer. Each suspended lamp cast its bright, mercurial light down in milky pools of shimmering molten ivory, illuminating various portions of the surrounding neighborhood quite well while leaving other areas swimming in cold blackness.

Random wisps alternating with full curtains of powdery snow blew past and swirled around the angular frame of the vehicle. Peterson gave up trying to finish his novel as the streetlights threw long and impossible shadows over the windows of his silently hovering vehicle.

While on surveillance watches such as this, he preferred the company of paperbound literature over that of the modern digital media. Sure, it may be easier to find and store any book you desired with the stroke of a laser stylus, but that wasn't the true intention of literature. Books were meant to be enjoyed in the format for which they were created—in print, on paper, and bound with cloth and fiber.

The whole experience of opening a book, feeling the texture of the pages, smelling the age and environment, left him feeling viscerally aware of the story within as if his senses helped to define the milieu of each tale. No two books felt or smelled the same, and each narrative had a unique voice that never changed over time no matter how many times the book was reread.

He carefully placed his tattered copy of Ray Bradbury's *Fahrenheit 451* in the small console between the front seats and pulled out the stainless steel flask of brandy he kept stowed away. As he spun the cap off the container he noticed movement across the street near the opening to a dark intersection. He took a long pull of the amber liquid allowing its warmth to cascade down his throat and settle like fresh viscous syrup in his stomach.

He watched for additional movement within the thick shadows across the street between the lighted pools of the hanging street lamps, beyond the darkened intersection and under Jonathan Webb's apartment.

After dropping Gionetti off in the Club District, he had returned here, to the Lower Town area, where the subject of his surveillance resided. The assistant detective was hopeful for an early sighting of Mr. Webb so he could report to Gionetti that the man was in for the night and then maybe head home himself.

He didn't mind the tedious and often mundane tasks associated with investigative work, and in fact, enjoyed the mild euphoria of assisting in closing difficult cases. This particular case, though, seemed rather cut and dry, and he failed to share in the growing skepticism of his boss.

However, Gionetti was adamant about close and thorough surveillance of their prime suspect. So, Peterson secreted himself among the thick inky shadows of yet another low income neighborhood, with a small flask and a good book; obedient, semi-vigilant and bored.

He scanned the surrounding area methodically as he took a second and then a third sip from the flask, before replacing its cap and returning it to its place of concealment.

He noticed one particular shadow pull away from the others and slowly slink down the sidewalk from one of the alley openings. He watched the silhouette glide purposefully toward the corner of Webb's building, and then halt at the lighted perimeter's edge, immersed in the gloom, as if wary to proceed into the light and up to the entrance. Peterson shifted in his seat and leaned forward to improve his view, but the figure remained cloaked in darkness.

He sighed, frustrated, and reached up to shield the interior dome light as he quickly and quietly opened his door, slipped out of the hovering vehicle and gently closed the door without a sound.

The AirRide bounced almost imperceptibly from the relief of his weight. He crept along the smooth fender toward the rear of the vehicle, using the shadows for cover.

The dark figure at the corner neither stirred nor showed any sign that he noticed Peterson's movements.

As Peterson reached the tapered tail of the vehicle he paused, quickly feeling through his coat pockets. *Shit*, he cursed silently. He left his digital plasma-graph on the front seat. He would need it to capture some clips and stills for Gionetti, and have them verified as images of Webb.

Peterson shook his head, disgusted with himself for his lack of preparedness and began to slink back toward the driver's door to retrieve his video device. He gently ran his hand along the cool, smooth plastic of the AirRide's frame as he slid back alongside vehicle.

With his eyes fixed on the still shadowy figure across the street, he stretched his arm out the few extra inches needed to reach the thumbprint latch imbedded within the surface of the door, his fingers swimming in air, seeking purchase. They briefly brushed at the powdery snow cascading across the slick plastic surface, and then felt the slight bulging irregularity of the tactile print-plate that would unlock his door.

He suddenly remembered that the interior dome light would illuminate upon the door unlocking and swinging open, surely giving away his position and ruining the surveillance altogether. He silently cursed himself again for forgetting the camera. His hand dropped away from the print-plate and he began to reassess the situation.

He turned to slide back into the darkness afforded by the rear of the vehicle as a cold, steely object pressed into his forehead.

Simultaneously, a firm hand grabbed the hair at the back of his neck and forced his entire head forward into the sudden sharpness of the object fixed into his brow. He felt, rather than heard, the soft, wet crunching sound of his skull being rapidly penetrated from front to rear, caught in a fatal vise grip as the blade drove deep into and through his brain.

Light exploded behind his eyes and then went black—nothingness.

His death was lightning quick and vacuum silent.

Peterson's limp body hung for a moment, suspended by his pierced skull between the powerful hands of the ghostly assailant, then slumped to the snowy asphalt as the lethal grip loosened and the blade slid back into concealment.

The dark figure across the street stirred gently, as if readjusting its cloak of shadows, and then proceeded into the entrance of Webb's building.

~ * ~

Jon Webb walked around the corner of his building and into the sharp November wind, fine granules of snow stung his chapped face. He would never get used to the new winters in southern California. He remembered visiting the west coast as a child with its year-round sunshine and warmth. Now, most of the warm weather foliage that had once graced the sunny coastal valleys had all but completely disappeared replaced by the sturdy conifers and perennial grasses that normally flourish in the upper Midwest.

As he approached the entrance to his building a sleek dark Boeing AirRide slid out of the shadows and down the street humming over the asphalt on a perpetual cushion of air. The vehicle cruised slowly and deliberately out of the neighborhood, its running lights extinguished until it reached the end of the block where it made a slow right turn, its lights snapped on, and it disappeared behind the distant architecture.

Webb paused, giving the departing vehicle only mild consideration due to the rareness of its make and model, and then continued through the glass doors as they parted in recognition of his eye-scan and palm-print identification.

Jon Webb stepped through the tiny stone foyer and into the elevator alcove where, again, he submitted to and passed a short number of personal identification security measures. Once completed, the 'vator doors snapped open in a quiet whisper of pressurized air.

Jon boarded the conveyance and spoke softly into the mesh screen imbedded in the faux-wood wall of the interior of the car.

"Seven-C. Tango. Uniform. Capricorn," he submitted the destination of his apartment and access code words for voice verification and acknowledgment by the Resident Artificial Intelligence.

The RAI, or "Ray", was a fully integrated, self-sufficient, locally contained meta-computer designed to fully interact with the residents of the building. Ray provided an extensive assortment of services ranging from simple personal messaging to elaborate maintenance and security measures. Ray essentially ran the building and everything within its walls.

A soft, musical tone, personalized for each member of the residence, rang from the elevator speakers to notify Webb that he had been acknowledged.

"Evening, Ray," Jon said absently.

"Good evening, Mr. Webb. I trust that your day went well. I was expecting you much sooner, being that it is Thursday. However, I understand that things do come up from time to time. I hope that any unexpected changes in your routine came as pleasant surprises."

Jon frowned morosely as he recalled the day's events.

Ray was programmed to learn from his interactions with his human tenants and realizing that some people responded well to the idea of having a sentient intelligence daunting over them, while others were certainly threatened, he tailored each relationship accordingly. Through the use of various genderized voice programs, accents, conversational personality archetypes and even generational slang, Ray could customize exactly how each tenant experienced his presence.

Mrs. Rafferty, the middle-aged widow on the third floor, preferred to experience Ray as a soft, yet powerfully confident and independent English woman perhaps to fulfill some self-perceived void in her own personal make-up.

To the couple living two floors above Jonathan, Ray presented himself, sadly, as an attentive and inquisitive adolescent male always eager to please and serve; their own fourteen-year-old son having been missing for nearly two years.

For Jon, though, Ray had yet to develop that certain relational character. Early on, during the initiation process, Ray trialed many of the standard avatars that had proven popularly successful with men of Jon's phenotype. The results were unquestionably negative.

In fact, after only a few days, Jon had asked Ray to cease his attempts to find an appropriate character and just stick to the neutral default. However, the young, soft spoken Southern belle with matriarchal tendencies did last nearly three days whereas most of the personalities were immediately aborted.

"You have twelve new audio messages awaiting you and five dig-vids," Ray informed in a caring, yet professionally detached masculine voice.

Jon sighed, regrettably expecting a flood of messages in the wake of the Corporate Campus murders.

"Would you like to review them now in summary or just identify the sources?" Ray asked.

"No," Jon answered. "Just sort by source. Delay all originating from Phoenix-Lamneth internal. Summarize all others."

Jon could wait to review any traffic from coworkers and curious associates depending on how much about the murders had already leaked out, although he believed that Lacombe and MacDonald had probably contained this particular situation quite tightly.

Jon yawned and rubbed his eyes as the OmniVator rose to his floor. Ray would have processed his request within seconds and the messages would be waiting for his perusal on the holo-disc in his apartment.

He needed a stiff drink first, then maybe a shower.

The 'vator doors slid silently open at the threshold of his apartment. Jon blinked as the foyer lights automatically flickered on and the identification panel on his door glowed to life.

He stepped up to the small screen and entered his password as a soft fan of orange coherent laser light scanned his eyes. The door hummed for a second then multiple clicks from deep within its interior announced his clearance to enter. The door rose quickly and smoothly into the ceiling and Jon stepped into his darkened apartment.

He had his 15mm Heston automag out of its shoulder holster in a split second, holding the weapon at arm's length in a two-handed combat grip, sweeping from right to left as he scanned the immediate darkness before him.

The apartment lights should have activated automatically upon his entrance. The fact that they didn't instinctively alarmed him.

"Ray, security record," Jon quickly requested that the resident computer begin an immediate multimedia record of the interior of his apartment thus capturing any current activity on official record. If he were to encounter any intruder, which was usually assumed unlikely considering the level of security protecting this residential building, the incident would be accurately recorded for legal history.

Jon then initiated the New Common Miranda Warning, which legally cleared him to fire his weapon first if need be, without questions or consequence. A direct result of the Safe-Self Law passed early in the past decade; the new Miranda Warning gave individuals the right to adequately protect their homes and families without fear of legal reprisal from the trespassers. As a result, residential break-ins and violations were rare.

"I am armed and will fire to kill. You are unwelcome. Show yourself in a non-threatening manner," Jon uttered the warning. The apartment lights remained out, and curiously, Ray had yet to respond or verify Jon's request for a security record.

"Ray, initiate security record. Verify," Jon repeated.

Still, the computer remained silent—the apartment, dark. Jon swept his weapon in slow, purposeful arcs, trying to allow his eyes to adjust to the blackness of the room.

There was a faint, mechanical click behind him and to his left. As he spun toward the sound, the cold metal of a pistol suddenly pressed into his cheek. He could feel the concavity of the barrel's opening dimple his skin. He felt the slight hum of the weapon's magnetic charger vibrate against his facial bones.

"Easy, Jonny. I had to be sure it was you and not the goons from outside," the familiar voice whispered.

Jon's own pistol vibrated in his sweaty hands, the fully charged magnetic coils ready to propel their hollow point trillium ferrous alloy rounds. Jon swallowed hard as his mind grappled with the fact that one of his employees, and his friend, had an electromagnetic auto-burst pistol jammed into his face.

"Max," Jon began. "What is—?"

"Ah, ah, ah," Max Donovan warned. "Power-down your weapon. Slowly. Then we can talk."

Jon flicked the power switch on his pistol with his thumb. It responded immediately with a soft, barely audible purr that wound down to silence as the magnetic field dissipated and the weapon placed itself in a safe mode.

Max reached over with his free hand and groped for the pistol in Jon's hands. In that brief moment, taking advantage of the slight shift in balance as he released his grip on the gun, Jon quickly spun away from Max's grasp, fell to the floor and rolled across the stone tile to the nearest wall where he regained his bearings in the dark room.

"Oh, come on, Jon. Relax. I wasn't going to shoot you. I told you, I was just being cautious, man," Max stammered in his speech slurring his words. "Look," he continued, "I'll put on the lights. Just relax, and don't jump me."

Max half chuckled sounding uncertain and shaky. "Hey, Jon? You don't have another gun on you, do you?" the man asked suddenly sounding more afraid than nervous.

"Lights are going on now, Jon. Do not shoot me, okay?"

The lights gradually came on, controlled by an automatic rheostat, indirectly illuminating the entire apartment from shadowy dusk to brilliant noon over a few seconds.

Max spun spastically about, eyes darting to every corner, every nook, trying to locate the elusive Jon Webb. As he completed a fully distressed and desperate turn, he froze, wide-eyed and quivering.

Jon held a plasma Fasor to Max's forehead and firmly depressed the charge button. The small weapon whined in response as it energized to six hundred joules.

Max's eyes were locked on the index finger of Jon's right hand as he held it poised over the discharge button that would release the entire amount of stored energy in a sharp plume of electric blue plasma. Six hundred joules from the Focused Amplification and Serial Optic Radiation weapon would liquefy his eyes in their sockets and evaporate his soft, moist brain tissue in a flash.

Max jerked his eyes from the gun to Jon's stern face and back again. He licked his lips and stammered again, quivering and pale.

"Easy, now Jon, easy. Let me explain—"

"I cannot believe you held a gun to my head, you ballsy little fuck!" Jon shouted.

"Man, it's not like that!" Max said. "I didn't know where to go. They've been following me all day. I've been trying to think through this whole situation at Phoenix. Man, I just needed to talk to you, and you weren't home. I tried your digcom, left a couple of messages." Max's voice hitched with emotion. "I couldn't stay at my place anymore; I could see the surveillance teams all over the neighborhood—fucking amateurs. I went out and they were everywhere. So I came here.

"They got your place under watch, too, you know." Max's breath was sour and heavy with oxidized alcohol. Jon blinked but said nothing. His grip on the Fasor never loosened.

"Come on, Jon, you know me. I just needed to see you. I'm sorry about the gun thing, really. I was just being cautious. I guess I'm a little paranoid."

Jon raised his eyebrow at this.

"Okay," Max admitted. "A lot. I'm scared, man. They think I did this." His lips were quivering with stress and emotion.

Jon narrowed his eyes at his friend and sighed heavily. The Fasor remained firmly pressed into Max's brow. "Max, you've been drinking. I'll allow you this. Once and only once."

"You ever point a weapon at me again, you better use it. Don't even think about going halfway. I will kill you in an instant. Are we clear?" Jon glared.

Max nodded against the pressure of the plasma weapon, his eyes locked with Jon's. A stiff moment passed between them, unspoken understandings took root, and then the Fasor was lowered. Max sighed and rubbed his forehead.

Jon took a few cautious steps back, kneeled and holstered the slender gun against his ankle. The weapon whined softly as it powered down to safe. He looked up at Max with a mix of confusion and disappointment.

"How did you bypass Ray and gain entry?" Webb asked Max.

"Oh, that old logic matrix was easy. I remotely inserted a Patriot virus and enacted a preliminary search-and-seizure under probable cause suspicion." Max explained referring to the technique of legally overriding personal residence security measures; an outdated, yet trustworthy method adopted under the Generation Four Patriot Act.

The law, an over-revision of the original Patriot Act that had been proposed during the first decade of the century, was enacted during the turbulent and paranoid period when global terrorism peaked and became a real and constant threat to all citizens. It allowed for law enforcement and governmental agencies to gain undetected access to any residential area via computerized security systems in efforts to flush out covert terrorists.

Jon nodded as if to confirm the obviousness of the act. He sighed and turned to enter the main room of his apartment. Max followed slowly, sheepishly.

"Hey, Webb," Max began, sounding apologetic and sincere. "Again, I'm sorry about the gun and everything."

Jon waved his hand dismissively and poured two tall glasses of dark amber bourbon from a bottle under his desk. The sharp tang of the alcohol vapors rose from the heavy glass as he passed it to Max.

Jon immediately took a long sip from his glass and closed his eyes as he swallowed slowly. He took a second, and then dropped down into the heavy desk chair behind the glass and metal work station housing his personal holo-disc and household controls. Webb entered a few characters on the keypad and watched the glow of the holographic LCD display. He took another drink as he motioned for Max to have a seat.

The LCD danced with activity throwing multicolored angular shapes across Jon's sharp facial features. He studied the screen in silence momentarily ignoring his guest. Max sat stiffly in his chair and nursed his drink.

After a few minutes, the LCD froze displaying an empty milky white field, blank except for the small blinking blue icon at the very bottom right. Jon touched the screen at the icon and a dark green grid oscillated into view, undulating and writhing across the flat panel in silent rhythm.

Jon took a sip from his glass and extended his open hand toward Max, leaving his eyes fixed on the screen. "Give me the override and termination codes for the Patriot," Jon demanded coolly.

Max sighed and began to recite the sequence of random words that would extinguish the Patriot virus and erase any history of its existence. Jonathan quickly entered the code as Max uttered the words, typing and touching the screen at the appropriate intervals.

After the last fragment of code was entered, Jon sat back in his chair and finished off his drink. He stretched his massive arms behind his head and spoke in a clear and loud voice.

"Hello, Ray?"

The resident computer answered immediately through the small speakers embedded in the work station's polished surface. "Yes, Mr. Webb?"

Jon nodded and rose to pour another drink. He spoke to the computer as he grabbed Max's half-empty glass and poured them each another drink, more hefty than the first.

"Ray, I'd like full digcom summarizations jump-loaded to my PDD, then fully delete my entire log. Everything. I then want you to disengage for this evening. Fully dissociate. You may return to minimal default functions at 0600, with the exception of messaging. Verify."

Webb now looked sternly at Max as he returned to his seat handing the glass over the table. Max accepted and sat back avoiding Jon's piercing eyes.

Ray responded, "Confirm request. You realize that by my disengaging, you remain without the highest level of security and protocol."

"Yes, Ray, and thank you. Verify and execute."

"Confirm and initiate," Ray answered. "Good night, Mr. Webb."

Jon waited for a minute, glancing about the apartment as if he could actually see evidence of Ray's physical departure. However, Ray's compliance would only be evidenced by the lack of his ethereal presence. He, of course, did not physically exist.

"Ray?" inquired Jon of the ceiling. "Ray?"

There was no response. Jon took another sip from his drink, and then turned toward his friend and fellow employee.

"Now that he's blinded, let's talk." Jon directed his attention to Max.

Max shrugged and drank from his glass. He wrinkled his brow as if working through a difficult mathematical problem. Finally, he spoke.

"I don't know where to start, man," It was all he could honestly offer.

"How about last night? Can you account for yourself during the time the murders occurred?" Jon asked pointedly.

Max winced at the question and looked up, wounded. "What, you think I had something to do with this?"

Jon shrugged and drank from his glass. "Hey, I know only what I know. And you would ask the same of me if I were on last night."

"Yeah, I suppose." Max relaxed a bit. He was visibly shaken. His eyes remained glassy from the stress and the alcohol. "Look, I finished rounding about 2300, and then went to the disposal bay to have a smoke and chat with Red." Max recalled the previous evening's events in detail, outlining his movements and activities up to and including his meeting up with Jonathan that morning.

"That's it, boss. I got triple paged from P-Mac to hook up with you and report to the Center. You know the rest," Max concluded.

Jon sat awhile in silence, and then asked Max, "So, what are your thoughts?"

"Shit. How in the hell could anybody without access even get close to that room, much less in and out cleanly," Max said. "Had to be an inside job."

"Yeah, that's obvious, I think," Jon agreed. "Problem now is, who and why."

"I get the feeling that MacDonald and Lacombe may know more than they let on. What did that detective—what's his name? What does he think?"

"Gionetti. I think he thinks it's an inside job as well, and that one or both of us is involved. He has to," Jon said sipping his bourbon. "I would."

Max shook his head. "Christ! What the hell is going on? I didn't do this, and I'm relatively sure you didn't."

"Thanks," Jon responded somberly.

Max smirked apologetically.

"Seriously, Jon. What do you think is going on?"

"I honestly don't know. But there are a number of things that concern me about this whole affair," Jon began. "First, we're obviously being set up to take the fall for this, though I can't see why.

"Secondly, those people were executed. Why? What is their connection? They were all together in one room; there has to be a connection. Which brings me to the kill mode."

"Kill mode?" Max asked.

"Yeah, it's what we used to call the method of execution. You investigate enough grisly scenes, you start using sterile clinical terms to keep a detached perspective. After awhile it just becomes routine to speak about death like you were discussing it with a computer."

Max nodded reminding himself about Jonathan Webb's past experiences.

Jon continued, "They knew their assailant. Knew him well, in fact. Well enough to all remain seated at the time of their demise."

"Yeah, that kinda bothered me, too," Max added. "No sign of a struggle or surprise. Like they were all shot simultaneously..."

Jon raised his eyebrows as Max paused suddenly realizing the revelation.

"That would mean more than one killer," Max concluded. "What, actually four different individuals, right? No way!"

"I thought about that, too. Actually the moment I saw the scene, I suspected something was wrong. But I still wonder about there being more than one killer. More than one person at anytime for anything is a conspiracy.

"This group of murders is huge for some reason. It is important to someone. Important enough to have been committed right under our noses, in our house, and was engineered to fall on to us," Jon paused, wondering.

"There's a purpose behind this. Someone wants to make a point, and the more people involved, the more opportunity there is for it to backfire.

You want to limit the number of people involved, and then distance yourself from the wet work," Jon explained.

He finished off his drink and carefully, thoughtfully, placed his glass down on the polished steel surface of the desk. "No, whoever engineered this has a grand design. I truly believe that there was only one killer, and I wouldn't be surprised if he hasn't been taken care of in the process."

Max shook his head. "But who? And how?"

"That's the billion dollar question. And to find the answer, we need to start asking why. Otherwise, we remain prime suspects number one and two." Jon looked at Max and waited for the younger man's response.

The stress had wreaked havoc on Max. He was half-drunk, jittery and paranoid. His whole world had come crashing down around him without warning leaving him defenseless. Jon empathized completely, having been there himself many times over the last few years, although Max lacked the internal machinery to forge the necessary emotional tools to begin reconstruction of his life. For that he would require close supervision and guidance; otherwise, he would certainly spin into defeated oblivion.

"What do we do?" Max asked, almost childlike in his desperation, openly wounded and fearful of the ambivalent environment broiling around him out of his control.

On observing the young man in this state, Jonathan was instantly glad that he hadn't Fasored him earlier.

"I suggest that we immediately cooperate with the investigation, offer to become involved in whatever capacity. There are enough loose ends yet that we haven't been formally charged, though, it's simply a matter of time. The best thing for us right now is to make ourselves fully available. We cannot act defensive — not yet. In exposing ourselves this way, we may also learn something," Jon said.

Max nodded somewhat reluctantly.

"We go to MacDonald first thing tomorrow morning and offer our assistance," Jon added.

"Do you think they're involved somehow?" Max asked hesitantly.

"Who, Lacombe or MacDonald? I don't know. I really doubt it. I mean, what could be gained from wasting your top engineers in your own back yard?" Jon asked.

"Too close to home, I think. But someone higher than us knows something. Again, someone with access." Jon shrugged and rose to his feet.

"Look, Max, get home. Don't worry about the surveillance and all that. You and I are at the top of a very short list. Accept it for now and keep reminding yourself that you can't control what other people think. Right now, what serious physical evidence could they possibly have?

After a pause, Jon answered himself. "Nothing, if we weren't there, right?" Jon grabbed the younger man by the shoulders and held him at arm's length.

"Remember Pyramid Dust-off?" Jon suddenly asked, referring to an almost forgotten operation during the Arabian War, a not-so long ago conflict full of forgettable days and nights.

Maxwell Donovan nodded, his eyes a little more clear with recollection.

"We took some heat for that little fuck up and saved how many lives?" Jon asked.

Max's eyes flickered with distant memories as remote events replayed through his mind at light speed. He nodded again, more confident and assured. He bit his lip and met Jon's gaze. Jon nodded firmly in substantiation.

Back then, it had been Max who had remained cool and in control. Now, the younger man seemed more easily upset and less in control of his emotions. Much had happened in both of their lives to change the men since those days in the faraway desert.

"Right on, my friend. We did the right thing then, and you need to stay proud of that. All of that. It wasn't in vain. This, too, will work itself out," Jon asserted. "Now, go home. Sleep it off and meet me downstairs with my vehicle at 0400. We'll get in early and be waiting for them. A sign of sincerity. Okay?"

Max nodded again and reached up to grasp Jonathan's shoulder. He gave it a hardy squeeze. "Thanks, Captain. For everything."

"No prob, Sergeant. Now take my car and get home. Carefully. The auto-glide voc-com is stuck in Spanglish. You'll have to type in your address." Jon handed the ignition disk to Max and escorted him to the door. At the threshold, he paused and turned to Max.

"By the way, points for using the Patriot. You went old school; I didn't see that coming," Jon said.

Max cocked his head to the side and smiled weakly. "I picked it up from some old guy I know, wanted to see if that ancient stuff really worked."

"Yeah, well if you would have paid better attention, you may have picked up that the old guy nearly sautéed your fragile brains with six hundred joules of plasma energy."

"I could've wasted you on the spot, Captain." Max smirked, slightly cocky, yet respectful.

Jon shivered with mock fear in his eyes. "I love your enthusiasm, son. But I'm glad that you don't have the eggs to shoot your friend and mentor in the head." Jon clapped him the back and sent him out the door.

Max waved over his shoulder as he entered the OmniVator. The doors whispered close. Jon returned to his apartment.

He manually fingered the interior lights down to a dull glow, sat behind his desk, poured another glass of bourbon and set about reviewing his messages.

As the text flew across the screen of the LCD monitor, he felt his eyelids starting to weigh heavy. He began to blink, slowly, allowed his eyes to remain closed for what he intended to be a brief minute and dozed. He slumped in the chair and immediately fell into a deep and fitful sleep.

~ * ~

The dream is horribly lucid, a playback of memories that are thick and hazy with the humidity of terror.

He recalls emerging from unconsciousness, rising from the murky depths through clotted black oil, clawing his way to the surface toward an even greater horror than the monstrous abyss of sleep below.

He's dismally aware of the terrible things around him. Knowledge and realization lurk at the periphery of wakefulness. His awareness roils and writhes buoyed in a turbulent current of suffocating darkness. His mind spins like a coin tossed on a tabletop, turning blinding circles about its axis, randomly meandering across a black, empty surface; wobbling as the momentum of the spin winds down toward an inevitable resting state.

As he braces for the eventual effects of entropy, flashes of gauzy white light assault his inner eye, seemingly random, yet increasing as the spinning mental coin of his awareness slows to a flat rest.

The sleepy darkness brightens with varying degrees of languid, milky opaqueness as he surfaces toward wakefulness. The essence of illumination, both visual and mental, is diffuse and shifting as if shadowed forms fluttered across the thick cataracts of his mind's eye.

He remembers sounds as well, deep, bass vibrations emanating from near, and then fading into vagueness. The sounds are structured, yet meaningless; and there's menace in their tone, a hurtful and purposeful intent behind the undulating waves.

In the dream, he becomes more aware of his physical body—in that he perceives real pain—his neck spasms with sharp, unpredictable tremors and his head throbs with a high frequency shriek. A thrumming rises in crescendo from a murmur to a baleful scream in his ears as blood pounds against the thin tissue of his brain in concert with his racing heart.

Suddenly, and without hesitation, his dream-self breaks through the ephemeral surface and into lucidity, shattering the fragile plane of unconsciousness like a breaching dolphin racing to the surface for a breath of cool, salt air.

With abrupt clarity, his ears become acutely tuned to his surroundings, his muscles fully aware of the damaged inflicted and his skin hums in response to the constant pain.

However, in the dream-world he remains blind. He recalls the sudden and instant fear of eternal blackness.

No, not quite.

When he blinks, his eyelashes brush against something making a soft, almost insectile scratching sound. A covering.

Blindfold. *Oh, Christ!*

His heart freezes with the fear of sudden realization and crisp memory; an inner terror that hooks icy barbs into his insides, pulls the viscera corpse-tight and shrinks the soul into a frozen vacuum. The terror is constant and cancerous, relentlessly tearing through him, ripping new gashes into the fabric of his being before the previous wounds ever have a chance to heal and scar over.

He is anxiously aware of the creatures before him, hidden by the blindfold, taunting him and reveling in their celebration.

He can smell their chemistry, the acidic tang of adrenaline, the salty musk of their sweat and sex, and the richly sweet fragrance of the Synth that they continually smoke. Their savagery grows palpable as their bravado gains potency from the inhaled synthetic opiate.

He remembers the sounds: the raspy draws off the pipe, the crackle of the powdered crystal as it burned under the flame and the throaty coughs as he imagines thick white plumes of drug-laced smoke billowing around their heads.

From the sounds of the toking and the ambient conversation, he recalls at least three beings in attendance, though there could have been more.

Occasionally, they paid him some attention, blowing smoke into his face or slapping him hard across the side of his head. At least one of the monsters urinated on him, spraying his face with the hot, rancid liquid and drenching his clothes. The acrid stench of the waste rose into his nostrils from his soaked shirt with the physical force of a screwdriver pushing into his sinuses. He willfully resisted the urge to vomit and swallowed hard against the heavy gag, realizing far too late that he had already ingested some of the noxious wetness.

His anger rose with the bitter bile, coating the back of his throat with a greasy film of rage.

The laughter around him was constant, and the celebratory environment swelled pregnant with anticipation of some savage climax. Their vocalizations were incomprehensible, a smattering of grunts and moans, cheers and taunts, and bastardized fragments of popular songs.

Through the cacophony, he registered a few bits of intelligible phrases, but most of the dialect was slurred by drug and hype. He was certain of one thing; the beasts were determined and of singular purpose. They were electrified, vibrating toward the satisfying completion of one goal: to satiate the cravings fueled by the drug.

He remembers wishing that he was wrong, but he knows better. He is utterly helpless. Propped against a wall, piled in a throbbing heap, he's unable to do anything to alter the situation. His drifting and wounded mind recalls each detail in vivid clarity, yet he remains frozen as a reluctant spectator within his own dream.

One of the demons spoke directly into his face, smelling of stale spice and sweet smoke. "Get rightly fucked! Terribly colorful and majestically soft. Yes!"

The language was Illuminese, an irregular pairing of adverbs and adjectives frequently used in the drug subculture by those under the influence of Synth drugs like Symphony. The intended goal, apparently, was for each user to try and elucidate their own heightened experience of the drug as eloquently and succinctly as possible. The chemicals released by the brain while creating and interpreting these vocabulary exercises then, in turn, enhanced one's overall experience.

He was all too familiar with the designer drug and its culture, and this knowledge did nothing to ease his anxiety.

A synthetic opioid neurocotic, Symphony was originally designed as an anesthetic, but quickly found its way into the field of alternative psychology as it gained notoriety in efforts to expand and even enhance overall human cognitive abilities. In essence, it was thought to make people smarter.

And it did, for awhile, until people started suffering from unexplained strokes, seizures and fatal cerebral hemorrhages. But that didn't stop the thrill seekers and street entrepreneurs from realizing and exploiting the recreational aspects of the drug.

Symphony also had one other peculiar side effect: it was a potent aphrodisiac in human males.

"Jess, ditty-do!" another voice responded. "Righteously velvet, flickering pink!"

More snickering and heavy breathing as bodies pressed in close to him. He could sense their scrutiny, their close inspection and assessment of their captured prey.

Other smells wafted across his nasal palate, mingling with the ever present stench of Symphony vapors; smells that are distinctly human and sour—tangy, metallic odors that carry a faint flavor with them, reminiscent of swimming pool locker rooms and old musty mattresses.

Someone yanked his head back by the hair, twisting left and right as if inspecting a large fruit for ripeness before picking it from the tree.

"Woefully engaged, eh?" Hot, acrid breath blew across his face as the creature spoke. "Blissfully reluctant. No. Willful rapture! Crimson and gold with rage. Yes! Taste the rage. And the fear." The voice squealed with childish delight.

"Ultra fuck! Now and then again! Fanciful impatience!" This third voice, less articulate and perhaps younger, was nevertheless inexperienced with the use of Illuminese. A loud, sharp smack immediately followed, as one of the others slapped the third.

"Scrap and hold!" someone shouted obviously chastising the eager member of the group.

Then, in a whisper next to his right ear, the voice spoke. "Ah, impatient youth."

A heavy, seductive sigh followed; sour and heavy from a fresh hit of Symphony.

"Wanton haste and lusty drippings. But what of the meal?" the voice whispered. "Enjoyment of the meal for the simple virtue of it being a meal?"

It seemed a rhetorical question, laced with allusions that he refused to contemplate. His mind raced to unravel a viable option, a way to resist, to escape, to fight.

The speaker grunted disapprovingly, and then batted him twice across the head.

"Obstinate reluctance! Fresh, flaky, frostingless cake," the voice shouted.

Then to the others, spoken as a permissive directive, the speaker commanded, "Violate and pollinate! Cotton candy will never last long in the raging torrents of this evening's downpour!"

With that, the blindfold was ripped from his eyes and the world glared scorchingly white in front of him. He blinked and struggled to take in as much as he could, quickly reassess the situation, and attempt to formulate a plan.

Then he saw the crumpled half-naked body sprawled on the floor before him.

His heart froze, and then collapsed into the vacuum of his imploding soul.

Then the dream spiraled away, as it always does, leaving him in expanding and woeful darkness.

Eleven

Paul MacDonald entered the CEO's large office through the adjoining door of the conference room. As he crossed the threshold, the last of the attendees were exiting the small room behind him via the exterior door in the opposite wall.

The emergency security meeting had shocked the junior and senior executives alike; but the heads of all of the major divisions, now fully briefed, completely understood the gravity of the situation and had left the briefing with a sense of urgency not unlike that of a major military operation. MacDonald was confident that the picture he painted was one of grave concern for potential catastrophe, and that the mission objectives he handed out were going to thwart any further degradation in the grander scheme of Phoenix-Lamneth and the corporation's attempt to resolidify itself in the wake of disaster.

MacDonald did what he was paid to do, put out fires and rebuild from the ashes. The irony of that task and the corporation's name was not lost on him, despite his limited capacity for poetic melodrama.

The door whispered tightly closed behind him as he approached the huge gold and mahogany desk. Barrett Lacombe sat behind the mammoth structure in a high backed leather chair with his back to his lieutenant. His small fisted hands kneaded his eyes, working away the exhaustion and tension as he slowly turned to face MacDonald. His reddened face screwed into a frown as he acknowledged the younger executive.

He sighed as he reached for a wide and squat crystal tumbler half full of golden brown brandy. Lacombe held the heavy glass in his left hand, hefting its weight as he watched the syrupy liquid swirl with the motion.

"So, how did they take it?" he somberly asked his second-in-command.

"As well as can be expected," began MacDonald. "R and D seemed surprisingly calm. Though engineering, as expected, was quite emotional."

"Of course!" Lacombe burst forth. "They—*we*—lost our top three architects! Christ, what a fucking mess." Barrett Lacombe shook his head for maybe the thousandth time in as many minutes.

The unfortunate victims murdered within his intellectual sanctuary less than twenty-four hours ago were the best and brightest of any of the teams he had ever created. They had been hand recruited by him personally, developed under his tutelage and guided through the murky waters of corporate politics to spearhead the most innovative technology production team the world may have ever seen. They were simply the unquestioned brain trust behind what could prove to be the most important breakthrough in mankind's short tenure on this unstable planet.

"Averson's concerned about media leakage. The obvious questions regarding the merger were alluded to but never addressed directly," MacDonald added.

"Good. We need to keep a tight lid on that. I'm thoroughly convinced that this tragedy is a direct attempt to derail the PI purchase. I just can't figure out how anybody outside of this office could have known about it." Lacombe again looked questioningly at MacDonald.

He never once even so much as insinuated that Paul MacDonald might be responsible for leaking the potential Polar Innovations merger. Paul had nearly as much to lose as Lacombe himself if the buyout failed. Together they had invested a nation's fortune in one single corporate deal. The deal of the millennium, it was hoped.

Yet, now it seemed that someone might be privy to the deal.

"What about Averson?" Lacombe asked. "Is he capable of something like this?"

MacDonald shook his head firmly. "Absolutely not. In fact, he has only just begun to see the proposals in censored detailed. If he suspects anything specific, it would be purely by blind luck and weak conjecture."

It was common practice to allow the corporation lawyers handling any significant purchases or mergers limited and censored access to pertinent information only. The material they received was intentionally ambiguous and often redundant, in efforts to protect the true nature and depth of any deal.

Business lawyers, in general, and those practicing within large, volatile corporations, specifically, were untrustworthy and prone to offering insider-trading tidbits to the highest bidder. Therefore, all of the material required to complete any significant transaction was usually delivered to the lawyers on the eve of the proposed activity, by armed and obvious chaperones, and merely hours prior to the signing.

These double-blinded legal secretaries were often sequestered upon receipt of the critical materials, and then frequently terminated immediately after the closure. They were, in turn, compensated quite lavishly for their limited involvement. There was never a shortage of short-term, temporary, corporate legal assistance.

Lacombe gestured for MacDonald to take a seat. He offered a glass and the brandy bottle. MacDonald politely refused. Barrett Lacombe was working on getting an expensive hangover.

"So, Paul," began Lacombe. "Regardless of how it happened, someone knew the identity of our engineering trifecta and essentially erased a number of lifetime's worth of work." He paused and took a thick swig from his glass. "Is our chief of security capable of this? Is Jonathan Webb our man?" the CEO asked blankly.

"Sir, he's more than capable. His military and law enforcement credentials support that. Hell, it's why he was brought in here in the first place. What's more, he has motive."

Lacombe glanced at his associate with a wide and questioning stare. He swallowed audibly and wrinkled his brow against the slight burn of the alcohol as it coated his throat.

"Do you mean his wife and son?" Lacombe inquired, knowing the history and just barely making the connection.

"Yes, sir." MacDonald was in his element now. Reveal, convince and execute. His job now was to leave little doubt in his boss' mind as to Webb's involvement, if not sole responsibility.

Lacombe remained silent allowing MacDonald to argue his point.

"His wife Sarah and four-year-old son Matthew have been patients up at the Rainey Clinic ever since he brought them here from the East coast. The clinic is the single reason that he relocated, in hope to provide them with not only the best in neurological care, but also to find a cure. A recovery. He's jaded from the lack of results and seems to have been quite vocal against the methods and philosophies of the Madison Progressives program.

"In fact," MacDonald continued. "According to my sources deep within the clinic, it would seem that he has come to the end of his rope, both emotionally and financially. Despite their best efforts over there, Mr. Webb has turned uncooperative and has actually had an extreme change of heart.

"Where he was once supportive of their interventional technologies, he has now turned another card."

MacDonald leaned against an ornate armchair and softly cleared his throat before continuing. Lacombe nursed his brandy.

"After his wife suffered an unfortunate and debilitating seizure, he never regained his trust of the technology. As a result, and just recently, it has been decided to remove his wife from the clinic and relocate her to Finality care. His son is to remain in accordance with the custody ruling."

MacDonald paused to allow Lacombe time to absorb the information. The CEO simply looked past him, focused on the far wall, actively listening.

MacDonald pushed on. "Sir, it's my position that Jonathan Webb is a man of many talents and resources. It's unfortunate about his personal situation; however, the Rainey Clinic has offered much in the way of pro bono medical and supportive care for his family. I believe he's an angry man, still confused as to how to manage his emotions after the many tragic events in his life. He's an emotionally unstable man, with a sociopathic personality and a vengeful bent.

"I believe that he used his position as security chief to gather information about our employees and eventually targeted those most responsible for our success in biotechnology and, in a fit of displaced rage and vengeance, lashed out against the technology that initially failed, and ultimately was refused his family.”

“Why not take me out directly? Or the Rainey Clinic itself, for Christ sake?” Lacombe wondered aloud.

“The Clinic still cares for the wife and son. It would harm them to bring his wrath down there. And you, sir, pardon me for saying so, are not a real solid target. There would be little lost if you were removed, sir.”

Lacombe waved off the statement with a look of disgust. “No, Paul, I’m not so vain to think that Phoenix-Lamneth lives and dies with me. No, the technologies created and perfected here—and elsewhere, for that matter—grow and live far beyond the lives of their creators. You’re right. Perhaps he thinks that my death would simply give the cause the power of martyrdom.”

“Yes, sir. And the fact that, as you said, he erased nearly three lifetimes worth of work in one act of savagery. All three of the architects were irreplaceably involved in the ASCI IV program,” MacDonald said.

“He was targeting the *future* of advance stem cell therapy? To what end?” Lacombe asked.

“Discrediting the Advanced Stem Cell Initiative, as a whole, would be difficult and time consuming. Besides, with the successes we’ve had in early eradication of Parkinson’s, ALS and Type I diabetes; it would be next to impossible to stir up any significant opposition. Not with Senator Douglass’ bill on the floor of the FedTech Congress this week. The world has already accepted the technology; the battle is over, and we have won. Politically and publicly.

“But to actually wipe out the architects of the future; well, that delivers a blow that’s difficult to recover from. At least immediately.”

Lacombe sighed and took a long sip from his tumbler.

“He’s irrational with rage and blinded by revenge. You saw him at the scene, sir. Completely numb. He viewed those bodies without a quiver of visceral response. I thought Donovan, on the other hand, was going to lose it completely,” MacDonald said.

“Yes, Maxwell Donovan. What are your plans for him, Paul?”

“If he is involved, which I strongly doubt, then he’ll be given the opportunity to come clean. I believe we can use him to locate, or even bring in, Jon Webb,” MacDonald explained.

"You had that poor boy shaking in his boots." Lacombe took another sip of brandy setting his teeth tight as he swallowed.

"I still had my doubts about Webb's guilt during the interview. But I quickly realized that this was way out of Donovan's league. This took skill and fortitude. Max is weak, and lacks the intellect and creativity for something of this magnitude."

"So, you really believe Webb acted alone? Motivated purely by emotion?" Lacombe asked.

"Yes, sir."

"And what of the merger, Paul?"

"I truly believe that he knew nothing of that. I think it was just unfortunate coincidence that he chose to commit these atrocities two days before the PI merger."

"Perhaps." Lacombe took a long swallow of brandy. A long silence followed.

"I have given this merger a great deal of thought, in light of the grisly developments," Lacombe finally said. "I think that if we are successful in containing this unfortunate event, we still may be able to proceed. The requisite technology is already physically manifested and the teams should be able to continue without Levy, Iiancote and Rhadma. It will be tricky but not impossible.

"Containment is the key, Paul. If Cronus gets wind of this, it's over." It was the first mention of Wyatt Cronus, CEO and founder of Polar Innovations. The mere inclusion of his name in the conversation made the potential merger real and the threat of loss even greater.

"Paul, what about this fourth body?" Lacombe asked. "Who was he, and why was he with my top three engineers last night?"

"Sir, I'm still working on his ID. There's nothing in the P-L corporate manifest for his DNA." MacDonald shrugged. "He remains a nobody for now. I initially assumed that he was involved with Webb somehow, but that just doesn't make any sense. Why would Webb kill his accomplice at the scene? I don't have a valid explanation, sir."

"What did you give that detective for ID, then?" Lacombe asked.

"Some bogus name from our ghost files, for now," MacDonald said softly. He was embarrassed at having to admit slight failure, but everything happened so fast. When he initially saw the bodies, he immediately recognized the three biotechnical engineers. The fourth body looked vaguely familiar, but without an ID badge, he couldn't place a name to the face.

It was the lack of the badge that alerted him and for some reason, perhaps raw instinct, he simply blurted out a vague name in response to Gionetti's inquiry. It seemed prudent that the top executives of the largest biotechnology company on the planet knew the identities of the four dead bodies discovered in the highest level of their securest labs. MacDonald couldn't have simply said *I don't have the slightest idea who that guy is* and brought himself to face his own reflection in the morning. It would be an admission of loss of control; something Paul was loathe to do.

So, offering the name of a long retired employee, who perhaps was already dead, may have solved the immediate dilemma, but it was sure to come back to haunt him.

Now, he realized, of all of the things that could go wrong during the aftermath of the murders, a simple check on a name, a ten or fifteen second MetaWeb search, and it all could come crashing down. If he was to keep this out of the media until the merger, and ideally, forever, then he needed to get the real identity of the fourth victim and prevent Detective Gionetti from discovering his lie.

He knew of some talented people in dark places within the city who could switch identities and vital statistics via the Ethernet, for the right amount of Credits. He just hoped that Gionetti wasn't too thorough just yet.

Lacombe simply nodded at the response and seemed distracted by another thought. "So, has Detective Gionetti been back in touch with us?" he finally asked.

"Not since earlier this evening. He was placing both Donovan and Webb under surveillance and was going to be in first thing in the morning to update us," MacDonald reported glad to move on, yet internally quivering at the mention of the detective's name.

"Is he going to formally charge and arrest someone?" Lacombe asked, rhetorically, obviously thinking of Jon Webb.

"That was left unclear, sir."

"Well, Paul, why don't we make it easier for him? When he arrives in the morning, I want you to bring him up to speed. I want you to present your Webb theory which, by the way, I am confident of and suggest a collaborative effort between our internal resources and himself.

"Let's suggest our desire to be discreet and have a speedy resolution to the investigation. Perhaps we can even entice him to allow us to handle the media, giving him, of course, full credit for solution and capture.

"You work the negotiations, Paul. I'm giving you carte blanche with the credits. Just get it done and ensure silence. When the details eventually do leak out, and they will, the purchase will have been completed, and we will have had some time to work out the softer angles."

"Yes, sir. And Webb? How should I inform Detective Gionetti that we are to pursue Jonathan Webb?"

"Explain to him that we would like to remain internal in our pursuit and apprehension. Of course, with his expertise and assistance. You said you had a plan. Act on it. I don't need the details, just results. And please, remember: Quietly."

MacDonald nodded and spun toward the heavy door leading out of the office.

"And Paul," Lacombe called out. MacDonald turned halfway around to face the CEO. "Solidify the relationship between the Rainey Clinic and Webb. Reach out to the staff there and establish a history for Webb's animosity toward the technology. I want this to be airtight. He's responsible for this, and I want him buried to the eyes in culpability."

MacDonald simply nodded again and strode out of the office.

Twelve

Jon awoke with a start to the musical pinging of the alarm on his holo-disc notifying him of a completed incoming download. He rubbed his eyes and stretched the stiffness from his neck as he slowly lifted his head from the cradle of his folded arms. The lingering emptiness of melancholy left by the long-departed dream temporarily consumed him. His heartbeat echoed dully in the dark chambers of his soul like the distant knelling of a Sanctus bell from within an abandoned cathedral basement.

He massaged the tingling fingers of his numb left hand with the other as he attempted to blink away the fog of sleep. The luminescent screen of the monitor glowed softly casting an aquatic blue-green haze over the small room.

He had passed out hours before, exhausted after his surprising visit with Max, and now struggled with the temporary disorientation of sudden wakefulness. The fragments of the dream faded along with the dangerous emotions associated with them.

He blinked a few more times and refocused his vision on the blinking cursor at the top of his displayed homepage. Ignoring the listings of previously unread messages at the right of the screen, he lightly tapped the highlighted cursor on the LCD and brought up a menu window prompting him for a password.

He typed the case sensitive code on the flat keypad and was rewarded with access into his MetaFiles. At the top of the screen, the sender's address was displayed in bold blue font: *WizardSeven@globalmetanet*.

It was a message from Robert and contained a rather large attachment.

Jon touched the screen on the appropriate icons and brought up the recently downloaded data. He smiled and shook his head as he read the short message and scanned the contents of the attachment. The file included all of the software required for Jon to begin composing his own personal message to Sarah.

The idea of recording anything that could be replayed and actually understood by a comatose individual still baffled him. If he hadn't witnessed the phenomenon with his own eyes, he would think anyone suggesting the possibility was completely daft. He would have to thank Robert graciously; he had been pretty hard on him initially. Aside from Max, Robert might be the only true friend Jon had.

He reread the message and the instructions for uploading the extensive document.

> *Hey old man; as promised... Merry Christmas! Attached is an Upload Wizard that will guide your HD through the install. First, scrub your holo-disc with the enclosed Cleanser (my own little creation). Then upload versions one (1) through four (4) of the Piracy Leash (another of my little masterpieces); that will partition and protect any and all material related to the Ice Cube Digital Composer. This is high-end stuff, and slightly illegal, I think. Be careful.*
>
> *Let the HD and the programs do the work. Should take about eight hours to load correctly. Once the blank disks are in your multideck, it's hands off until complete. The HD should reboot and then you are set. I'll bring by the actual recording apparatus when you call. Take your time and compose something special. You both deserve that.*
>
> *Later, R*

Jon initiated the functions required for opening and installing the necessary programs. After a few minutes, his computer screen took on a strange orange glow and a message box materialized in the center:

> *Touch screen once with each of the four fingers on your left hand, beginning with the last digit to the upper left hand corner and continuing CLOCKWISE around the screen; touching each corner with each consecutive digit. Finally, touch your left thumb to the center of this box.*

Jon did as he was directed leaving behind ghostly whorled fingerprints after each of the touches. When he finally touched the center of the screen with his thumb, the screen flickered and went black. He gasped and instantly assumed that he had fouled up the instructions. He was about to start frantically pounding the keys of the touchpad and attempt to reboot the HD when his PDD phone hummed at his waist. He reached for the phone and flipped open the thin cover.

"Webb here."

"Hey, you got it started! Great. Don't freak out and try to reboot. The black screen is normal. It hides the magic from prying eyes." Robert's voice was musical and full of pride.

"How did you know that I just started it?" Jon asked.

"Put in a little signal program to send me a d-alert when you initialize. Kinda like a receipt."

"Oh," Jon replied innocently.

"Hey, man, this is cool stuff. Trust me. Just let it do its thing. It'll take awhile, so go to work or whatever. I'll be checking on it remotely from time to time."

"Is this safe? I mean, will this crash my system? My God, Robert, an eight-hour upload at lightfiber speed. How big is this program?"

"Programs. Plural. And yes, it's safe," Robert replied somewhat defensively. "This is only the foundation for editing the material, a fraction of the memory space needed for the entire program. I have the Ice Cube, remember? That's where the memory ad infinitum lies. Jon, your HD will never be the same after this. It'll be millions of degrees better. Trust me."

"I do, Robert, I do." Jon sighed.

"Gotta run, Jon. I'll bring the rest over to your place tomorrow evening. That'll give you some time to get your composition together."

"Yeah, that'll be good. And thanks, Robert, for everything. Really."

"Don't mention it," Robert said with a pause, and then added, "Really. Not to anyone. Not a word."

Jon laughed. "You bet. I'll see you."

Thirteen

Paul MacDonald folded his hands in front of his face, elbows resting on the dark wood of his desk as he steepled his index fingers and brushed them against the sides of his rigid nose. He peered at the man seated across from him with unblinking authority and palpable impatience.

"Do you fully understand all that is being asked of you?" he inquired after a long moment, speaking sternly through his tented fingers. His eyes narrowed in anticipation of any faltering response. MacDonald sat tensely forward, poised to pounce if the man wavered even the slightest.

The man slumped back into the plush leather of the high-backed chair rocking it slightly. His head slowly cocked to one side as he absently fingered the loose papers that had spilled from the folder lying across his lap. He was willfully forcing his gaze onto the strewn documents before him, avoiding having to make immediate and direct eye contact with McDonald's intimidating stare.

He consciously fought the urge to sigh, to blink or to even rub his hot, dry, tired eyes. He knew he was at a significant and perhaps fatal crossroads. The situation had melted from a simple professional dilemma to an impossible circumstantial labyrinth in the time it took for him to open the folder and peruse the documents within.

MacDonald had him by the balls, and he saw that his choices, as symbolic and meaningless as they were, were quite clear and extremely limited.

"In retrospect, I'm wishing that I'd not called this meeting," MacDonald began. "Don't make me ask you again, or I will seek alternate means to accomplish my goal. As it stands, I'm doing you a favor. Your hesitance only belays your weakness. You have this one opportunity to redefine yourself. How will you finish living your life?"

The man finally brought his gaze up to meet MacDonald's cool and damning stare. He fought back the moisture threatening to cloud his vision, struggled with the thick clot forming deep within his throat and despite the internal vertigo of his insides flipping and tumbling; he managed to softly croak his response past cracked lips. "I understand."

"Good," MacDonald said as he allowed his hands to fall gracefully into his lap. He swung his chair to the left as he crossed his left leg over his right knee. He methodically smoothed the creases in his pant leg as he spoke.

"I'm glad that you can now see for yourself the other side of the man. The complete Jonathan Webb." Paul MacDonald casually swung his gaze toward the man cowering in the chair across from his desk, then to the strewn papers of the spilled dossier in the man's lap. He shook his head slightly and offered a condescending smirk of pity and sympathy.

"You shouldn't allow your past loyalties to cloud your responsibilities to yourself. A great many things have changed since then. For both of you. Your paths have taken two distinctly different courses," MacDonald explained as if tutoring a small child. "You have the ability to do what is right and just. You can evolve, and in doing so, improve your station in life, despite whatever foolish choices you've made or unfortunate transgressions you may have found for yourself. "

The man attempted a shrug and peered mournfully at the sheets of paper strewn across his lap.

"The truth lies in front of you." MacDonald gestured over the desk at the rifled pages of the folder. He managed another baleful smile and narrowed his eyes at the younger man. "I can make some of what's in those files disappear forever. At least the stuff about you. You know, the felony drug and lewd acts charges. Even the manslaughter. Gone." MacDonald paused, rubbed his cleanly shaven chin and pursed his narrow lips.

"However, the stuff about Webb will remain etched in stone for all of history. And, of course, any link that he may have had with you can be strengthened or weakened by what is in your own little history. It's sink or swim, boy!" Paul MacDonald sighed, leaned back in his heavy black leather chair, stretched his arms to the ceiling, feigned a yawn, and set his jaw firm as he leveled his piercing gaze on the beaten man before him.

"Now, tell me again all that was said. What are Webb's thoughts? His intentions?"

The younger man stretched his neck to both sides, took a deep breath and leveled his eyes at Paul MacDonald. He spoke clearly and succinctly gaining confidence with each word. Before he would finish, his transformation and complete betrayal would be solidified. He would seize this one opportunity and remake himself: successful, confident, and strong.

Paul MacDonald listened intently as the man shared all that he knew about Jonathan Webb.

Fourteen

As Jon rode the OmniVator to its destination, he allowed the events of this morning to replay at random through his head. Though he was moderately surprised at the ease for which he was allowed to access the secure 'vator, and then proceed directly to Paul MacDonald's private office, he was even more perplexed when the security office gave him the pre-authorized code to enter the newly secured executive wing unescorted, stating that the VP was actually expecting him and would personally receive him at the threshold of the sanctuary's entrance.

Equally astonishing was the news on Mandatory Media this morning as vague reports of the fatalities and a citywide manhunt for suspects were revealed to the general public. It would appear that either an unplanned leak occurred or there was real truth to the reports of former employees seeking some sort of vengeance.

Either way, it appeared that Barrett Lacombe and Paul MacDonald were no longer operating under the cover of discretion; whether or not the outing of the tragedy would harm Phoenix-Lamneth in any way was a prime question, however, not nearly as vexing as the question of who or why.

Jon could not immediately think of any former or current employees who not only held such a grudge against the corporation, but also possessed the technological prowess to carry out the elaborate deed.

Again, it seemed to inexplicably fall back onto himself and Max Donovan, and few alternatives provided any logical explanation that would account for the breach of exclusive security. It was a puzzling and frustrating position to occupy, and Jon hoped that in meeting directly with the heads, he could establish his ignorance and innocence, regain trust and offer assistance with the investigation.

Jon sighed as the 'vator shifted into its horizontal trajectory with a soft shudder and faint sideways acceleration. He thrust his hands into his pants pockets and fiddled with his car's ignition disk. He began to think about Max.

Jon had given him his spare disk to drive himself home last night, and then return to pick him up this morning. When Max failed to show, Jon wasn't overly concerned considering how much the younger man had drank that evening.

However, when Jon went down to the garage and saw his leased Hybrid Spirit still parked in the same stall where he left it, he began to wonder. Obviously, Max hadn't driven home, and although on most occasions where a friend has had far too much to drink this would be a favorable result, Jon held a modest amount of concern for his friend's demise. He hoped that the young man had not tried to walk home and met with some unfortunate fate. He held on to the thought that Max had chosen to take a cab or even the unreliable Public Access shuttle and was now sleeping off a raging hangover.

However, the fact that Max wasn't at his apartment, or at least wasn't answering his calls, was curious and mildly worrisome. It would probably be better, after all, if Jon handled his negotiations with MacDonald without a hung-over and ruby-eyed accomplice.

The 'vator glided to a halt, its doors whispered open and Jon stepped out into the brightly lit reception area of the corporate executive offices. He softly strode toward the unoccupied reception desk just as the young woman emerged from a small hidden room to the right.

"Oh," she exclaimed, mildly surprised by his sudden appearance. "Can I help you?" She quickly regained her composure as she slid smoothly behind the desk and eased her hand under the marble top undoubtedly fingering the safety of some concealed weapon. Her smile was practiced and left little doubt in Jon's mind of her willingness to vaporize any unwelcome guest should the need arise.

Outwardly, she reflected a soft, pleasing feminine aura intentionally meant to distract and sedate the routine and oblivious guest. But to Jon's practiced eye, she was a well-trained watch dog—a softly packaged, petite agent of protection, perfectly willing to quickly and proficiently dispatch any troublesome interloper by any number of gruesome means.

He returned her smile with guarded professional etiquette and introduced himself. He stood tall and firm with a slight air of impatient confidence.

"Ah, yes, Mr. Webb," she confirmed as her posture relaxed, yet her hand remained beneath the desktop, apparently poised over the covertly placed weapon. "Mr. MacDonald *is* expecting you. If you could please have a seat for a moment, I'll notify him of your arrival." She gestured with her sharp eyes and a faint tilt of her head toward the deep bucket seat of a single leather chair.

Jon nodded once, obligingly, and moved to the chair. He lowered himself into the plush cradle of softened leather and folded his hands carefully in his lap. He was acutely aware of the Doppler and quantum phase scanners silently and methodically searching his body for weapons and recording devices, concealed or otherwise.

He, of course, unlike most of the visitors to this office, was fully aware of the security protocols in place and freely allowed the necessary steps to be taken. It bordered on paranoia, but that was the reality of high tech business.

As he waited, he reflected on his current position and the few options available to him. He was certain that MacDonald or Lacombe knew more about the circumstances surrounding the murders than they were allowing. He was also fairly confident that, for whatever reason, he was being implicated in the commission of the fatal deeds and it would be only a matter of time before formal charges were brought against him.

What puzzled him most was the elaborate way in which the crimes had been committed. It smacked of forced intention, almost overdone; as if someone tried too hard to make the murders seem like they were meant to illustrate some passionate or emotional statement.

Jon didn't buy that for a second. He had seen far too many acts of blissfully committed carnage, as well as coldly calculated acts of premeditation. There was no doubt in his mind that these people were executed, and for some important reason. Regardless, he knew that his best approach would be to directly confront his potential accusers and offer his opinion and assistance. Besides, his alibi was watertight, and once that has been established, and he has been able to shrug off any cast of doubt, he assumed that he would figure greatly in the investigation process.

"Mr. MacDonald will see you now," the demure guardian said, her eyes unblinking and coolly assessing.

Jon rose to his feet, acknowledged the young, pretty pit viper with a gentle nod and walked through the slowly opening grand wooden door silently wishing to never have to tangle with the likes of her in a darkened alley.

As he passed through, the thick wooden door automatically swung shut behind him. He continued forward toward Paul MacDonald's desk with a deliberate and controlled stride.

The Vice President and Chief executive assistant to the CEO calmly waited for Webb, leaning against the front of his desk wearing a confident, yet hesitant smile. His legs were crossed at the ankle, the tailored cuffs of his light linen suit hung perfectly over soft imported brown leather shoes.

While one hand cupped a thick coffee mug from the bottom, the other remained behind his back, supporting his tall frame as he leaned against the dark wood and marble of the large desk. His stern eyes blinked once as he raised the mug and took a small careful sip. He silently smacked his lips and sighed as he finally addressed Jon.

"Mr. Webb, have a seat. Please." MacDonald didn't gesture to any chair in particular, as there were none in the immediate vicinity.

Jon looked around the huge office for a seat, finally locating one in the farthest corner of the room. It was a folding chair made of black metal, without a cushioned seat cover, leaning against a closed door.

Webb turned his gaze from the chair to MacDonald, raising a questioning eyebrow. MacDonald bit the inside of his cheek, pouted his lips and shrugged casually as if in apology. He sucked his teeth as he rocked himself from his semi-recumbent stance, gracefully walked around the desk and took his seat in the overstuffed, high-backed commander's chair. He was firmly entrenched at the helm of his office, clearly enjoying the display of Alpha-male dominance.

Jon sighed and moved to retrieve the rigid folding chair. As he brought it from the corner of the room to the front of the desk, he quickly tried to think of tactics for regaining some control and dignity in the situation.

Things were not going as Jon had hoped, yet MacDonald was dictating the environment. Jon had no choice but to react defensively.

He placed the chair to the side of the desk, then quickly spun it around and simply rested his left foot upon the chair's metal seat. By remaining standing, Jon placed himself physically higher than MacDonald, shifting the momentum of the game slightly.

Jon leaned forward resting a forearm on his bent knee. He slowly curled his dangling fingers into a tight fist as he glared at the executive.

"Do we pull out our dicks next and measure?" Jon asked tersely.

MacDonald glared at the man leaning into his space actually amazed at the defiance. He shook his head slowly and placed his hands flat against the cool, clean marble desktop. As he studied his hands, he slowly addressed Jon in a detached and almost bored manner.

"If that's how you want to play this, fine. I was hoping for a more mature and professional exchange." The executive pinched his face tight and narrowed his lips as he continued, "I don't like you very much, Webb. Never really have. And now that we've finally exposed you for the infiltrating spy and saboteur that you are..." A dramatic pause followed as he slowly turned to look Jon straight in the eye. "Well, I, for one, am quite ready to be done with you."

A door opened at the rear of the office, slowly and carefully. Jon looked up at the sound of the door's latch clicking open. It was the same door from which Jon had secured the folded chair and emerging from behind the swinging wooden shield was a sight that froze Jon's heart and turned his mouth to dry ash.

He turned back to MacDonald to verify the shocking scene, but met only with the dark, unblinking muzzle of a large bore magnetic pistol.

Jon reacted instinctively at yet another handgun being pointed in his face. He slapped the hand holding the pistol sideways and up as he simultaneously thrust his other arm out, ramming stiff fingers into the front of the VP's neck.

In a fraction of a second, Webb was on, over and then under the inexperienced MacDonald, pulling the man over him by his expensive coat sleeve in an arc as he tumbled in a controlled roll over the back of the executive's chair, landing behind the large desk.

Jon seized the weapon from Paul's stunned grip with a practiced twist and pull, just as four rapidly fired projectiles whined overhead and slammed into the rich mahogany wall behind the desk, throwing large smoking splinters of wood and plastic over their tumbled bodies.

The shooter had fired from the center of the room as he entered through the door, but was now circling around the front of the desk to cut the angle of attack and perhaps even fire through the thinner, front face of the desk.

Jon rolled back on top of MacDonald and grabbed him around the lower jaw as he shoved the muzzle of the gun into Mac's now forced open mouth.

Jon hissed through clenched teeth, "Have him stand down. Now! Or I'll waste you right here and use your corpse as a fucking shield!" MacDonald's eyes were wide. He shook his head feverishly as he choked; spasmed breaths racked through his fractured windpipe. Jon pressed the muzzle of the gun deeper into the man's mouth as the shooter from across the room finally spoke.

"Jon?"

Webb remained silent, yet continued to press the gun against MacDonald's straining palate. He grimaced and repeated his demand as he spat the words across the man's pale face.

"Call him off or die!"

In that moment, MacDonald realized his fate and relinquished. He closed his eyes and between shuddering gasps and hitching breaths, he nodded compliance.

"C'mon, Jon. Where you gonna go? What are you gonna do?" the shooter cajoled from across the room, his voice heavy and sweet from intoxication.

Jon removed the pistol from MacDonald's mouth and nodded once. Strings of saliva hung from the tip of the barrel and stretched to his quivering lips. MacDonald tried to clear his throat to speak with some authority, but the words merely rasped out in a weak and gravely whisper.

"Back off!" he wheezed. "He has my gun." Another stridorous breath. "Just. Back. Off."

A brief pause, as the shooter seemed to think things through and then responded obviously surprised and indecisive.

"Jon, there's nowhere to go. There's no room for explanations. I've seen the documents, Jon. I know about the East coast killings. You had motive and means. And now you think you have a hostage." He paused.

Jon could hear the muffled whisper of footsteps as the shooter gently shuffled across the carpet, trying to gain an advantage in position, just as he had taught him to do many years ago.

"You don't know shit, Max," Jon shouted angrily. "And you're wrong!"

With that, Jon raised up, pulling MacDonald with him, keeping him close and in front of him, the muzzle of the mag-pistol firmly pressed to the back of the man's head. Jon was all but completely hidden behind the quaking executive. MacDonald stared wide-eyed as Max Donovan instantly drew a bead on the two men.

"I *do* have a hostage." Jon gritted his teeth and crouched tight and low behind MacDonald's large frame.

He stared unbelieving as his partner and friend aimed a semi-automatic mag-pistol back at the two men; the dull black metal of the weapon a surreal extension of his gloved hands, the long barrel unwavering in Max's firm grip.

The moment of silence stretched into a brief eternity, each man measuring the seconds with quick and steady pulses. Jon's mind raced with possibilities while struggling to grasp the unreality of the present. He willed his senses to focus on the immediate threat, to analyze the hard, concrete facts of the situation as a whole, formulate a plan of action and execute.

He needed to remain visceral and wholly instinctual. Now was not the time for emotional responses. But, his longtime and intimate friend once again held a gun on him, and this time seemed wholly intent on using it. It defied reason and understanding.

"C'mon, Jon. You're in a classic stand-off, and you know you can't win." Max was talking, trying to lead him into making a mental mistake and offer an opening; another tactic Jon had trained his protégé on many years ago.

Jon wasn't about to bite.

"You don't negotiate with a hostage taker, Max. You know that. You lie and you manipulate, but you offer nothing. You take your shot when you can." Jon never flinched and barely breathed above a shallow sigh.

"Jon," Max repeated his name, another tactic to personalize the moment and confuse the perpetrator into reacting to the situation emotionally. "No doubt you have a lot of things in your head right now. Mind numbing questions. It's a lot to process. Frankly, Jon, this is not the way to go about establishing your innocence."

Jon ignored the additional psychobabble and interceded.

"Shut up, Max. You're wasting everyone's time. Paul here is going to die of cardiac arrest if his heart keeps up at this rate." Jon pressed the weapon solidly against MacDonald's skull, forcing a weak, raspy whimper from the tall VP. "You crossed a line now, Max. One that cannot be taken back. You need to make a choice, right now. Take your shot. Or stand down."

Max blinked. His eyes twitched and vibrated suspiciously. The gun wavered ever so slightly as he swallowed. His response was a second too slow, and the hesitation was all the answer that Jon needed to choose his next step.

"No, Jon. You're the one who crossed the line. When you took the law into your own hands, first in Boston, and then here. And now you have a hostage. Face it, man. You're desperate. *You* need to make a choice, not me. Alive or dead, you are coming out of this room with me." Max slurred his words and his voice held a hint of fear and uncertainty.

Jon had already made his choice. Now it was time to act.

"I told you the next time you pointed a weapon at me, I'd kill you." Jon looked into Max's eyes and saw instant, raw fear crystallize, like time-lapse images of cataracts forming.

In a fraction of the next second, Jon shifted his weight imperceptibly to facilitate swinging his weapon around MacDonald's head for the kill shot.

He had already visualized the fatal round piercing Max's brow, cleaving his long time friend's face and ending his life, mercifully and quickly. The instant Jon committed his muscles to the act, the great wooden door to the office burst open and a figure flashed in the doorway.

A fiery burst of three rounds burped from an auto-mag, spraying the wall behind Jon just as he leveled his pistol and fired. The single shot that would have struck Max squarely in the forehead missed by mere centimeters as he dove down and to the right. The hot magnetic missile scorched across Max's scalp, gouging and cauterizing in the same instant, embedding itself in the wall behind.

Jon registered the movement and subsequent fire from the doorway even as he fired off the single shot.

The receptionist.

She dropped to her knees, cradling a bright silver handgun and prepared to execute a perfectly tight tactical roll in an attempt to shrink her profile and make a smaller target. However, she was a millisecond too slow, as Jon had already redirected his aim and instantly acquired the woman's form as she began to tuck for the inevitable roll.

Two shots exploded from the muzzle of his gun in sizzling synchronicity, finding their mark as silent wet splashes erupted from the woman's body in mid-roll. Her body's inertia carried it through the somersault, only to flop to eternal rest in a heap of blood soaked rags, the wall behind dripping in crimson gore.

Max was gone from the immediate field of view, perhaps seeking cover or hugging the floor, no doubt counting his fortunes and blessing his luck.

Jon again reacted instinctively, dropped MacDonald's limp body and bolted for the open door. He didn't know if the VP was hit during the fray or just collapsed in fear, and at this point could have cared less.

He threw down a volley of suppressive fire over his shoulder as he launched through the door and into the reception area. No one returned fire nor made any effort to give chase just yet. In seconds, Jon was careering down the hall away from the battlefield in the office and towards—*what?*

Where was he to go?

Not the OmniVator. Silent alarms were surely sounding and the security force was being mustered. He had a minute or less to secure an escape; else he would run himself to exhaustion within these corridors and succumb to what could only amount to a deadly capture.

Something unconscious drove him deeper into the labyrinth of the executive suites, further back into the maze of hallways past locked doors and empty alcoves until ahead and to the left, he came upon the double glass and marble doors of CEO's executive suite: Barrett Lacombe's name emblazoned in carved granite over the threshold, bordered by highly polished brass and stainless steel.

Jon wheeled his arms around as he stopped short of the entrance and risked a cautious glance back down the hallway when suddenly, almost calmly, he experienced another epiphany.

Realization and hopeful salvation flooded his mind as he remembered: *The pod slide!*

He fought the urge to smile at his unconscious recollection and set about to put together a plan.

The pod slide had been installed in Lacombe's office months ago in response to the man's nagging request for one. Apparently, he had heard of them being installed in some of the higher politician's offices as a means of securing a clandestine escape during disasters, both natural and political. Potential events that justified such a contingency ranged from the absurd and unlikely—perhaps the altered global consequences of a comet raining down from the sky—to the more probable, like an uncontested military coup. The pod slide provided the owner with essentially a mobile safe room.

Jon had supervised the installation himself, and although the final version of the system's controlling communication and long-term security were still weeks from being implemented, the structure itself was intact and functioning. The fact that the unit was not yet wholly linked to the main security grid was actually a boon for his escape. He only hoped that he could activate the pod itself.

He swung the mag-pistol around and with a firm two-handed grip, fired repeatedly into the glass face of the double doors. The rounds pierced the smooth glass surface in puckered and wrinkled holes, spider webs of minute cracks fanned out from each punched out iris. After ten or twelve shots, the glass was frosted and pockmarked. Jon turned sideways and kicked mightily at the heavy door, stressing the fractures and shattering the glass into thick crystalline nuggets.

Fortunately, this deep into the executive territory of Phoenix-Lamneth, it was assumed that the need and cost of unbreachable glass was precluded by the gauntlet of security prior to reaching these esteemed halls. If you got this far, it was reasoned, you were welcomed and posed no real threat.

Jon ducked through the opening. Fat jewels of leaded glass crunched under his boots as he slid and scuffed across the stone floor toward the main room of the suite.

The massive room contained a mammoth desk, flanked by towering gothic wooden pillars soaring into the shadowed heights of the vaulted ceiling. The room was perfectly round and the walls wrapped around in great arcs of marble and thick dark wood, unbroken save for two doors at either extreme of the circle. The main office was, of course, empty. Lacombe would never be in this early, and his time spent here was actually quite limited. He preferred the quiet comfort of his four-bedroom apartment adjacent to the Executive Spa and Gym one floor down.

Jon ran across the wide curving expanse to the door on the right where, from experience, he knew the lavatory existed. He threw open the heavy wooden door and the fluorescent lighting within flickered on with a soft click and vibrant hum.

He heard the shouting and commotion of distant chaos coming through the shattered hole in the glass doors. He mentally calculated a minute or less before the first of the heavily armed security agents discovered his forced entrance and locked down this office; men and women he trained, officers of unquestioning commitment and unequaled proficiency.

If they were quick enough to employ the sub-sonic Anvil—so named for one of the auditory ossicles it liquefied—it would be over before he could blink. Once the Anvil's ultra-acoustic pulses pulverized his inner ear, rendering him helplessly languid, they would descend upon him with electrochemical restraints and he would be reduced to mental jelly.

But they could not activate the Anvil until they knew exactly which room he was in. Wide-spread and unfocused use of acoustic apprehension would be dangerous to all, for there was no known method of shielding one's ears from susceptibility. Covering or plugging the ears simply wasn't adequate. The highly energized sound waves penetrated bone, flesh and most solid surfaces for the duration of the broadcast.

A focused transmission into the interior of a room resulted in complete paralysis of any human being within, while those outside of the broadcast field remained safe from the effects as the pulsed waves did not reflect or refract in the manner that most sound waves behaved.

Jon reached up to the large mirror covering the whole of the facing wall, touching the reflective surface nearly in the center. The surface rippled slightly, becoming lucent, then iridescent. The mirror took on a greenish-blue electronic glow, transforming into a giant plasma screen. A bright white cursor blinked near the left hand side of the screen.

Jon quickly touched the cursor, causing it to become a solid white horizontal line. He then began tracing out seemingly random characters with his index finger, moving across the horizontal from left to right.

In the wake of his scribing finger, letters and numbers appeared in recognition of the intended entries: a random temporary code Jon had created for the initial installation of the pod slide, allowing him and the technicians to finish the details of the install. Ultimately, the unit would only recognize the finger and code of Barrett Lacombe, but for now the unit was open, and Jon was eternally grateful for small favors.

The last character illuminated on the screen and with a jolt and whine of hidden mechanisms, the pod came to life. A reverberating thrum pulsed through the interior of the bathroom, the water in the toilet vibrated in tiny oscillating waves. A smooth metallic wall slid across the opening of the doorway separating the interior of the lavatory from the wooden threshold of the office behind.

Jon dropped the toilet seat cover down, the top of which was specifically contoured in firm yet pliable foam, reached behind the narrow concave tank, also padded with the thick molded foam, and retrieved two leather straps from hiding. He secured the harness across his lap with a slender metal buckle, leaned against the cool water tank, allowing the foam padding to contour to his body, and braced himself for the twenty story drop.

The pod would plummet down the slide's rail into the depths of the building's basement, and then out horizontally to a well hidden egress nearly two miles from the center of the campus. Once the pod separated from the coupling holding it suspended above the precipice, it relied on gravity alone to generate the energy required to complete the journey. As it fell along the slide rail, magnetic fields generated to charge the unit's internal reserve battery.

Upon completion of the drop and subsequent horizontal glide along frictionless rails, the pod would come to rest in a safe station, well concealed and protected from the external environment. There, the pod and its occupant could remain for weeks while the unit interacted with the safe station and evaluated the world outside.

It was elaborate and relatively ingenious in its simplicity. Trials of various pods had shown that a man could survive quite comfortable in his hideaway while the world raged outside. Exiting the pod took merely a command request from the occupant.

Jon anxiously waited for the audio prompt, signaling the initiation of the drop sequence, when he suddenly remembered that the audio interfaces had yet to be installed. With no forewarning, the drop would happen unannounced and could jar the unexpecting occupant quite severely. Jon braced for the surprise release and the inevitable drop, his eyes clenched shut, jaw set tight.

He also fully anticipated the telltale tingle in the roof of his mouth and the dull vibration of his scalp that would precede the acoustic assault of the Anvil.

Time within the pod became palpable, each breath an arid vacuum, every swallow a sticky bitter rope of phlegm. For all Jon knew, security forces lurked just outside the pod, preparing to either disengage or vaporize it.

Drop, already! he screamed to himself. All this way, seeing and surviving the things that he had, and his ultimate fate rested on the random release of three steel locking bolts, that when finally toggled, would drop him into gravity's waiting maw.

Christ, he hated free fall.

Back in his Army days, he nearly puked every time they jumped into action. Of course, he never let on to his instructors or fellow soldiers. If he hadn't jump qualified, he would've been relegated back to regular ground infantry, and back then, that meant nothing more than joining the masses of forward crawling dune-tunnelers. Those boys rarely got out of the shifting sand-dune firefights alive without the intervention of extreme close-air support and a few squads of well armored Rangers.

That was where he had met Sergeant Maxwell Donovan, a young kid from Houston, with fleeting and conflicting morals and even less conviction. But when it came to loyalty and commitment, to his comrades or his duty, Max was utterly dependable.

Or at least, so Jon had thought.

Then today...

Gone was that young man that Jon knew so well. The pragmatic realist who, when once faced with the ultimate existential dilemma, had gathered a lifetime's worth of ethical and philosophical experience from one single, crystal clear moment before it had shattered into unrecognizable splinters.

Jon had finally realized, years ago, that it wasn't the precise moments in time that change a man but rather the molecular eons that follow. They hadn't merely experienced a watershed moment out in the blistering sandy wasteland of Saudi; they went one entire evolutionary step beyond.

They had helped create it, he and Max had.

Years ago, Jon thought sadly.

Together, within the surreal atmosphere of a Pleasure Pyramid called *Bacchus Plateau,* they had crossed into a nightmare landscape of indescribable human terror and had made choices and taken actions that forever altered lives—theirs and many others.

And in the microcellular ages that followed, Jon and Max were forever changed.

Max, however, it seems may have come full circle, completely and forever lost in the oppressive wake of his own continuum.

Now, waiting for the Pod to drop, Jon mourned the loss of his good friend to the voracious appetites of the Fates. He fearfully wondered what lay ahead. For both of them.

Jon's scalp began to crawl, quiver and vibrate with a low and insistent grating. The rough surface of his upper palate tingled as if the roof of his mouth was covered with microscopic hairs and they are all standing on end in response to some source of static electricity.

The Anvil!

With a sharp pop and a metallic whine, the locking bolts disengaged. The pod hung suspended for a quantum eternity, a frozen second, then plummeted as the forces of gravity swallowed it in great, Newtonian gulps.

The floor of Jon's stomach rose to fill his mouth and then crashed back down through the bowl of his pelvis. The pod fell freely and silently without so much as a quiver or shake. Jon's arms floated gently at his side in the artificially created zero-G of freefall.

Jon struggled to remain coherent, trying to recall the science involved with mass and gravity's effects on bodies in motion. The mathematical value of some gravitational constant lingered teasingly at the periphery of consciousness, and then was swallowed by the shadows of an abyssal sleep.

Jon blacked out. His last coherent thought was of the Pyramids at sunset. He dreamed.

And he remembered the desert.

Fifteen

Pyramids and Principles

...and he remembered the desert.

Great swirling eddies of tan dust danced across the top of the dune as the vehicles slowed to a halt. Billowing clouds of sand settled around them filtering the early evening sun to a deep blood red. Sharp, flickering shadows leapt across the smoky curtain of the sand plumes, backlit by the setting desert sun; as from within the enveloping cloud men dismounted their vehicles and gathered in the drifting motes of dusty talc.

As the veils of dust grew thin, details of the vehicles emerged: wide black tires with thick, knobby treads supporting broad, squat aluminum Kevlar shells wrapped around ionized titanium skeletons. Painted in traditional desert camouflage, six Army Foxtrot-Class Assault Tacticals (AFCATs) sat idling on the shoulder of the desert road, their engines rumbling low and throaty.

A few of the men had shuffled to the rear of their vehicles rummaging through the cargo holds for ammo, cool drinks and cigarettes.

One man walked to the front of his vehicle, placed a suede leather boot on the bumper cage and stepped deftly up onto the hood of the

AFCAT. He faced forward holding digital optic goggles to his eyes with his gloved right hand while shielding his face from the glare of the setting sun with the other.

"What's up, L.T.?" a young soldier asked from the ground beside the truck. His face was obscured by wrappings of thin brown and green cotton scarves, his eyes completely covered by round polarized goggles and his uniform was a faded tan and gray patchwork of random digital patterns almost completely bleached by the desert sun.

"Sir?" the younger soldier repeated.

The man stepped down from the hood of the truck and tossed the high-powered digital binoculars to the waiting soldier.

"Pyramids, Dickerson. Fucking Pyramids," he replied as he walked back to the driver's side and swung back into the vehicle. Private Dickerson looked after the lieutenant, fumbling with the optics as he attempted to stow them back into their carrying case. Upon completing the task, he walked back toward the other side of the vehicle slinging the binocular case over his shoulder.

As he rounded the front of the truck, another soldier emerged out of the sandy haze and bumped him roughly in the shoulder nearly knocking off his weapon and the optics case.

"Watch your cherry-ass, Private!" grumbled the new soldier stooping to light a cigarette in the steady wind.

"Hey, Sergeant Donovan," Dickerson remarked recognizing the NCO. "What did the L.T. say about pyramids?"

Sergeant Max Donovan took a deep drag from his smoke, stretched his neck from side to side and lifted the goggles from his face. His eyes sparkled in the growing gloom, filled with the wisdom and confidence of experience, yet spiked with a curious mischief. He rarely took anything, including himself, seriously. The corners of his mouth were always slightly twisted into a smirk as if he were contemplating his next practical joke or saw some humor in a situation that would simply take too long to explain.

He elected to go through this particular portion of his life blissfully ambivalent and silently chuckling to himself.

"There aren't any pyramids in Saudi," Private Dickerson hesitantly reasoned. "They're in Egypt, or some shit, right?"

Donovan winked and then spat some sand from his lips. He smiled as he spoke.

"That's right, Dick-head-erson. Very good." Donovan put his arm around the young private, giving a patronizing hug as he pointed toward the north, indicating the general direction in which they were headed.

"But as you will soon see, lad, over the hills and far away, there indeed lay, the Great Pyramids of Saudi Arabia. Where we will feast on honeydew and drink the milk of Paradise." He grinned mischievously as he waxed poetic, glancing sideways at the private and looking for a spark of recognition. "Before your time, I suppose," he sighed as Private Dickerson's face went slack.

His tone changed, his smile regrettably faded. "Way before your time. Mine, too, I suppose." He took a drag from the shrinking butt.

Donovan shrugged then chuckled at his vain effort to bring a little culture into the younger soldier's lives.

He explained, though, more for himself than anyone else. "I just always think of that obscure little lyric every time I see the Pyramids. It goes back to the days before holographic or even digital media. Albums on vinyl if you can believe that."

"Huh." Private Dickerson shrugged pausing in thought as he looked out past the drifting yellow sand. He stood still for a moment struggling to process the new information.

He let out a pensive and staggering sigh as he turned toward Sergeant Donovan, looking confused. "But I'm sure that—"

"Oh Christ, Dickhead, relax. You'll see," Donovan exclaimed in a rare burst of impatience. "Jesus, you fucking kids! You've got no vision. No capacity. It's a goddamn good thing that you're a crack shot, Dick-cheese, or you'd have no redeeming qualities what-so-ever." With that, Donovan flicked his dead butt on the ground and worked his way back to his vehicle. As he passed the lieutenant's window, the grinning officer ribbed him a little.

"They just don't get it, eh, Sarge?"

Donovan paused and looked back at the young private. He was still staring out toward the northern horizon obviously trying to work something out. Max glanced back to the lieutenant, shaking his head sadly.

"I tell ya, L.T. These young guys—I don't know."

"Shit, Max, what are you, twenty-two, twenty-three?"

"Yeah, but it's not about age, sir. It's about class and style. You know, the kind of classic, original flavor that outlasts an era.

"I could totally see myself in the Nineteen-fifties you know, with James Dean and Elvis. Or the Seventies and Eighties with Steve McQueen and Mel Gibson. Now those guys defined the world around them. They created their own mystique, L.T."

"I suppose. Though I'm not so sure that every age has its icon, you know. Maybe you really are the model of bravado for our time, but you're shielded by your admiration of the past and unable to express your own originality." Donovan actually gave this considerable thought, pausing to reflect and dissect what the lieutenant had just offered.

"Of course," the lieutenant continued with a smile growing across his face. "Those guys were studs. Always getting laid and never missing the opportunity. They always had it right, you know?"

"Yeah," Max added softly smiling. "What the fuck am I doing here, sir? I should be out there carving my niche, right?"

"You are, Sergeant, you are." The lieutenant winked nodding toward the young private standing in front of the truck. "You help me keep these young cherries alive. And from killing us or one another."

Donovan looked at the officer, lips drawn tight and eyes narrow.

"That, Sergeant Donovan, is class and style of a sort that has been immeasurable throughout history. Ever since the dawn of man, we've taken up arms against some enemy. And there have always been men of style and class during those times. You just don't hear too much about them because they always seem to die young. When this shit is over and you rotate back, it'll be hard for you to fill the void left by all of this."

Max nodded, sighed lightly and readjusted his goggles over his eyes. He threw up a quasi-dramatic right-handed salute and turned to leave just as the loud, abrasive voice of the unit commander erupted from behind them.

"Lieutenant Webb! What the *hell* is going on up there? Do you have a Sit-Rep for me or am I supposed to read your fucking mind!"

Lieutenant Jonathan Webb sighed heavily and returned the mock salute, sending Donovan on his way. As he prepared to radio the situation report to the colonel, he shouted one last thing through the window to his noncom.

"*Xanadu*, though lyrical and vivid, lacks the epic visionary elements of *2112*, which is by far Rush's best album from the days of vinyl." He was referring to the obscure lyrics uttered earlier.

Without looking back, Sergeant Max Donovan waved his middle finger over his shoulder in response.

Lieutenant Webb smiled, shook his head and then keyed the mic on his headset to send an encrypted message to his commander waiting impatiently three trucks back.

While Webb completed the transmission, Private Dickerson returned to the AFCAT, unshouldering his weapon as he slid into the passenger seat. He removed his tinted goggles and looked at Webb questioningly.

It was the private's job to drive the officer's vehicle, particularly in combat. However, Webb seemed to prefer driving himself, and most of the time completely ignored the young Ranger. Dickerson often wondered if the L.T. would rather he mount up and ride in back with the rest of the grunts manning the crew-serve weaponry. For the time being, though, he figured he'd remain in the main cabin of the truck until told otherwise. At least that way he stayed out of the scorching sand.

"Don't worry, Dickerson," Webb said sensing the young soldier's curious manner. "You'll have plenty of opportunities to drive across this Godforsaken desert. Think of it this way; if we run into any rag heads, you'll have your hands free to throw some hot metal down range. Maybe even earn yourself a medal or something."

Dickerson smiled at this and turned to address the lieutenant. He thought better of it when he noticed that Webb wasn't smiling at all, but instead appeared deadly serious and intently distant.

The truck lurched slightly as Webb shifted and accelerated back onto the hard packed sand of the road.

The vehicles pulled forward and continued their convoy north. Rolling clouds of sand and exhaust billowed in their wake. The long, black barrels of the hyper-magnetic rail-guns mounted on the rear of each tactical swept right and left, covering their movement. Private Dickerson settled into his seat and through the smeared windshield studied the empty orange horizon ahead.

~ * ~

Within minutes, small black peaks appeared in the distance, ratcheting the otherwise unbroken yellow dunes with perfect artificial angularity.

The Pyramids.

They weren't actually pyramids at all, at least not in the classic sense. But that's what they were called by the soldiers of the World Economic Coalition.

Years ago in the early stages of the Middle Eastern Campaign for Democracy, Economic Freedom, and Eradication of Global Terrorism—the politically correct blanket-label for any organized military effort in that particular theater—it became painfully obvious that modern Western involvement in southwest Asia was going to expand over at least two generations.

In fact, once the United States began numbering its various military exercises like Super Bowls, it was evident that a persistent American military presence would forever redefine the character and culture of the desert nations.

During Saudi Savior IV/Persian Gulf Guardian VII, better known as the New Crusades for Global Alliance and Unification, forty-six self-sustained, permanently entrenched U.S. military bases were constructed across the sprawling deserts of Saudi Arabia, Iraq, Iran and Kuwait, dotting the rolling arid planes with long, squat buildings surrounded by high walls and deadly barriers. These heavily populated islands of western culture were connected by a network of paved roads and highways, weaving through vast arrays of highly secured communication towers, satellite dishes, and concrete encased ground lines.

The oil-wealthy country of Kuwait, its sovereignty eventually crumbled by repeated invasions and occupations, continued to serve as the main port of entry and exit for the Middle Eastern theater. However, with crude oil as its only significant natural resource, the transformation of Kuwait into a viable platform for the sustainment of nearly two million troops and families stationed there required the implementation of advanced Western industry and technology.

Of course, with that, came the self-indulgent influence that epitomized the Muslim's negative perception of a brusque and godless America.

While the outlying frontier regions of the country resembled the dank, iron-gray skeletal works of any North American industrial-heavy community, Kuwait City itself pulsed with the neon opulence of a Nevada resort. Within the city, around any corner, as well as bleeding into the surrounding suburbs, one could find alcohol, drugs and illicit sex in all of their wicked forms.

America, version 2.0, had sprung up right in the heart of the Muslim world.

Ironically, a powerful fraction of the wealthy minority in the Muslim community had been secretly enjoying the decadent rock and roll lifestyle of the West for decades; all while the orthodox masses toiled under the strict laws of their faith and struggled to comprehend the convoluted and contradictory doctrine fed to them by their leaders.

As it turned out, and coming as no surprise, the few religious zealots who were constantly misguided by the loose interpretation of their scriptures were themselves wallowing in the same self-absorbed depravity that they decreed as spiritually felonious. Eventually, and after much exposure and ridicule, their religious credibility vanished; replaced by the reality of financial desperation.

The entire Middle Eastern oil cache was now under the full control of the World Economic Coalition and that alone justified the necessity for continued Western occupation of the desert lands. As a result, generations of inherited Muslim family wealth was draining out of the sand and into WEC pipelines.

So, out of desperation and realization, these few, yet powerful religious hypocrites embraced their true god—money.

Once they discovered that the personal pain suffered from their spiritual failures and the loss of King Oil paled in comparison to the elation they experienced when the flow of money returned, they began to turn a tidy profit from soliciting sin to the ever-present soldiers.

As Kuwait grew into an international military resort, the stain of western culture and depravity spread into the desert, pulled across the sand in the wake of rapidly deployed military forces.

Behind every combat and support element that moved through the Middle East, there followed gypsy communities of entertainment and recreation, complete with organized gambling and prostitution, abundantly rich with the agents of excesses like alcohol and designer drugs.

The American-dominated WEC swept through the vast deserts of Kuwait, Iraq and Saudi Arabia, chasing rogue terrorist factions and independent oil holding tribes, securing oil field after oil field and establishing small outposts whenever they settled for longer than a week. These outposts would usually remain once the military moved on, awaiting the next wave of western influence to sweep through and sprinkle the seeds of colonization.

The outposts were constructed from sturdy lightweight desert-tempered hardware, and from a distance the steep conical design of the fiber resin structures did indeed resembled tall slender pyramids. Up close, however, the angularity of the rapidly deployed perm-a-tents was broken up by tentacles of flexible tubing and cables supplying each structure with water, power and environmental control.

In essence, the outposts evolved into self-sufficient oases peppered across the desert sea, offering a buffet of western delights for every taste and teasing the palate with exotic flavors of local influence.

Lieutenant Webb's vehicle passed through the outer gate of the outpost just as the desert sun was kissing the flat tan horizon. The dark crimson disk faded from an intense radiant blast to a diffuse warm throb as the AFCATs followed single file through the narrow and winding entryway.

Tall, electrified coils of concertina wire bordered the serpentine gate for two hundred meters before giving way to an open roadway that quickly funneled into the single narrow portal cut into the thick concrete inner wall of the outpost. Four heavily armed sentries guarded the entrance and immediately took up defensive positions as the vehicles slowed to within twenty meters.

"Prepare to transmit authorization and verification!" commanded a synthesized mechanical voice. The heavy bass boomed over loud speakers and reverberated through the air around the port, simultaneously crackling loud and distorted over the vehicle's internal-to-external communications.

"Cut I-to-E comm. Go to short range mobile," instructed the disembodied voice of the unit commander over the vehicles' radios.

Lieutenant Webb thumbed a keypad on the instrument panel and the internal communications snapped off. Private Dickerson immediately activated two small handheld phones and handed one over to the lieutenant, furrowing his brow in question as the officer quickly checked the phone's front panel LCD, and then secured it to his web-belt.

"All ciphered external communication is prohibited within the Pyramid Zone. Only un-encrypted handhelds are authorized," Webb explained to the private. Dickerson nodded his understanding as he turned to gaze out of the side window.

The sentries had multiple large-scale mag-weapons trained on the small entourage of tacticals, their faces and bodies concealed beneath flowing wraps of rags and torn uniforms. The weapons emitted a low, incessant hum indicating that they were fully charged and presently off safe.

"Transmit ether-code to channel four. Now," boomed the mechanical baritone. Within the onboard computer of the commander's vehicle, a silent game of electronic twenty questions took place between the security system of the outpost and the Army's most advanced mobile processor. Within seconds, they were identified and authorized entry. No messy interpersonal interaction. No interrogation and no passwords. If any question arose as to their authenticity, the vehicles and the men inside would have been instantly and completely vaporized without hesitation.

"Enter and proceed to immediate disarm and physio-scan." They drove forward at a slow idle. The sentries' weapons tracked their progress through the open portal until the final vehicle disappeared into the blackness of the tunnel.

Once inside, the soldiers would surrender their weapons to the guardians, and then submit to a brief, yet thorough, physical health evaluation. Once cleared by the guardians, they were free to move about the one hundred twenty-five acre interior of the outpost.

"So, this is a Pyramid?" exclaimed Private Dickerson.

"One of many in theater, yeah," said Lieutenant Webb. "But this is the only one in this sector of Saudi."

Dickerson watched silently as the darkened tunnel before them began to lighten as they proceeded deeper. Irregularly spaced flickering fluorescent tubes in the curved ceiling revealed outlines of pipes and conduits running the length of the walls and ceiling.

A man in civilian attire was waving them forward from a small alcove to the side of the narrow passage. He unslung his shoulder weapon and held it casually at port-arms as they approached and coasted to a stop. The man smiled and sauntered over to the lead vehicle. He leaned in through the open passenger window.

"Hey," he began as he looked over Dickerson and then Webb.

He quickly recognized Lieutenant Webb's rank and continued more formally. "Welcome to Bacchus Plateau, sir. What unit are you guys from?"

"Two-three-six, FRF," Webb lied. Their identification and mission were highly classified even though they had completed their assigned sweep over a week ago. The commander insisted that they remain incognito as they moved back through the Controlled Zone.

"Forward Reaction Force? Man, I thought you guys were long gone," the man said. "Well, welcome anyway. Staying long?"

"Not sure," Webb offered hoping his ambivalence would bring an end to the conversation.

The man leaned back out and quickly scanned the grouped vehicles, mentally tallying their numbers. Webb hoped that he would hurry. The commander was not a patient man, and Webb didn't want this well-meaning, one-man welcoming committee to bring about the wrath of the colonel. One of his unfocused tirades could last an uncomfortably long time.

"Okay, I count six AFCATs and what, fifteen bodies?" the man asked.

Webb nodded.

"Looks like you guys are packing a lot of hardware. How much locker space will you need?"

"Full personal load times fifteen, plus the crew-serves and some specialty items. I assume we can leave the sensitives intact on the vehicles?" Webb spoke succinctly.

"Yeah, that's fine. Actually, you lucked out. We're pretty light at the moment. I can give you guys a full lock-down vault. Keep it all together in there."

"Outstanding," Webb acknowledged with a single nod. "Let's get it done."

The man glanced back at the fully outfitted vehicles and seemed to teeter on the brink of submitting to his curiosity. Before he could ask any more questions, Webb interceded.

"We really have to get moving." Webb tilted his head back indicating the vehicle behind him. "Old man really needs to unwind. Know what I mean?"

The man nodded knowingly and smiled. "Oh, yeah. Sure. Just follow the remote and you're all set. About forty meters in.

"Hey, check out the new casino if you get a chance. Some great new games." The man winked at Dickerson as he added, "And some tasty new Synth over in Highland." He stepped back and waved the column past.

A small hover-remote met them at the intersection, floating a meter above the packed sand and led the way to the security vault. As the trucks followed the robotic airborne guide through the dusty labyrinth, Lieutenant Webb addressed Private Dickerson. "Dickerson, how old are you?"

"Nineteen, sir."

"I'm going to give you some advice, private, and it's not the kind of advice you may have received from your old man back home about not fucking the coach's daughter. This is the kind of advice you really need to pay attention to."

He glanced over at the young Ranger, ensured that he had his undivided attention, and held his eyes with a stern unblinking stare. The vehicle never wavered, though his full attention remained on the boy.

"Watch your ass in here," Webb said. "Stay close to one of the NCOs."

Dickerson cringed a little chewing on the inside of his cheek.

"I know, I know," Webb continued. "The last thing they're gonna want is some cherry tagging along, but you've already proven yourself out there and in the end, they would rather have you for a shadow than off running around by yourself." Dickerson raised a questioning eyebrow.

"Look, private, all of these guys have been to the Pyramids before. It can be overwhelming for a newbie, and quite honestly, a little dangerous. They may mean well, but sometimes things can get heavy and out of hand. They forget that it's your first time." Dickerson visibly bristled at the insinuation of his vulnerability and inexperience as a weakness. He was oozing youthful machismo, indoctrinated alpha-male competitiveness and denial.

"Relax. I'm not calling you a puss or anything. You need to approach your first Pyramid experience like you would any combat scenario, cautiously and methodically. Learn from experience. And son, I am the voice of experience. I've seen seasoned combat vets die tragic, very un-heroic deaths in these places."

Dickerson sat staring at the instrument panel. Webb continued to drive following the remote as it wound through a maze of internal roadways, his eyes darting between the road and the young solider.

"Have a good time, man. Drink, get laid, piss away all of your credits at the gaming tables. Just watch your ass. Stay away from solicitors and refuse any business mergers. The vendors will rob you blind before you can even shake their hand and close the deal." Webb paused as he negotiated a tight turn in the road. He hesitated before continuing with his warning.

"And stay away from the Synth." He looked over at Dickerson, caught his eye and held it again with a stern glare. "I mean it, man. Stay the fuck away from anything like that. Dopa-nepherine, Fenta-nepherine, Clear, Fright. All of it. Avoid Highland all together."

Dickerson looked blankly at the lieutenant.

"Are we clear, private?"

Dickerson nodded. "Yes, sir."

"I know we have some Synth-heads on board, but they're small time compared to the Neuro-junkies floating around in here." Webb took a breath and continued, "Murphy and Tollifsen, those guys can probably handle some of the harder shit, and that's their choice." He was referring to the squad's small internal clique of synthetic neurophilic stimulant abusers.

"Do yourself a favor and don't get involved with that shit."

The silence hung between them like a humid fog, barely stirring with each breath. The remote had stopped at a large reinforced door hovering silently as the line of tactical vehicles pulled up alongside. The oval shaped steel door began sliding up and cheers arose from the vehicles. Webb shook his head and sighed.

He glanced sideways at Dickerson whose eyes sparkled with wonderment and childish anticipation; unblinking and wide as he watched his comrades scramble from their vehicles. The men ran about like players on a football field after winning the Super Bowl in double overtime, and Dickerson visibly ached to join in the revelry.

The young private finally snapped out of his trance, broke his wide-eyed stare and turned toward Webb. The officer raised his brow and impatiently shrugged, awaiting a response from the awe-struck soldier.

Dickerson swallowed hard, averted his gaze slightly and answered hurriedly, "Yes sir, I hear you. We're cool."

With that Lieutenant Webb frowned and hung his head in futility.

This was supposed to be his last mission...

Sixteen

The whine of the cranial saw dropped in pitch as the high frequency oscillating teeth sliced a thin channel through the bone of the skull. Clear fluid leached out from the sharp edges of the groove as a pair of well-trained hands guided the small saw through an arc, circumscribing the entire irregular dome of the exposed skull. Fine clouds of bone dust settled on the inverted scalp flap and thin rivulets of cerebrospinal fluid collected in the soft dampness where the scalp was reflected back on itself and met pale bone.

The saw automatically clicked off as it completed its round trip excision across the calcified globe; and with the aid of two sharp, pick-like bone forceps, Dr. Tabitha Gunnerson carefully lifted the skullcap from the top of the cadaver's head. Gently placing the bony bowl upside down in a shallow container of saline, she then reached for a pair of smooth tweezers-like forceps and a fresh scalpel. Turning her attention to the thin, yet tough outer membrane that covered the brain proper, she carefully pinched up a segment of the duramater, gently sliced through the fibrous sheath and created a wide, continuous flap, which she progressively reflected back as she sliced.

With the surface of the brain now fully exposed, its convoluted folds and crevasses glistening like salmon and rose-colored gelatin, she could proceed with a gross examination of the brain and cranial vault.

She ignored the obvious deformities of the brain's normal cauliflower appearance and instead focused on the areas not obliterated from the path of the bullet.

A ragged, yet fairly straight gouge ran across the sloping surface of the right hemisphere. The obvious track of a projectile tapered from the back of the skull and extended forward; flaring wider as the bullet must have tumbled once it pierced the bone of the posterior cranium. The bullet had tunneled cleanly through the material of the right brain and exited the skull with enough explosive velocity to macerate the entire anterior aspect of the head.

The left frontal lobe and entire left hemisphere remained intact, and apart from some tissue edema from the adjacent trauma, were fairly well represented in her meticulous dissection.

It was this skillful preparation and exposure that made it extremely easy for her to identify the gross anomalous mass that was literally embedded within the pale contours of the uninjured side of the brain.

Tabby paused, her breath caught in her throat just below the root of her tongue, causing a flood of metallic tasting saliva to fill her mouth. She swallowed hard, blinked and shook her head in attempts to either clarify her vision or wake herself from an illogical dream.

Yet, there it remained, shimmering moist and alien underneath the bright autopsy lights: a smooth, pale strip of thin tissue about two millimeters by six, perfectly rectangular with precise margins and distinct segments. It lay across the normal brain tissue in a front to rear fashion, near the central fissure dividing the right and left hemisphere. Tiny vascular tendrils extended from the sharp margins of the foreign flap of tissue, as if it had been grown in place and developed a vascular supply from the existing anatomy.

Tabby was stunned and instantly fearful, actually worried for a moment that the strange segment may suddenly begin to pulse and throb, pull free from the underlying brain matter with a sick, wet tearing sound and leap from the dead man's opened skull to her face, cover her mouth and suffocate her with writhing tendrils seeking purchase within a new host.

She involuntarily backed up a step and gathered her wits before she realized that the next thing she needed to do was to photograph this bizarre finding *in situ*. She sighed heavily, exhaling a shaky and apprehensive breath.

She went to a low countertop across the lab and retrieved the digital recorder. She decided to record everything from here on and checked the device for adequate memory space.

Tabby positioned herself at the head of the recumbent cadaver, again taking in the bizarre and impossible sight.

What was she looking at? Tumor? Cancerous growth? Normal variance? No. The structure was surely organic, yet linear and sharply defined. It was symmetrical, for Christ's sake! Perfectly rectangular. Not a natural growth at all.

She couldn't help herself from slipping back into fantastical thinking. Considering the artificial, obviously manufactured appearance it seemed only logical that the segment of tissue was purposefully placed. *Alien implant? Secret governmental experimentation? Shit. Ridiculous.*

She slipped the recording glasses on over her eyes and activated the holo-drive DVR in the narrow bow of the glasses. She took her time, choosing her words carefully and selecting the best approach before beginning her dictation.

Eventually she slid into the familiar, natural rhythm she was accustomed to during any routine autopsy; though this was anything but.

"Addendum to post mortem dictation dated November tenth by Dr. Bernard Flavham. Dr. Tabitha Gunnerson presently recording initial post mortem craniotomy on Phoenix-Lamneth fatality number four. Official reference identification Kilo-Lima-Foxtrot one-four-seven-seven."

She spoke clearly and succinctly for the record, more out of habit than necessity. She was unsure who would actually be reviewing this recording, but was certain that Detective Gionetti would be one of the first. She assumed that keeping it objective and professional would be in her best interest.

The detective had been adamant about her staying low and out of sight, and especially about avoiding work, but something had been nagging at the back of her mind since their talk, and she had finally succumbed to her scientific inquisitiveness.

Carla had begged to come along, but after an hour of fighting and then negotiating, Tabby finally agreed to call Carla at the beach house every thirty minutes until she returned. If Tabby failed to report in, Carla would notify the police and Detective Gionetti.

Tabby was initially unsure about the true extent of any real danger she may be in, but now after exposing the fourth victim's brain she was suddenly convinced that whatever was going on, it involved some extreme science.

And with extreme science, came extreme risk.

"After complete craniotomy was achieved through the usual circumferential excision of the skull cap, the cerebral hemispheres were exposed in their entirety through the standard Penfield dura flap.

"Upon gross examination, the cranial vault contains the complete right and left cerebral hemispheres, with severe through-and-through ballistic trauma to the right hemisphere extending posterior to anterior..."

Tabby described the damage inflicted by the passage of the bullet in specific medical detail, reciting for the digital recorder in dry clinical monotone. She picked and prodded at the obvious track of the bullet, carefully and methodically assessing the specimen in order not to miss anything while consciously ignoring the glaring abnormality resting on top of the left half of the man's brain.

Stay focused, Tab. Don't miss the trees for the forest. Finish the right side first and then consider that fucked-up impossibility on the left!

Tabby paused, rubbed her eyes and shook the distraction from her mind. She continued dictating her gross findings on the right hemisphere for another fifteen minutes. Finally, she turned her attention to the left hemisphere and its unusual patch of extra tissue.

She took a breath, closed her eyes and set about to try to objectively collect as much of all the data that she could. She leaned in close to capture as much detail as possible for the DVR. She began speaking more animated and descriptive than previously, struggling to remain neutral for the record.

"...apparently organic in nature, though seemingly artificial or, manufactured, in origin. The margins are crisp and linear. Razor straight and perfectly symmetrical. There seems to be evidence of neovascularization surrounding the graft..." She paused at the sound of the word coming out of her mouth.

Graft.

That's exactly what it looked like, a graft.

A cerebral graft?

She continued, actually thinking out loud now with little regard to the legal ramifications of the content of her recording. She was captivated by the overall mystery of the grafted tissue.

"…if it's a graft, then why? What for? And what was grafted? Consider seizure foci or, I don't know, CVA, tumor site. Maybe it's topical therapy for cancer?

"I want to excise it, or at least a portion, and do a full histological exam. Should I—Shit!" She reached up and flicked off the DVR as she suddenly realized her rambling stream of consciousness.

She sat back on the raised rolling stool and rubbed her eyes beneath the DVR glasses, considering all of the possibilities confronting her when her phone began vibrating on her hip, startling her. She flipped the face open and saw the ID.

Carla. She forgot to call.

"Shit," she mumbled to herself bracing for the verbal lashing she rightfully deserved.

"Carla, I'm fine." A pause. "Yes—all right. Everything is fine, hon. I'm sorry, I lost track of the time. I'll remember to call—yes, I promise. I'm so sorry. I love that you worry, but really, just relax. Yes, I know." She nodded to nobody as she held the phone to her ear with one hand and removed the DVR glasses with the other.

Her mind drifted, unable to focus completely on the phone conversation. She remained fixated on the work ahead of her tonight.

"Look, Carla. Please, just listen. I have a lot to do tonight. Yes, it has to be tonight. The sooner I get at it, the sooner I can get back home to you.

"Why don't you call me every half hour if you like, instead of waiting for me to call? You know me, I'll get wrapped up in something and forget and you'll make yourself sick with worry. Okay? Deal. About three hours, four max. I know, I know."

She listened, placating her partner for a few minutes then found a moment to bring the call to an end. "Okay, look baby, I have to get to work now. I love you, and I'll expect your call every half hour, unless you fall asleep again in front of the fire." She smiled, listening.

"I know you do, hon, and I promise this will all end soon. Okay? Good night and don't worry. Bye." She punched the phone off, placed it in her hip pocket and turned back to the exposed brain.

She gathered her instruments and walked over to the counter pulling on a new pair of latex-free gloves. She toggled a few switches and pressed a number of buttons on the equipment littering the surface of the counter as she geared up the sensitive microscopic and scanning instrumentation.

~ * ~

The digital signal scrambler beeped, hummed and chirped in three distinct tones before the connection went clear and the electronically altered voice spoke.

"The game just went into overtime."

"How?" asked the man seated in the shadows of a vacant Washington, D.C. office suite.

"MacDonald got creative and called an audible. He got the other one to turn and work for him. Tried to scare the prime," the robotic voice warbled through the tiny speaker of the decoder.

"End result?"

"One dead and the prime is loose."

Silence.

"We've put our players back into the game, but MacDonald won't keep the amateurs on the bench."

"We must ensure discretion. Options?"

"Few. I recommend complete sterilization. An all-out blitz. We can have control of the game by COB tomorrow."

"Close of business will be too late. Besides, the coach wants the prime to take the dive. His implication is critical to achieve the goal."

"I understand."

"I agree with the blitz, though. Erase all associations and discover as much as possible in the process. However, clean sweep the prime, past and present, front and back. Stay near and wait. The coach has a plan to flush him out."

"I understand."

"Call a time out and huddle with all of the players. The prime is not to be hit. Any and all organic associations are to be fully debriefed in the field, and then thoroughly cleaned. All commo will go through you. This office will remain central until phase two. You now have discretionary authority for all local activities."

"I understand."

The connection went dead, the signal decoder hummed and then powered down. The man in the shadows rubbed his head vigorously with both hands and groaned out a long, aggravated sigh.

Seventeen

It was supposed to be his last mission...

...and they were less than a day's travel from their extrication point, yet instead of driving on, calling for a pull out and getting home, the colonel insisted on a layover at this particular outpost. No explanation was given, other than some well-deserved R&R for the boys. Webb was all for unit morale and God knew the men deserved some downtime after the past three months, but he was short and due for a full discharge upon returning stateside.

He kept reminding himself what it had been like when he was fresh in-country and in need of some seriously well-deserved mental decompression after the stress of combat; and repeatedly chastised himself for his selfishness.

But there was something else, vague and shadowy, lurking just beneath the surface and it made him skittish. It felt like the longer they hung around, the more likely their chance of running into something wickedly awful—something darkly permanent.

Perhaps it was just short-timers' paranoia, but over the years he had learned the value of trusting his instinct. Today, his instinct was thrumming like a high-tension power cable in an electrical storm and it was screaming at him to police up his men and un-ass this desert Eden.

They entered the spacious vault, parked the vehicles and dismounted. The soldiers scurried about, dropping the heavy battle gear from their backs and securing their weapons and equipment in large personal lockers. Their loud energized voices echoed off the curved walls and high ceiling as they high-fived one another, slapping hands and heads playfully amidst boisterous laughter and raucous male humor. The atmosphere was as loose and full of testosterone as any victor's locker room.

Private Dickerson quickly disassembled his own gear, eagerly stealing glances at his frenzied comrades as they grouped together at the rear of the vault, smoking cigarettes and re-telling stories. Webb slowly pulled his own gear from the back of the truck, watching the men gather as they anxiously waited to be formally dismissed.

Dickerson hesitated obviously waiting for the lieutenant to release him.

"Go, Dickerson," Webb said through a tight smile.

"Yes, sir," he said breathlessly. "Um, can I help you with your stuff?" he asked half-heartedly.

"No, thanks. I got it."

Dickerson nodded quickly and took off at an excited jog.

"Hey, Dickerson!" Webb called out suddenly. The private stopped and spun around, mildly exasperated.

"Sir?"

"I mean it, dude. Watch your ass, okay?"

Dickerson faltered slightly and then smiled wide. Too wide. And dangerously innocent.

"Roger that, sir!" Then he sprinted off toward the men.

"Hey, Dickhead-erson! What the fuck, cherry!" the fraternal shouts met him as he joined the group and traded slaps, gropes and arm-punches.

Webb continued assembling his combat pack and securing the vehicle, his mind reeling with concern for the young man specifically, and an overall ominous feeling in general. He willfully struggled to squeeze out the shadow of impending doom that had begun to seep under the surface of his otherwise steely resolve. It blew through him in smoky wisps like a warm infectious fog seeking out cracks in the seals with its cancerous tendrils and choking him. He couldn't completely shake the chill left by the icy fingers of doubt and foreboding intuition.

"Lieutenant!" bellowed the colonel.

A weary, gaunt form sauntered up behind Webb, hands on his hips, a slim leather case under his arm.

"Handle the men. Usual briefing and all that. I'll be out of the AO for awhile. Keep your phone close, but don't expect to hear from me for at least twenty-four hours." The colonel's eyes were distant, wild. He already appeared to be somewhere else entirely. Webb nodded and responded.

"Yes, sir." Jon glanced in the direction of the men. "How long do you want to give them?"

The colonel's eyes jumped and twitched. He worked his tight jaw as he gnawed on the inside of his cheeks. He finally answered absently and without real conviction. "Doesn't really matter." Then he caught Webb's immediate concerned look and amended, almost casually, "Oh, lieutenant, I don't know, give 'em at least three days. They've earned it."

Webb nodded and then sighed.

Three more fucking days until pull out, he thought.

And what was going on with the colonel? He was definitely distracted with something.

The commander spun on his heels and quickly strode toward the exit as he flipped open his thin phone and brought it to his ear leaving Jonathan Webb in his wake.

Webb turned to walk toward the men as Max Donovan approached from behind the rear of the vehicle. He had lit a fresh cigarette and took a long drag, winking at the lieutenant through a cloud of blue smoke.

"Twitchy fucker today, eh?" Donovan offered watching the colonel leave.

"Hmmm." Webb shook his head lightly as he studied the hard-packed orange sand at his feet.

"I tell ya' what, L.T.; I think that guy passed over into the Twilight Zone a few weeks back. I mean, he's all thirty-one flavors of fucked up, if you ask me. Like he's in some kind of shadow land."

"Yeah, maybe."

"No maybe about it, sir. He isn't right, and this is the last place on earth for a soul like that."

Webb suddenly looked up and caught the flicker of fear and doubt in his sergeant's eyes; a faint glint of dark worry shadowed the usual confident steely gray and then vanished. He recognized the look and was instantly confident that if he gazed into a mirror right now that same look would stare back at him from his own exhausted face.

"All right, Donovan," Webb shifted the topic and redirected the non-commissioned officer. "Let's get these guys debriefed and released. The colonel wants to give them three days..." He shook his head defiantly, and then continued, "Give them the usual brief-down. Emphasize the buddy system and clean commo. I want them back here in forty-eight hours, not seventy-two. Clean and sharp."

Sergeant Donovan nodded his acknowledgment.

"And Max," Lieutenant Webb added. "Keep a close eye on the Synth heads. And Dickerson, okay?"

Max rolled his eyes at the mention of the Synth abusers. "Yeah, I got a personal beef with Murph anyway. I think he and his crew may pull last weapons watch. Force them to stay clean. Or at least cleaner."

Webb nodded as he softly sighed, and then began to repack his gear. Sergeant Donovan moved sternly toward the restless gaggle of men bellowing for them to assemble.

Soon they would be released into the dark, decadent shadows of Bacchus Plateau, northern Saudi's only recreational Pyramid—young men, fresh off the battlefield, oozing testosterone and bravado, their appetites rumbling and their pockets swollen with unspent credits. Every brothel and gaming parlor, an exotic and tempting bastion; every bar and holographic tattoo club, a promised fulfillment of mythical proportions.

In exchange for their hard-earned salaries, and at criminally high prices, they would quench their thirst for flesh and emotional release, seeking instantaneous, albeit temporary, serenity in the escapism afforded by the buffet of delights spread before them.

Webb could appreciate the need for emotional and physical decompression and the importance of adequate R&R for the combat weary soldiers. He strongly advocated it, in fact, and was comfortable in allowing his NCOs to keep control of the men, ensuring that moderation prevailed.

Yet, nothing about this last mission or the colonel's obsessive insistence on this sudden retreat to the Pyramid sat well with Webb. He knew better than to ignore his instincts, and right now that little voice was screaming for attention. He had kept his mind sharp and senses clear in hope to discover some signs, a clue as to what specifically worried him. However, his efforts had been fruitless, and aside from the colonel's queer behavior, everything else had gone textbook perfect.

Lieutenant Jon Webb stowed the last of his gear in the assigned locker and followed the last soldier out of the vault. The young man turned to the lieutenant and smiled as he asked, "Hey, L.T. Join us for a few over at the reception hall. The guys are all starting off there before cutting loose. Gotta drink to the team!"

"Thanks, Benson, but I have the Committee staffers to debrief, and then some business to take care off." Webb shrugged apologetically.

He then reached into his cargo pocket and withdrew a flat black leather wallet, opened it and fingered through a few items before coming out with a slim plastic holographic card. He quickly swiped it across the face of his phone and deftly typed some numbers into the glowing keypad. He swiped the card a second time and flipped it toward the soldier, who caught the spinning card in a swooping arc.

"First and last round are on me, and I don't want to see that card come back with any credits left on it. Got it?" Webb smiled and winked at the soldier.

"Yes, sir! Roger that! Thanks, L.T." The young man swiped the card across the face of his own phone and viewed the amount of credit value displayed on his small LCD. "Oh, shit, sir! Wow!"

"Get the hell out of here, Benson." Webb waved the soldier on as he walked away.

"Warrior Ranger!" He called out the first part of the unit's motto.

"All the way!" replied Webb.

Jon's easy smile faded as he watched the young soldier jog out of the vault and into Babylon.

Three more days, he thought.

Christ.

Eighteen

After nearly four hours of tedious dissection and meticulous examination under the harsh limelight of the autopsy lamps, extensive cellular and biochemical analysis and some old fashioned text research, Tabitha had enough hard information about the strange patch of pink tissue to scare the shit out of her.

She fielded one last call from a wound-up and distraught Carla before closing the skull and putting together a report for Gionetti.

"Yeah, I'm essentially done here. Just got to clean up, organize some of the data, and then I'm out of here. I know, it's late. I'm sorry, baby. Hey, I'll make it up to you when I get home, okay? Hmm? Yes, if you like." She smiled mischievously as Carla responded seductively to her suggestion. "Okay, I'll see you soon—oh, wait a sec!" A sudden thought came to her as the last piece of the puzzle fell into place.

She grinned even wider, taking some well deserved self-pride in her ingenuity. "Listen, I'm going to ether-load some files from my PDD to your holo-disk there at the house in the next few minutes. It'll be kind of large, so when it's complete, do me a favor and just compress-bundle it into an encrypted metafile and save it to two disks. Put one away somewhere safe and keep the other one as backup for my PDD. Can you do that? Yeah, thanks, hon. I'll see you soon. Love you, too."

She hung up the phone and went to work closing up the mysterious head. As she deftly sutured the skullcap back on and stapled the scalp back in place, she marveled at the results of her evening's work.

Though many questions were answered through the forensic revelations, just as many new uncertainties had been uncovered. She shook her head as she allowed her mind to drift and consider the conceit and audacity of those involved to actually carry out such a fantastic and bold stunt. She would put together a brief and concise report for Detective Gionetti and attempt to send it to him via his own PDD. He had given her his personal number and she hoped that he would have the capabilities to receive the large amount of data that she needed to show him.

If the transfer went well, she could purge her own PDD and rely on the backup she would send Carla momentarily and eliminate any local trace of her investigation and findings.

She settled in at a small workspace along the low counter next to all of the lab equipment, the instruments and scanners just now completing their communication with her personal digital data device. The PDD's mini-plasma screen flashed lime-green to indicate successful transfer of all the data from the peripheral devices.

Tabby rechecked the function application to verify the overall size of the file, and once satisfied with the transfer, began rebooting and purging all of the lab instrumentation, scrubbing any evidence of her work from their existence.

Once completed, she swiftly began typing across the keypad of her PDD, entering a short and descriptive narrative to tack onto the file, breaking down her discoveries into layman's terms for the detective. She completed the task in minutes, and then activated the ether-connection to the meta-web and searched for Carla's beach house-based holo. The signal was found in seconds, a secure connection was made, and with a few deft touch strokes across the glowing flat panel, the transfer was initiated.

While the file uploaded, Tabby washed her hands in the low stainless steel sink working a thick lather of antimicrobial soap between her fingers. She turned her wrist to check the time on her watch as she rinsed her hands and arms under the warm running water.

Just a few more minutes and she would be closing up the lab, probably for the last time, she somberly thought. The chances of her remaining at this job after all that she recently discovered were remote. Hell, when the dust finally settled from this particular windfall, there might not even be a forensics department, at least not in its current incarnation.

Of course, Tabby just might emerge from this a true hero, and if that happened she could quite possibly be in line to rebuild the entire pathology team from the ground up. There could even be a solid argument for her to assume the directorship. She allowed herself a small mental congratulation, and then returned to reality as the PDD beeped in response to completing the upload.

She dried her hands on her jeans, and retyped a second transfer request. This time the device searched for Gionetti's PDD signal.

She was still a little nervous about the situation, though now she felt empowered with the truth of her findings. Somebody had quite a bit of explaining to do and if her hypothesis was correct—

She flinched at the crashing sound of stainless steel bouncing off tile. Her head snapped to the left toward the sound, her eyes darting about the lab, searching and finally coming to rest on a thin silver tray lying on the green tile floor just beneath a semi-recumbent cadaver.

The dead man's arm had slipped from out of the mesh harness that secured the body to the wire frame of the autopsy table. Normally, the stiffness of rigor would prevent the limb from simply falling and dangling free, but the right shoulder of this particular corpse had been disarticulated by one of the residents during a practical exam on the complexities of the brachial plexus, and now the arm swung quite freely if not properly secured.

Tabby saw that the arm had indeed slipped free of its harness and had knocked the tray loose from one of the many mobile Mayo stands scattered about the table. She caught her breath and stepped over to the table, stooping low to retrieve the tray, grasping the cool steel in one hand as she swept a short lock of hair from her eyes with the other.

She rose and turned with the tray in her left hand to replace it on the Mayo stand as the sharp steel point of a long thoracic trocar pierced her abdomen in a swift upward arc.

Strong arms drove the pointed tip of the trocar through the soft viscera of her coiled bowel, slicing smoothly across the purple surface of her liver, lacerating it deeply and finally coming to rest firmly pressed against the resistance of the fibrous diaphragm that separated the thoracic cavity— containing her heart and lungs—from the abdominal cavity.

Rich, dark blood flowed freely from the wound spilling over the leather-gloved hands that held the trocar in place. Tabby gasped, open-eyed and instantly in shock. Her terrified gaze rose from the glinting metal of the surgical instrument protruding from her belly up the powerful, darkly clad arms of her assailant. She managed a confused and questioning stare as the man's face swam into clarity from beneath the floating gray spots that coalesced in front of her, an ominous visual sign of impending unconsciousness.

He was a stranger to her, though strikingly handsome, she thought, which was unusual for her considering her preferential orientation. *But truth be told*, she reasoned dreamily with shock-induced calm and certainty, *if she was ever to consider sleeping with a man, he was physically attractive enough.*

She weakly shook the disconnected and distracted thought from her mind.

Dimly, behind the incoherent, rambling thoughts of approaching death, a single shred of lucidity dug its claws into her awareness. She knew that she was sliding into darkness. She strained against the persistent tug of the shadows closing around her because the man was speaking, forming words with his sinister, yet beautiful mouth—sounds that barely made it through to her cognizant self.

She concentrated on the thin, chiseled lips of the man with the steel spear in his hands.

"Ah, doctor. Don't pass out on me just yet. I need to have the encryption code for the data file you just sent." The man narrowed his eyes as he lifted the trocar slightly, bringing her involuntarily up on her toes.

"You *will* die tonight, but it's up to you how long and painful that may be." Again, he twisted and tweaked the steel rod ever so slightly.

The darkness receded from her mind, replaced by searing agony as the collection of severed nerve endings in her belly suddenly overcame their initial shock and began firing all at once and in a continuous barrage.

She gulped and gasped, each minute breath adding fuel to the roaring inferno throughout her bowels. Her eyes jumped from the man's shadowed face and wide brow to the strong hands clutching the deadly instrument.

A barely audible beep sounded from behind the man emanating from her PDD. He quickly shot a glance over his shoulder at the thin device, its face opened to him, yet at such an angle that he was unable to read the plasma display. Tabitha glanced over his shoulder and quickly surmised the message on the glowing face of the display without being able to actually read it. She recognized the red color of the screen, hazy as it was from her disadvantaged angle.

She slumped a bit, seemingly defeated, as the man snapped his attention back to his prey. He held firm to the trocar as he lowered his face to within inches of hers, his jaw set, teeth firmly clenched. He whispered through narrow white lips, his breath sweet from spearmint gum.

"Who all did you send this to? How many now know what you know?" He waited grinding his teeth behind tightly drawn lips.

Sweat rolled freely down her face. She tried to blink the stinging salt from her eyes as she felt the darkness creeping back. The furnace in her belly was fading, not in intensity, but in meaningfulness. She felt her mind begin to softly snap the fragile strings that tethered it to her soul.

She made one last decision that was entirely her own before the phantoms of darkness descended and swept away her mind. With one last bolus of will-induced adrenaline she straightened her head, squared her face with the man's stony glare and parted her lips to speak.

He noticed the effort and drew even closer to the shaking woman, their noses touching. She blinked a few times in rapid succession, took a deep shuddering breath and strained to vocalize.

She slowly, carefully, reached around the man's waist with her trembling arms, hanging them out in space. As the words fell from her lips she quickly, and with surprising agility and strength, grabbed the man around the midsection and jerked him close, thrusting the trocar deep into her, tearing through the thick fibrous diaphragm and puncturing her aorta.

"Fuck you." She exhaled weakly, yet her last lucid thought remained silent and unspoken. *Oh God, Carla. I'm so sorry!*

She fell limp in his embrace as her entire blood volume pumped through the torn wall of the great artery in just a few fluttering heartbeats. He stood stiff and stunned holding her flaccid body in his leathered arms. Gouts of precious crimson spilled out of the hole in her midsection as he dropped her lifeless shell onto the tiled floor.

He spun around and approached the flashing PDD resting on the counter. As he picked it up in one massive hand and flipped the plasma screen to read the message, he knew before he saw the words trailing across the screen that his hunt was about to become more challenging.

Against a deep rose-hued background, pale white letters marched across the flat matte of the small plasma display:

> *Failed to complete entire transfer. Inadequate disk space at SGionetti-lapd.globalnet.metaweb.*

Nineteen

Three more days.
Christ.

~ * ~

Blanketed in soft blue light from the Officer's Club back bar, Jon Webb settled into the deep, plush leather of the bucket recliner as he rocked back and crossed his feet up on the low tabletop. He swirled a large crystal goblet of warm cinnamon brandy. The sweet spiciness of the rare liquor rose out of the bell shaped vessel and tickled his nostrils with wisps of fragrant flavors; some full and candied like caramel, almost chewy, while others teased his aromatic palate with insinuations of cedar and pine, vague and tenuous.

The atmosphere of the small club thrummed around him with the low bass beat of some unidentifiable old rock tune. He preferred the older, retro clubs to the more popular multi-phase clubs frequented by the younger soldiers. Here, he could enjoy a nice stiff, yet pleasant drink in the company of nobody, surrounded by sights and sounds he could understand, and not feel pressed down by the weight of the surging reality that engulfed his current world.

He savored a long pull of the golden elixir from the smooth lip of the goblet, allowing it to swim around his mouth, numbing his tongue and lips, tingling the insides of his cheeks before gently swallowing. His teeth were becoming anesthetized and his head nestled into the soft fuzzy blanket of a good, warm buzz.

A young, dark girl across the room had been watching him for some time, and now caught his eye and winked slowly offering a suggestively shy smile. Webb blushed and returned a smile that acknowledged the compliment. He softly shook his head once and then shrugged. She visibly sighed and raised her eyebrows in both appreciation and disappointment. He chuckled and took another mouthful of brandy as the girl shifted her efforts to another promising mark.

Webb recrossed his feet and went to work on finishing his drink before the waitress returned with his second.

A firm hand landed on his shoulder and gently spun him around in his chair. His feet fell limply from their perch. He tilted his head to the side and smiled wryly as Sergeant Max Donovan dropped into the seat next to him.

"Still got a thing for that syrupy air freshener shit, eh?" Max inquired nodding to the half-full glass in Webb's hands.

"Properly aged, aromatic brandies are rare these days. Though I prefer the mellow vanilla bean to cinnamon, this is the best they could do on such short notice." He took another sip, speaking into the wide bowl of the goblet as he did. "You uncivilized, nose-deaf cretin." Webb was smiling as he swallowed the sip.

"*Nose-deaf*? What the hell is that? Nose-deaf." Max feigned irritation and distaste. He sniffed to accentuate his defense.

"Yeah, nose-deaf. You couldn't tell the difference between camel shit and fresh pumpkin pie, let alone discern the subtleties of hand crafted fragrant ballantines."

"You're absolutely right. I hate pumpkin pie, so I make no distinction in that case. They both smell equally unappealing." Max paused raising his finger for effect and dramatic emphasis. "Now, a good single malt scotch or a fine merlot. Well, now there we have some olfactory rewards."

The waitress arrived as if on cue with two fresh glasses for each man, the diffuse light glinting off the meniscus of the golden liquids. Max retrieved his tumblers of scotch as Jon secured his brandies. They both smiled a sincere "thank you" to the young lady and waited for her departure.

They held their respective glasses high and touched rims.

"To the end of another bullshit assignment, and another day toward retirement," Max offered.

"Fuck that," Webb countered. "To the moment." He paused and held his friend's soft, curious gaze, then continued. "And to those again who share in it."

Max Donovan smiled and shook his head in admiration taking a deep swig from his glass.

"Bastard! Always one-upping me. Even in toast composition."

Jon Webb smacked his lips lightly after his drink and winked confidently. The men shared a comfortably silent moment.

They had served together for nearly thirteen months, through nine major missions and countless fire fights. Their relationship matured rapidly from superior and subordinate to a trusted brotherhood bound through endless trials of loyalty and courage. Their mutual respect for one another and unwavering trust set the tone for the men they commanded and lent to the unit's cohesiveness and success.

Max finally broke the silence.

"So, I'm curious. What's your take on the colonel's irrepressible need to drag us into this shithole rather than high-tail it cross country to the pullout point?"

Jon looked over the rim of his glass into the dark shadows of the club and pondered his response. He'd been wrestling with that very topic all afternoon and kept coming up with the same conclusion.

There really was only one logical reason anyone would bypass immediate extrication and electively spend days buried in the shadows of the Pyramid's ecstasy.

"He's got something on the side and beyond the regs."

Max nodded as if confirming his own suspicions and raised his eyebrows.

"Drugs or pussy?" It was the next most logical question.

Webb shook his head narrowing his eyes. "I honestly don't know. The man's too flaky for any kind of long-term girl thing. Either for himself or anyone else." He thought a moment, and then added. "Drugs make the most sense, but not for him, you know what I mean?"

"Yeah. He's fluffy-weird and fairly disjointed. But I agree. I don't see him getting all hopped up on the latest melon craze. He just doesn't have the—what, what's the word."

"Cerebral integrity," Webb finished.

"Yes! That's it. He definitely lacks the cerebral integrity".

Classically, the users and eventual abusers of synthetic neurophilic stimulants were actually quite heady. The designer drugs, collectively called Synth, were manufactured to heighten cerebral function and magnify intellectual experiences to an almost orgasmic state—referred to by aficionados as blooms. The thrill was in walking the fine line between ever-increasing blooms, and full blown electro-chemical meltdown of the delicate neural pathways of the mind.

Donovan shrugged and asked, "Then what?"

Webb finished off his goblet of cinnamon brandy and wiped his lips with a satin napkin.

"The one thing that lures any and everybody." He winked. "Money."

Max sat, swirling his scotch, watching the amber liquid film the sides of his crystal tumbler.

"He's got something cooking, and if it's coming out of here, it can't be good."

"Or long-term," Max added. "Committee control changes hands around here faster than a case of clap."

Webb nodded solemnly then placed his empty glass on the low marble table. He leaned back into the thick leather of his chair and laced his hands behind his head. He stretched his neck to each side as he spoke.

"I don't know, Max, the guy really scares me now. There's something not right with this whole visit. I've felt shitty-bad about this from the moment we pulled in."

Max nodded in agreement.

Webb continued as he reached for a new glass. "Man, I just want to police up our shit and get the hell out. We can R&R back in K-city." He shook his head in dissatisfaction.

"So, what do you want to do, boss?" Max inquired over the rim of his thick tumbler.

Jon raised an eyebrow and savored the last sip from his goblet before he spoke. "Get nice and mellow with a good friend, I guess. Then sleep for an uninterrupted eight." He finished off his drink and tapped the short stem with his finger. "After that, let's get the boys together, chase down the Colonel and un-ass this place."

"I'm with you, Jon. Where you staying tonight?"

"I got a small loft up in New Reno. You?"

"Nothing that fancy, I assure you. I was hoping to score some clean local love, and maybe just crash there for awhile." Max winked slightly embarrassed.

Lieutenant Webb shook his head as he smiled. "Well, don't let me stop you."

"Naw, I've got some time to kill. Besides, it's still early. None of the guaranteed honeys are out yet."

Webb nodded and took another draw from his second glass.

"Hey, remember that little makeshift oasis just off the Tigris, right after Lavender Push?"

Jon paused, then closed his eyes and laughed at the memory of the long ago post-mission celebration, shaking his head and flushing slightly over the recalled images. The two men rolled with laughter as they breathlessly revisited earlier escapades, sharing well-worn anecdotes and tales of self-embarrassment.

For the next two hours they drank and laughed like brothers at a reunion, temporarily forgetting their concerns. They were stuck at the Pyramid for at least a short while, so they might as well enjoy the rest.

Twenty

"Two bodies in the car. No ID for either, but when we ran the tag on the vehicle, well, you know…" The young detective's voice trailed off as he held up the plastic barricade for Sal to duck under.

Red and blue LED police beacons strobed and flashed in rapid, dysrhythmic pulses, illuminating the misty, snowy darkness of the early morning. Thin, wispy veils of sleet and curtains of fine snow alternated through the air fluttering on surging gusts of wind. Winter's chilly breath bit into exposed skin like an electric shock, first enlivening the flesh and then bringing about persistent numbness.

The two men walked side by side across the pavement of the closed road striding through standing puddles of icy water, the long tails of their coats fluttering behind them in the breeze. Intense, bright spears of limelight pierced the night around them, sweeping in quick, jerky movements as men with handheld flashlights and forensic drones searched the cordoned off area for additional clues. The crackle of static and terse, muffled voices over radio intercoms echoed in the damp frigid air.

As they approached the vehicle—its doors ajar, men and women scurrying in and about it like ants on a discarded candy bar—a short, plump man parted from the crowd and rapidly approached them. He waved absently, almost angrily, as he shouted above the noise.

"Inspector Detective Gionetti! Any fucking idea why your partner's been found dead with a naked girl in your car?" The Chief Investigator of Western Division spoke sourly, squinting against the glare of the throbbing strobes bursting all around them. His ruddy cheeks swelled with anger, colored by the freezing air as much as his hypertension. Small, dark beady eyes drilled into Gionetti's empty expression as he waited for a response.

"Take your time, Inspector Detective. Think it through. Unless you want to invoke your goddamn Miranda now."

Sal hated it when the Chief referred to him by his full title. It smacked of resentment and personal distaste. He didn't need a constant reminder that the Chief despised him, and that the numerous petty reasons lacked any actual validity.

Someday, Sal assured himself, the sarcastic little troll would get his.

"No idea, Chief. Who is she?" Remaining professional, Sal managed to ask the most obvious question while still processing the shocking reality that only twenty minutes ago, he had learned that he not only lost a loyal partner of two years, but a true and solid friend.

In time and much later, he would be able to grieve privately and appropriately. For now, though, he had the barracuda of Division making a hearty lunch out of his ass.

"She's naked as the night is cold. No ID. DNA pending, of course," offered the younger detective who had escorted Sal, attempting to be helpful, but instead earning a furious glare from the stout Chief.

"Jensen, why don't you go over there and start separating the rain from the snow, okay?" The young man looked blankly at the chief, about to add an explanation before getting violently cut off.

"Get the fuck out of here so I can properly ass fuck the good Inspector Detective here! Christ!"

The fat chief rolled his eyes and flapped his arms at his sides. His hands in the pockets of his coat made the open garment flap like the heavy wings of a prehistoric flightless bird.

The young detective spun on his heels and smartly retreated catching Gionetti's arched brow expression of thanks before striding into the misty darkness.

Gionetti turned back to the Chief just as the fat man was putting the finishing touches on what he considered his best hard ass expression—an overly practiced, melodramatic pursing of the lips while simultaneously sucking in the cheeks.

Most of the cops in Division have had the unfortunate opportunity to experience this asinine display of *persona bravado* firsthand, and the general consensus was that the portly son-of-a-bitch probably rehearsed the facial windup daily behind his closed office door. His attempt to conjure a stern glare of undeniable power and confidence only resulted in reducing his appearance to resemble that of a pouting, flamboyantly homosexual blowfish.

Sal Gionetti felt his anger rise as he watched his boss size him up and down for a full five seconds before clicking his tongue against his palate, snapping it annoyingly, and then indicating with a tilt of his round, misshapen head for Sal to follow him.

The chief waddled in a painfully stereotypic manner and it took real concentration to walk with him and match his stride. Sal buried his hands deep in his coat pockets in an effort to slow his gait and remain at the man's side.

"We're gonna play this as a John and Jane Doe for the fucking media," the chief said. "At least until I know more about your partner and the dead bitch. The last thing I need right now is a fucking circus with a strung-out cop and his junkie hooker girlfriend as the main attraction."

The chief continued wobbling toward the floodlit vehicle, stealing occasional sideways glances at Gionetti. He was trying to stir up some emotion, get a rise out of Sal.

"Where're you at with the whole Corporate Campus murder thing?" the chief asked. "That fell to you by sheer luck; you know that, don't you? Keller paged the wrong fucking DOD that morning. It should have been Doyle's case." The chief snorted and shook his head, over dramatizing his dissatisfaction with Gionetti's assignment.

Sal had been just coming off call that morning in question and the assignment director couldn't get a hold of the incoming detective-on-duty, Daniel Doyle, a close and personal friend of the chief. In desperation, the assignment director paged Gionetti just as he was finishing up his shift.

He simply caught the Phoenix-Lamneth case by default.

"Still working some leads," Sal began. "Pete was tailing one of the primes last night using my car. His vidcam and shit should still be in there," Sal answered softly, cursing himself for leaving Pete without backup.

"Nothing but two frozen stiffs, Dago." The chief frequently regressed to racial and ethnic slurs when addressing the men. Mostly it was taken as a crude form of endearment. It only bothered Sal because it came from this particular pig's mouth.

He usually bristled at the man's comments and would say something corrective, but tonight his mind was elsewhere and the dig passed without so much as a wink or furrowed brow. The chief was visibly surprised and disappointed.

"We swept the entire vehicle and found nothing." The chief shook his round head, puffing out his reddened, veiny cheeks. "High profile case like Phoenix-Lamneth and I got the wet backed-WOP and his now dead and apparently nefarious partner working the details. Christ!"

Sal had suddenly had enough.

"If Doyle hadn't been nursing a hangover at his girlfriend's and lost his pager in her toilet, he could have had the damn case. Hell, he can have the fucker right now!" Sal's voice stayed steady though it rose gradually as he finally defended himself and his partner.

"What did you say?" The chief paused, swung around and looked up at the taller detective, his eyes wild but his face thankful for the confrontation, finally.

He thrived on exercising his power, or at least his perception of power.

"Listen here, you Mexican-Italian piece of shit, I don't ever remember asking you for your opinion. On anything!

"I *can't* pull your ass off the investigation because the old man doesn't want any reassignments; otherwise, I would! He thinks it looks bad, doesn't present a unified and cohesive division. Dumb nigger fuck wouldn't know a clue if it bit his fat-assed lips."

Sal simply stared at the man, feeling sad that he had to waste so much of his time and energy appeasing him and his pathetic existence.

And to think he was married. The poor wife: what must she be like?

"You just be sure not to fuck anything up." The chief snorted. "Just get the facts straight, secure a viable collar, solidify a case and be done with it."

The fat man began walking again; still pursing his lips and narrowing his eyes in the frown that he mistakenly took to portray himself as a stalwart hero cop. Sal simply followed alongside and tried not to openly mourn his friend.

"Gionetti, this smells like an I.A. feeding frenzy. I want to know what kind of shit Peterson was into, and who he liked to play with."

Sal clenched his teeth and swallowed the bitter urge to strike the rotund little pecker for even insinuating that Pete was dirty. Internal Affairs was sure to get involved, as they always did when there was a mysterious police fatality; but Sal knew Peterson like a brother and was absolutely positive that he was as clean as the Virgin Mary.

"So, asshole. Who's the ginch?"

They had arrived at the open driver's door of Gionetti's black departmental Boeing AirRide. The chief was gesturing casually with his stubby hand toward the interior of the vehicle where his partner and a young woman lay naked against each other in the back seat.

They were both obviously dead—eyes frozen open, lips chalk blue, limbs stiff with rigor. Pete looked to have been stabbed cleanly through the head. Both entry and exit wound appeared sharp and distinct. The rest of his pale body seemed unblemished. There was no blood on or around his body.

His partner. His friend.

There was no question that the woman—the ginch, as the Chief referred to her—was Tabitha Gunnerson. She appeared to have been through a great deal more suffering than his partner. Her abdomen looked as if it had been torn through by some vicious predator. As with the other body, there was no blood to be found on or near her either.

His mind suddenly flashed to the missed transfer of some file she had attempted to send him only hours before. He hadn't had the opportunity to upgrade his PDD with more memory yet, though he'd been intending to do just that the next time he was in the station's tech shop.

Then, of course, he got the initial call to Phoenix-Lamneth and from that moment on, time stood still.

Could that have gotten her killed? A file? What had she found?
And Peterson?

Pete didn't even know about Tabby.

Sal Gionetti sighed and swallowed the painful guilt as he fully realized the truth—this had absolutely nothing to do with Pete or Tabby, and everything to do with Gionetti and the Phoenix-Lamneth incident. They were simply unfortunate, innocent tokens on the periphery of something much more complex and sinister. The macabre display of his murdered partner and prime witness was put together for his benefit to let him know that someone understood the connection between them all.

And that he had gotten too close. Sal had put both his partner and an innocent young woman at risk, and now they were dead.

Assassinated.

"Well, slick? Do you know the broad or not? She one of your snitches or just one of his snatches?"

This time, Sal snapped.

Darting out one hand, he tagged the fat clown square on the left ear. Blood instantly welled up in the shallow cup of the chief's puffy ear. His face cringed in surprise and a whiny, almost shrill yelp escaped from his mouth, but before he could form any coherent words, Sal brought his other fist forward in a lightning quick jab that shattered most of his front teeth in a dark spray of blood and spittle.

The fat man fell back against the rear quarter of the AirRide, pinwheeling his arms as he slid along the smooth surface slick with freezing sleet. His heavy ass impacted the slushy ground with a wet splash as Sal moved cat-quick to straddle the fallen man.

Gionetti placed the heel of one well-worn boot firmly in the chief's crotch, and reaching down with his dominant right hand, he grasped the front of the man's throat. With his left hand twisted into the mop of stringy wet hair, Sal pulled the man's bleeding face up by both scalp and larynx, stretching the man's body against the pressure he applied with his embedded boot heel. He brought his own face down to look directly into the chief's fractured snout.

"You're done, fat man. This is the end. Of you and of me!" Sal gritted his teeth and ignored the surprised gasps of the other people surrounding the crime scene.

He continued, more for the benefit of any good cop in the vicinity of his voice that may have the smarts to pay attention than for his bloodied boss.

"They were both assassinated by the same sick twist who did the P-L hit. She was my main lead in an investigation that was leading me to believe some thick shit was in the works. Now I know for sure, and I don't think that they're finished."

"You—your, your career is finished. Fucked!" The chief slurred the words spitting them through broken teeth and clots of blood.

"Like I give a shit." Sal dismissed the threat with a firm shake of the fat man's bulbous head. He finally looked around at the stunned faces of the uniformed and plainclothes police that were staring in bewilderment and shock. He nodded softly, more to himself than anyone else. He only knew a handful of the officers present.

Sal held tight to the chief's neck and scalp though he stepped off his groin and repositioned himself into a crouching straddle. With one smooth pull, he raised the fat man to his feet and propped him against the side wall of the car. He turned the man's face toward the open door of the AirRide and readjusted the grip on his throat. He spoke through gritted teeth, loud enough for all present to hear.

"Samuel Peterson, who preferred to be called Pete, was an honest and dedicated cop. He died in the line of duty while investigating a murder. Write it up!" He shook the chief by the neck and scalp for emphasis.

"Dr. Tabitha Gunnerson was a smart and caring physician who chose to do a very brave thing and believed in the truth. She also died in the line of duty. Write it up!" Again, a firm and violent shake to accentuate the point.

He turned the chief's swollen and bloody face back to look him directly in the eye. The man's small, beady pupils swam wildly in a huge, wide pool of terrified whites. Sal narrowed his own eyes to slits and spoke directly to the man.

"You or Division want my resignation? My badge? I'll bring it to you personally." He slowed his breathing in three short, deep sighs, and then continued, "But not before I find out who and why. I will close this case, and then you can charge me." He released both of his grips with a quick violent toss.

The chief stumbled in the slippery muck, slipping backwards, falling hard on his ass again. His hands shot immediately to his face and throat, gently palpating the damage. He looked up to Gionetti with crazy yet terrified eyes. He tried to form words, put together some kind of witty retort or threatening counter punch, but instead only succeeded in a strangled murmur and a garbled cry of agony and embarrassment.

Gionetti shouldered his way past the gathered patrolmen and detectives, only to look back once upon the miserable hump of a man sitting in the slushy mud, bleeding against his car.

"Fucking coward," was all he said as he walked into the dark morning.

No one came forth to aid the chief.

Twenty-one

They were stuck at the Pyramid for at least a short while, so they might as well enjoy the rest.

~ * ~

"L.T.!" The voice echoed off the close walls of the small room.

"L.T.! Shit! C'mon, lieutenant, wake up, man!" A firm hand shook his shoulder as the echoes solidified and he swam back into wakefulness.

His eyes snapped open and he reached for the hand as he spun to his side, rolled out of bed and up to his feet—the unconscious act of a combat veteran. Jon Webb blinked twice. His eyes adjusted to the dark and he quickly assessed his surroundings.

He slowly released the young man's hand as he registered his environment. The small loft he'd rented was pitch dark, save for the dim entryway light that shone just behind the partially open bedroom door. Two soldiers were standing just inside, their backs to the main door of the apartment, their heads drooping low and tired.

The third soldier, who had obviously and reluctantly drawn the dubious wakeup detail, stood cautiously at a distance after waking the lieutenant, his gray form enveloped within the blacker shadows of the darkened room.

"Right!" the soldier exclaimed in a near breathless whisper. "Hey, L.T. You gotta come. Now."

177

"Williams?" Webb asked recognizing his soldier. "What the fuck? What time is it? What's up?"

In seconds, Jon was fully alert and focused—the product of many years of training and close combat experience.

His gut twisted tight and shrunk with the icy cold realization that nothing good could come from a panicked, personal wakeup.

"It's Dickerson, sir. He ain't doing so hot. Sergeant Donovan sent us for you."

Private Williamson visibly shook and continually shifted his weight from one foot to the other, agitated and impatient. He looked and sounded like he was revving down from a pretty potent high. As the two men moved from the darkened bedroom into the dimly lit foyer, one quick look into the young soldier's bloodshot eyes and pinpoint pupils confirmed it. The other soldiers avoided his scrutiny and kept their gazes down and away.

"Shit," Jon mumbled as he opened the door and herded the men out of the apartment and into the hall.

~ * ~

The room, small to start, was now cramped with the sweaty and disheveled bodies of seven young men. Lieutenant Jon Webb crowded past the hot stinking bodies and into the humid, dank room.

"Make a hole!" a soldier bellowed upon seeing the officer elbowing through the mass of soldiers.

Max Donovan was kneeling at the side of a low cot, his back to the door and Webb. The squad medic, Anderson, was feverishly working at securing a plastic bag of intravenous fluid to the end of a clear line running into the neck of the unconscious Private Dickerson.

Max turned suddenly and met with Jon's stare; his eyes were wide and intense. Jon's face asked the silent question that Max answered as he rose and looked upon the supine soldier drenched in blood and sweat.

"The guys found him in the Holo-Tat parlor where they had left him two hours before," Sergeant Donovan whispered.

He shot an icy, angry glare at the gaggle of men crowding the doorway; their eyes misted with instant guilt, and their faces paled with the fear of consequences.

"Apparently, they felt the need to desert their buddy and go sightseeing in the Liquid Zone," Max hissed.

Webb spun around to face his men and narrowed his eyes at the trembling group. His stare bore through them like a sharply honed laser.

One soldier spoke up softly in a lame attempt at a defense, obviously fueled by the lingering remnants of the confidence provoking Synth he had done earlier.

"Sir, Dicky—er, Dickerson—Private Dickerson wanted to get a tattoo, but we all wanted to explore some of the newer scenes, you know. And well, anyway we all got our Holo-Tats and really didn't want to wait around for the cherry to get his ink.

"I mean, we knew where he was and told him not to go anywhere, to wait for us and we'd be back in a few hours. You know, figuring the tat-job would probably take at least that long. So, we—" Donovan stopped him cold with a deadly glare and the gentle raising of his finger.

Lieutenant Jon Webb spoke softly and clearly, slowly turning away from the ghostly men and assessing the limp body on the bed before him.

"Secure your shit and get back to the vault. I want full load and prep in fifteen. Scott, you clean?"

"Yes, sir," responded a quiet voice behind him.

"Scott, assume number one until you hear from me and only me. Establish comm and set up egress options." There was an echoing silence that followed.

Webb turned his stern face over his shoulder, revealing a chiseled profile. His voice dropped even lower in tone and volume. "Now! Get the fuck out of my sight."

There was a scurry of uncoordinated shuffling as the men hurried over one another to exit the humid room. Not a sound was uttered from the stunned and frightened young men. Max and Jon held each other's gaze momentarily before turning their attention to the frenzied medic.

"What's the deal, doc?" Jon asked.

The medic sighed as he uncapped a syringe and pushed half of the cloudy contents into the IV line. He never made eye contact as he continued through his treatments and repetitive assessments.

"He's fucked up, sir. Best guess is Synth O.D., though it's hard to pinpoint which one. Treatment is very specific for the different types.

None of those fuckheads has a clue as to what he may have taken. If I knew, I could treat him better. Right now, it's all just supportive. That's the best I can do."

"I overheard Tollifsen mention something to one of the guys about his arms and legs. He mentioned 'vamping'. What's that?" Max asked.

"Yeah, I checked his extremities for tracks and fresh punctures. Hard to say with any degree of certainty, what with all of the swelling and vasoconstriction, but I think he may have popped something into his left antecube. There." Anderson indicated the fold of the antecubital fossa in the bend of the left elbow. "There's just so much edema. You can see I had to throw a neck line in him. I couldn't get anything peripherally."

"What's vamping, Anderson?" Jon asked impatiently.

The medic finally made eye contact with the lieutenant. He held the look, and then sighed as he shook his head and spoke in a defeated tone of despair. "Synth, in general, wreaks havoc on the body's filtration system. It's metabolized in the liver and the nasty byproducts are excreted via the kidneys. Even in small, infrequent recreational doses, you can end up with significant liver and kidney damage.

"So, in an effort to reduce that problem, the architects of the various neurotropics, collectively known as Synth, have been trying to manipulate the synthesis of the drugs so that they're more user friendly," Anderson explained as he retaped the length of tubing to the side of Dickerson's neck.

"They haven't been very successful. So in the meantime, some psychotic genius came up with a way to offer a version of certain Synth extracts that have already been through some of the degradation processes. In essence, they've purified and concentrated the active components of the drug."

"So, they've found a way to bypass the adverse affects on the body," Max attempted to clarify.

"Negative." The medic shook his head emphatically. "The drug, in its original synthesized form, still must pass through the liver and kidneys, whether it's smoked or injected, before it exerts its effect on the central nervous system. It's called the first pass effect. There's no way to avoid that."

"But you said that there are purified forms out there and that—"

"The so-called purified extracts have indeed gone through first pass metabolism." The medic glanced at both men solemnly, and then continued almost reluctantly. "Just not in the end-user's body."

He paused to see if the men were following him. He sighed and then elaborated.

"They inject Synth into a host, whose body initially metabolizes the drug through the first pass effect, and then offer that host's serum, which carries the purified extract, to the user. It has to be transferred via direct blood transfusion because they can't separate the active components from the plasma proteins." Jon and Max stared at the medic in disbelief.

"I've only heard about it; never actually seen it. Apparently some of the Pyramids in Afghanistan have turned quite a profit from it. The added thrill, of course, is the risk you take with blood type matching, unknown potencies and blood borne pathogens. You truly put your life in the hands of the supplier. Some have likened vamping to the deadly delicacy of eating Japanese fugu. One screw-up during any step in the preparation will kill you." Anderson was adjusting the flow rate of the IV, shaking his head in frustration.

"So, there are people out there supplying bags of blood doped with Synth for the sole purpose of getting the high without the risk of metabolic damage." Jon Webb was stunned and growing angry.

"Well, I wouldn't say it's without risk," Anderson responded. "I mean, if they type you incorrectly and infuse the wrong blood, you'll die from hemolytic shock. Most of the suppliers try to utilize O-positive hosts. Those are considered universal donors and are generally accepted by everyone, but that's not always the case. If sources are scarce they just may take what they can get."

He sat on the floor beside his patient, crossed his legs and lit a small cigar. The fresh blue smoke plumed around his head as he continued. "Then you have to consider the physiologic fact that not everyone metabolizes the drugs with the same efficiency. You never really know just how strong or dilute each preparation might be. And then, of course, there are biologic contaminants. Nanobot screening may have eradicated the HIV/Hep class viruses, but there are plenty of other treacherous little bugs out there."

Anderson puffed heartily on his cigar as he laid his hand across Dickerson's pallid forehead and opened the closed eyes, checking the pupils.

"Where do the hosts come from? Who does this?"

"Anyone desperate enough for quick cash and dumb enough not to know better. They think they're getting paid to enjoy the rich man's high. You think the suppliers are going tell them that their kidneys will shut down in a year's time? Or that their liver will harden and rot, leaving them to die yellow with jaundice and crazy with encephalopathy?"

"Jesus," was all that Max could manage as he glanced at Webb.

"No shit." Anderson agreed.

"Max, work the street and find out where he could have scored this and from whom," Jon directed. "Meet me at my loft in two hours. Stop by the vault; check on the unit and then outfit yourself appropriately. Bring me some equipment as well."

Donovan nodded and made for the door. Webb flipped out his phone and thumbed it to life. He quickly scrolled in the colonel's number and activated the auto call. He didn't expect an answer and was, in fact, more interested in the global positioning feature of the search and locate software. With this technology he could locate anyone with a similar phone to within precisely four meters, even if their phone was inactive.

Almost immediately, a fine meshwork of thin blue lines knit a grid across the face of the small flat screen. Coordinate points flashed and danced at the margins as the intricate array of military satellites high above the earth squinted in search of the colonel's thin silver phone. Webb made mental notes of the plot points racing across the milky screen as he turned from the medic and the comatose Private Dickerson.

"Hey, doc," Jon called over his shoulder. "I want this boy to make it home, okay?"

Anderson shrugged and sighed. "Roger that, sir."

Twenty-two

Inspector Detective Sal Gionetti pushed the stolen police Cadillac hybrid to its limits, screaming down the frosty slick ribbon of pavement toward the coast.

He would have preferred his sleek and quiet Boeing AirRide Deluxe over this ancient four-wheeled behemoth with its rough vibrations and nervous quiver at anything over two hundred kilometers-per-hour. He appropriated this particular unmarked police cruiser from the scene in what he simply viewed as an even trade, considering that his vehicle was now bound for an eternity in the impound and evidence destruction lot.

He kept his hands firmly on the steering wheel, making the natural and nearly unconscious adjustments of a seasoned driver. With churning high-grade synthetic tires scoring the pavement, the heavy car tended to drift more on the sleet polished asphalt surface than would a hover car cushioned on a mattress of magnetically stabilized air.

His eyes remained narrowed to slits and unblinking as he focused not on the road ahead, but at points in time far removed, as well as those yet to come. Considering all frames of reference simultaneously, he allowed the flow of thoughts and feelings to come freely and wash over him in heavy, suffocating waves. He had loosened his mental and emotional collar and removed all of the protective filters from his perceptive senses.

As a successful detective, he was inherently talented at multi-tasking his mind.

He piloted the groaning Caddy on through the freezing night, headlights pierced the darkness in twin cones of bright halogen, the slanted tracers of hard, frozen snow and sleet flashed across his field of view. The wide grill of the car cleaved the frigid air in oscillating screams and whines of racing wind that changed in pitch from shrill to low grumble. His mind raced like a disembodied spirit rapidly whispering in his ear from lofty currents high in the thin blustery atmosphere.

At least six murders—all inexplicably, yet undeniably linked. And I'm firmly cemented in the middle of it all. By design or sheer blind fate?

He clenched his teeth and began to mentally sort and file the facts. He struggled internally with an accelerating need to allow the relenting chaos to assume control of his thoughts and force what was left of his analytical mind into a degrading spiral. Sanity momentarily prevailed as he considered the brief history of events and attempted to put down a coherent and logical approach.

The four dead bodies at Phoenix-Lamneth looked to be an obvious inside job, for which he liked Jon Webb's involvement.

At least, initially.

The ex-cop's actions and demeanor, however, painted an entirely different picture and now had Gionetti's instinct humming with curiosity. His head for details and deduction told him to follow the logical path, yet his heart reminded him of the subtleties of human nature and warned him of logical pitfalls and deductive traps.

The nature of the murders alluded to passion and severity, the location limited the suspect pool to a few, and with the mysterious twists revealed by Tabby's persistent pathology work, the profile now included professional and technical skills that far exceeded anything common.

At first glance, Jonathan Webb certainly fit the bill, at least for ability and method. The method and means of any murder were easiest to pinpoint. It was the most important variable that eluded the best of investigators—the motive.

The why.

There was an insistent will applied in the killings, an approving, almost personal satisfaction in their commitment. Someone had carried out orders, of that, Sal was sure. And that didn't fit Jon Webb at all.

In fact, Sal was now willing to bet that Webb had never been in that room before this morning's walk through. Webb had cased the room like a seasoned detective, sniffing out the less than obvious, looking beyond the blood and gore.

Sal was convinced that the man had discovered something other than the fourth body was missing a badge; and was being cautious about revealing too much as he knew he was being considered a prime suspect.

Sal also believed that Webb was probably a much better detective than he; and Sal considered himself pretty sharp.

So that left Webb's buddy, Max Donovan.

Capable?

Yes. Their shared military backgrounds gave them both solid MO's for the killings, but that's where the similarities diverged.

Donovan was more emotional, with a shadowy past that left many years before and after his stint with the Army full of holes. In fact, there was a period of time during both of their Middle Eastern tours that seemed suspiciously manufactured. The only reason the narrative account of their last mission together struck Sal when he read it was because it read word for word like an entry in his own military portfolio.

It was a standard blanket narrative created to fill gaps in accounts of activity where the truth was edited out. The government would claim it was all for the sake of national security; however, the lies had more purpose than that. They were used to cover up the evidence of our boys crossing the wrong line into the wrong place at the wrong time to kill the right people.

Usually.

Of course, "unintentional collateral damage" also resulted, and then had to be frosted over with a sugary glaze of democratic goodwill and global patriotism.

As a member of the elite covert forces known as The Black Hands, Sal Gionetti knew all about the generic fluff placed into military files. Something happened to Webb and Donovan over in the Big Sand Box. He doubted it had anything to do with current events, but it went far in explaining and justifying the men's relationship.

Sal doubted Donovan's involvement on sheer intuition alone. But, he knew little of the man and needed to uncover more before entirely ruling him out.

Now he considered Pete and Tabby, both ruthlessly assassinated and placed in Sal's car to be easily found.

A clear and distinct message.

Sal couldn't help but choke on a bitter swallow of guilt at the thought of their bodies lying naked in the back seat of his car. Pete was a cop, and yes, took the risk as any cop does. But, Tabby, young and innocent, was only trying to do the right thing. Now they were both dead because of Sal's direct involvement in the case.

And who knew of his involvement?

Webb, Donovan, and the head boys at Phoenix.

Again, conventional wisdom was pulling him the direction of the two security agents. *But...*

It just felt trite. Like they were being handed to him.

He shook his head to clear his thoughts and try a new angle. Before he could solidify a new starting point, the exit rose over the horizon and his emotions came hammering home. He turned right onto the exit ramp and veered the car into the gradual cloverleaf turn, heading toward the beach house and a meeting that he dreaded.

He couldn't recall the exact number of times that he had had these types of meetings, though he knew there were a lot—tearful smiles, convulsive sobbing racked with torrents of angry tears, silent and wide-eyed shock, abrasive apathy, vehement denial. People exhibited all types of emotional responses when told that a loved one was murdered and that, though they would do their best, the vast majority of them would go unsolved. He never relished the conversation and in fact had prepared a canned spiel for every possible scenario.

Tonight, however, he was overwhelmed by his proximity to the victims and was painfully unsure how to proceed. He was completely unprepared and more uncertain than ever in his life. *Must be getting old*, he thought as he turned the car onto the long gravel drive that led out to the flat cold beach. Even in the changing west coast climate, people cherished beachfront property.

He brought the Caddy to a shaky halt, allowed the engine to idle down, and then turned off the bright halogen beams. Dimly lit from the soft blue light of the instrument panel, the interior of the car was cast in a ghostly indigo haze, his features sallow and apocalyptic as Sal gazed into the rearview mirror.

The low white house stood out against the dark ocean and gray sand. The wind blew currents of wispy snow across the hardened sand, picking up the finer grains and threshing them against the aluminum siding.

A sad buttery-yellow light clicked on within the house, and from behind a single window, a drape was pulled back. A shadowy figure swept long hair from her face as she peered through the frosted glass out into the drive. She slowly rubbed a circle in the frost-encrusted window and brought her face, cupped within her hands, against the glass for a better view.

Sal watched as the woman tried to recognize the strange car. His stomach tightened, then flipped and loosened and flipped again as he opened the door casting bright light on his face for her to identify.

He stepped out of the Cadillac, rose to his full height and began the slow march toward the house. The rhythm of the beeping alarm from the open car door kept cadence to his agonizing stride as he struggled with the emotions that choked the breath from his swollen throat. After thirty seconds the Caddy's AutoOff disengaged the alarm, cut the lights and softly pulled the driver's door closed.

The chilled night was suddenly silent, reverent.

The snow and sleet stung his face, his eyes.

The front door opened, and Tabitha's friend Carla stood wrapped in a colorful quilt, her feet clad in thick, patterned wool socks. Her somber face and red, tired eyes stared openly. A painful grimace began to twist her lips, then her eyes, as she simply shook her head and pleaded softly, weakly, "No, No—"

She collapsed into Sal's arms.

Twenty-three

Max met Jon Webb at the front entrance of his rented loft as the lieutenant was locking the door behind him.

An unconscious body lay across the narrow passageway just to the left of the entryway. The tatters of his outdated military uniform were knotted beneath his still form and small gnats flitted around the man's filthy unshaven face. Dried blood caked the corners of his twitching lips. A few small beetles and spiders scurried through his stringy hair and ratty beard. His respirations were slow and shallow and the stench of humid sickness rose from him like a heat mirage hovering over hot asphalt.

Max stepped over the derelict, grimacing as he handed a stout magnetic pulse rifle to Webb. Jon accepted the weapon as he turned from the door and quickly strode toward the side exit absently checking the load of the rifle as he shouldered his personal bag.

Max followed silently, two duffel bags strapped over both shoulders and a second pulse rifle slung across his back.

"What's the op plan, boss?" Max asked.

"Are the guys loaded and prepped?"

"Yeah, it's cool. Scott has everything secured. We placed Tollifsen and Murphy in restraints and sedated them for the pull out. They'll sleep for a day," Max assured catching up to the lieutenant's fast pace.

The two men burst through the heavy glass door, bouncing it off the wall and rattling it on its reinforced hinges. They stepped into a blinking, hazy, fluorescent-lit alley that stretched both right and left into the distant shadows, fading from blurry to black. Smoky, open doorways bordered the wide corridor, gaping like the toothless maws of demon sentinels on the banks of the river Styx. Waves of incoherent voices and mechanical music assaulted the shores of the senses, ebbing and flowing from within the exotic shops and clubs.

Sex parlors and drug dens, dance clubs and holographic art vendors all lined the interior alley like some nightmarish carnival midway erected on the molten frontier of Dante's Seventh Ring of Hell. Not a single person was visible at any of the doorways, but screams and shrieks of either despair or enrapture echoed from deep within the dark, glowing depths of hidden rooms.

The cacophony awoke dark, icy shadows beneath Webb's breastbone like fine dust vibrating on the floor of a deserted building just as the subsonic sound waves from descending missiles pushed out the air ahead of them leaving in their wake a silent, empty vacuum—a frozen pocket of nothing.

The raucous noise was vertiginous, stirring in him a sense of foreboding and despair like a silent, invisible squall of fear.

He felt something was not only coming; but had already arrived.

As dimples of goose flesh tightened the skin across his stomach, Jon scanned the corridor up one direction, and then back down the other. He gripped the pulse rifle with firm determination his knuckles white from the effort.

The men soon eased down the alleyway with Jon in the lead. Max lingered slightly taking in their bizarre surroundings.

Eventually, a small, rail-thin girl emerged from the blinding darkness of one of the doorways, her gait weaving and staggering. Her face was pale, nearly translucent, and her eyes lacked focus and attention. She approached the men; a ghostly waif wrapped in tattered metallic ribbons of shiny fabric that barely concealed her body.

She raised her glassy eyes to meet their gaze, the empty orbs jumping wildly from face to face. A hesitant smile crept across her dry, cracked lips in an attempt to feign seductiveness. Behind tightly clenched lips, she tried to conceal and internalized what may have only been a belch, but also could have been partially liquid, forcing her practiced sexy smile into more of an alien grimace.

She took an unsteady breath and opened her mouth to speak. Dry skin pulled apart and left clinging remnants on both of her thin pale lips, flaky bits of dermis that quivered in the shaky breath of her exhalation. Before she could give voice to whatever scrambled thought was waiting to escape her pathetic mind, Max Donovan interrupted in a polite, yet stern inquiry.

"Where can we find Aristotle Leary?" he asked pointedly.

She flinched at the suddenness of his voice and firmness of his request. Her eyes fogged, moving independently of one another and then resynchronized into the familiar rhythmic twitching of acute intoxication referred to as nystagmus.

She rocked gently from left to right led by some distant alien music only she could appreciate. Her small hands trembled as they floated from her sides and caressed the scratched and bruised skin of each arm. Her slender fingers trailed along the pale, cracked flesh toward her shoulders and quivered as they sought the comfort of her breast. No warmth would be found there, however, as the shabby swaths of silver and bronze cloth fell from her avian shoulders revealing perfectly enhanced breasts.

Cold and taut, the geometric domes of her surgically altered bosom barely dimpled as she stroked them from base to permanently erect nipple. She allowed her lifeless eyes to flutter closed as she attempted to allure the men with an almost comical plea of dreamy sensuousness.

"Lap the milk of dreams," she droned. "Sweet, sweet sugary satin. Hmm." Her voice trailed off as she continued to rock and caress.

Her Illuminese was heavily accented with a thick Middle Eastern influence, though her nationality clearly appeared European—French or perhaps even Italian. She couldn't have been more than sixteen years old and was already in the death grip of the Pyramid lifestyle.

"No thanks," Max dismissed her sales pitch, reached out, firmly gripped both of her shoulders and squeezed hard. The sudden pain refocused her, and she glared frightfully into his eyes for the moment it took to repeat the question: "Leary. Aristotle Leary. Where. Is. He?" Max enunciated each word keeping her directly in his grasp.

Her eyes darted crazily up, back, left, right and up again. Then she caught a glimpse of their short stocky weapons, and her eyes began to wind down to a faint resting tremor. She opened her mouth in a revelational "Oh!" and cocked her skeletal head to the side.

Before she could have a chance to process any perception of their possible intent, Max continued, "We have a special delivery of some of the very best new Synth for him. We're fulfilling a huge order of gray-matter batter that will simply blow him away." He feigned a smile and winked conspiratorially toward Jon.

She gasped and quickly looked to Webb for verification.

Jon nodded and licked his lips while adding, "Righteous orange-blossom flannel."

Max blinked and stiffened at Jon's lame attempt at Illuminese. The girl seemed to buy it, though, as she grinned and sucked in a laugh like a toddler just discovering a dropped cookie underneath a sofa.

Max glanced quickly toward Jon and arched his eyebrows. Jon shrugged.

"Oooh," she began to plead, pathetically. "A taste?" she begged.

Max shook his head, softly smiling. "Leary first. We must make the sale. Then you'll be one of the first. I promise. We'll come find you."

She engineered a pout meant to be fetching and seductive but only succeeded as a terrifying, hollow death mask.

"The Liquid Lounge," she finally revealed. "Ary is almost always at the Liquid. Lower level where the rest of the bottom feeders are."

The obvious animosity was the first and only sign of sincere emotion she displayed. She carefully and hesitantly pulled at the thin banners of her wardrobe attempting to conceal what she could. She quickly tired of the effort and started to amble away from the men down the wide alley, one breast still fully exposed and shimmering in the dull neon. She never looked back, again and forever still, lost within her own mind—the walking dead.

"Leary?" asked Webb of Donovan. "That from a good source?"

"Yeah, he's Tollifsen's connection. I beat it out of the little prick before we sedated him."

Jon simply nodded, shouldered the rifle and followed Max as he began down the misty iridescent alley.

~ * ~

The Liquid Lounge was a neolithic, cavernous, industrial themed holo-club popularized by the abundance of affordable depravities to be found within its stone and iron walls. Inside, diffuse red and indigo LED lighting vibrated and undulated through a spectrum of intensities, matching rhythm with the eerie electronic music.

At four in the morning, few patrons were present; and those who were remained mired in the smoky shadows preoccupied with their hallucinations and inner musings. The long curving bar was empty and a tall, thin, olive-skinned man with long white hair and matching braided beard wiped down the chipped marble surfaces and repositioned half-empty bottles on a three-tiered shelf along the back wall. The skeleton of a man raised a bony, bent finger in their direction as the two men entered the room from the darkened foyer.

"Hey! No weapons allowed! You know the laws! Now, get out! Felix!" the man shouted in broken English. "Felix!" he yelled more excitedly as he stretched to look past the two men and into the foyer from where they just emerged.

"Felix, is it?" Max Donovan asked quickly gesturing back over his shoulder. "Big Samoan dude with one good eye? Yeah. Well, old Felix won't be able to join us. Having a bit of a nap right now." Max glared at the bartender; Jon Webb stiffened at his side.

The man behind the bar made a half-hearted attempt to reach under the marble counter just as a high pitched whistle shrieked throughout the room and a number of glass bottles exploded behind the man raining fragrant liquor and splintered shards of glass down over the wincing barkeep.

"No, not tonight, Hajji!" exclaimed Jon Webb—his pistol drawn, held in a tight combat grip and vibrating from the discharge. He pointed the weapon directly at the center of the man's forehead. Three laser hash marks inscribed a small red triangle on the man's furrowed brow.

Jon and Max quickly and efficiently closed the distance between them and the bar, Jon keeping his pistol sighted on the bartender while Max expertly reconnoitered the remaining interior of the room. There was not a single rustle of movement, no response to their entry or the fired round.

Two men reclined in one corner of the establishment completely oblivious to their surroundings. Another figure—a woman and probably a prostitute—was rummaging through the pockets of a comatose soldier and barely paused in her pilfering to briefly gaze toward the bar. Determining that the activity had nothing to do with her, she resumed robbing the young man that was nestled between her legs.

Jon leaned over the bar, pressed the muzzle of his pistol into the flesh of the bartender's forehead and with his free hand, gathered the loose collar of his shirt and drew the trembling man close, pulling him down into the reflection of the scratched marble countertop.

"Now, no bullshit, Hajji. Are we clear?" The man stared unblinking. Sweat rolled off his brow and collected in the concavity between the pistol's twin barrels.

"I want to see Aristotle Leary. Now. And I want it to be a surprise."

Max had worked his way around to the back of the bar and leaned in from behind the barkeep. He breathed heavily across the man's hairy ears, which smelled strongly of sweat and curry.

"Is Ary here?" Jon asked.

The man rolled his eyes, straining to see Max behind and to the right of him. Jon pressed the gun harder into his brow blanching the surrounding skin white. The man closed his eyes against the pain of the pistol as he slowly nodded.

"Good. Now, where? Exactly," Jon inquired softly.

The man's lips trembled, and he swallowed hard, his eyes darting and unblinking. It was obvious he was thinking up a lie, and before he could form the words, Max shot him in the back of the knee.

A brief burp from the silenced mag-pistol blew the pulverized fragments of bone and cartilage in a gory red splash across the stone floor. The man's mouth formed a scream, but the suddenness and shock prevailed and he was left breathless and stupefied.

Before he could regain the opportunity to inhale and properly scream in agony, Jon deftly removed the pistol from his forehead and shoved the gleaming black barrel into the man's wide-open mouth. He gagged at first, and then bit down to prevent further intrusion.

There was the distinct sound of teeth grating against metal, and then breaking off in muffled snaps. The man's eyes locked wide, his potential screams wavering on the brink of semi-audible decibels.

"Scream, and die. For sure. You mean absolutely nothing to me," Jon remarked in a stern whisper.

"Now. Is there a back room? Just nod."

The terrified man shook his head, his lips pulling the pistol from side to side, his eyes streaming with tears of dread and searing pain.

"Upstairs?"

Again, a trembling shake of the head. Sweat streaked, stringy white hair flopped across the man's brow. His finely braided beard was matted with globs of bubbly saliva.

Jon sighed. "Then downstairs?"

The man's eyes brightened a little; he nodded feverishly. He rolled his eyes to the left and down, indicating a spot just below the liquor shelf where Jon had earlier fired his weapon into the bottles.

A small indentation in the wall suggested a door, sealed flush with the finish of the bar's back wall. Max walked over and pressed upon the panel. It swung open easily on smooth assists. The opening was wide enough and tall enough to accommodate an average-sized adult. The interior looked to be pitch dark. Max looked at Jon and arched his eyebrows as he knelt down to peer into the passageway.

"There's light down a ways. I think I hear music. Distant, but not far." He rose to his feet and turned to the others. He gazed sympathetically at the shaking, sweating bartender for a moment, then at Jon. He nodded and reached inside the front of his jacket.

"What are the chances that Ary heard us up here?" Jon asked the man. He shook his head emphatically, rolling his eyes toward the pistol hanging limply from Max's free hand.

"Silencer? The walls are sound-proofed, is that it?" The man closed his eyes and nodded slowly, sighing through his thickly running nose. Mucus and tears ran down his cheeks and chin.

"Now, you know that I can't just simply leave you here, alone and able to call for help, right?" Jon mentioned the obvious to the man as he raised his drooping head by elevating the pistol wedged in his mouth.

The man kept his eyes closed, the lids tensed under the stress— clenched in realization and expectation of his fate. He sighed again, resigned to endure only a brief moment more of sheer pain before it would all end mercifully.

Jon nodded to Max, who withdrew an article from beneath his coat and touched it to the man's neck. There was a flash and a brief electrical crackle. The man convulsed violently for a second before crumpling to the floor trailing strings of saliva from the pistol's mouth as he fell. Jon grimaced as he wiped the muzzle of his weapon on his pant leg, and then slid it neatly into its leg holster.

"He'll sleep for hours. That leg wound self-cauterized." Max explained. "He'll live through us, but I'm not so sure about the loyalties of the regulatory committee here in Eden, you know."

"Fuck him," Jon said. "You lie with dogs, you get fleas. Let's go."

Twenty-four

Gionetti stared into the dying fire smoldering in the brick hearth. Waves of red and orange heat danced across the glowing lumpy embers. He succumbed to the hypnotic throb of the translucent flames and allowed himself to be slowly drawn into a soft trance.

A shadow fell across his lap and from deep within the cloak of a quilted comforter, a slender pale arm extended a thick, wide mug of steaming coffee. He blinked his wide, staring eyes twice to break the trance and, looking up at Carla's stony face, accepted the dark blue cup from her shaky hand. He held her solemn gaze for a second, offering a careful half smile that he hoped was both thankful and apologetic.

Their fingers remained in contact for a brief moment as he accepted the heavy mug—his warm and dry, hers icy cold and stiff despite the warmth of the freshly poured coffee. Her return smile was tentative and dismissing, almost defeated. He dropped his eyes to the mug as he took it and cradled it in his lap.

She quickly turned away, her long wavy hair flipped back over her shoulder obscuring her sunken features. She flopped into a plush overstuffed leather chair, pulled her bare slender legs underneath her and fidgeted with the thick quilt with one hand as she balanced her own coffee mug with the other.

"The fire's dying," she stated casually, the last word hanging in space like a prophetic omen spoken across the ages by some ancient oracle. Her eyes held moisture, but little life, as she stared blindly into the bed of shifting embers.

Silently, Sal rose from his chair, carefully placed his coffee cup on the side table and walked over to the fireplace. He methodically grabbed two perfectly quartered wedges of dried wood from the wire bin next to the hearth and drew back the ash screen. The gently placed logs stirred the glowing embers from a deep crimson glow to a fiery orange blaze in a shower of sparks that cascaded upward in random, frantic swirls. The wood caught immediately and the warmth from the freshly kindled fire spread quickly and evenly into the darkened room.

As he turned back to his seat, he saw that her wide-eyed gaze remained fixed on the dancing tongues of fire that consumed the fresh logs. Orange and yellow light flickered and jumped across her slumped and huddled form. Her features remained colorless and still, a hollow porcelain impression of unfettered beauty.

He found himself admiring her natural classic look and, despite the deep pain and sorrow etched at the edges, her narrow face held a certain cut and poise that transcended her environment. She was strikingly handsome, and he suddenly felt the guilty pull of remorse and regret as Tabitha's face swam up from the depths of memory. His stomach knotted and tightened as he looked upon Carla.

She suddenly broke her intent stare from the fire. The power of her deep gaze held his for a moment. He saw twin images of dancing flames reflected in her dark eyes as she searched his face desperately, frantically, seeking explanation.

He immediately felt ashamed and uncomfortable, like a conquered stranger allowed to enjoy the comfort of his enemy's home, unsure how to act in the wake of the victor's graciousness.

Then her eyes softened, losing all accusation and anger. She blinked slowly forcing the moisture into small perfect tears that hung just at the rims of her lower lids. She smiled softly as a healthy ruddy glow suffused her anemic cheeks. He felt the tension ebb out of her and into the air, thinning out, diluted from the warmth of the fire. In that moment, he sensed her forgiveness.

"That's nice. Thank you," she said, referring to the fire—and perhaps something more.

He nodded and offered a nervous half smile.

"She loved fires, you know," Carla began, staring back into the blazing hearth. "I never really learned to enjoy them much growing up in Nevada. Always seemed like a lot of work, you know. But Tabby, she was originally from Michigan. Upper Peninsula. Gets pretty frigid up there in the winter."

Sal had returned to his chair and was sipping the coffee: rich and creamy. Vanilla with a hint of brandy.

"She wanted this house so badly. I thought that it was a mistake, and would have preferred a nice modern loft in the city. But she convinced me of its rustic charms after a long ski weekend up in the mountains, before they closed them down a few years back. Of course, it's all avalanche country now with the climate shifts and all." She took a long sip from her mug and smiled to herself at some internal memory.

Sal remained quiet, watched the pulsing fire and sipped from his own mug.

"She loved her work, too, gruesome and morbid though it may have been. She truly believed in making a difference. Getting the answers. Finding the truth." Carla shook her head.

The steam rose into her nostrils as she inhaled softly then gently blew into the mug. She took another sip, savored the flavor and closed her eyes.

"She was killed at the lab, wasn't she?" she asked suddenly without looking at him.

He was surprised to find his voice, though not to hear it crack like a teen wrestling with puberty. "I honestly don't know."

Carla nodded. "I'm sure that she was. Killed doing her work—because of her work, really."

Gionetti cringed, and she must have perceived the flinch because she quickly looked at him and added, "I don't blame you, detective. Really. No more than I could blame myself for falling in love with her."

Sal continued to stare into the safety of the flickering fire. He felt her eyes upon him but was too ashamed to face her. Again, she seemed to sense his unease and turned back to her coffee. He felt even worse as he realized that she was as capable of easing his anxieties as she was at handling her own grief.

"She gave me something to keep safe, you know."

Sal was quiet.

She sipped again, and then continued, "She sent me an encrypted digital file right after our last phone call and instructed me to keep it somewhere safe. I had no idea what it meant at the time, but now I have to believe that it probably got her killed." She caught his eye as he finally turned toward her.

His lips parted to speak, but he remained silent. His eyes were wide and instantly wondering. She bit her lip and raised a single eyebrow before speaking again; and when she did, the strength had returned to her voice.

"She trusted you, detective. And despite your instruction to stay low, she couldn't rest until she uncovered the truth. I pleaded with her to wait, to at least get you or somebody to provide her with protection before she ran off on some heroic quest.

"But something kept nagging at her. She said it was like watching a movie where you swear you know an actor's name, but just can't quite remember it. You can name all of the movies and appearances you've ever seen him in, but still his name eludes you.

"So you watch the stupid movie—and it's usually a fairly bad one— until just as the credits roll, right before his name scrolls up on the screen, you suddenly remember it."

Sal nodded softly.

"Just like that, two hours of your life that you'll never get back." She chuckled softly, again shaking her head. "Well, she said she didn't want to wait through another ugly movie until the end. She needed to scratch the itch and finish the job that should've been done in the first place."

She produced a thin, square, black leather sleeve from beneath her quilt and held it on end in front of her. She tipped it slightly to the side and three gold digital data disks rolled halfway out into the palm of her other hand.

"It looks like she found it," she stated simply.

Sal Gionetti just watched her as she tipped the leather sleeve back and forth sliding the disks in and out.

"I'm no pathologist, but from what I can gather from the information on these disks..." She paused, narrowed her eyes at him and set her jaw firm. "You have quite a little freak show to chase down."

He cocked his head to the side and pursed his lips.

"There's no safer place, in my opinion, than with you, detective." She suddenly flipped the leather sleeve toward him. It landed on the side table with a dull slap. He reached out and palmed it, bringing it into his lap. The disks had inched out from the protective case and shimmered gold in the dying fire light.

"As I said, she trusted you and believed in finding the truth. I have to believe that whatever is on those disks will help you solve your crimes and find her killer." Her lips were tight and the color had drained from her face. She was once again icy pale and trembling.

He nodded, cleared his throat and spoke in a respectful whisper. "Tabby tried to d-mail something to me earlier this evening, but my PDD didn't have the memory to fully upload the material. So, it—I never..." His voice trailed off as he began to process the reality of the situation.

Suddenly, his eyes opened wide and he shot a hard, worried glance at Carla.

"Carla, how did you receive the data? Was it over the MetaWeb? GlobalNet?"

"No. It was Ethernet routed through the mainframe hardpac at the studios, then encrypted into secure bundles via my secured holo-disc here. Why?"

"The studio?"

"Yeah, Mandatory Media. The breaking news division, you know, where I work," she explained somewhat confused herself and surprised at his uncertainty.

Of course, Mandatory Media! That's where he recognized her from. Carla Robinson! The news anchor. How could he have been so dense?

She suddenly smiled realizing from his expression that he finally worked it out for himself.

"You didn't know who I was, did you? The other night at the club? Today?"

He blushed and shook his head. "I thought you looked familiar, but..." He shrugged.

"Huh," she managed tongue in cheek as she stared at the fire.

"I don't watch the broadcast much. I'm sorry," he tried to explain.

She waved him off and wrinkled her nose. "Don't, please. It's refreshing to know that I may still have some degree of anonymity."

"Look, Carla. Whoever…" He paused wanting to choose his words carefully. She nodded softly to assure him that it was okay and that she appreciated his concern for her sensitivity. "Whoever did all of this probably has Tabby's PDD. We have to assume that they do, anyway. They'll be able to find you through the address history of the download." He paused again and held her attention. "You're not safe here."

"I'm perfectly safe here, detective. That data was routed through the system at M & M first, encrypted and sent to a secure holo-disc. It's completely untraceable. I insisted on secure routing to my home because of my work. I have received threats and hate mail from any number of seedy characters," she explained.

"We've exposed quite a few shitheads over the years. Trust me, detective, no one can crack my encryption or trace any digital traffic to this place."

Sal sighed as he fingered the thin black disk case.

"That may be, Carla, but I'm not taking any chances with you. I already feel responsible for—"

"Detective." She smiled and cocked her head to the side. "If they know how to get to you, then it's already too late. They probably followed you here."

Sal swallowed hard. He had already thought of all that, and it made him sick to think that it never occurred to him to just simply avoid Carla for her own protection. His sense of honor and duty overpowered his reasonability.

"I think if they wanted you dead, that would have been their first option," she continued. "It seems to me that they want something from you." She indicated the disk in his lap with her coffee cup.

He nodded slowly. "Yeah, I've been considering that all evening. I just don't know what."

"Detective?"

"Sal. Please. I don't think after tonight I'll have much justification in referring to myself as a detective."

She tilted her head questioningly and glanced at him through the thin curls of steam rising from her mug.

He caught her look out of the corner of his eye and quickly dropped his gaze out of embarrassment. He shook his head and chuckled nervously.

"I burned some important bridges earlier."

She raised her brow and silently encouraged him on.

"Beat the shit out of my asshole boss, for starters," he said. "Then pretty much sealed the deal by stealing his car." He chuckled again thinking of the Caddy outside.

"Detective—Sal, I think you should take a look at those disks." She took a deep drink of her coffee, set the heavy mug on the table and rose to her feet. The thick quilted comforter slid off her lap and gathered in a lumpy heap on the hardwood floor. She padded across the room to the far corner and waved her hand in front of a creatively hidden flat screen. The dull gray surface of the LCD display instantly glowed and rippled with swirls and waves of intense colors. She reached beneath the desk surface and booted up the remote terminal.

"C'mon." She waved at him. "Bring the disks over here. Maybe together we can make something out of this."

He rose and moved to her side handing over the black sleeve. She deftly shook the three disks into her hand, loaded them all into a multideck and then slid it closed with a soft press of her finger. The hard drive hummed and the screen suddenly jumped to life as text and graphs and diagrams flicked and flowed across the shimmering flat surface.

Together, Carla and Sal perused the contents of the disks absorbing Tabitha Gunnerson's last words and thoughts. As the information unfolded, Sal slowly began to doubt everything he had ever known about human nature and the realities and possibilities of the universe.

Twenty-five

~ * ~

Aristotle Leary was a moderately built, tall African American with an air of aristocracy punctuated by a lofty Indo-British accent. His droopy eyes and sluggish body language suggested a lazy, carefree attitude—effective camouflage for the ruthless, tyrannical methods with which he built his little empire.

Ary, as he was known in his circle, may not have been the man solely responsible for the existence of Bacchus Plateau, but he certainly was the man responsible for its overwhelming success. From booze and women, to drugs, art and entertainment; Leary was the beginning, middle and end.

Today, he sat on a soft leather recliner with his bald head resting against the carved wood of the office wall. His eyes were closed as he breathed deeply and slowly, holding each breath for a moment before exhaling, trying to maximize the effect of each inhaled molecule of precious oxygen. The large veins in either side of his glistening neck throbbed with his drumming heart. The rapid pulsations betrayed any outward appearance of calm as he internalized the anger and surprise.

"It's simple, Ary. I want to know everything about vamping," Jon stated.

He and Max stood in the center of the large semi-circular room, their pulse rifles whined in sub-audible decibels as they powered down from the recent fire fight. Eight bodies lay strewn about the room in various stages of dismemberment and death. Only a few moaned and pled for mercy in their dying breaths, the rest lay motionless in thick, clotting pools of blood.

Ary's men had fought hard, but poorly, and consequently briefly.

Aristotle Leary folded his long, bejeweled fingers in his lap as he slowly opened his eyes and stared stoically at the two soldiers. The whites of his large eyes were the color of unstirred cappuccino, a swirling blend of dark brown and pale caramel, as heavily pigmented as his dark chocolate skin. The pupils and irises of each globe were indistinct from one another, giving the appearance of perpetual dilation and thus an intimidating intensity. His wide mouth was outlined by unusually thin lips, which he licked repeatedly before he spoke.

"It would appear that you've defeated my best. And that will be costly." His voice was mellow and deep, the British accent almost comically stereotypic. "Unfortunate," he whispered sadly.

"Yeah, well, you need to retool your recruitment criteria," Max commented as he gazed about the room and the fresh carnage within.

Ary cocked his head and drilled Max with a laser glare.

"These men were Black Hands, one and all. Though you should feel proud of your victory, young man, they deserve the respect due any fallen warrior." Leary then blinked and returned his deep, hypnotic gaze back to Webb.

"As for your inquiry, Lieutenant, I'm afraid that you have killed some fine soldiers in vain. I know nothing of this vamping." His eyes were still as he spoke, his face drawn tight.

"Nevertheless, you will tell us what you do know," Jon replied.

"Or what?" A faint smile touched the dark man's lips drawing the corners into a wide, almost vaudevillian grin. "You will kill me? Or perhaps torture me?" A light chuckle rumbled from within the man's wide chest. "Please." He waved dismissively.

Silence hung between the men like an invisible hive of bees waiting for a stick to strike and shake loose thousands of irate insects.

Ary simply sat motionless waiting for Webb to play his next piece. His patience was practiced and nearly pathologic. He was obviously used to situations like these and was content to wait for his competitors to commit the inevitable error that would ultimately bring their demise.

Max walked over to the seated Leary and reached down to finger a wide silver medallion that hung from a thick chain around his neck. Ary simply followed his movements with bored curiosity. He did not try to stop the man from invading his space to touch the ornate pendant, nor did he flinch when Max suddenly snapped the chain in two and held the shimmering medal up to the light before his eyes.

Ary blinked once, and then cocked his head.

"Interesting. I've seen this before." Max squinted his eyes feigning deep concentration as he twirled the medallion in a tight arc, winding the chain tightly around his finger, and then unwinding in reverse.

His eyes suddenly popped open in melodramatic discovery and sudden revelation. "Yes, of course!" he exclaimed, his performance seasoned with sarcasm.

"The big faggot Samoan upstairs." Max pointed at Jon, the chain wrapped completely around his index finger. The pendant dangled from the tightly wound spool and danced as he wiggled his finger. "I told you this was a Union Cleat."

He made dramatic cow eyes at Leary as he glanced sideways in mock disapproval.

"Ary—my, my. And such a *big* man, too." Max winked at the now visibly stunned Leary. "When did you two tie the proverbial knot?"

Aristotle Leary glared indignantly at the mockery, but the steadily increasing pulses in his neck betrayed his false stolidity. Max had found an exposed nerve and pressed down relentlessly. "Business must be pretty good to promise yourself eternally to such a man. I mean, the Union Cleat pretty much ensures his rightful place at your side. A little bit more than business partners, eh?" Max clicked his tongue within his cheek and winked again.

Leary refolded his hands and sighed as he slowly closed, and then reopened his eyes. He remained silent.

Max walked a wide circle about the room. He swung his pulse rifle dramatically as he continued to work at Leary's crumbling veneer.

"Yeah, not exactly my ideal choice in life partners, but, hey..."

He paused and turned toward the seated man. "Well, hell! Congratulations, you old dog. Really, congrats and all that Hallmark shit."

He then turned to Jon.

"Jon, ol' Ary here and our large-and-in-charge bouncer friend upstairs are—or, were—an item. How about that?" Max exclaimed, the melodrama thick and flowery.

Jon Webb simply nodded keeping his gaze and weapon trained on Leary. Aristotle finally broke his damning stare from Max and slowly turned to meet Jon's calm eyes.

At the moment their eyes locked, Jon recognized his narrow window of opportunity. Max had performed perfectly, dragging the experimental rodent through the maze of existential possibilities, dangling the likelihood of dark fate just in front of him. Now it was time for Jon to offer up the cheese, the reward of potential hope.

"You know, we left him alive," Jon said softly.

Leary's face remained hard and uncreased, but his eyes glinted with a barely perceptible hint of moisture.

"He's unconscious from a tranq-stun, but aside from some bruises and what-not, he is quite alive."

Leary swallowed, his prominent Adam's apple bounced with the effort, but otherwise he remained still. His gaze remained fixed and angry. Jon let the strength of the silence work its way into the room.

Finally, Ary broke his mannequin act and blinked several times as small round tears welled up in his eyes. He ground his teeth and clenched his jaw in efforts to stymie the emotion that filled him.

Max brought his hand to his mouth in an over-the-top Hollywood gesture of surprise and regret.

"Oh, my God! You thought—Jon, he thought that—Oh, I'm so sorry, Ary, baby." Max oozed fake sincerity. "You thought all this time that your sweetie was killed during all of this craziness. Oh, you poor, silly, sod. No, no, no. He's fine. A little banged up, maybe, but I'm sure nothing unlike some of your more romantic interludes with the big, lovable lug."

Max smiled playfully.

Ary snapped a murderous look toward Max, held the man's eyes for a few full seconds. His glare burned with rage and hatred.

"Easy now, big fella. You don't want to spoil the moment." Max wagged the finger wrapped with the chain and medallion.

"Ary?" Jon said.

Leary hesitantly pulled his eyes from Max and focused on Jon. For the first time since their arrival, Leary's gaze considered the prominent pulse rifle in Jon's steady hands.

"You give me what I need and you get Felix. Simple as that. I don't give a shit what happens after that.

"But if you continue to eye fuck me like you have, acting all bad ass, I will kill him. You will watch, and it'll take a long fucking time. Max is a very sick dog, Ary. I won't have to give him much encouragement." Jon cocked his head and waited for a response.

Leary contemplated; his face never changed, and his eyes never wavered. His fingers tensed in his lap, then suddenly loosened and flexed. He had decided.

"Show me Felix. Then we'll talk." Aristotle Leary allowed his moist eyes to find Max, and he glared with a defiant vengeance.

Max shook his head as he tossed the medallion and chain back into Leary's lap. "Relax, love."

He nodded for the man to rise and indicated for him to lead them back out to the front of the Liquid Lounge.

~ * ~

Lieutenant Jonathan Webb and Sergeant Maxwell Donovan kept their word, and upon seeing that Felix—the large Samoan bouncer—was indeed alive, though badly beaten, Aristotle Leary reluctantly gave up what he knew about the social and recreational phenomenon of vamping. The whole of Leary's knowledge on the subject consisted of a single name and a location.

The name was Logan Slousad.

It was probably an alias and meant nothing to the men. Ironically, however, and as Jon had suspected, the location given to them matched that of the coordinates he retrieved from his directional phone when he scanned earlier for the Colonel's whereabouts. Somehow the Colonel was involved with the Pyramid's drug business and was now considered to be officially AWOL with criminal intent.

Their plan was to search for and secure the Colonel, arrest him on conspiracy charges, evacuate the still comatose Private Dickerson, and then immediately move the unit out of Bacchus Plateau and to the extrication point.

Once back in Kuwait City, they would then turn the Colonel over to the Coalition authorities and let the system handle him. Hopefully, the MedCom in K-City would be able to help with Dickerson's fate.

The Parliamentary Cradle, as the local population of Bacchus Plateau liked to refer to their command and control center, was located just a few hundred meters from the Liquid Lounge, and Jon and Max made the jog in just minutes. The Cradle housed the offices of the governing bodies as well as quartered the Pyramid's management and maintenance elements and a small, antiquated medical facility.

The building itself was plain: gray-black brick and smoked glass. It stood without any grand architectural theme, and rather than rising with importance from the central hub of the man-made resort, it rested anonymously along the outer wall of the Pyramid's perimeter, at the end of a barren causeway.

A few haggard men stood at the entrance, draped in tatters of ripped and mismatched uniforms, makeshift and modified weapons held lazily or slung carelessly. Diffused light dripped thickly from neglected neon and fluorescent tubes suspended from the shadowed heights along the walkway and around the building, casting a ghostly red/blue/yellow haze about the immediate area.

Apart from the small group of gathered men at the top of the short staircase leading to the entrance, the building appeared deserted. Jon and Max halted a good fifty meters from the building and expertly unslung their weapons, simultaneously fingered off their safeties and prepared for yet another firefight. The only sound was the whispering whine of their pulse rifles cycling to full power.

The scraggly gaggle of armed men floated across the stairs of the building's entrance like bored and exhausted specters searching for a portal back to the land of the dark and dead. Their presence and poise spoke of anything but menace and action, yet their eyes focused intently on Jon and Max.

One of the thin phantasms broke from the quivering, disheveled flock and approached the two men, his weapon still slung loosely across his shoulder. The spook of a man descended the stairs with a jerky and swaggering gait. His arms hung limply at his sides and his head swayed as if it were a balloon caught in a steady shifting breeze. He stopped at the foot of the stairs and bent to sit on the first riser, more falling than purposefully sitting. He cocked his head to the side and assessed the two soldiers.

Jon and Max were certain that Ary Leary had phoned ahead and alerted somebody to their arrival, but there was nothing in this man's manner or action that appeared confrontational. He finally worked his cracked face into a strained smile, the effort clearly draining as he addressed the men.

"Army or Marines?" His voice crackled like a broken radio transmission slurred with a thick unrecognizable accent.

"Rangers. Forward Reactionary Force," Jon answered succinctly but without aggression.

"Ah, Army then." The man scratched his head violently and for a long time, and Jon was sure that he would draw blood.

"Well, Army Ranger men. I am supp's'd tell ya ta git da fuck out here. Now," The man slurred.

He grinned widely and inspected the fingertips that were just digging into his scalp. He did in fact draw blood and perhaps a bit more from his delighted and surprised expression.

"But, I tired. Hell, we is aw tired." His eyes jerked toward the lingering zombies above him as he brought his fingers to his mouth and began sucking and chewing on the gnarled tips and nails.

He mumbled around his fingers, "B'sides; I dunno wanna die today. Not here in dis shit pool." He arched his eyebrows twice in a knowing and sharing gesture.

Jon simply allowed the silence to prevail and struggled to keep his gorge down. The man before him was creeping him out in more ways than just his physical grotesqueness. There was a frightening lucidity to his obvious madness, and even though Jon was certain there would be no resistance from this ghostly platoon of men, he shuddered at the interaction.

"Da man. Ya come ta see da man, right?" He nodded as he answered his own seemingly rhetorical question, still gnawing at his fingers.

"Fucker's long gone. Soon after da udder Army Ranger man come. Ya know him, eh? He yous man, no?" His hand dropped from his mouth trailing a long silver web of saliva from his cracked lips. His eyes searched their faces frantically for an answer to this last question.

"Yes, sure. That man is probably our man. A colonel, if it matters any," Jon quickly added.

He waved Jon's response off like an annoying gnat and began picking his nose in earnest. "No matter if he Prezdent to me," he replied nasally. "Sick fuck, jus' da same."

Jon nodded softly suddenly wishing for an abrupt end to this eerie exchange.

"Inside, top floor. Da man—yous colonel, he all melted up on da top floor." The man inspected his finger for extracted nose treasures, his eyes distant and dreary.

Jon and Max shared a questioning and somber look, and then began to slowly walk toward the stairs. Jon half expected the man seated at the base of the stairs to suddenly leap up and begin blasting with a well-concealed weapon; but when he didn't, Jon became even more frightened. Max visibly tensed as they approached, and then passed the man and ascended the stairs.

The man never looked up from his fingers and had seemingly forgotten about the two men. Just as Jon began to think that he was clear of the frightening specter and growing comfortable with the prospect of putting him behind them, the haunted man spoke up without turning.

"That one wicked crop they grow, in der." He slowly turned to meet with Jon's surprised gaze. The man's eyes were suddenly clear and lucid, shining with wisdom and experience from beneath the cloudy cataracts of indifference.

"Der are many battlefields, Mr. Lieutenant. I see enough evil for two lifetimes, ya know?" He nodded wrinkling his brow and narrowing his eyes as if he had just shared some sacred fact with them.

He continued, cryptic, yet steady and convincing. "Evil is a crop dat only man can plant. Once it grow, den only man can harvest what he grow." He closed his eyes, and then opened them slowly. "Dat is a bitter harvest."

Jon allowed the man's words to float and then evaporate into the night. He nodded to assure the man that he understood and concurred, to not upset him, but the man had already turned away and was slowly and unsteadily rising to his feet. When he stood erect again, he motioned absently for the remaining ghostly bodies to follow as he ambled away from the stairs and the building.

As the other men descended the stairs in much the same exhausted fashion as their leader, he spoke again, over his shoulder, to Jon and Max.

"Happy harvest, Army man! Happy harvest." The man's frame shook with concealed snickers and chuckles. He shook his head slowly as he sauntered away with his decrepit squad of sleepwalking phantoms following closely behind. Apparently the building was theirs now, with no contest or battle.

Max glanced at Jon and laughed nervously as he shook his own head. "We have got to get the hell out of here and soon. I've had it with this whole creep show. I mean, shit, man!"

Jon simply nodded and sighed.

"I hear ya', brother. Let's go." The two men ascended the rest of the stairs and entered the building through the blackened revolving doors.

The interior was cast in smoky shades of pale gray and black, lit only from the faint ambient light of the just arriving dawn and the flickering spasms of dull blue and red neon that bled through the curtains of filth that filmed the exterior windows like a dusty skin. The footfalls of their heavily treaded boots echoed in dull rhythm as they carefully strode across the open expanse of the marbled foyer.

Towering stone columns, sloping walls and a soaring ceiling opened before them in a grand and awesome modern design. Although the exterior of the Parliamentary Cradle building was bleak and neglected, it seemed no expense was spared in outfitting the interior in lavish opulence.

Elaborate stone sculptures and intricate woodcarvings adorned every wall, interspersed with ornate and vibrant tapestries. Tactfully spaced throughout the great lower level were stone and marble fountains of various sizes and themes, ranging from the gothic and magical creatures of mythology to the classical Roman characters frozen in nude melodrama. The founts were still, the waters quiet and the finely crafted figures unquestioningly inanimate.

Throughout it all, small date trees spouted up through perfect holes cut into the shimmering floor surrounded by expertly grouped fronds of palm, climbing ivy, orange, apple, cherry, peach and olive trees bearing ripe, colorful fruit. In all, the scene was breathtaking in its opulence and extravagance, but painfully surreal. It was alien to them, as it must seem to anyone, walking through those doors from the outside—as out of place as a colorful and festive bar mitzvah celebration would have been in the middle of a Nazi death camp.

"Nice digs, eh, sir?" Max craned his neck as he spun around and took in the amazing wealth of the great room. Their high-powered halogen lamps pierced the darkness with swords of pearly illumination washing everything in pure white. They paused to get their bearings, and then brought their lights to shine upon the long arc of a low wooden reception desk framed in bronze and gold trim.

The semi-circular table was the only visible piece of furniture in the cavernous room: centered at the base of the rear wall, flanked by two heavy iron staircases gracefully winding up and into the shadows.

They approached the desk, rounding either side, and scanned behind for signs of recent activity. The narrow, flat work areas were bare save for a few strewn empty bottles, broken syringes and crumbling piles of white ash—spent Synth cooked in shallow glass dishes.

The place appeared abandoned just long enough for some recent partying, but not long enough for true decrepitation to settle in. The intact fruit trees, unmolested statues and intact artwork were evidence to that.

A single blue plastic binder lay open on the seat of a leather chair. Jon picked up the ring binder and thumbed through the pages.

"Some kind of directory." He scanned for further signs of organization or evidence of records. "There're no computer terminals, phone jacks, intercom. Nothing. No hardwire anywhere."

"Wireless?" Max offered. "No traceable evidence. Very mobile."

"Yeah, probably." Jon returned to the binder and paged through the thick pages more carefully.

"Lots of numbers. Could be code. Looks like some dates and times, but I can't be sure," Jon observed.

Max nodded absently and traced his spotlight along the course of one of the staircases, following it up into the darkened heights. "Up?" he asked.

Jon sighed, closed the thick blue binder and traced a finger across the embossed lettering etched into the rigid cover: *Slousad Protocol - 3.1.* He carefully placed the binder on the desk. "I suppose."

"Hey," Max asked. "What do we do when we find the old man? How do you want to handle it?"

"Yeah," began Jon hesitantly. "Been giving that some thought." He walked toward one set of stairs motioning for Max to take the other.

"And?"

"I honestly don't know."

"What are the chances he'll even come with us? Without resistance," Max asked as he mounted the first riser.

"Unlikely. Like I said, I don't know what to expect." Jon and Max continued their ascent of the stairs training their halogen beams up and around the curving steps.

Eventually the stairs ended at a common landing that extended deeper into the building. The path ahead lay completely immersed in shadow; their brilliant search beams pierced the blackness like shining needles through ebony sponge. They forged ahead through the darkness, following the smooth floor and wide, empty hall. The walls remained smooth and unbroken, the ceiling lower than below, but still very high.

Eventually, the hall opened into what appeared to be another room, again long and narrow, yet with evenly spaced doors running the length of both sides and extending ahead into the darkness. In the distance, to the left of the hall and just at the limit of their lights, a figure crouched low to the ground.

As they slowly approached they unslung their weapons and prepared for surprise. The figure remained crouched, or crumpled, and still. Bathed in the unearthly whiteness of their lights, details began to sharpen as they drew nearer and were able to identify the form as human.

The figure's head was buried in its lap, arms thrown over in what appeared to be a protective posture. It remained unmoving and unresponsive to their approach.

"Hey!" Jon yelled breaking the vacant quiet of the deserted building. His voice did not echo, but fell flat and dull in the thick air.

"You! If you can hear me, rise slowly with hands extended and open!" Jon commanded. Max peered intently at the figure, trying to sense even the slightest movement or response.

Nothing.

Jon sighed, and then together they slowly inched closer to the unmoving figure.

"US Army Coalition command!" Jon said. "You are in a secure and unauthorized area! Rise and respond!" Max looked at Jon; they both shrugged.

"Colonel Arrington?" Max finally asked in a loud voice. "It's Lieutenant Webb and Sergeant Donovan, sir. Is that you, Colonel?" The figure remained motionless.

The two men advanced with tactical precision, mirroring one another, Max back-stepping with his attention focused on their rear, Jon shuffling forward while keeping his weapon trained at the center of the crouching man before them. They reached him seconds later, and Max turned carefully around to join his lieutenant to engage the still human figure.

"We're clear to the rear," Max announced automatically as he had hundreds of times before.

Jon raised his eyebrows and looked curiously at the curled up man at their feet. He licked his lips and spoke one last time. "Colonel Arrington, sir. I'm going to reach out to you. Don't be surprised."

He reached toward the man and pulled one of his arms away from his face.

The limb fell away limply and the shift in weight caused the man to tumble backward off his haunches and land splayed out, supine on the floor. A grunt of air escaped from between the man's lips, but he was otherwise silent and non-responsive.

The men reflexively recoiled and instantly brought their lights to shine upon the man's face.

The colonel didn't appear to be dead, but was indeed unconscious, his face sallow and pasty gray. His buzz cut hair shone ghostly white in their lights. His nostrils flared ever so slightly with shallow and infrequent respirations.

For that, Jon was grateful, for he could easily see that the man was indeed breathing.

Jon had no intention of touching the man to assess for breath or pulse. Not with the thick amber slime that covered the colonel's skin or the hundreds of tiny spiders and beetles that scurried about in the gelatinous goop.

Vile mucus coated the man's face, neck and forearms: a foul smelling marinade of putrid syrup. Max and Jon both cringed and choked back their gorge as they pressed the backs of their hands against their mouths.

"What the fuck?" Max managed between gags and swallows.

"Plasma distillate," remarked a soft, masculine voice from behind. "Quite harmless, I assure you, but rather rank when it sours. Though it seems that the indigenous wildlife savor its bouquet."

Jon and Max spun around in rapid, well-controlled combat pivots and brought their lights and weapon sights to bear on a young man standing just outside one of the doors that flanked the long hallway. He carefully closed the door behind him, turned to face the men and their weapons as he squinted into the lime whiteness of their lights.

"I am Aristotle Leary. I've been expecting you."

~ * ~

"Freeze!" Max commanded with guarded surprise concealing his panic.

"Keep your hands in plain sight and away from your body!" Jon added equally as tense.

The thin, young Middle Eastern man simply smiled as he complied with their request. He slowly raised his arms, palms up, in a graceful sweeping arc from his sides—an angelic pose. The loose sleeves of his light cream-colored shirt billowed open as he fanned his arms out, adding to the impression of a sentient being stretching heavenly wings. His features were soft, dark and smooth. His hair was short and perfectly groomed in a close swept-back fashion. He spoke in a clear, soft tenor flavored with perfect Oxford English.

"Gentlemen, I'm unarmed and mean you no harm. As I said, I've been expecting you. My faithful friend phoned ahead and filled me in on your noble quest. It would seem that we share a common goal."

The man flashed a genuine smile, warm and inviting, as he continued, "I assure you that I am who I claim. The gentleman—the other Aristotle Leary—is a close personal acquaintance to whom I have trusted much of my enterprise. Our relationship extends back to our roots in London, and he has proven both loyal and industrious.

"He has taken to represent me in most, if not all, of my endeavors here within Bacchus Plateau. I owe you both a debt of gratitude for sparing him and his colleague; for to lose him now would cause me great and terrible sadness." He paused, closed his eyes and allowed his smile to evolve into a stern mask that spoke both sincerity and humility.

He bowed dramatically from the waist, his arms wide. "Thank you for your discretion and wisdom." He rose slowly from the deep bow as the wide smile again spread from his lips and recaptured his bright, dark eyes.

Jon and Max were visibly shocked and confused, clearly uncertain as to how to proceed. Max was agitated, shifting his weight and furrowing his brow. Jon slowly rose from his combat crouch and lowered the pulse rifle from his marksman eye. Max eventually followed his lead and relaxed his posture, though both weapons remained perfectly trained on the young man before them. The laser sights from both weapons painted twin triangles across the young man's chest, wavering slightly from their rapid, shallow breathing.

Aristotle Leary casually glanced at his chest, watching the small laser-red pyramids quiver and dance on the soft cotton fabric of his linen shirt. He continued to smile and seemed unfazed by the fact that he was clearly and expertly targeted.

"If I may be so bold as to politely suggest a significantly less aggressive posture, I believe that you'll be very interested in what I have to share with you." The man cocked his head in a quizzical manner, widening his smile.

Jon blinked a few times, considered his next move and then quickly decided, more out of pure instinct than common sense or battle-hardened training.

"Sergeant, pat the man down for weapons and wires. I'll cover." Then to the man, he said, "One crazy move and you're a smoking hole in the floor. Are we clear?"

"We are," the man answered. Max moved forward to frisk the man as Jon held his ground and remained alert, the weapon held high and ready.

"Clean and clear," announced Max at the completion of his search. He had slung his rifle, but held a stout mag-pistol to the man's side as he escorted him back toward Jon. Jon slung his own rifle and widened the beam of his halogen light to act more like a lantern than a search light.

The hallway was now more fully illuminated and the three men cast long wavering shadows against the smooth walls. Jon motioned to the body of the supine and comatose colonel.

"What's the story, Leary?" Jon asked.

"Your man, the colonel, was—is, I suppose—a very sick and twisted man. Although his initial motivations began admirably, as they most often do, his tastes ran a little to the left of conventional." The men gazed upon the colonel's still form; the light glistened off the slimy mess that covered his head and arms.

The real Leary continued as he shook his head in either disgust or remorse. "A smart man, to be sure. He recognized early on the amount of money to be made from aiding in the Americanization of Synth, as we like to refer to it.

"He quickly understood the role of the American military in bringing the popularity of the synthetic neurocotic experience home to the shores of America. The successful export of the Synth culture would bring fortunes to those of us orchestrating its globalification.

"However, the good colonel became involved with a man whose vision was a bit more skewed. Warped, I suppose, would be a better descriptor. Anyway, Logan Slousad, the man for whom you and I both seek, recruited Colonel Arrington for means both morally and ethically beyond anything we were comfortable with."

The young man glanced hard at Jon, captured his eyes and held them with cold intensity. "Yes, Lieutenant, even the fabled underworld has a certain code of ethics."

"I thought there was no honor among thieves," Max added wryly.

"Nor among purveyors of expensive designer narcotics, Sergeant. But what these men were proposing to do would simply destroy the future of our business. You don't kill off your customers with the product. You keep them coming back for more. It's simple economics," Leary explained.

Jon and Max exchanged glances. Max rolled his eyes, and Leary noticed but did not react.

"So, this Slousad and the colonel are responsible for vamping," Jon attempted to clarify. "And you and your associates were concerned that that may be too extreme and eventually ruin overall business?"

"No. I am ultimately responsible for the vamping technology," Leary answered coldly. "I stumbled upon the idea while working with designers in attempts to purify the drugs and make them less toxic to our delicate compositions. I soon realized our mistake and fought to destroy the concept. Slousad was a significant financial contributor, and at the time a powerful ally in the industry. He wouldn't let go of the idea, and held on to the fading promises that vamping offered.

"Despite the evidence and the obvious facts that transfusing human plasma loaded with pre-metabolized synthetics was killing the end users, he forged ahead on his own. He broke free from the established community and went rogue with his grand plan: to bring purified human catalyzed Synth to the free world and apparently turn a quick profit from insidious murder."

Max and Jon stared at Leary eager for elaboration.

"Once we realized his intent, and the consequences, we targeted him for removal. All we knew of him was that he was operating out of China somewhere, and that he was very close to introducing the vamping phenomenon into the mainstream. We knew that he would utilize the military as a main vehicle to spread the cause. We had to wait until he surfaced to know for sure. Unfortunately—or fortunately—he showed up right in my backyard as it were. Kind of poetic, I suppose." Leary took a deep breath, and turned from the colonel's crumpled body and gazed at the two soldiers.

"I wish that I could apologize for your colonel's demise, but there's no denying his involvement. You were hoping, I'm sure, to bring him to justice within your flawed system. But accept this fact—the man got what he deserved. My men assured me that when they found him, he was already up to five micrograms of Dopanyl in one sitting. That, my uneducated friends, is quite a lot.

"He didn't even realize it when they slid the needle into his arm and infused four half-liter bags of untested plasma. He's alive in that he's respiring and his heart maintains a perfusing rhythm; otherwise, he is beyond salvation." Leary glanced over his shoulder at the refuse of flesh on the floor and grimaced sourly.

"That slime is spilled, thawed plasma my men wasted as a message to Slousad. However, that demon must have disappeared days ago. I can only assume that he took any real evidence with him. We will find him, though. He'll leave a trail of bodies; of that, I'm sure. That is unfortunate, but we will not allow vamping to leave this continent." Leary's eyes burned with conviction and angst.

Jon and Max stared at the young man before them. During the shocking revelations, they both had unconsciously lowered their guard. Max's weapon hung limply at his side. Leary eventually noticed the soldiers' relaxed posture and smiled openly. He spread his arms invitingly and gestured for the men to follow him back down the hall.

"Gentlemen, if you would follow me. I have something you need to see for yourselves."

~ * ~

Through the hall door from which Leary had first emerged, they followed him into the shifting shadows and down a short and narrow corridor that opened into a square low-ceilinged room.

Leary led the way solemnly with the aid of their spotlights, striding briskly yet cautiously, as if on an icy road and seeking shelter from an oncoming storm, his previous confidence and bravado now fading under the heavy cloak of something both morose and enraging.

As they entered the darkened room, Max and Jon paused in the habit of seasoned combat veterans and scanned the immediate interior of the room before them, while Leary continued confidently to the far end of the room. The younger man turned and addressed the two soldiers, his voice quiet and sober.

"Come forward and see for yourselves."

Dim lights flickered, sporadically spaced throughout the room at uneven intervals along the dingy walls. Here and there, fluorescent bulbs popped and hummed, and shadows danced in the jerking dysrhythmic glow.

Nearly forty steel beds lined the perimeter of the room, spaced evenly apart and dressed on one another in tight military order. Most of the beds were empty, yet shown obvious signs of recent use with crumpled, disheveled sheets, lumpy pillows and piles of worn clothes strewn about.

In the few beds that were occupied, the forms lay still beneath thin covers. Slow, heavy breathing resonated across the room and settled upon them in heavy, humid snores.

Max and Jon turned about slowly, taking in the room and its grotesque furniture. Presently, a few short, staggering figures emerged cautiously from the shadows near the back of room and slowly worked their way toward their respective beds. They appeared to be young children, some no more than three or four-years-old. They wobbled like sedated trolls, without purpose or direction, but rather moving according to some ancient instinctual drive.

They didn't look to be healthy children in general, with hazed rheumy eyes, pale bruised skin and bony limbs covered with tatters and rags of patchwork clothes.

A few older figures now emerged from the shadows, ambling with the same intoxicated gait toward their respective beds. One or two of the older beings, apparently young adults, gazed curiously at Jon and Max, yet completely ignored Leary as they walked directly by him. When they reached their beds, they slowly lowered themselves into the messy nests of dingy blankets and sheets. Once supine, they seemed to slip immediately into deep sleep, breathing slow and shallow, as if anesthetized.

Jon looked to Leary with an open expression, hoping to receive an explanation other than what his mind had already deduced—that these were vamping hosts.

Leary smiled sadly and swept his right arm across the room, as if casting a spell over the wretched souls that dwelled within. "Forty beds, but we can only locate twenty-six of them." He sighed as he moved across the dim room to rejoin the soldiers. Jon and Max remained silent and wide-eyed.

"There are eight children, three under the age of four. It seems that they are presumed to be the best candidates as hosts due to their virgin enzymatic systems. Their liver and kidneys haven't yet been exposed to the toxins that we normally experience through our lifetime struggle into adulthood." Leary's face twisted into a bitter grimace as he gazed about the room.

Jon whispered under his breath, "A bitter harvest indeed."

"Who are they? Where did they come from?" Max asked softly.

"We're not completely sure. Some are Asian, Chinese, perhaps. Others appear to be Middle Eastern—Iraqi, Pakistani, whatever. There's no identification and none will speak, not even the adults. Their features have become somewhat distorted from edema and discolored from jaundice. Most of the adults we've found are in full-blown liver failure. Cirrhotic, mad with encephalopathy from elevated ammonia levels and slipping into renal failure. It's neither reversible nor treatable. Their end will come slowly and painfully without some mercy."

Jon shook his head. "How could this have happened right under your nose?"

At first Leary bristled at the accusatory tone, tensed his lean arms and clenched his teeth. He then regained his composure and nodded in reluctant agreement.

"As I've said, Lieutenant, we were unsure where Slousad was operating, and until some cases of Synth-vamping actually surfaced, we could not act. We discovered this operation only four days ago. Your arrival and the Colonel's involvement are merely coincidental.

"And perhaps unfortunate." Leary gazed intently at the men, measuring their response and gauging their reaction.

"Unfortunate, how?" Jon asked raising his eyebrows, clearly and immediately concerned.

"Well, frankly, we're concerned about how you'll act from here on. There are steps that must be taken, and there must be a certain degree of discretion exercised by all. Now that you and the good sergeant are most definitely involved, we need some assurances about your position in this matter." Leary folded his hands carefully before him, interlaced his slender fingers and hooked both thumbs in the waistband of his trousers. His gaze remained fixed on the farthest row of beds against the darkened back wall.

Max spoke up, agitated and defensive. "Just what the fuck are we talking about here, rag head?"

Leary slowly turned to Donovan and squarely faced the sergeant.

"I am of Indian and Egyptian decent, born and raised in Great Britain, educated in America at Stanford and Brown. I am not Muslim nor am I affiliated with any terrorist cell. In fact, I'm agnostic and rather prefer American football to soccer or even English cricket," Leary countered in what sounded like a practiced retort, though he smiled and continued in a quiet matter-of-fact tone. "Sergeant, I'm a businessman—an entrepreneur, if you will. Not a rag head, a camel-jockey nor sand-nigger.

"Now, you may not agree with my specific market interests, and that's fine. That is a debate for a different place and time. At this moment, however, we do have a shared goal—the prevention of a plague, very real and very evil, and the elimination of the man who will stop at nothing to bring it upon humankind." Leary turned his gaze to Jon who merely watched the exchange between the two men.

"Now, gentlemen, with your colonel resting in eternal and drooling mental bliss, I need to know, what are your immediate and long-term intentions regarding all that you've learned here today?" Leary fixed the men with a stern look, and for the first time displayed a sense of power and dynamic conviction.

"I guess that depends on your intent, Ary," Jon simply stated choosing diplomacy over confrontation. Jon sensed that if it came to blows, right now, they would probably be out-gunned by any number of hidden warriors faithful to Leary's command. And not the nearly comatose zombies they met on the way in, either.

Leary shrugged and pursed his lips for a moment; then answered in a clipped and business-like address. "First, we'll need to euthanize the hosts. Then—"

"Whoa! Wait a sec. Euthanize? You mean kill them, right? That is what you mean to do to these poor souls?" Max lowered his voice to an excited whisper, glancing about as if the slumbering dead could hear and comprehend what was being discussed.

"Kill them?" Max repeated.

He looked to Jon, exasperated. Jon glanced at him, nodded softly and turned to Leary.

"All of them?" Jon asked.

"The adults, yes. My medical people assure me that they are quite beyond saving. In most cases the hepatic encephalopathy is far too advanced to hope for any significant recovery. They'll just continue to live in oblivious misery until they slide into complete systemic failure. The only humane act is one of mercy.

"The children, well, they're not so sure of." Leary's eyes glistened with sincere empathy and conviction. "Look, I don't believe in any sort of afterlife, but I have to think that for these unfortunate ones, existence in any plane other than this must be an improvement."

"That remains the eternal debate, doesn't it? Existential metaphysics. Heaven, Hell and Earthly existence, not necessarily in that order," Jon added curtly.

Leary sighed and shrugged. He seemed to be choosing his words carefully in response, then simply shrugged again and spoke softly.

"What can we do?"

It wasn't a question, but an attempt to place their dilemma in some cognitive, yet simplistic perspective.

"Well, I agree with you. Mercy is indicated." Max flinched at Jon's statement quickly shooting the lieutenant a shocked and disapproving glare. Jon raised a hand and closed his eyes. He cocked his head in understanding as he continued.

"But for the adults only. The children will be air-evac'ed by our military and taken to proper medical facilities. They will be given that chance." Jon looked sternly at Leary anticipating his disapproval.

"We cannot allow news of vamping to leak into the mainstream," Leary cautioned. "We must remain vigilant and covert in our pursuit of Logan Slousad."

"I'll offer some cover story to explain the children," Jon countered. "If they remain in the military system, it should be contained. However, I cannot guarantee that some smart and industrious young Army doctor won't grow curious and pry a little deeper. You should find and eliminate Slousad quickly, if that's your intent."

"Our intent is to eradicate any evidence of his existence." Leary wrung his hands as he spoke, eyeing Jon with a mix of respect and careful doubt. "I can assume from your statement that we will be allowed to exercise freely in our quest to bring Logan Slousad to terms. That we will not experience any Coalition entanglements and that our existing operations may continue without pause? After all, we'll need to generate revenue to finance the hunt."

"I never saw you and know nothing of the workings of Bacchus Plateau. Colonel Arrington is MIA as of yesterday, and I'm requesting immediate air-evac of eight orphaned children discovered on the outskirts of the Pyramid complex. They'll send in an investigative team immediately upon my report, you know that, don't you?"

"Yes," Leary admitted soberly. "We'll be long gone before you clear the Zone. All that will remain will be ghostly myths and legends spewed by the incoherent masses."

Jon nodded then looked at Max to ensure that the sergeant was following the exchange. Max, though still somewhat baffled at the sudden evolution of events, nodded in understanding.

"All right then," Jon concluded. "I'll leave the distribution of mercy to you and yours. We'll need some assistance with securing and preparing the children. I'll call for the dust-off when you have cleared the Cradle and established adequate cover. Once we part from here, you're on your own. I will hold no responsibility for anything you run into from here on in. You can, however, rest assured in my promise of silence about these events." Jon motioned to Max to follow him from the center of the room.

He approached one of the steel-framed beds. A small boy of about four lay supine with his head turned to the right. Dark brown hair spilled across a prominent brow—pale and yellowed with jaundice. His breathing was erratic but slow and deep. Jon stroked the tangle of hair from the youth's brow, ran his hand down a dry cheek, along his thin neck and cupped the boy's small frail head in his large hand. He gently raised the boy's head, easily and without resistance.

The collar of the boy's tunic fell open, revealing a freshly healed surgical scar just below the left collarbone. A small, perfectly round artificial bulge immediately beneath the skin confirmed the placement of a Port-a-Cath: a long-term, easy access venous port through which intravenous fluids could be administered or blood drawn off as easily as popping a needle through the flexible self-sealing diaphragm of the device.

Jon set his jaw against the welling anger and glanced up at Max. They both shared a silent moment then Jon spoke directly to Leary as he laid the boy's head back on the thin, stained pillow.

"Find him, Leary. Find this Logan Slousad." Jon turned to exit the room, Max was at his elbow as they strode purposefully toward the corridor.

Leary glanced at the boy, and then called out after the men.

"If there is a Hell, there will be a place set for him."

Jon nodded as they disappeared into the shadows of the corridor.

~ * ~

The rhythmic thumping of the helicopter's rotors beat the surrounding air into submission as the twin turbos accelerated the four spinning blades into a blurry gray disk that vibrated over the top of the sleek aircraft. The high-pitched whine of the jet engines became a heavy bass roar that vibrated the ground as the MedEvac chopper rose into the early morning light of a hazy desert dawn.

Great swirling cyclones of sand and fine tan dust completely engulfed the shadowy figures scattered around the landing zone as they crouched low to the ground and shielded their faces from the blast of the rotor wash. The awkward Kevlar bird veered off in an extreme sloping arc, rapidly ascended, and accelerated out of the Zone.

With the vibrating beat of the rotors still palpable yet fading, the men slowly rose to their feet and began dragging the makeshift cloth litters back to the doorway of the shelter through the slowly settling clouds of orange and yellow sand.

On the horizon, two more aircraft appeared, black and angular, fluttering just above the smooth red sand a few kilometers away. Just as their presence was confirmed through the eyepiece of long range, digitally enhanced optic monoculars, the distinct chop and rumble of their rotors could be felt. A nearby radio lying in the sand against the wall of the shelter crackled and beeped with the traffic of secure and encoded conversations.

"Zephyr Two, Zephyr Two. This is Iccarus Four requesting approach clearance into Bacchus Plateau restricted zone for Pyramid Dust-off," The wavering and raspy voice of the incoming MedEvac pilot crackled over the secure communications channel.

Jon Webb trotted over to the radio and stooped to pick it up as he signaled to one of the other soldiers with his free hand. He raised the slender radio to his mouth and spoke loudly into the fine mesh of the transmitter.

"Iccarus Four, this is Zephyr Two. The LZ is secure and you are clear for dust-off. Your approach on final is marked with IR strobe and tether. How copy?"

"Roger that, Zephyr Two. I copy infrared strobe and laser level tether on final. I got two birds and lots of class two and eight. I'm trading you supplies for wounded," the pilot responded, his transmission ebbing in and out as his reproduced voice oscillated in pitch and quality.

Jon continued to frantically hand signal at the scurrying soldiers as he holstered the radio. He finally got Doc Anderson, the squad medic, to acknowledge his summons.

"Hey, Doc." He threw an arm around the medic's shoulders and walked him toward the outer boundary of the landing zone. "You ever land a chopper before?"

"Yeah, couple of times in school. But never anything out here." The young medic glanced at the lieutenant through his smeared goggles.

Jon handed the soldier a slim gray box that contained the controls for the infrared and laser indicators. He nodded toward the approaching aircraft.

"Just like in school, Doc. Once the pilot has lock on the strobes, he'll take it from there. I've already called in the nine-line; you just gotta load him." The young soldier nodded eagerly in understanding and acknowledgment.

"Listen, Doc," Jon continued shouting over the rumble of the incoming helicopters. "I want you on this last bird with Dickerson, okay?"

Doc Anderson nodded again, licked his lips and glanced over the lieutenant's shoulder at the screaming aircraft racing low across the desert toward them.

"And Doc." Jon grabbed the young man's shoulders by the equipment straps and shook him to gain his undivided attention. Anderson locked eyes with Webb through dusty eye shields. "I don't need to remind you to keep quiet about what happened here. No mention of vamping or any of that shit! Clear?"

"Clear, sir." Anderson straightened up and snapped off a rigid salute. Jon returned the salute and patted Anderson on the shoulder as he ran off in a crouch toward the shelter's doorway leaving the medic to land the MedEvac and load the last of the children and Dickerson.

The young medic would ensure that the dust-off concluded without event, and that the children would receive the appropriate medical attention in Kuwait City. Hopefully, Dickerson would also be taken care of without calling too much attention to their unit or the mission.

Webb was certain, however, that in short order, some serious questions would arise regarding Dickerson's state and the circumstances surrounding the children. Webb simply hoped that Anderson could stall long enough to delay any significant investigation into the unit's recent involvement with Bacchus Plateau.

Jon knew that eventually he'd have to answer many questions related to the Pyramid and his discovery of the children. He also knew that he would have to answer for the Colonel's actions and that, he hoped, would be a non-issue.

His intent was to make the colonel disappear into the dark shadows of the Pyramid's underworld, simply write him off as MIA or criminally AWOL.

A good and safe plan.

That was, until the investigative officer bounded from the belly of the last chopper before it even settled onto the sandy ground.

The man was dressed in durable civilian attire, yet still sported the high and tight haircut of a true Ranger. He flashed past Doc Anderson and the litter bearers without even a curious glance at the face of the young patient bundled onto the stretcher. He raced up to Jon and immediately identified himself and began demanding things.

"I'm Major Simons with the IG and WEC Provost. I need to speak to a Col. Arrington ASAP!" the man bellowed over the thrumming overhead rotor blades.

Jon Webb shrugged and shook his head indicating that he didn't hear the man. Frustrated, the man reached out to grab Webb's baggy uniform sleeve, but stopped short as Jon flashed him a stern, narrow look and shifted the slung weapon across his shoulder. The man hesitated, unsure how to proceed and clearly unhappy about even being here.

"Is there somewhere we can go to talk?" He leaned in toward Jon's face and shouted merely inches from his ear. "Inside? Can we go inside?" He gestured behind Webb at the door to the shelter, eyes imploring Jon for some slack.

Jon grimaced and shouted back. "Let's go inside! I can't hear a word you're saying!"

The man rolled his eyes, and then nodded enthusiastically. Jon could hear the man perfectly; he just didn't know what to do with him. He really didn't think they would send out an investigator so quickly. This guy was obviously prior service, but now, according to the laminated plastic ID badge twisting from the braided chain around his neck, he was playing field operative for the controlling civilian branch of the Coalition Corporation.

In Webb's opinion, this Simons represented the worst in wartime bureaucracy, a young military officer lured into early retirement by the seduction of financial greed and the promise of power. In reality, however, most of the unfortunate Corporation recruits ended up with modest, albeit guaranteed, civilian contracts and the illusion of control over circumstantial events that have been decided well in advance.

To have sent him out this fast, they were trying to protecting something or someone. But, this guy was already too late; he just hadn't realized it.

Jon Webb led the small, stocky man through the doorway of the shelter, out of the blast of noise and shower of sand generated by the hovering choppers and into the dark, arid interior of the temporary shelter. Gray, smoky shadows swam through the room as men moved silently yet quickly about, dismantling pieces of equipment and packing up various bundles.

The civilian investigator stumbled over the scattered aluminum cots and low wire-mesh tables that remained strewn about the small room. He turned a full three hundred-sixty degrees as he regained his balance and his bearings. When he turned back to find Webb, the lieutenant was already seated at a short folding table with a steaming stainless steel cup of coffee. Jon Webb smiled and narrowed his eyes in the gloom, slowly sipping from his mug.

The Major, as he insisted on referring to himself, moved forward and drew a deep breath as he puffed out his chest and attempted to reassert himself.

"Yes, well, lieutenant, as I was saying. I am Major Sim-"

"Simons. Yeah, I heard you the first time. Sit the fuck down, won't you?" Jon indicated a short steel chair on the other side of the table. He continued to sip his coffee as the Major glared intently before cautiously moving to his seat.

"I'd offer you some coffee, but I really don't want to. Truth be told, I don't think our conversation will last all that long anyway." Jon looked over his shoulder at the men quietly scrambling to bundle up and remove all evidence of their ever being there. He rubbed his eyes with both palms and spoke slowly into the hollow of his cupped hands.

"Now, what the hell does a Coalition Corporation lap dog like you want with our operation?"

"Lieutenant, you're already treading on very thin ice here. Your confrontational tone is unappreciated and will be officially noted in my report." The short man leaned forward and spoke with all of the vehemence of a seasoned combat veteran. "Unofficially, you are really starting to piss me off with your attitude. I need to speak with your commander, Col. Arrington, right fucking now.”

He leaned back again and continued more conversationally. “Now, you really need to be made aware that I’ve been authorized a ridiculous amount of latitude in this matter. That means that I can waste as much or as little time and resources on you as I deem necessary. You understand what that means, don’t you, lieutenant.”

Webb nodded softly. “Yeah, yeah. You’re a bad dude with lots of powerful people backing you. You can pull my fingernails out with your teeth if you want, and there’s nothing I can do about it, right?”

Simons simply stared at Jon, tense and growing impatient.

“Arrington’s missing,” Jon finally said. “Been AWOL for nearly two days now. We searched the entire Pyramid without success. I’m finishing up here with this dust-off, moving to the extrication point and pulling my men out of this shithole desert. You want to talk to Arrington, you go find him. I don’t have time for your corporate team gangbang.”

Jon sipped from the mug, and then continued, “Arrington’s filthy dirty. I know it. And you must know it; otherwise, you wouldn’t have come so far, so fast.” Jon rose to his feet and polished off his coffee.

He turned to leave the room, and then halted when the major suddenly spoke up.

“Give me Aristotle Leary, Webb. We know someone from this unit was in contact with the drug dealing sand-nigger. You and I both know it begins and ends here.” Simons paused waiting for Jon’s response.

Webb remained still, his back to the Major.

“Listen, Webb. You’re a smart and talented young officer. Don’t kill your future over this. We don’t give a fat fuck what happened here or what you got yourself involved in. But with one quick call, I will have those choppers diverted over the gulf and they will purge their cargo into the sea. Are you reading me, Lieutenant?”

Jon turned slowly around and faced the Major.

Though Simons’ face remained in shadow, the tension was apparent in the solid set of his jaw and his rigid stance. He chewed the inside of his cheek and waited a moment, milking the anxious atmosphere for momentum.

“You want those kids to arrive safely in K.C.?” Simons challenged. “You give me Ary Leary. Now.”

“Why?” Jon croaked softly almost whispering.

Simons snickered and shook his thick head. "Not your concern, soldier. What the fuck do you care, anyway? You cut a deal with him or something?"

Jon remained still, tense and engorged with anger.

"Jesus Christ! What is it with you guys? A whole new generation of stubborn, pussy officers! Webb, I have neither the time nor the desire to sit and explain myself to you! You will give me Leary. Now!"

"Fine, you want him." Jon leaned into the dim light revealing his firmly lined face. "Follow me, he's in here."

Simons rose to his feet and pulled out a short, slender mag-pistol from his pants pocket. He checked the magazine and flicked off the safety. "About fucking time. Let's go, asshole."

Jon stopped the man with a solid hand to the chest and pressed firmly. He lowered his face to the Major's and with their noses just centimeters apart, spoke directly into the man's face.

"First, I want some assurance that the dust-off was successful. I want to know that those choppers make it to K.C." Jon eyed the Major intently.

Simons' smirk slowly melted into a stony glare. He never hesitated and spoke in a harsh whisper. "Fuck you, Webb. Those birds were never going anywhere but to the fucking ocean. They have instructions to tip all cargo overboard fifty clicks out over the Persian Gulf. Now get out of my face or I will remove whatever balls you have left! Are we tracking, Lieutenant?"

Jon blinked once, dumbstruck. His entire face went slack and for a fraction-of-a-second he felt completely cold, numbed by the realization that he'd been involved in a game far more advanced than he ever imagined. He'd been duped and played, manipulated by powers beyond his comprehension.

He stood dumbly as Major Simons pushed by and marched through the interior opening and into a secondary room all the while mumbling obscenities.

"You're a worthless piece of shit, Webb. Did you really think you were doing the right thing? Fucking pussy!" Jon could hear Simons stomping and throwing out orders in the other room, frantic to reach his objective.

"Get your ass in here, Webb! Where the fuck is Leary? You, soldier. Yeah, you…"

Jon turned, walked into the room and joined the ranting Simons. He ducked his head as he passed through the low hanging threshold, ambled over to a fuse box mounted on a thick, upright metal bar and flicked a few switches.

More lights flickered on, brightening the room as Jon sauntered silently over to another bank of relays and thumbed an entire row of toggle switches down. Somewhere within the walls of the room machinery quietly geared up, sending minute vibrations through the stone floor. Cool air began to blow through the overhead vents around the room.

That was the agreed upon signal.

Jon gazed at the four soldiers standing in the room, previously occupied with various tasks, but now frozen by the surprising entrance of this armed stranger in civilian attire. The soldiers traded glances with one another as they sized up Simons, and then looked to Jon for guidance.

"I don't have all fucking year, Webb. Leary. Now!"

"Gentlemen, Major Simons is from Command and has requested an audience with our host. Would you mind escorting him to Mr. Leary?" Two of the soldiers looked dumbfounded and before they could do or say anything, Webb reasserted.

"Taylor. Jensen. If you would please escort Major Simons to the Liquid Lounge. And do it quietly."

Simons joined the two young Rangers as they walked by Webb, raised their eyebrows and shrugged ever so slightly.

As Simons passed through a second narrow threshold on his way out, he turned back over his shoulder to say something to Webb. "You know, Webb, you really aren't that bad of an officer. You've got a good track record and all. You just have a problem with authority. But then again, so did I at first.

"Tell you what, when I get back, maybe you and I can work something out. Long-term type of thing, okay?"

Jon closed his eyes and sighed heavily. He didn't reopen them until Simons was completely gone.

"Goodbye, asshole," Jon murmured to himself.

~ * ~

"Through those doors and down the hall, sir. You can't miss him." The private indicated the direction with a slight tilt of his pulse rifle.

Major Simons nodded, leaned forward and cautiously peered down the dark hall. He looked right, then left, and then turned to speak to the two soldiers who had escorted him to this place. They were already halfway out of the deserted bar when Simons called out.

"Hey, you lazy grunts! Get back here and provide me with appropriate cover."

Privates Jensen and Taylor traded curious glances, paused only to chuckle, shake their heads and then continued out the door and into the street. They were gone before Simons could act.

"Shit! Fucking pussies," he mumbled as he took a deep breath, rechecked his mag-pistol and slowly sidestepped down the dark corridor. He swept his weapon back and forth with overdramatic intensity, squinting into the shadows ahead. His breath was rapid and wheezing, and thin beads of sweat sprung from his brow and stung his eyes.

Eventually, a dim light appeared at the end of the corridor, soft and yellow, flickering like a candle or lamplight. By the time he realized the flickering was caused by moving shadows, the three men were already approaching, crouched low and moving with surprising agility and speed toward him.

He stopped, took up a wide shooter's stance and prepared for confrontation.

"Stop right there! Freeze!" Simons bellowed, a little louder and a whole lot shakier than he had intended. "I represent the Coalition Corporation, and I wish to meet with Mr. Aristotle Leary."

"Who da' fuck is dat?" was the only response. The approaching men paused for a moment, turned their heads toward one another and then full out sprinted at Simons.

Taken completely by surprise, Major Simons turned on his heels and sprang in hasty retreat. In three blind strides, he ran into a solidly built, tall and very large man, his face immediately buried into the big man's chest. A shimmering medallion bounced against the Major's nose as his wide, terrified eyes quickly followed the silver chain up to the man's face.

The large, round face of what appeared to be a Samoan glared back at him. The larger man's eyes were swollen and blackened, his face badly scratched and marked with irregular contusions. He had obviously taken a recent beating and was grimacing in either pain, frustration or both. Simons was frozen with surprise, rooted to the ground by terror.

"Mr. Leary sends his regrets. He won't be able to see you today," Felix said. His soft eyes held Simons' horrified stare.

Two hollow shots rang out echoing down the hall in dull harmony. Major Simons flopped backwards onto the stone floor. The empty gourd of his skull bounced once and splashes of thick blood cascaded down the gradual incline of the sloping floor.

Felix turned and walked out of the hallway, administering calm orders over his shoulder to the remaining men.

"Leave the body. It's time to move. Quickly and quietly. Let the Boss know that we're done here."

~ * ~

Sergeant Max Donovan ducked under the sleek, tapered barrel of the magnetic rail-rifle that jutted from the side of the vehicle, tapped Webb on the shoulder and leaned against the side of the Tactical as he lit a cigarette. A fresh plume of blue smoke curled around his head. The fag balanced at the corner of his mouth jumped and jittered as he spoke.

"Teed up and ready to load and go, sir."

Jon didn't answer, but continued to secure his pack to the rear of the driver's seat.

"Jon, you couldn't have known that they would have set us up like this. Calling for the Evac was the only thing you could've done." Max rubbed his eyes with balled up knuckles and sighed. "It was the right thing, man. How could we have known about the choppers?"

Jon rose from his task and stared hard at the sergeant, his eyes red rimmed with exhaustion and emotion. He suddenly plucked the cigarette from Max's mouth and took a deep drag, closing his eyes against the harsh drifting smoke.

"Yeah, sure," Max mumbled. "Help yourself, man."

"It's a fucking waste, Max. A fucking waste."

Max shook his head and accepted the cigarette as it was offered back. Both men leaned against the idling AFCAT and gazed back at the soldiers finalizing the upload of the gear and warming up the vehicles.

"A tragic, shameful waste. No doubt. But Jon..." Max turned slightly to get the lieutenant's attention. "It's pretty obvious that this game involves players that are way out of our league. I mean, we literally stumbled into this. And now we know more than they—whoever they are—probably would like. We have to worry about ourselves now."

Jon turned to Max, fingered the short smoking butt from him, took the last drag and flicked it to the sandy ground. He remained quiet, forlorn and angry.

"Jon, you told me recently that to fulfill my niche, all I had to do was help you get these sorry assholes home alive. Well, let's get it done, boss.

We can discus the philosophic ramifications of our actions once we're home, sucking on an ice cold beer at a Labor Day picnic with our kids running around screaming and our wives nagging at us."

Max held out his hand balled into a fist. "Let's get out of here, sir. Today."

Jon glanced down at the sergeant's fist, cocked his head and sighed deeply. He brought his own fist up and tapped Max's repeatedly, in typical Ranger fashion.

"I have every intention of doing just that, Sergeant Donovan. And you're right, we need to get moving. Just one more thing to take care of."

"If it's about Col. Arrington, forget it. I took care of it."

Jon started with surprise and an instant of fear and dread iced his bowels tight. He continued to glare at Max as he asked a question that he knew he shouldn't ask.

"What do you mean?"

"The Colonel's been taken care of. Now let's motor." Max pushed himself upright and began to move toward the rest of the men. Jon reached out and snatched his loose sleeve, spun him against the truck and pressed him flat. He brought his face within inches of Max's wide and stunned eyes.

"What, exactly, are you talking about, Sergeant?"

"Hey, L.T.—Easy. I said it was taken care of. Don't worry. No loose ends, okay?"

"Aw shit. Donovan, you didn't. Tell me that you didn't."

"What, whack the Colonel? You want me to tell you that I didn't whack the Colonel?" Max was breathing heavily, rapidly. Jon grit his teeth and shook his head; more in sorrow and remorse than in anger.

"Jon, we have to erase our presence here. Completely. When that Company dude showed up and dropped the bomb on our dust-off, man, it was over. You see that, don't you? We can't win. But we can survive. I had the last loose end tidied up. It was a merciful act for a suffering soul, Jon. Christ, you saw the old man."

"You executed a field-grade officer who was—"

"Who was involved in a major experimental narcotic plot that had proven to be quite fucking lethal! Jon! We didn't ask for this, but now we have to get out. Alive. This is no different then you sending that Simons cat to the Liquid. You knew his fate. Just because Arrington was our commander, that doesn't absolve him."

Jon loosened his grip on Max's uniform and backed away. He knew in his heart and soul that Max was right. It just went against everything that he trained for. He'd been forced into action and now was dealing with the ramifications.

He kicked at the ground with his boot, swung a blind fist into the air before him and grunted. In the mini-dust cloud that ensued he stood defeated and silent. All of the strength and wisdom earned from his years of training and experience seemed to leech out of him in a flush of frustration and helplessness.

It should have been me, Jon thought. *I should've cleaned up the Colonel. Not Max.*

A soft, dejected, "Shit," was all he could manage.

Max nodded slowly in empathy as he thrust his hands into the deep pockets of his trousers.

"Yeah, it sucks, sir."

The two men stood that way for many long minutes, each staring into the grainy sand, searching for answers that weren't there. Eventually, their minds accepted the harsh reality and their hearts consumed the guilt of their acts.

Packaging the nuggets of facts and deeds into tiny bundles of causal relations, their souls processed and stored the events of the last few days into shadowy storage bins deep within themselves. Over time, those dusty bins were sure to swell from the ripening of the old and forgotten past.

Soon, they simply looked at one another, nodded solemnly, and moved to their vehicles. The squad pulled out of Bacchus Plateau that afternoon, under the partial cover of a minor sand storm. The journey to the extrication point was uneventful and by dawn the following day, they were enroute to France.

Their time in the desert was finally over.

Twenty-six

Awakening

Thin, glistening streamers of frozen rain floated down from hazy heights, swirling in the winter downdrafts created between the tall steel and glass of the city's towering buildings. Shifting artificial light from myriad sources bounced and vibrated against the gossamer veils of sleet and grainy snow; as throngs of pedestrians splashed and scampered their way through the cold, wet streets, their collective shadows dancing irregularly across neon washed blacktop and concrete sidewalks. Deep blues, piercing reds and soft amber illuminated the night in a continuous seizure of color and intensity, reflecting off the soaked pavement and the damp polarized glass of the surrounding structures.

The frozen mist clung to his overcoat in minute beads and frosted the hair on his exposed hands like dew on a silky spider web. A small drop of melted sleet collected on a single eyelash, hanging perilously from the tip, refracting the surrounding cacophony of light and blurring his immediate vision with prismatic halos.

He blinked and shook his head abruptly to clear his vision.

He stood on the edge of the curb before an intersection teeming with shadowed figures that slouched in the misty sleet—gray ghosts bundled against the frigid wind, shuffling through slushy puddles. He turned up the collar of the stolen overcoat, pulling it tight around his thick neck, and then thrust his bare hands into the deep pockets. There, he fingered the cold metal of the mag-pistol, brushing the smooth steel finish absently.

Jon Webb had been walking aimlessly for a few hours, but still felt no need to rest, no need to declare a destination or set a plan in motion. His head still reeled from the recently recalled memories of the Pyramid, Max Donovan, their vivid experiences together in that distant desert, and now, the abrupt reality of his friend's betrayal.

Since waking from the free fall induced blackout and emerging from the relative safety of the secure vault of the pod slide, he'd been acting on pure instinct, driven by a survival mechanism as ancient as man himself. Fueled by fear, rage and uncertainty, he quickly fled the safety of the pod and dove blindly into the shadows of the city.

As he had sprinted through the flooded alleys and splashed through the liquid black streets, the lucid images of his past remained etched into his waking mind, peeled back like the healing flake of a scab. The memories struggled with each other for precedence and clarity, randomly streaming and repeating like a digital playback defaulted to shuffle mode. He quickly became numb from the ever-increasing emotions stirred up by the total recall, growing immune to their potency.

So for lack of any considerable option, he had run.

He ran, from the inevitable physical pursuit, but also from the past and the consequences that lay far within those caverns. As he ran, he regained some semblance of order and control over his capsized life. Soon the icy chill of the winter evening bit into his bones and Jon stopped halfway down another dank alley.

There, he had nearly stumbled over the prone form of an unresponsive vagrant lying in the middle of the narrow passageway, his stubbled cheek pressed against the wet, oily asphalt. The unconscious man wore a thick, long, wool and leather overcoat. The garment appeared to be of high quality—obviously found or stolen.

Jon never hesitated as he stripped the heavy cloak from the sleeping skeleton of a man and threw it on in a grand sweeping motion. The bum would surely die in hours if left exposed in this weather but Jon had nothing to offer in fair trade. He quickly checked all of the pockets and immediately withdrew a thin pipe of clear glass and white ceramic.

The slender device used for smoking Symphony lay gleaming in his palm. He could detect a faint whiff of bitter maple, the signature stench of spent drug. His lips curled in a grimace as he gazed down at the man.

Maddening anger flooded Jon's chest as the past again downloaded from the shadows of his mind. He chucked the Synth pipe against the wet ground. It shattered into hundreds of tiny clear and white shards, clinking and tinkling across the alley.

Fuck him! Jon had thought vehemently. *Fuck them all.*

Now, hours later, he gazed from beneath his hardened, furrowed brow at the undulating masses before him. Standing on the curb, shielded from the icy mist of the evening by a stolen overcoat, he began to contemplate his next move. Purpose and direction solidified within him as he watched people dodge in and out of clusters, splash across the street in unathletic jogs and clamber down slippery sidewalks.

They must race toward some meaningful goal: some venturing out into the freezing rain for a late dinner or a drink with a colleague, perhaps even a first date; while others are hustling through the city's maze to get home where it's warm and dry and a lover's bed awaits, children beg to be tucked in and various household chores remain undone.

Jon Webb clenched his teeth and gripped the barrel of the weapon nestled deep within the warm pocket of the coat.

He'd had his life turned completely inside out on more than one occasion; usually by people he never knew nor cared about. And yet, now it seemed that those closest to him were looking to completely shut him down.

He was through being a passive victim. This time he would fight and expose those responsible. And if he couldn't win, then he'd die in the effort.

He rolled his shoulders back, took a deep breath and searched back into his past for the necessary experience and training to carry out his next course of action.

Like a flick of a switch, he was back on duty. The soldier. The cop. The warrior.

He reached into the inside pocket of the coat, flipped out the billfold he found there, recounted the cash and tallied the total credits on the displays of the three debit cards. He had enough to begin his mission: a stroke of luck for him, bad news for the poor soul from whom the overcoat was stolen.

Jon stepped off the curb in a confident stride, floating across the puddled pavement in long, purposeful steps. He turned onto a side street and walked briskly toward the nearest public garage, slicing through the shallow puddles, coat tails billowing out behind him.

~ * ~

Sal Gionetti piloted the Cadillac through the hazy wet streets of the city, traveling in a gradual circle of about fifteen blocks across, drifting in and out of varying degrees of concentration. His mind wrestled with the facts, both new and old, as he drove from deserted industrial parks up into the expensive and prestigious high-end real estate, and then back through the slums.

He tried to piece together all that he'd learned since unwittingly falling into this evolving puzzle; yet despite all of the painstaking efforts, he couldn't seem to reach a solution. It was exhausting just to digest the technological aspects of the apparent scheme, much less the motivations of the participants. He had a real career maker here. Unfortunately, his career was spinning into oblivion.

The first DigVid came across his PDD soon after he arrived at Carla's beach house, but he ignored it until he was back inside the Caddy and speeding back into the city. Internal Affairs was initiating an immediate investigation into the situation at the latest murder scene, between himself and his ignorant Chief.

It appeared that, though nobody present reached out to help the blubbering fat prick, many of the cops present were willing to testify that Sal's assault of the Chief was unprovoked.

Assault, I guess, no matter how you twist that one around; it is what it is. And I assaulted the fat son-of-a-bitch. He shook his head and internally berated himself for losing his cool.

The Commander of Western Investigations was next to call: no DigVid, just audio. The Commander was old school and avoided any and all technology. As abrasively distrustful and paranoid as he was fair and intelligent, the Commander laid it all out for Sal in a succinct and unquestionably chaste message.

"Gionetti, get your ass into Cathedral Plaza. Quickly, quietly and voluntarily. I don't want to hear anything from you or any lawyers until IA has completed their look. You are on immediate lock down. Drop whatever you're involved with and get in here. Now." Click.

That was all.

He had beaten the shit out of his boss, and that would result in serious charges against him. His days as a cop were over.

Sal knew that he was probably screwed five ways to Sunday, but he just couldn't let this one go. This case held something more important in the balance than his future as an Inspector Detective. The potential for global catastrophe lurked just beneath the surface, and he was very close to understanding and comprehending the entire scope of it all. If he was correct in his assumption, then nothing else mattered but to expose the truth and stop the villains.

Besides, as cliché as it sounded, even to him; things had gotten quite personal.

He suddenly cranked the wheel to the right, sliding and fishtailing into a narrow side street. Spinning tires sent fan sprays of slushy water into the darkness. He throttled the Cadillac beyond a safe speed for the conditions and put together his plan.

He needed help. He needed clarification and he needed an ally.

He drove through the heavy misting sleet toward Phoenix-Lamneth.

Twenty-seven

Dawn brought a gray dome of filtered early morning light over the drenched city. The blowing sleet had turned to thick, heavy snow in the dropping temperature, blanketing the sleepy metropolis in fuzzy wet fur.

A few pedestrians plodded through the dirty slush on the streets surrounding the corporate campus building, collars turned up against the slanting tendrils of the winter storm. The falling snow grew heavier by the minute, and the dim light of emerging dawn seemed to forecast no immediate break in the day's accumulation.

Sal Gionetti adjusted the slender earpiece of the phone over the loop of his right ear, shifting his weight behind the wheel of the idling Caddy. He nudged the car's heater control toward the red and watched the digital display of the internal thermometer slowly rise. The wipers smoothly cleared a fresh arc across the windshield pulling wet snow with a soft, hollow squeak.

"No, I'm still waiting," he spoke impatiently into his phone.

His eyes automatically scanned the smooth smoked glass of the tall building looming before him. Thick, irregular globs of snow interrupted his view as they slanted down from the gun-metal gray sky, landed on the steaming windshield in soft splashes of white fluff, melted and then were periodically whisked away by the thin rubber squeegee action of the intermittent wipers.

"Mr. Gionetti, this is Agnes Roman, Mr. MacDonald's personal assistant. As Bethany explained, Mr. MacDonald will be unavailable today. I'm sorry if this presents a problem for you; however, if you would like to give me a number where you can be reached I'll be happy to set up an appointment at his earliest convenience."

How many assistants did this guy have?

Gionetti pressed his eyes closed, set his jaw against the growing frustration and tried to calmly address the third "assistant" in as many quarter-hours.

"Look, miss. I know that MacDonald is very busy and that his time is valuable. But I'm sure that if he knew I've been waiting in your little phone screening tangle-net, he would be upset. I have important information regarding an extremely sensitive matter. If he knew that Detective Gionetti had called on him, he would want to take this call."

The woman sighed audibly, as if expecting this response, and replied tersely, "Please hold." Click.

Jesus!

Sal rubbed his eyes with both balled up fists, a low growl rumbled in his throat. He blinked and returned his gaze to the towering glass facade of the Phoenix-Lamneth office building. Halfway up the smooth dark glass, the corporate logo stood out in three dimensions from the unbroken surface. Spanning two full stories and cast in coppery gold, the image was of the rising phoenix, ablaze from eternal fires, surrounded by the perfect sphere of planet Earth balanced on the cresting waters of the Fountain of Youth. He marveled at the opulence and implied power of such a token.

He again felt the anxiety and trepidation he experienced on the ride over. He was taking a gamble coming back to MacDonald, but if his suspicions were right, then this would verify it.

His earpiece clicked and hummed with another remote connection. He shifted again, expecting yet another hurdle in the phone gauntlet.

"Please wait for Mr. MacDonald." This time, a fourth voice—male and mechanically direct—asserting an obvious air of reluctant compliance.

Whatever, thought Gionetti.

"Gionetti? It's nearly five AM. What couldn't wait until civilized business hours?" MacDonald's gravelly voice instantly betrayed him:

dismissive, edgy and far from sleepy. It had the timbre and melody of a practiced voice-over announcer. He sounded tense and jumpy, even a little terrified. Paul MacDonald was a lot of things in his guarded corporate world, but convincing actor was not one of them.

Gionetti lied, sort of. "Just thought you'd like to know that we've had a break in the case."

A pensive pause. "Really." MacDonald sounded doubtful and almost disappointed.

"Yeah, looks like we may have some latent prints off the bodies. I guess our guy wasn't so careful after all." A full out lie.

There, the line has been cast; the bait is in the water.

"Huh, that's great. I didn't think you guys would be able to lift anything from the scene. I mean, your forensic guys seemed pretty bleak about it. Have you got a positive ID?" *Forced, Paul. Very forced.*

"Well, yes and no. We really can't confirm until we have all of the completed pathology data. Later today, probably. But I can move with what I have. I just want to know how you and Mr. Lacombe want to proceed as far as the media is concerned. This will be big once it unfolds." Gionetti smirked at his own creativity.

"Mr. Gionetti, I was under the impression that you were no longer on this particular case. Frankly, I'm quite surprised to hear from you. Was I mistakenly informed? Am I to understand that you're still chief investigator in this matter?

"Otherwise, you can understand my hesitancy in accepting anything that you may have to offer." MacDonald's voice shifted in tone from concerned surprise back to cool, authoritative control.

Had Division already contacted Phoenix-Lamneth about Sal's sudden suspension? It had only been hours ago. Or was there something else, a mole within Division, or even at Phoenix. Sal bit his lip and thought quickly, contemplating his next move. *Maybe MacDonald was bluffing. Why?*

"Gionetti? I'd like to know what your status and official position is regarding this matter." MacDonald was instantly back in control. Sal felt panic welling up in his throat. Metallic acid flavored his saliva; his heart froze for an instant.

Then he remembered something, and more on instinct than rational judgment, he softly blurted out his last trump, a big lie to catch a bigger truth.

"It was Max Donovan," he said. "His prints were all over the scene. Webb looks clean." Sal bit his lip harder and waited, unconsciously squinting his eyes in anticipation, half expecting his ruse to backfire.

The silence over the wireless connection was piercing, and Sal could almost hear MacDonald's pulse rate accelerate.

"That's impossible," MacDonald spat in a hasty whisper. "Webb was in here yesterday morning. He shot the place up when confronted. Nearly killed me!"

MacDonald was racing, his voice scratchy now and without confidence. It sounded as if he was suffering from a bout of laryngitis and was previously masking the crackling vocalizations with a well-practiced false baritone.

"The bastard took out one of my aides and trashed the executive suite in the process. Fucker got away in Lacombe's little hideaway escape pod thing. Didn't even know that existed." He was rambling now, and Sal took it all in.

What the hell had happened? Did MacDonald try to confront Webb on his own?

"MacDonald. Paul! What are you talking about? What happened?" Sal attempted to redirect the babbling exec, but sensed that it might be futile.

"Shit!" MacDonald shrieked. "Are you telling me that Donovan was really in on it? That they both played me?"

"Paul, where is Webb now?" Sal asked firmly.

"How the hell should I know? He made it out in that pod-slide contraption. Shit." MacDonald was losing steam, and with the defeat, his voice took on a wounded, grating sound.

"Donovan? Where is Donovan?" Sal asked.

There was silence for so long that Sal thought MacDonald may have cut the connection. Then in a raspy, gravelly whisper, "He's out hunting Webb. On orders to execute."

There was the distinct click of the connection being terminated. Static for a moment, then dead air emanated from the earpiece. Sal reached up, tore the device from his ear and tossed it on the wet carpet of the passenger side of the car. He fingered off the slim phone that was docked in the PDD port of the Cadillac's dash and stared out at the early morning blizzard.

It would appear that MacDonald had taken it upon himself to act on his own suspicions and confront Jon Webb directly, and that mistake ended in obvious disaster. Now, Webb was on the run, and his friend and protégé was hunting him down.

The one glaring question facing Gionetti was not whether Webb was guilty or innocent—he felt fairly confident he knew that answer—but whether or not MacDonald acted on Lacombe's behalf or of his own accord.

Sal put the car in gear and spun the tires in thick, slushy snow.

~ * ~

Paul MacDonald slumped in his chair, head buried in his hands, the thin arc of the earphone dangling from his splayed fingers. The desk before him was littered with crumpled papers, shiny shards of broken digital disks, fragments of discarded pastries and torn strips of glossy photos. He mumbled, almost imperceptibly, into the hollow of his cupped palms, slowly rocking his head from side to side.

There was a soft double knock at the thick oak door to his home office followed by a whispering creak as it swung open. MacDonald slid his head up from behind his hands, pulling the skin of his face down with his fingers as he did. His thin cheeks pulled his lower eyelids into droopy troughs, which then sprang back into their natural anatomic position. The flesh around his nose reddened from the pressure, his eyes purple and wet from exhaustion.

He unconsciously rubbed at the swollen bruises that circumscribed his neck and cleared his throat in a loud, moist cackle. He attempted to right himself into a seated poise of authority and control; however, the effort was tired and unconvincing.

He cocked his head and addressed his visitor.

"Averson, yes?" His voice cracked, and he continually cleared his throat against the swollen sensation of obstruction.

The lawyer cautiously approached the trashed desk; stepping over bits of food, paper and notebooks that littered the floor. He eyed MacDonald soberly, then regained his focus and spoke quickly and succinctly.

"Everything's in order from a logistics standpoint. I just need to go over a few fiscal issues with Mr. Lacombe. Share dispersal and dividend allocation, that sort of thing.

"I, uh, also need to talk to you about your end." Averson blinked, nervously shifted his weight from foot to foot and diverted his eyes to the frosted window behind the desk.

MacDonald blinked dully, spread his hands out in an impatient gesture and shook his head numbly.

"Yeah, what's the problem?"

"Well, I'm concerned with your ability to back your end of the merger."

Paul stared dumbly at the lawyer before him as if the man were speaking a foreign language.

After a few seconds of silence, Averson realized that he was expected to come clean. He sighed and continued, nearly stuttering. His eyes darted from item to misplaced item strewn about in disarray on the desk. He avoided making eye contact with MacDonald.

"Well, Paul, it seems that your shares in Phoenix-Lamneth have been sold," the lawyer finally said. "Um, they're locked in guaranteed virtual accounts scheduled for complete liquidation at the open of market day after tomorrow. That's after the merger, Paul."

MacDonald stared at the man before him, his mouth agape, a thin string of saliva hung from top lip to bottom. It barely quivered as Paul involuntarily held his breath. His eyes appeared to have instantly dried out, and the flesh of his face grew red and raw. The swollen skin around his neck flushed with a sudden increase in blood pressure. He remained frozen.

"Yeah, I had the same response. I even tried to track the transaction activity, but all of your accounts have been frozen. Everything, Paul. Pure stocks, mutuals, core cash, even personal savings. Locked as tight as a drum." Averson shook his head and chanced a furtive gaze at the shaken executive. MacDonald remained frozen, shocked.

Averson seemed to gain some courage in the silence, so he continued. "Look, Paul. I can't do anything for you until you clear this up, and frankly, I'm not sure I want to remain involved. Not after all that's happened. I don't know who froze your accounts, and I probably don't want to know.

"Lacombe is paying me a pirate's ransom to complete this deal, so I will. Hell, I hope to retire after this gig. But you have some serious issues, Paul. I just thought that you should know." Averson waited nervously for a reply, a reaction, anything. But MacDonald just sat behind the chaotic desk and stared forward like a terrified mannequin.

"Yeah, well, good luck." Averson turned to leave shuffling through the debris covering the hardwood floor. He stopped, turned back and asked one last question.

"I haven't been able to reach Lacombe anywhere over the last few hours. I've tried both of his private lines and his urgent pager and got nothing. Any idea where he might be?"

MacDonald finally blinked, brought his gaze to meet that of Averson and closed his mouth slowly. His hand went to his lips, rubbing them methodically as tears welled up in his eyes. He blinked a few more times, forcing the moisture down his flush red cheeks.

He never replied.

Averson paused, considered the broken man before him, momentarily feeling something close to pity. He then shrugged, spun on his heels and left the room.

The wide door of the office swung closed slowly in the wake of the exciting lawyer.

~ * ~

"If anything, Paul MacDonald is predictable."

The voice crackled and warbled over the small speaker as the digital scrambler decoded the fragmented transmission and replayed it in a genderless, mechanically fabricated voice. The sound echoed dully off the worn, battered furniture of the cramped and secluded office. The man sat alone as he took the call.

"Yes, I believe he has outlived his usefulness. Has he been neutralized?" the man asked of the speaker.

"Essentially. We cut him off completely."

"Good, then he should pose no problem as long as he remains isolated."

"I agree."

"What about our detective?"

"He's smart. He immediately confronted MacDonald. Bluffed him into revealing our little safari."

"So, Donovan is actively pursuing Webb?"

"As we speak. Should play out nicely. The smart money is on Webb. He's got the edge on intangibles. Either way, once the media leak hits the mainstream, the damage will have been done."

"And when can we expect the tip to hit the air?"

"Sometime tomorrow afternoon, just before market close."

"Are we concerned about the data transmitted by the good doctor prior to her demise?"

"I don't think so. The hard evidence has been cleaned, and any data that found its way to the cop will only be as valuable as he is credible. And he's on the fast track to complete loss of credibility."

"When can we expect a clean house? Entirely."

"By close of business today."

"That includes full retirement of all active players?"

"Absolutely."

"How is the Madison Protocol package?"

"Matheson over at Rainey assures me that everything is in place, and it will perform as promised."

"Make certain there are no loose ends over at Phoenix. Webb may prove to be more of a challenge than you anticipate. Expect the unexpected with him."

"Certainly."

The connection clicked off.

The three tones from the digital encoder chimed as the device cycled through a program purge and cleansed its hard disk, erasing all evidence of the conversation and eliminating the convoluted pathways of the anonymous routing addresses.

Twenty-eight

He counted four outside, slowly walking the perimeter of his building and trying hard not to seem obvious. They were amateurs, through and through, from their dress to their tactics. Each cleanly shaven, well-groomed agent was clad in designer leather overcoats, sported fashionable, yet impracticable footwear and lacked warm headgear. They purposefully meandered around the building, carefully sidestepping slushy puddles and frequently brushing the thickening snowfall from their hair and shoulders.

They stuck out like turds in a punch bowl. The men didn't even conceal their digcom devices when checking in with whoever was running this half-assed surveillance.

Judging from the previous group that entered the building an hour ago and having not yet returned, he figured at least two more were inside, trying to break into his holo-disk, tossing his apartment and making a general nuisance of themselves.

Jon Webb shook his head with humorous disgust at the pathetic show of confidence across the street. If they sincerely hoped to snare him with these stooges, they were in for a long afternoon.

He shifted quietly under the weight of the garbage he had piled on top of his prone form as he lay in the greasy slush of the alley directly across from the entrance to his building.

He had already made two reconnaissance missions to the rear of the building, hoping to gain access via the delivery door, but was foiled as one of the well-dressed boys proved lazy enough to take a seat directly on the narrow ramp leading to the entrance.

In his stealth, they failed to detect him, but he was growing impatient and was beginning to wonder if it would come down to a show of physical force after all. He was confident that he could take down all four—or six—of them easily and quietly, but he didn't want any more violence than necessary. He wasn't so naive as to not consider the very real possibility of having to deal a deathblow to one or more of the men assigned to bring him in, especially once things started moving at combat speed.

He was also growing more certain that these men may not be the retrieval crew, but rather the extermination team, which might explain their lack of concern over being inconspicuous. They may simply be looking for a hard target.

Two of the men met at the corner of the building and shared a laugh at something one had uttered as the other fished out a box of cigarettes. Having lit both smokes off a single lighter, they each enjoyed a long drag as they casually peered about the neighborhood. Another laugh, a lingering chuckle and they each resumed their strolls in opposite directions.

Jon weighed his options and began to formulate an attack plan. He was sure that his next move would have to be on the offensive. He needed to get into the apartment and to his holo-disk. Hopefully, Robert's program uploaded completely, and was as ironclad as advertised. What he needed was nestled safely within the crystal circuitry of his computer.

It was then that events took on the surreal speed and focus of a dream, accelerating through space in quantum leaps, while also slowing to an imperceptible crawl.

Jon's senses jumped and sizzled with the acuity and velocity of super-excited neurons firing out of sync. Yet the events that transpired before him seeped into progression like watching slow-motion time-lapse imagery of a plant emerging from loose soil.

A jet cycle silently pulled to a hovering halt just to the left of the front entrance to the building. The rider throttled down the whispering turbos. He slowly let out the clutch and the cycle jittered to a stop, resting firmly in four inches of fresh snow, compressing the powder under its narrow frame. The arrival of the cycle caught the attention of one of the smoking sentries, and he returned to the front of the building in a jog speaking into his digcom as he trotted around the corner.

The cyclist unbuckled his sleek helmet and removed it, revealing Robert's young and energetic face.

Shit, thought Jon.

He had completely forgotten that Robert had planned on bringing the Ice Cube technology over this evening for Jon to learn. Now Robert had walked right into the middle of what Jon could only hope was a political witch-hunt and not a fabricated murder setup.

Jon, however, feared that the latter was closer to the truth.

The sentry had tossed his cigarette and was waving Robert over to him, casually smiling and reaching inside his coat with his other hand. Robert shifted the helmet under his arm and turned to step off from his straddled position across the bike.

The man had produced a slim black billfold and was flipping it open, extending it forward in the manner of all plainclothes authority figures as they identified themselves with credentials, fake or otherwise.

Robert placed his helmet on the narrow seat of the cycle without looking. He appeared to study the credentials the man held out in front of him as he closed the distance between the two. The man's smile widened, and he said something that Jon could not make out.

Jon's eyes shifted, just for a fraction of a second, to the other side of the building. The second sentry had already rounded the far opposite corner, behind Robert, and was quickly and carefully moving toward him. As he moved, Jon saw the shimmering black metal of a mag-pistol in his gloved hand held barely concealed behind his back.

Jon's gaze snapped back to the man facing Robert, the two men now only fifteen meters apart and closing. Robert waved innocently, prepared to extend his hand in anticipation of a professional handshake; the other man reached behind his back, under his long coat and into his waistband.

Jon reacted in an instant, though his actual movements through space seemed to take an eternity. He erupted from the pile of fetid trash in a silent explosion of paper, rags, rotten food and accumulated snow. Fresh, flaky powder billowed up and around him in a cloud of whiteness as he leapt to his feet like a scene in a violently shaken snow globe.

He brought his mag-pistol up in a practiced arc and expertly sighted the red laser-targeting beam. The men across the street simultaneously jerked their heads toward the sudden noise Jon had made in his emergence from the floor of the alley.

Robert's eyes widened, and he stood rigid with surprise and fear. The sentry, however, stared for a moment too long, his hand still frozen behind his back in the aborted effort to secure the weapon concealed there.

A tiny, star-shaped pinpoint of red laser light danced faintly across his forehead, tracing minute figure-eights as Jon applied the necessary pressure to the trigger of his pistol that would loose the high caliber ferrous missile and cleave the man's brain in two.

A sudden, unexpected cry of painful surprise halted Jon from exerting any more force against the sensitive trigger. The pause lasted only another second, but was enough for Jon to register that the second sentry had been brought down by a giant bat-like creature and was instantly incapacitated.

Jon dropped his aim, refocusing his full attention back on his target, and at a distance of nearly eighty meters, blew out both of the man's knees with two rapid, consecutive blasts. The man fell like a doll thrown to the ground by an angry child and cried out in agony.

The bat creature rose from the sidewalk in a billowing flap of tattered wings and soared over to the writhing figure of the now kneeless man. The movement cast fluttering shadows over the unconscious man at its feet. The black wings of the creature enveloped the screaming man for a moment, muffling his cries. There was a slight jerking, twitching of the man's legs and his screams suddenly stopped. He lay still beneath the rising form of the bat-creature.

Robert stood in terror, watching the caped form of the dark creature as it turned its head first toward him, then back down the alley at Jon.

Jon tried to sight in on the creature's face, to get a glimpse of some features, his targeting laser inscribing jittery, irregular ovals over the rippling dark form. The bat raised its arm and pointed a similar weapon at Jon, the reddish-orange shimmering brightness of the second laser flittered across Jon's eyes, causing him to squint against the blinding glare.

The two thin laser beams intersected some distance between the two warriors. Heavy snowflakes fell through the twin cords of light, sparkling and twinkling with iridescent crimson and neon orange.

Jon sensed power and confidence throbbing in the air between them, and he instantly knew that this was to be a moment of action and not merely a standoff.

He prepared to fire blindly into the creature when it spoke.

"Webb! This is Detective Gionetti, hold your fire!"

An eternity flashed by in an instant. The microseconds stretched and morphed into eons. Time raced and space folded, ripples of reality ebbed and reflected back on themselves. Eventually—and immediately—the fabric of the present caught up with itself and all of the scattered molecules of the instant fell back into place.

Jon blinked, cleared his head from the euphoria of surging adrenaline and refocused on the here and now. He cocked his head, keeping his weapon—his aim—true and steady.

He could just now make out the physical form and familiar facial features of Detective Sal Gionetti beneath the dark cloak of his tattered and ripped overcoat. Gionetti stood rigid and sure, his weapon held high, the beam of the targeting laser steady.

"Gionetti?" Jon croaked.

"Webb, lower your weapon. I didn't come to take you."

Jon remained silent as he considered his options and consequences. He trusted no one, except for maybe Robert.

But, whatever the reason, Gionetti was indeed here. That was no coincidence.

"Webb, I need you to listen. Please, lower your weapon."

"I'm not responsible for any of this!" Webb blurted, more to hear himself say it than anything else. It felt good to say it, to give the thought a breath of life. It made it real, somehow. Nearly believable.

"I know, Jon. I know," Gionetti said softly with genuine concern.

"I'm being setup and I don't understand it!" Jon was sliding into a gray fog of emotions, and his frustration and anger could easily lead to a loss of control. Even though Jon sensed it happening, he was powerless to stop.

"Max has turned against me, and now they hunt me like a dog! What's going on?"

"Look, Webb. I'm placing my weapon on safe and securing it." Before he could complete the sentence, Gionetti powered down his pistol.

The thin orange beam of the targeting laser winked out as the handgun's magnetic impeller wound down with a low whine. Sal pocketed his weapon and motioned for Robert to join him as he carefully took a step off the curb and into the street toward Webb.

"I'm coming over to you, Jon. I'm unarmed. Just relax. Don't fucking shoot me, okay?"

Jon hesitated, noticed Robert at Gionetti's side and slowly lowered his own pistol. The bright red targeting beam reflected off the blowing, drifting snow that swirled at his feet. The beam flicked off after a few seconds and the pistol hung limply from his hand.

Jon inhaled deeply, closed his eyes and let the breath out in a shaky sigh. Gionetti and Robert approached, seeming to float across the top of the swirling snow.

Jon took a tentative step toward them as Gionetti's face became clear through the thick slanting snow. The detective's smile was wide and warm, and he held out an open hand toward Jon.

"A lot has happened since we last met."

Jon accepted the offered hand and grasped it firmly. He felt the warmth and held tightly, squeezing security from the friendly touch. Gionetti's deep green eyes shimmered with sincerity and strength. Jon felt instantly welcome and safe in their gaze.

He returned the smile with a head-shaking half-chuckle of his own. He pulled Sal closer and slapped the man on the shoulder, squeezing the fabric of the leather coat between his bare fingers, testing the realness of the moment and gaining assurance from the feel of the fabric and the solidity of the man beneath.

The two men simply looked at one another for a brief second, and then Jon turned to Robert, who was obviously still numb from the shocking events of the past few moments.

Jon smiled at Robert, threw a long arm around his shoulders and hugged him close.

"Robert, good to see you. I'm so glad that man didn't shoot you," Jon stated as casual as an everyday greeting.

Robert blinked, looked at Jon with an air of wonder and concern; then replied almost defensively, "Yeah? No shit? Me, too. Jesus Christ!" He shook his head, wide-eyed, shaky, and still attempting to process the whole scene.

"What the hell?" was all Robert could manage after another moment of contemplation.

Gionetti gathered the loose tails of his billowing coat about him, wrapped it around his narrow frame and thrust his hands back into deep pockets. He indicated back over his shoulder with a tilt of his head, nodding in the direction of the lumpy, still forms of the downed men.

"They'll be out for awhile, but this cold may revive them sooner than we'd like. I suggest we come up with a plan and act on it, soon." The smile returned to his sharp, narrow face. His eyes continued to sparkle as if he may actually be enjoying this.

Jon recognized the look from the adrenaline-filled days of his past. Perhaps they did share some commonalties.

"Unfortunately," Sal continued, "I hadn't thought much past this point."

"I need to get to my apartment. There may be some information on my holo-disk that will help." Jon suddenly stopped short and turned to Sal, remembering the number of men he had counted during his survey of the building.

"What about the others? In back?" he asked quickly scanning the sides of the building for approaching conflict.

Sal calmly shook his head.

"Taken care of. PulseTranq." He patted his hip pocket. "Sleep for at least thirty minutes, but like I said, in this cold," he shrugged, "who knows?"

"Right." Jon nodded. "I think there may be two upstairs. What do you suggest?"

"Direct retreat. Chances are they may already know about their friends. We should really move."

Robert shook his head and weakly pulled away from the men.

"Yeah, well, good luck and all that. I'm way out of here."

Jon reached out, grabbed Robert by the collar and brought him close.

"Robert, I'm sorry that I got you involved in this, but it's too late to undo that. I can't explain how or why, not yet. But I'll need your help. You may be the x-factor in this whole mess."

"What?"

"There's a good chance that they, whoever they are, don't know about you or our relationship. That gives me—us—the edge." Jon glanced at Gionetti, who raised his eyebrows, pouted and shrugged softly.

"Besides, if they do know about you, then you're safest with us."

"Great," Robert replied, void of enthusiasm.

Jon peered desperately at Gionetti. "You really don't think we should at least try to enter the apartment?"

Sal continued shaking his head and leaned into the growing wind. "Jon, there's a good chance that whatever you're searching for up there is long gone or even destroyed. All that's waiting for you in your apartment is a whole lot of trouble that I'd just as soon avoid."

Sal's eye's searched Jon's face, scanning for any sign of rational acceptance and logical, linear thought. He knew that Jon was shaken and not thinking clearly.

Jon eventually nodded his compliance and pocketed his weapon speaking rapidly as he folded the flapping tails of his overcoat around his waist.

"All right, then. Where to?" Jon asked.

Gionetti bit his lip, looked quickly from side to side, and then seemed to settle upon a plan of action.

"Okay, let's grab Robert's cycle and toss it in the alley. Cover it with debris. Hopefully, no one will find it for at least a few hours."

Robert flinched and began to protest. " 'scuse me, but..."

Jon spun toward Robert and spoke sharply, yet with compassion and sympathy. "I'm sorry, but he's right. They find your bike, run a trace and link you to me." He paused, slowly shook his head and then added, "These guys don't like loose ends."

Jon arched his eyebrows and pursed his lips for emphasis, until Robert reluctantly nodded, defeated and solemn. Jon patted his friend on the back and led him toward the jet-cycle. Gionetti fell immediately behind them continuing with his plan.

"We'll take my car. It's stolen, but they shouldn't expect me to have been here. They figured on you, Jon, coming back. Leave your vehicle where it is. It'll look like you attempted to breech their trap, but got spooked and fled."

The three men hefted the two hundred-sixty kilogram cycle and started to carry it back across the street. Their flickering shadows crept across the unconscious men lying crumpled on the sidewalk. The bleeding had stopped from the two pulverized knees; dark crimson clots of gelled blood dyed the fresh snow in deep hues of red and fading pink.

The twice-injured man moaned, barely audible, yet remained completely still. Robert glanced wide-eyed and worried at Gionetti as they carried the bike. Sal nodded and muttered softly, "Yeah, we should probably hurry."

They picked up the pace, and within another minute were piling bags of garbage and loose debris over the shape of Robert's only mode of transportation, his one-year-old Harley-Davidson Falcon AirGlide.

"Christ," Robert grumbled. It was all that he could manage through the increasing numbness of his lips and tightness of anxiety in his chest as he gazed sadly at the pile of filthy rubbish that blanketed his ride.

When they finished burying the cycle, Jon glanced over at the sidewalk. The second man—the one with his knees still attached—was stirring, trying to raise himself on trembling arms. He collapsed after the strained effort in a huff of exhaustion and pain. Jon looked back at the other two men and wrinkled his brow.

"Well, where to?" asked Robert.

"Your place," Jon answered nudging Robert back out of the narrow alley and toward the street. Gionetti sprang into a moderate run, taking the road immediately to the right, down the block, and away from Jon's building.

Jon followed, snagging Robert's sleeve as he passed.

"Come on!"

Twenty-nine

Revelation and Recourse

They kept Robert's small efficiency studio dark with the exception of two well-used candles flickering at either end of a narrow coffee table. Robert sat cross-legged on the floor, his face illuminated directly from the candle on the table. Jon and Sal slouched deep within the soft cushions of two mismatched recliners; the fabric thrones flanked the coffee table at haphazard angles.

Robert took a long pull from a thick bottle of maple-colored scotch, grimaced slightly, blinked against the involuntary tearing and then passed it up to Gionetti.

Gionetti leaned forward with some effort, reached long for the offered bottle, snared it by the neck and flopped back into the plush chair with a grunt and a sigh. His green eyes still sparkled, flecked with gold in the twitching candlelight. He took a slow, well-measured sip from the half-empty bottle and closed his eyes against the fluid warmth that coated his throat. He sighed and cradled the bottle in his lap, head back, chest rising and falling rhythmically.

The three men sat in exhausted silence, mentally chewing on the recalled events and digesting the complexity of their shared situation. Gionetti had just finished recalling the harrowing story of his evening:

from the discovery of his partner's murder and the confrontation with the Chief to the surreal and disjointed path that eventually brought him to Jon and Robert's aid.

"Tell me about this doctor, the pathologist," Jon requested as he reached for the bottle.

Gionetti opened his eyes as he turned toward Jon and leaned sideways to pass the bottle of scotch. He shrugged his eyebrows and softly sighed.

"Tabitha Gunnerson was the deputy medical examiner who assisted the M.E. on the post-mortems of the four murder victims from Phoenix-Lamneth," he began as he shifted in his chair and propped himself on one elbow.

"She took me aside that evening and said that she suspected foul play, that the M.E. may have been a fraud. So we met later that night, and she revealed her concerns; some interesting and carelessly overlooked facts and a very plausible hypothesis."

He stared into the darkness of the apartment, again saddened by the memory of his lost friend and partner, and the innocence of Tabby. The image of Carla grieving beside the dying fire reflected onto the back of his mind.

"They must have been following me," he whispered. "I don't know how I didn't realize it. I guess I'm getting careless."

"Sounds like circumstances beyond your control," Robert interjected. "You were doing your job, man. I don't see a reason for you to blame yourself."

Sal smiled, as if to say *thanks for the vote of confidence, but two people are still dead because of my involvement.*

Robert merely shrugged and accepted the bottle as it made its way back to him. He held it between his crossed legs, but did not drink.

Jon continued, "So, you believed her. What was it?"

"Long story short, they were assassinated with some kind of anesthetic drug, a paralytic that's almost impossible to trace, and then shot execution style in a passionate statement. Someone wanted them dead, but wanted it to look like emotional or political motivation. Now there's no doubt in my mind that someone wanted you, Webb, to take the fall."

Earlier, Jon had shared with the two other men the complete story of his escape from Phoenix-Lamneth. As they drove away from the defeated ambush at his building, across the city to Robert's place, he recounted with stunning clarity the unexpected gun battle with his traitorous friend, the killing of the receptionist and the Pod slide.

"But why? Why me, and to what end?" Jon asked.

"I wish I knew, brother. I wish I knew."

Sal Gionetti shrugged, looking sleepily at Jon through the flickering candlelit shadows. He motioned to the blue binder lying on top of the coffee table before them.

"It's all in there, including the results and conclusions of Tabby's final PM. Somehow, it all ties together but I can't make sense out of it."

Robert fingered the document folder, reluctant to become further involved in what appeared to be a conspiracy of grand design. He stared at the thick binder as Sal and Jon continued.

"Well, this is big enough to involve the methodical extermination of anyone involved," Jon said.

Robert flinched at the grim statement and took a long pull from the bottle, his eyes glued to the blue folder.

"So, let's put our heads together and figure this thing out before more people get killed." Jon sat up wringing his hands as he did.

Sal slid the binder toward him as he reached for it. Jon opened it and immediately began rifling through the pages. Most were bound to the spine of the folder, but a few loose sheets fluttered out and see-sawed to the floor. Robert leaned over and snatched at the individual papers. He began reading the text on one of the sheets, paused, and then slowly proceeded to gather the remaining dropped pages. His eyes darted from paragraph to paragraph as he paged back and forth, reshuffling the papers and trying to put them in some sort of order. As he read, he became anxious and edgy; he sat more erect and readjusted his legs beneath him.

"Jon, let me see the rest of that binder," Robert asked suddenly without taking his eyes off the documents. He had fanned them out in his hands, like a competition poker player during the final hand of a high-stakes tournament.

Jon paused in his perusal and glanced at Robert's intense, rigid face. Robert abruptly looked up and caught Jon's stare.

"C'mon, c'mon!" Robert wiggled his fingers impatiently at Jon encouraging him to hand over the complete document. Jon did so with a raised eyebrow and a look of annoyance.

"Shit, I need more light." Robert leapt excitedly to his feet, snatched the blue binder from Jon's loose grip and skipped clumsily over to a wall-mounted light switch. Bright, ivory fluorescent light flooded the previously darkened room. Jon and Sal squinted against the flare of whiteness, hooding their eyes with cupped hands.

Well, thought Robert defeatedly, *I'm in this now.*

He sat back on the floor, binder fully opened on the nappy fabric of a well-worn throw rug, the loose sheets spread out and in order before him like tarot cards. He studied them intently; his eyes jumped from page to page, rapidly ingesting the contents. He occasionally shook his head and sucked in short, surprised breaths.

Jon and Sal watched as the young man devoured the contents of the document over the next fifteen minutes, never moving and never saying a word. The bottle passed between them only twice during that time, and they wondered silently if Robert would ever pause to share his revelations. They feared that to interrupt with inquiries might stun him out of whatever productive trance he was in.

Robert finally halted in his studious attack of the folder, staring into the blur of words on one of the pages. He slowly paged back to a colorful graph flanked by columns and tables of numbers. He fell back on his heels, rolled to one side and pulled his legs out from under him. He rubbed his eyes with one hand and reached for the bottle with the other.

Gionetti obligingly handed the remaining scotch to Robert, who took a huge swallow without a grimace. As he wiped his mouth with the back of his hand, he finally spoke. "This is scary shit, guys."

Jon and Sal simultaneously widened their eyes and leaned forward to encourage immediate elaboration. Robert looked at each of the men, his unblinking eyes jumped from one to the other.

"And if this is correct, involves some of the most important technology of our time."

Robert gathered his thoughts, took a smaller swig from the bottle and continued, "It seems that they, and I'm presuming Phoenix-Lamneth is 'they', have found a way to manufacture and graft brain tissue into living, functioning humans."

Jon and Sal simply stared at Robert not quite fully understanding what he just proposed. Robert sighed in exasperation and consulted the gathered sheets of data before him.

"According to your pathologist, an anomalous strip of neural tissue was found grafted—transplanted—onto the surface of one of the dead guy's brain. It seems that this piece of tissue was grown, or manufactured somehow, harvested, and then grafted onto the cerebral cortex of a living host.

"If I understand her correctly, it was obviously foreign tissue and purposefully placed there." He paused for a moment, and then continued in a tone of confusion and fear. "This mass was a completely perfect, biologically intact, fully functioning strip or patch of specialized neurologic tissue."

Robert swallowed thickly as he said the words. He licked his lips and added, "If this data is authentic, then this is a miraculous and terrifying discovery."

"So you're saying that she found a brain tumor, or mass, in one of the Phoenix-Lamneth victims?" Jon asked looking from Robert to Sal.

"No, no. Not a tumor or anything that grew out of the native brain tissue. This is an organized, highly specialized mass of neurologic tissue that was artificially manufactured, cultivated and purposefully grafted onto the surface of someone's brain.

"It was placed there," Robert asserted.

"What?" Sal exclaimed.

Robert nodded emphatically. "I know, I know. It sounds crazy. The stuff of sci-fi. But as I said; if this data is genuine and can be trusted; well, then..." He spread his hands and shrugged. "The possibilities are frightening."

Sal narrowed his eyes, bit the inside of his cheek, and frowned before shaking his head and asserting, "No, I have to believe that the data is pure. I trusted Tabby. She was killed for uncovering this, and I have to believe that what she discovered is the truth."

"Wow," Jon whispered. "So what does this really mean, Robert?"

Robert shrugged. "I don't know. The possibilities are staggering. But you can bet that someone does not want this to go public."

"I don't understand. Is this sort of thing possible? I mean, can we do this type of thing now?" Sal asked.

"Evidently," Robert answered. "You'd be surprised what we've achieved over the past decade, especially with the advent of optical processing. Anything is possible." He glanced at Jon, who caught his look and flashed sudden recognition as he remembered the wondrous revelation of Robert's phenomenal success with the Ice Cube technology when applied to Sarah's cerebral Halo.

Jon let his gaze falter and shifted in his seat.

"I guess I shouldn't be so surprised after all," Robert said as he fingered the folds of paper on the ground before him. "With all of the successes in advanced stem cell technology, I really suppose that this was inevitable. They've been trying to grow neurological tissue from stem cells since the beginning.

"For years, they've attempted to regenerate neurons in efforts to repair and rebuild damaged spinal cords. They even tried to regrow optic and acoustic nerve cells in efforts to cure various forms of deafness and blindness. Most of the endeavors failed, however, primarily due to the fact that they've been unable to coax any generation of stem cells to fully blossom into a viable neuron."

"So what's the difference between that and the stem cells used to eradicate diabetes or leukemia?" Sal asked.

"Those aren't neurological tissues," Robert answered. "Look, all of the embryonic stem cells utilized in modern therapies have evolved from one of two prime stem cell lines developed during the last decade of the twentieth century—the Thomson or the Murdoch lines. Many stem cells lines have been generated, but those two are the root of all subsequent, successful generations.

"What makes those particular cells special is their pluripotency—their potential to develop into any type of cell. Basically, you extract the nuclear contents from the target cell—that particular cell you wish to develop— and inject it into the undifferentiated stem cell. Through various biochemical, and just recently, nanoelectrochemical techniques, you can program the stem cell line to grow into whatever cells you desire.

"Diabetic stem cell therapies were successful because they found the right combination of protein matrices to initiate and support the development of the insulin-producing pancreatic cells. Same with leukemia though it took a little longer to perfect those cell lines because of some complex immunologic issues."

"So why are nerve cells different?" Sal asked.

"One of the more popular hypotheses is that neurons are so specialized that they actually have to learn how to become differentiated neuronal cells. That somehow, at a time early in their development, they needed some sort of coaching on how to become a certain type of neural cell beyond whatever was written in the genetic code of the nuclear DNA. Something told one neuron to develop into a motor nerve, another into a sensory nerve, and yet another into a pain fiber.

"In nature, two completely identical nerve cells, each sharing the exact DNA template, will nevertheless develop into two very different mature nerves. Even in adulthood, they will demonstrate their shared genetic heredity, yet they can wind up being totally opposite from one another in their biochemical and physiological function. There are just way too many specialized neural cells to pinpoint any commonality in their early development.

"No matter how they tried, they couldn't get the embryonic stem cell lines to cleanly differentiate into predictable and viable neural cells. Every time they wanted to grow a sensory cell, they got a motor neuron or vice versa."

"Well, it looks like someone figured it out," Jon said glumly. "What about Parkinson's? That's a neurologic disease, and we've completely cured that."

"Actually, we never cured Parkinson's disease. We just found a suitable cell line that predictably and efficiently produces dopamine, a naturally occurring neurotransmitter in the central nervous system. Dopamine alleviates the Parkinsonian symptoms caused from under production of the same chemical in damaged areas of the substantia nigra in the brain.

"It's not the same as repairing severed spinal cord tissue or rebuilding functional centers of the brain damaged by stroke or tumors. That would require developing cell lines that spawn all of the specialized target neurons that are capable of handling the complexities of neural signal transmission specific to each physiologic need. They haven't been able to do that. The problem of the neuron has been a major obstacle in the advancement of stem cell utilization.

"At least until now." Robert wrinkled his brow and silently considered the new possibilities.

His audience of two sat quietly, lost in their own private thoughts as they, too, contemplated the shape of a new world in the wake of such profound technology and the consequences of this newly discovered reality.

"So, how did they do it, Robert?" Jon asked pointedly.

"I don't know. You would need vast amounts of data processing space to even begin to engineer a solution. Serial-parallel optical processors, multi-factorial logic matrices, unlimited access to purified stem cell lines and test sub—"

Robert's face drained of color as his voice trailed off. His eyes grew wide and watery, his lips quivered. He swallowed hard against his shrinking, yet rising stomach. He slowly glanced at Jon, hoping that he wasn't following the same line of reasoning as he.

Jon narrowed his eyes and considered Robert's peculiar transformation. Before he could verbalize his curiosity, Sal interjected, "So, they have somehow perfected this brain clone, and now want to kill everyone who knows anything about it.

"Did those scientists at Phoenix-Lamneth have anything to do with this? If so, why were they killed? And now, once again, who is responsible and why?" Sal's voice grew more intense as he spoke, anxious to bring the conversation immediately away from the science and back to the real issue at hand.

Robert blinked a few quick times and refocused in an instant. "This isn't really a clone, per se. But the idea is—"

"I know, and I appreciate your elaboration and education. You obviously know your shit, and seriously, I really do appreciate it. Sometime, later, I want to fully understand it all. But right now, I want to find our killers. I want to find out why. And I want to stop them from doing any more." Sal softly and succinctly asserted his position.

Robert calmly nodded and conceded the point.

"We may find answers to all of our questions once we find out whom and why," Sal added.

Jon nodded solemnly, trying to catch Robert's eye, but the nurse was busy rereading the reports in the file folder. There was something in his last comment, his evasiveness. Jon made a mental note to reinvestigate Robert's curious pause.

"Well, let's refocus on the murders then," Robert suggested as he pulled out and separated the initial notes on the murder victims, and then added Tabby's amended post mortem notes to the top.

"What do we know? The facts," Sal began.

"Very few people could have gained access to that office and committed those murders," Jon said.

"Right. Now, Jon, you definitely have a theory on this. I saw you casing that room like an old pro. What did you see? How did you feel?" Sal asked.

Jon hesitated, then shrugged and folded his hands neatly in his lap. "I don't know, it felt too staged. The hit was way too clean. No signs of struggle. They just sat there and took the bullets. And the bodies weren't moved or repositioned after the event either, of that I'm sure."

"How do you know?" Robert asked.

Now it was his turn to seek enlightenment from the experts in their field. Where he excelled in understanding and explaining the medical and technological details to the two cops, he equally lacked in grasping the subtleties of forensic and investigative work.

"Splatter patterns and the quantity and quality of the congealed blood surrounding the victims. There's no way to move those bodies around in that amount of spilled blood without leaving obvious tracks," Jon explained shaking his head. "No, they were shot and they died in place. I just can't accept that four people sat calmly while a single killer systematically executed them all."

"Unless they were dead already, or near dead," Sal added. "Robert, what's your take on Tabby's assertion about that anesthetic?"

"I just finished that part." He tapped the paper with his finger repeatedly, squinting in thought.

"Yeah, I got to hand it to your lady doc here, she's sharp. No way to trace succinylcholine unless you know to look for it. She did. And by the looks of this lab work, three of the victims died from massive cardiac infarction secondary to sudden hypoxia from the neuromuscular paralytic, succinylcholine, before they were shot in the head. That's clear."

Robert sniffed, cleared his throat and flipped back a few pages. "What is also clear is that none of those three had any gross abnormalities found on their autopsies, unlike our friend with the brain graft. Who, by the way, did not die from succinylcholine induced heart attack, but rather from a speeding bullet placed through the back of his head."

"So, we have four bodies, three of which appeared to have been purposefully poisoned, and then shot to throw us off the trail, and one unpoisoned, yet shot as well. Only he has some kind of weird brain graft." Sal recapped the facts and sighed.

He shook his head and considered the possibilities aloud. "Multiple perps seems unlikely, and in light of the clever use of the drug probably unnecessary. So one killer, with knowledge and ability. Probably known by the four victims. Also able to get in and out cleanly."

He spread his arms and looked to Jon.

Jon returned the look and pursed his lips. "Lacombe or MacDonald," he said soberly. "And my money is on Mac."

"Mine would be, too, if it weren't for the fact that he has an airtight alibi that corroborates with Lacombe. They were both in the VIP room at Synth-Sations that night until two a.m. Over fifteen witnesses place them there, enjoying a fully comped evening courtesy of some executive assistant from Polar Innovations," Sal said with a tone of bitterness.

"There is one other possibility," Jon offered as he stared at his interlaced fingers. "That the killer was also one of the victims."

He allowed the idea to float above their heads in the thick air of the stuffy apartment. Eventually, he elaborated, explaining what he had suspected from the start.

"The guy with the brain patch could be our killer. In fact, I'm sure of it, now."

"How is that possible?" Robert asked.

"Yeah," Sal added.

"Murder suicide, plain and simple," Jon began. "He either knows that the three doctors are meeting or he himself sets it up. He walks in after everyone has established themselves. No one moves out of their seat as he enters; they know him and are expecting him. He works his way around the table, shaking their hands." Jon pantomimes pumping invisible hands like a politician practicing for a campaign tour.

"The drug is injected with each hand shake. He sits down and waits. Perhaps he waits until they're completely dead before shooting them, but from the amount of blood in that room, I have to believe that he went about the executions just before they lost consciousness, but were fully paralyzed. He wanted them to feel the end when it came, the crushing agony of a massive heart attack followed by the piercing heat of a bullet through the brain." Jon grimaced slightly, and then wiped his mouth with a dry hand.

Sal simply stared into space as he considered Jon's theory.

"Huh," Robert murmured.

"So, what, the guy shot *himself* in the back of the head afterward? There was no weapon found, Jon," Sal explained.

"There's an incinerator access door located a meter off the floor, directly behind the chair in which he was found." Jon mimicked holding an inverted handgun, an older firearm that didn't rely on palm print encoding within the handgrip to activate the auto-safe features as on all modern weapons.

A pistol from the early part of the century could have easily been turned upside down, held inverted by the fingers alone and fired into the back of one's head, if one was so inclined. That simple act couldn't possibly occur with a newer weapon.

Jon then opened his hands and allowed the imaginary gun to fall out of his grasp and behind him as he fired a phantom round into the back of his own skull.

Sal watched. His green eyes sparkled in amazement and a slow smile spread over his face.

"Positioned carefully in front of the incinerator drawer," Jon explains. "He leans back and fires the final round into his own head, the gun falls into the incinerator and the drawer closes on a defaulted timer after one minute."

"I'll be damned! You noticed that while you were peeking behind the dead guy. You suspected that immediately, didn't you?" Sal asked.

Jon shrugged and looked solidly at the detective. "Well, the guy didn't fit in with the rest of the picture. No lab coat, no badge. He was pushed away from the table, leaning back and not forward or onto the table. You saw that, too."

"Yeah, but I never would've thought of the incinerator. That was good, Jon."

"Are you serious?" Robert asked. "You think this guy went to Phoenix-Lamneth, killed these high-profile scientists and then staged an elaborate suicide to frame Jon?"

Robert shook his head. "It sounds crazy just to say it."

"No, I think that he was already at Phoenix-Lamneth. I think he was the guy I replaced as head of security. I can't be certain, but he looked familiar."

"I buy it, Jon. I really do. Instinctively," Gionetti affirmed as he nodded confidently. "Going to be hard to prove, though. Besides, who is this guy, and what is this weird brain tissue? How does it all connect?"

Jon shook his head solemnly. Robert continued to peruse the bound documents and lab reports, searching for more clues, facts and answers.

"The big question is why," Sal said. "That'll give us who. The answer is in there, I think." Gionetti pointed to the folder in Robert's lap. Jon gazed over to the blue binder and nodded slowly.

Robert glanced up and sighed. "I think you're right, but there are more questions here than answers."

He carefully unfolded his legs from beneath him and slowly rose to his feet grimacing slightly as he tested his tingly, nearly numb limbs. He held the fanned contents of the file folder in one hand as he reached for the remainder of the scotch on the table.

"Give me a couple of hours to run through this stuff, clean out the distracters and try to make some sense out of the labs and PM's."

He grasped the bottle by the neck and sloshed the golden brown liquid as he turned to move into the deeper shadows of his small studio. He sauntered toward a small recessed workstation situated on the back wall of the apartment between the cluttered bedroom and the modest half bathroom.

Silhouetted against the bright blue-green iridescence of twin, wide screen LCD monitors, Robert's shadowy form sat silently before the glowing workstation. Already, his fingers danced lithely across the keyboards of the two parallel processors, clicking and clacking as he began to work in his medium.

Sal and Jon considered one another with shared caution and skepticism, each calmly eyeing the other, measuring and evaluating. Gionetti broke the silence with a simple statement that succeeded in both gaining Jon's trust and offering a clean opportunity for a segue into something that desperately needed answering.

"I know the basics of the unfortunate events that surround you and your family." Sal's gaze held Jon's for an instant, then casually and comfortably drifted to the darkened windows. Snow flicked against the frosted pane, sometimes sticking, though only lasting a brief time before melting and cascading down the glass. Sal had the strong, sure gaze of a friend and confidant who knew enough about you to speak the truth, no matter how hurtful, yet never offered judgment or criticism.

It was an energized look of both patient acceptance and eager understanding. It was the look of someone with whom secrets about the past could be shared without fear of reprisal or reprimand; and plans for the future could be discussed without concern for disdain or discouragement.

Sal spoke after a full minute had passed. "I know about the assault, the injuries and the long weeks in the critical care unit. However, like most, I know very little about the time during which you disappeared, though I suppose that's the way it should be."

Sal shifted in his seat, still watching the snowflakes paste themselves in random fashion across the ink-black slate of the rectangular windowpanes. Jon stared at his hands, quiet and still, barely breathing.

Gionetti looked at Jon, waited until the man sensed the pause and met his gaze. When Jon finally brought his eyes up, they were red with exhaustion, yet sparkled from both moisture and remembrance.

Gionetti smiled softly and said, "Jon, I know things seem hopeless and contorted right now, but if you help me to understand, to see the world through your eyes, maybe I can actually help."

Jon's mind retreated into the past. Memories and emotions flooded his consciousness in turbulent waves of images, sounds, smells and feelings. Some of that which was recalled was vivid and lucid like a perfectly edited digital moment forever captured in crystalline clarity.

But most of the memories remained murky and vague, mysteriously ephemeral. He sensed that he was balanced at a precipice, toes hanging over the edge of a cliff that was constructed entirely from the unstable, grainy sands of the past.

The intensity of the past twenty-four hours showered down around him from the apathetic heavens in torrents, a heavy rain of unyielding reality. The insistent deluge would soon wash the loose soil of the past beneath his feet, and the shifting ground on which he carefully trod over the years would soon become soft and unstable. That soil, bubbling and frothy, would begin to flow over his feet as his weight would force him to sink deeper into the repressed past.

He felt as if he didn't take a purposeful step back out of the softening slurry of the dissolving ground, that the quicksand of the past may just wash him, unbalanced and stumbling, over the edge and into the waiting maw of the abyss below.

Intuition struggled with both self-preservation and foolish pride in a constant eternal battle, yet somehow, deep under the granite veneer of his stoic facade, he relented and saw an alternative, and perhaps an opportunity to achieve peace.

Amidst the bizarre circumstances of recent events Sal Gionetti had magically appeared before the sinking man, wide-stanced and on firm footing as he extended a strong, sure grip.

Jon could turn his back on this one chance and again dig his heels into the unstable, loosely packed foundation of his past. He could continue to pray that the ground beneath would hold and not wash him over the edge; or he could take hold of the lifeline, step out and away from disintegrating history and begin to understand his station in the grand architecture of the universe from a new perspective.

"Five years ago," Jon whispered hoarsely, "I did what most men claim they would do if faced with similar circumstances. However, most men lack the capacity to act."

He continued, more as an explanation than confession, but clearly implying both.

"In emotionally charged pronouncements men will often, and rather eloquently, deliver oaths of revenge as if they were some kind of doctrine etched out in frozen testosterone. Yet, they somehow fail to act." There was no tone of remorse or sorrow in his voice, but rather a gentle almost editorial quality to his smooth words.

"But I had killed before. I've done many things in the name of democracy, to complete the mission and preserve our own universal vision of morality." Jon gazed up from his hands to see Gionetti now watching him as he spoke.

The detective's eyes were sharp and narrow, yet his face drawn and loose as if he were suddenly allowing some of his own demons to listen in on the conversation.

"Most of the time, it was kill or be killed. In combat, either during the war or in the street, it was self-preservation, a trained response to initiate an acquired skill. It happened because the parameters of the situation dictated the outcome. The details were all too often lost within the wider definition.

"People die in war," Jon said. "Usually the enemy, but also many helpless innocents. But even the innocent victims could not claim ignorance. They understood the parameters; they knew the consequences of remaining in hot zones. Morality never had a chance in the war."

Sal slowly nodded in agreement, sad and thoughtful.

Jon looked for the bottle of scotch and realized that Robert had taken it with him. He chuckled lightly and shook his head dismissively. "I operated under that illusion for awhile, until morality found me." He smiled though it looked painful and out of place on his face.

Gionetti remained silent and riveted.

"Actually, it was humanity—and humility—that found me," Jon explained. "In the desert. At an R&R Pyramid in Northern Saudi called *Bacchus Plateau*. Max Donovan and I were in the same Ranger Reactionary force back then. We were tight, Max and I..."

As Jon retold his tale of the three days within the Pyramid, Sal listened silently occasionally nodding in recognition or understanding of certain military details. But as the story unfolded, Sal Gionetti grew increasingly agitated and restless. He reacted viscerally to the horrors Jon revealed, swallowing hard and rubbing his face with clenched fists as Jon spoke of clandestine government sanctioned narcotic operations and the reality of human filtration crops used in the processing of potentially lethal recreational drugs.

When his story was complete, Jon rested his forehead against a closed fist, balanced on two knuckles, staring at the shadowed floor of the dim apartment.

Sal swallowed and cleared his throat. His voice cracked slightly, yet held an unmistakable strength of conviction. "We had heard rumors of renegade high potency drug entrepreneurs throughout Asia, but nothing that seemed important enough to involve the STR.

"Black Hand ops were strictly political not economic. Yet, I suppose everything reduces to money." Sal licked his lips. "Shit. They used people?" He shook his head in disbelief. "If I didn't hear it from you, Jon, I wouldn't believe it."

"I still wonder if it really went down the way I remember it," Jon admitted. "Max and I would get together periodically and talk it over, just to make sure that we had it right. Every once in awhile we would have to reassure one another that we did the right thing, you know."

Sal nodded. He didn't immediately respond, but it was evident that he completely understood perhaps even empathized.

Eventually he asked, "So, whatever happened to this Slousad character? He ever surface?"

Jon shook his head. "Not personally, no. Though I could feel his presence in the evil that I would come to witness; sense his impact on the evolving trends in society. He was still out there—powerful and influential.

"Logan Slousad." The name carried bitterly off his lips, familiar and sour. "I continue to firmly believe that what we did was right. That, somehow, it made a difference," Jon added as much for himself as for Sal.

"Of course. Shit," Sal remarked somewhat shocked that Jon would even hesitate.

"It's just that I only doubted my motivations after the demons took my wife from me." Jon's statement hung in the air, empty and incomplete. Sal twitched and blinked looking at Jon for clarification.

"I mean, after she went down, I lost all sense of time. Of space." He stared out the window into the black void of winter's evening. Thick doily coasters of snow fluttered against the framed black squares of glass.

"Five years ago, three complete strangers entered my home and made the mistake of leaving me alive." Sal watched as Jon's face hardened and softened with each deep, shuddering breath. He allowed Jon all of the time he needed to say what needed saying.

"Well, they were strangers to me, but they were sent by someone who knew me all too well. Someone who knew my past and wanted me forever removed from the equation."

Jon wrung his hands as he continued. "I was deeply involved in an investigation of a string of high profile assassinations on the East Coast. Four very influential congressional lobbyists were hit in a highly coordinated effort that involved some of the most original and creative tactics I'd ever seen. They were executed with extreme disregard for surgical precision.

"Though they lived at the four extreme corners of New England, separated by hundreds of miles and hours of driving time, they all died brutally within minutes of one another."

He continued to work his hands, twisting them against one another in his lap. "They all could have been taken out carefully and precisely without all of the collateral damage. But someone wanted to speak and be heard."

"Kind of like our little situation here," Gionetti said carefully.

Jon nodded, pursed his lips.

"What was the connection?" Sal asked.

"The lobbyists? They made up the driving force behind the most powerful and vocal opposition to the advancement of stem cell research."

"But stem cell therapy is legal; has been for nearly two decades. What was their beef?"

"Advancement and evolution. They already conceded that stem cell therapy was a reality; and however reluctantly, they also admitted that some—even most—of the medical applications were in fact not only successful, but the closest thing to a miracle that we were likely to experience in our lifetime," Jon explained. "That was the problem. The opposition may have evolved philosophically out of ethical and religious zealousness, but it was financed by the technology and pharmaceutical communities—the same science circles that spawned the stem cell revolution in the first place."

Sal winced as he tried to comprehend the revelation. "So, the same companies that were relying on stem cell science as their cash crop were also funding the opposition?"

"Sure. Have been for years," Robert answered from across the room as he spun in his chair. He had obviously been listening to their conversation and evidently had some input.

"All during the Great Debates, while the world watched with a collective gasp, the scientific pioneers and the moral ethicists fought the deciding battle. They dueled across two decades armed with fact, faith, scientific models and religious doctrines only to finally come to the conclusion that despite what anybody really feels about anything, man will still find a way to create God in his own image," Robert explained.

"So?" Sal inquired.

"Exactly. Who cares, right? The scientists and theologians have been arguing back and forth for generations. So, let them. Any attempt to unify their views is ludicrous," Robert answered.

He took a deep breath. His hands were still now, lying folded in his lap. "Then someone finally took the time and broke it down for everyone, at least for those with the money and time to spend it.

"Orchestrate the Debates. Give the topic a good long thrashing; complete with highs and lows for both sides. Victories and defeats, revelations and rebuttals. Just like evolution versus creation. Keep everyone interested over the years, but not enough to actually care. As long as there's adequate representation for both sides, let them fight it out. And ultimately, the victor, and presumably the right and ethical position, will prevail."

"It's like the old wrestling shows," Jon added. "The WWE or whatever. Huge, gothic sagas carried out over generations. Two sides, battling against each other in well-choreographed, grappling matches. Characters switching allegiances and philosophies, even coming back from extinction or in some cases, death."

"Right," Robert agreed with a nod. "Nobody cared who won just as long as the battle raged. And when the despised villain was finally bested, everyone suddenly cheered for his eventual atonement and recommitment to rise and conquer that which defeated him. It's a screwed up metaphor for the world. But it works."

"So, the Great Debates over stem cell science were choreographed—actually madeup?" Sal asked, bewildered.

"Essentially. I mean, think about it. What better way to ensure the outcome of any fight than to control both sides. And after all of the exhaustive debating and years of testimony, when it was finally decided that the pros outweigh the cons of stem cell science, and that it will therefore be endorsed by our great leaders, well, we accepted that. After all, the greatest minds of our time toiled over the topic for nearly three decades."

"So the controversy wound down to exhaustion, and we were ready to move on. It's ingenious, really. And we bought it hook, line and sinker, once again." Jon concluded.

"What do you mean, again?" Sal asked.

"Taxes, toll booths, medically assisted suicide, therapeutic abortion, legalization of marijuana. Whatever embattled topic you want to choose. All of it highly controlled, well thought out ad campaigns. The outcomes of which were predetermined long before anyone had an opinion one way or the other."

"A little paranoid, wouldn't you say?" Sal offered, soon regretting it.

Jon bristled, then shook his head and sighed as he chewed the inside of his cheek. "Yeah, maybe. I don't know and I really don't care. It's far beyond my control anyway. And if I am paranoid, I believe I've earned that right."

"Tell me about the men whom you believe ordered the assault on you and your wife. Was it this Slousad?" Gionetti redirected the conversation away from the disorienting material of metaphysics and conspiracy theories and back to Jon's tragedy.

Robert remained perched on the wide armrest, but turned his attention to the sheaf of printed papers in his hand.

Jon took a deep breath momentarily energized by the liberating release of repressed thoughts and agonizing truths.

"No. Not directly." Jon rolled his eyes and fell back into the deep chair. "It was Aristotle Leary."

"The drug czar from the Pyramid?"

Jon nodded. "Yeah."

"How did you know?"

"The monsters that came that night were high on Synth. Crystal Symphony, to be exact. And they spoke Illuminese throughout the ordeal."

"But Jon, Symphony was huge back then, and Illuminese is as common among the Synth-heads as Chinese is to the Orient. I mean, they could've been any number of random losers out for a hyped thrill."

Jon shifted uneasily, agitated with the direction of the conversation. "You don't think that I already thought about that? That it may have been just coincidence? That Sarah was just another unfortunate victim of senseless, random violence?"

Gionetti looked at his feet embarrassed at his insensitivity. "I'm sorry, Jon. I just—"

Jon waved a hand and smiled sadly though remained visibly hurt. "No, I understand. Hard to break old habits. Logical and deductive reasoning are part of your makeup. It's what makes you who you are. I was there once, too.

"It was what they said, not how. The drug culture just triggered flashbacks to the war. Déjà vu," Jon explained. His dreary gaze wandered to the frosted window and the dancing tufts of snow outside.

He spoke softly, yet with a quiet strength that sounded at first strained, but then grew confident and resolved over the minutes.

Jon told them of the sudden and violent breech of his home, the crashing of glass and soft thump of the tranquilizer darts. He remembered aloud the waking dream that he relived each night, the hazy recollection of being drugged, bound and blindfolded. He explained the disorienting emergence from unconsciousness into the horrifying world of reality, the demonic presence of the three Synth heads babbling in their nonsensical and flamboyant tongue, the bitter fumes of smoked drug and the underlying aromas of spilled body fluids.

He repainted for them the vivid images that struck him as the blindfold was removed and he regained his full senses—his wife's limp form, sprawled across the dark hardwood floor of the study, more undressed than not, tatters and shreds of colorful cloth revealing most of a bare thigh here, a full breast there. Her pregnant belly hung lopsided and skewed as she lay on her left side, still and seemingly dead.

How he had stared at her pale exposed breast for what seemed like a lifetime, waiting for it to rise with a breath, to move in response to his frantic mental attempts to telepathically send her a motivational, lifesaving message: *Breathe, honey, just breathe. It's okay, I'm here. Just breathe. Oh God, please, just breathe. Breathe. Breathebreatheohgodbreathe.*

After what must have been eons—timeless, empty, dark ages—Sarah Webb had finally taken a shallow breath. Her beaten body had shuddered with the effort, the tight skin of her round belly wrinkled from the strain.

He tried to share with them how it felt to wait, and watch, while the monsters circled and talked and smoked and masturbated. He tried to convey the level of anger and hatred that rose from deep within as they reinjected him with the cocktail that left him physically helpless, yet cognitively aware. How they positioned him against the wall so that he could fully observe them.

He had no choice but to watch them as they reveled in the unexpected and sudden revival of Jon's unconscious and pregnant wife. He explained that the drugs caused him near complete paralysis of his extremities, yet left him hyperaware and uncontrollably euphoric. His mind had raced, disjointed, and yet was still able to focus on any and every particular detail until it cut into his memory like a crystal edged scalpel. He resisted the euphoric and hypnotic effects with all of his will, but in the end found the struggle useless.

He described for them the horrors of the serial rapes, the hours of vile and dehumanizing acts perpetrated against his young wife. Though he attempted, he fell widely short of expressing the full extent of the hot rage that boiled in him as he helplessly watched the utter breaking of Sarah.

The drugs had prevented him from even closing his eyes against the carnage.

After some time he finally, somehow, mentally disconnected and withdrew from the terror displayed before him. However, it took much longer to disconnect his sense of hearing. The sounds of the repeated ravaging persisted, despite Jon's self-induced blindness.

He explained how, when he finally awoke from his desperate cocoon, he was surprised at the amount of strength that remained in his limbs despite being chemically and physically restrained for what seemed like days. He noticed immediately that Sarah's body was missing and began crawling around the small apartment in search of her. He told them of the stains and smells he encountered as he dragged his weakened and trembling body around the four-room flat.

He told them where he finally found her and what she looked like. She was breathing shallowly and he embraced her, careful not to squeeze so hard as to accidentally cause her to cease respiring.

The medics found them like that, one day later, sprawled out on the kitchen floor lying in a pool of fetid water that collected from the open door of the defrosted refrigerator, swirled with the bloody discharge that trickled from between Sarah's legs.

Jon was taken to the hospital in a separate ambulance from Sarah, and he recalled for them his first and only coherent thought since losing awareness. He vaguely remembers thinking that they were merely taking her to the morgue, and that he would have to call her parents. He dreaded the call, not because of the subject matter but because he knew that they would blame him for the death of their only child.

It wasn't until days later, as he began to morbidly accept his new home in the critical care unit and was warming to the idea of finishing his remaining days as a resident there that he learned of Sarah's survival. He took the news numbly and offered no desire to see her. It took weeks to accept that not only was she alive, but that the fetus within her survived as well.

Once he finally understood the reality of things, he immediately began his struggle back to the land of the living, where terribly strong and dangerous emotions inhabited the shadows around every corner— emotions like love, anger, remorse, guilt, and revenge.

Guilt and revenge seemed to rule the land.

Jon finally described the weeks and months following The Incident: the hospitals and treatment centers, the diagnoses and prognoses, both damning and hopeful. He spoke of the move from east to west, and of the involvement of the Rainey Clinic. He revisited the birth of his son, Matthew, and the enrollment of Sarah into the advanced care of the specialists at the Clinic.

In the end, he told them of his return to New England to enact his revenge. How he had hunted and brutally executed the men involved. His confession was clinical and cold.

Jon shared it all with Sal and Robert, and left nothing unexposed. The facts came out clearly and smoothly as if he had waited his whole life to perform a well-written and oft rehearsed soliloquy. He talked for nearly two hours, and expecting to end exhausted and drained, he actually seemed more alive. He felt energized and more awake then he ever had.

So he folded his hands across his lap, smiled and wept.

~ * ~

Jon had finished describing, for the first time ever, the tragic and graphic events that left his life torn apart and his family imprisoned. Robert and Sal sat in somber silence, neither wanting to be the first to break the frozen moment. Jon rubbed his eyes raw with trembling hands and spoke softly through his moist fingers.

"One of you, say something, please."

Robert sighed and spoke first. He was the closest to Jon and knew some of the story before Jon revealed his scarred soul. However, even with the little previous knowledge he possessed, the complete tale left him feeling empty and numb, weighted down with a chunky mixture of shame and grief. He placed a steady hand on Jon's shoulder and squeezed.

"Man, I am so sorry. I didn't realize the extent... the violent purposefulness. Jon, I'm sorry." Jon leaned into the younger man's hand and fell into an embrace. Robert hugged his friend feverishly catching the racked sobs on his shoulder.

Sal quietly rose from his chair and walked to the twin computers at the back of the small apartment. He retrieved the bottle of scotch left there by Robert and returned to the two men. Robert had risen and was self-consciously wiping his own eyes. Jon sat stiffly in the plush chair, taking purposeful deep breaths, attempting to regain control.

Sal Gionetti handed the bottle down to Jon, uncapped and tilted slightly forward. Jon blinked at the glistening opening and slowly shook his head.

"No, thanks," he croaked.

Sal shrugged and tipped the bottle to his lips, taking half of the remaining last third in two deep gulps. He never tasted a drop. The bottle landed ungracefully, yet upright, on the scratched wood as Sal fell back into his chair, guiding the bottle in the general direction of the low coffee table. The pale brown liquid splashed up the sides of the bottle leaving filmy trails of meniscus running down the smooth glass.

"I'm finished with the force," Sal finally said. "After this, I'm done." He nodded as if to convince himself as well as the others of his decision. "I've had it. The senseless violence. The corruption. The pain and injustice. I'm through."

Jon looked up to the man seated across from him. Sal met his gaze. Moisture glazed the detective's eyes. He stared intently at Jon until, when he finally blinked, the thin trail of a single tear tracked down his left cheek.

"What you did back east," he said to Jon, "took courage and love."

Jon didn't look up, but answered softly, yet firmly. "I murdered three men out of revenge. Hunted them like animals. That's still a sin, and I suppose that I'll have to answer for it.

"Did it take courage? Love? I really don't know, Sal. I really don't know. It simply had to be done, for whatever reason. I don't feel any better as a result. Never have. I guess I thought that it would bring some balance, some sense of justice, to the overall equation. But all I ever felt was loneliness and loss for what should've been. I mourn for the potential."

"The world is better off without those animals," Robert said as he stood before the darkened window. Snow continued to swirl in the light cast through the frosted panes.

"That may be true, but in the end, does it really matter?" Jon sighed and stretched.

Thirty

Sal woke with a start, his eyes popped open with painful quickness. He was instantly aware of the kink in his neck, the beginnings of a sharp cramp in his right calf and the oily gumminess of whatever had decided to grow on the surface of his tongue overnight. He carefully unfolded himself from the fetal position and sat on the edge of the short and narrow couch.

He was still in Robert's dingy apartment, and the lights were low enough to lend a dim cast of yellow over the cluttered interior. Sal craned his head toward the window in hope to intuit the time from whatever light may exist on the outside. The overstretched muscle trembling in the side of his neck twitched, protesting the movement. He turned his whole body around in compromise. The window remained as dark as the previous evening, though the frosted black panes held no evidence of snowfall. Semi-lunar arcs of frost adorned each of the window's four corners.

"Morning. Hair of the dog?" Robert asked from the shadows as he poured a modest bolus of scotch from the abandoned bottle into a wide glass mug of coffee.

Sal shook his head, waved the offer off and softly grunted, "No thanks."

"We have a big day ahead of us, and it looks like it's just you and me," Robert said matter-of-factly.

Sal scratched his head and looked at the young man quizzically. He jerked his head from side to side, audibly cracking the vertebrae in his neck. Robert winced at the sound of the reorganizing cervical joints.

"Yeah, that's good for the posture. Good luck with that when you're sixty." Robert shook his head and sipped his coffee. He grimaced against the harsh bite of the scotch.

Then he gasped, sighed and smacked his lips theatrically. "Ah, good shit."

Sal cleared his throat. "What do you mean, just us? Where's Jon?"

"Look's like our boy found himself some purpose," Robert said into his mug as he took another sip of the spiked java. "And perhaps a hard target."

"What?"

Robert motioned to the back of the room's long interior wall, to the flat LCD of his wall-mounted multimedia center. The sound was off, but the screen was alive with the image of two figures seated behind a desk, engaged in an animated conversation.

Robert grabbed a thin remote on the side table. The screen shimmered as the resolution and brightness sharpened from dim to crisp. The audio gradually increased as well until they were watching and listening to the early morning edition of the local Mandatory Media news updates.

The news anchors spoke eloquently and with enough practiced dramatic flair to capture and retain even the most casual viewers:

"...so, despite the tense atmosphere of ongoing investigations into the shocking quadruple murders at their corporate campus, executives at Phoenix-Lamneth Enterprises remain optimistic about the future of the company's leading technological advances." The alarmingly beautiful woman on the television wrapped up her portion of the story with a smile, a seductive flip of hair and a purposeful nod toward her equally stunning male co-anchor.

The handsome young man fielded the perfectly engineered segue with a well practiced grin that suggested enough youthful innocence to render anything that he uttered as Gospel, yet carried a smirk of mischief sure to appeal to any curious and doubtful romantic.

It made Sal nauseous, the contrived and presumptuous nature by which the manufactured talking-heads so easily and so effectively affected the masses.

However, seeing the Mandatory Media logo superimposed in the lower left corner of the screen made him immediately think of Carla. The image of her natural and unrehearsed beauty aglow with fire light from the crackling hearth rose in his memory like ceaseless dawn, making liars of the product endorsing synthetic pieces of molded narcissism on the screen before him.

He relished the image for only a moment, and then was brought crashing back to reality by the breaking news ticker that ran the length of the screen along the bottom of the picture.

The male anchor droned on:

"... long known to be a strong supporter and proponent of advance stem cell techniques, Senator Dolan Douglass will not postpone his scheduled address on the future of stem cell legislation. The multimedia event, set to kick off from the spacious Main Atrium at Phoenix-Lamneth Corporate Campus, will include presentations and colorful debates from the world's leading scientists in the field of biotechnology. A reception to follow this morning's activities will include celebrities from around globe sharing their own personal experiences and success stories..."

The plain white text of the running ticker had changed to a deep violet as the content of the story shifted from the weather to breaking sensation. Sal read the streaming news intently:

> *Breaking News Facts: Officials close to the ongoing investigation of the quadruple murders at the Phoenix-Lamneth facilities in downtown LA reveal that a citywide manhunt is currently underway for Jonathan Webb—the prime and only suspect in the shocking execution-style murders of the biotechnology company's top scientists. Webb was the head of security at the company's corporate campus and was highly regarded as one of the best in his field. However, after a tragic accident left his wife brain dead and comatose, Webb became reclusive and paranoid...*

A small square of scrambled pixels materialized in the lower right corner of the screen as the ticker continued to run its streaming string of lies. Sal stared in anger and awe, mouth agape as the shimmering waves of dancing pixels organized themselves into a crisp digital photo of Jon Webb. It showed a stern, chiseled face, the requisite hard stare of a soldier. It was an enhanced picture from Jon's military file, complete with the dark blue beret of the Special Rangers Battalion canted at a severe angle atop his shaved head.

The photo achieved its purpose and depicted Jon as a cold and calculating killer, a professional warrior. Small lines of information typed themselves out in bright yellow text across the photo—Jon's demographic data to include height, weight, eye and hair color, distinguishing markings, all marched out on the flat screen in unmistakable digital clarity.

Jon's physical attributes gave way to his military accomplishments: awards, decorations and campaigns. Then his police history printed out next, complete with types and amounts of arrests, shootings involving suspects, successful and failed investigations. It was both amazing and appalling the level of detail and amount of work put into the presentation. However disturbing to Sal, though, the effort achieved its purpose and painted the desired image of an emotionally unstable, very dangerous man with an extensively violent history.

"They're prosecuting him on live TV," Sal said to nobody in particular. He continued to watch as the live anchors droned on about the reception and the senator's self-hype circus.

"...the senator's admittedly favorite movie star also shares his appreciation for the four star chef's culinary creations. So at the Oscar winner's request, and as a last minute addition to the already loaded menu, Chef Bounteaux will make a guest appearance at the head table, whipping up what he calls 'impromptu heaven'." The young male co-anchor paused as a pasty smile spread across his face.

On cue, the scene faded to an interior shot of a busy industrial kitchen. An extremely fat and pompous looking man in requisite chef's attire began speaking, flamboyantly waving his arms and rolling his eyes. Sal turned to Robert.

"They're serving him up for a slaughter."

Robert nodded solemnly. "Yeah.

"Where is he?" Sal repeated his earlier inquiry looking about the small apartment.

"Don't know," Robert offered. "He was gone when I woke up. I fell asleep at the wheel." He motioned back toward the twin computers humming at the back of the room. "I was running some searches and put my head down for a quick rest. Must have fallen out for a while. When I woke up, he was gone."

Robert raised his eyebrows and gestured with his hands fanning them open. "Along with some of the printed results of my searches."

Sal looked at Robert impatiently and spread his hands. "And?"

"I reprinted the results and, like I said, I think he made a connection. I think he went there." Robert pointed at the TV screen where the talking news models were back.

The small photo of Jon was gone and the scores from the most recent football games were projected in its place. The constant ticker that ran below the jabbering news anchors now elaborated on Senator Dolan Douglass's historical presentation at Phoenix-Lamneth:

> *...in the history of the corporation's long-standing relationship with the Senate Steering Committee on the advancement of stem cell therapies. Senator Douglass's opening remarks are scheduled to begin at 10:00 this morning. The address promises to "recapture the world's attention and illuminate a fresh and wondrous path down which the future of neurology and behavioral science will travel hand in hand." The actual content of the Senator's address is being kept highly guarded; however, sources close to the chairman and founder of the Committee on Stem Cell Advocacy affirm that the Senator will "once again take a bold step to the forefront of biotechnology and blaze exciting trails toward the brave new future of stem cell advancements." Details are vague, but experts have suggested that Senator Douglass may have the inside scoop on some revolutionary technology that may forever change the face of stem cell science...*

"What? He went back to Phoenix?" Sal asked.

"He went to find Douglass," Robert affirmed.

"Why?"

Robert handed Gionetti three pages of tightly compressed text. Sal flicked the small paper clip off with a fingernail and leafed through the pages. They contained lines and lines of jumbled nonsense, groups of letters and what appeared to be foreign words separated by uneven spaces.

"What's this?"

"Anagrams."

Gionetti simply looked at the pages and shook his head.

"Anagrams are alternate words made from the same letters of one word. You know, 'stop', 'pots', and 'spot'," Robert explained.

"Yeah, okay?" Sal was growing impatient, edgy.

"On a whim, I ran a GlobalMeta search on the names from Jon's past. After his story last night, I got to thinking that Logan Slousad and Aristotle Leary were probably aliases."

Sal nodded cueing Robert to elucidate.

"Anyway, I figured Aristotle Leary was obviously contrived, and as I expected, all I got were the obvious references to the ancient philosopher and Dr. Timothy Leary—the LSD pioneer of the nineteen-sixties. Creative, but not stunningly original."

"And Slousad?"

"Well, I got nothing. At least not directly. What I did get, far down in the search string, was a site for creating and solving anagram puzzles. It was some grad student's homepage for brain teasers and cerebral exercises. I think the search hit on it only because of the sing-song rhythm of the syllables; 'Log-an Slou-sad'." Robert shrugged.

"Anyway, I hit the site, more out of curiosity than anything, and typed out the name. Hit the solve tab and seconds later I get this." He tapped the three pages.

Sal looked up at him, then down at the dense text:

landsggolasalsadogladglgoalgnslogandg.

On and on, line for line, endlessly.

He shook his head again and rubbed his eyes. "Robert, it's gibberish. It looks like a word search puzzle."

"Yeah, I know. I messed up. When I printed it off I accidentally hit a prompt that formatted it into just that, a word search puzzle. Up, down, diagonal, backward. All that." Robert sighed apologetically. Sal eyed him scornfully.

"But, here, look." He reached over and flipped to the next and last pages.

There, among the compact text of seemingly jumbled letters, highlighted and underlined by the computer, were the hidden words running up, down, diagonally throughout the page.

"I found the solve tab for my inadvertently created puzzle. Once I solved the word search, we can see all of the full and partial anagrams for Logan Slousad. To include proper names."

Now Sal could see highlighted across the page:

salad...land...go...salsa...glad...goal...slogan...gals...dan...

Robert nodded and pointed to one particular word on page two, and then flipped to page three and indicated a second. The first read left to right on a downward diagonal:

nolan

Sal narrowed his eyes. The second word ran right to left on an upward diagonal and was therefore harder to interpret until Robert traced it out for Sal: *salguod* read *douglas* when Robert dragged his finger backwards across the page.

He stopped and looked quietly at Sal anticipating both astonishment and enlightenment.

There was none.

Sal continued to stare at the puzzles, alternately flipping back and forth between the two pages. He frowned as he silently mouthed the two words: Douglas... Nolan...

Robert watched the detective work through the mystery, softly whispering the words and rocking his body in rhythm to the words: douglas... nolan... douglas...

"Oh, shit!" Gionetti suddenly hit on the connection just as the female news anchor spoke the name:

"...Senator Dolan Douglass now at the Hyatt Excalibur, downtown. Nancy?"

The video feed disintegrated and quickly reformed showing the opulent dining room of the posh hotel behind a tall, attractive Latin American reporter demurely making adjustments to a tiny throat mic situated in the hollow at the base of her neck.

The camera smoothly pulled back on cue and showed an equally tall, well-dressed man with sharp narrow features and close-cropped snow-white hair.

"Thank you, Elish. Nancy Feugo here, live from the elegant breakfast buffet at the grand Hyatt Excalibur. With me and equally as elegant, as always, is Senator Dolan Douglass. Senator?"

"Why, thank you, Nance. Standing next to you would make any man look more appealing." He smiled, confidently, and placed a hand on the reporter's shoulder. Nancy blushed on cue and batted her fake eyelashes.

Sal looked at Robert wide-eyed, uncertain. "Dolan Douglass?" he repeated.

"Yep," Robert answered.

"Pretty weak."

"Maybe. But Jon thought it strong enough. He took the original solution and bolted."

"Dolan Douglass. Logan Slousad?" Sal asked himself aloud, rolling it around his mouth, exercising the possibility.

~ * ~

The stifling sense of déjà vu persisted despite the difference in his attire and motivation for being there. The last time he stood in this room had been some time ago; and he had been dressed in a nondescript, off the rack, charcoal gray suit complete with deep hidden pockets that concealed his two standard weapons—a 15mm Heston AutoMag and mini plasma Fasor, a set of slidelock cuffs and the small digcom transceiver that fed a hair thin wire into the earpiece wedged in his left ear.

He remembered standing at the periphery of the great reception hall like it happened yesterday, serenely scanning the crowd for signs of mischief or confrontation allowing his presence to be felt, yet not actually seen.

And so it was, that nearly a year ago, he'd found himself in charge of that security detail—standing semi-rigid, hands clasped behind his back, gently rocking back and forth, heel to toe—watching the well-dressed guests wander about the elegant ice sculptures; greeting and groping one another for the better part of the afternoon.

It was the exact same day that he had recalled just recently at the Rainey Clinic—struggling for clarity during that moment of nagging revelation when he last saw his son, Matthew, playing in the observation room.

Now, of course, he wore a uniform very different from that poor fitting suit, and although the thin linen fabric pulled tight across his broad shoulders and the pants rode up short enough to expose his unmatched socks, he felt that he blended well enough with the rest of the wait staff. The poor bartender from whom he "borrowed" the attire was significantly smaller than Jon, but was the largest of the staff that he spied as he entered the back of the kitchen over an hour ago.

Presently, Jon was topping off a tray of crystal champagne flutes with pale Mimosa. With a teal-colored linen cloth draped over one arm, he hoisted the oval tray shakily to waist height. He paused a moment to test the balance of the tray, and then with dramatic and effeminate flair he flipped the locks of the false bangs out of his face, scrunched up his nose to reposition the fake wire-rimmed spectacles and primly sauntered out of the bar and into the growing crowd.

Breaking back into Phoenix-Lamneth proper was going to prove to be impossible, but Jon knew that if he were able to infiltrate the reception staff, he might have a chance at getting close to his target in the Atrium. Though he didn't exactly have a plan and wasn't sure he trusted himself or his emotions when, and if, the opportunity actually presented itself, he knew instinctively that he needed to get to Senator Douglass.

Operating on pure instinct from the moment he'd made the connection at Robert's; Jon slipped past the security net at its loosest point. Paying two street junkies to create a diversion at the loading bay of the campus kitchens, Jon eased into the shadows behind the four security agents stationed there as they responded to the curious commotion of the two naked vagrants.

Once within the back rooms of the catering services, Jon quickly worked to fit in with the hustling drones laboring to bring about a successful reception. From carrying boxes of fresh fruit to assisting with a sudden plumbing emergency, Jonathan Webb easily and smoothly worked alongside the men and women behind the scenes, chatting up talkative gossips, joking and complaining like any other hourly blue-collar employee asked to work the special event. All the while, he observed and waited for a window of opportunity.

When he finally saw the tall bartender primping in the men's locker room, dusting his gaunt face with foundation makeup and affixing eyeliner, Jon knew he had found his Trojan horse, so to speak.

The bartender went down too easily, and would not regain consciousness for hours. In fact, Jon was initially worried that he may have inadvertently killed the man, until his slow deep respirations confirmed his physical resolve.

With the aid of many cosmetic enhancements borrowed from the bartender's locker, Jon transformed himself into a passable, if not overly flamboyant, waiter. One quick self-assessment in the full-length mirror confirmed his metamorphosis; the only glaring fault lay in the ill-fitting cotton white uniform. But with an adequate amount of character play and attitude, Jon felt confident that the discrepancy would lend credibility to his colorful portrayal of an eccentric struggling actor/waiter.

He began working his way around the great room counter-clockwise, avoiding collisions with careless guests, pausing here and there as a disembodied hand blindly exchanged an empty glass for a fresh one from his teetering tray. As he had hoped, no one paid him any mind, ignoring his existence as one would a piece of furniture or the members of the string quartet tucked into the far corner who played just above the level of human auditory perception.

Jon was observant and made mental notes of the positions of all of the security agents stationed throughout the room. In the aftermath of the murders, there were many and their presence was anything but unobtrusive—large, ugly, poorly dressed men with equally large bulges in their jackets.

He counted twenty, and he had only made it halfway around the room. All were strangers to Jon. He didn't recognize any of the young faces as being from the security forces that he had, once upon-a-time ago, trained and led. Apparently, they dismissed Phoenix-Lamneth's security personnel, opting instead for the Senator's own chiseled walking slabs of granite.

His beverage tray was empty by the time he saw Max Donovan.

Jon's breath caught in his throat, and he instantly ducked behind the nearest couple, roughly bumping the lady and splashing a few drops of Mimosa from the tall crystal flute pinched between her gaudily manicured, bird-like talons. He met her glare of indignation with an equally pompous arching of his brows and a dramatic, "Madam, your pardon?"

She gasped and stammered as she searched for the most appropriate insult, turning to her male acquaintance for assistance. However, he was momentarily distracted by something apparently hanging from Jon's face. It wasn't until the man offered a sly, sensuous smile that Jon realized he was being hit on.

He returned the man's smile with a quick nod that he hoped was both apologetic and dismissive. The last thing he needed was to stick out from the rest of the staff, to strike a staying image with anyone. He deftly maneuvered out of the couple's space, the woman clicked and sucked her tongue in a condescendingly punitive fashion; the man's stare bore into Jon's back.

His instinct reminded him to play it cool and to continue to act as if he owned the place, like he belonged. Yet, he was paranoid that Max would turn and their eyes would lock; and that, for a moment, all time would grind to a halt.

Then the glint of pistols would flash, and it would be over in a millisecond.

Jon eased his way back to the kitchen as if he was the senior waiter on staff, excusing himself between groups and nodding casually at fellow wait staff. He returned to the bar and began the task of replacing the used champagne flutes.

He needed a plan and needed one fast.

Thirty-one

"Right. I see you now. Yeah, okay. On your cue. Thanks." Sal thumbed the "end" button on his PDD terminating the short call as he pocketed the thin device.

He turned casually over his shoulder and spoke to Robert in a near whisper, "Just follow my lead and nod. Look arrogant and pissed off, but don't say a word."

Robert nodded and stiffened up a bit, tugging at his suit jacket and adjusting his tie.

The two men allowed the flow of bodies to carry them toward the narrowing entryway ahead as the river of people ebbed with organic rhythm. Three across and tens deep, the ribbon of well-dressed humanity pressed upon the glass-walled partitions and velvet ropes of the security controlled entrance into the atrium of the Phoenix-Lamneth Corporate Campus.

At least ten security officers were visible, manning the stationary infrared and fluoroscopy scanners at the head of the line, visually and physically inspecting each guest as they squeezed through the narrow aisle created at the point of entry. Digital photo ID's were compared with computer generated guest lists, and then verified by the security watchdogs. The invited were granted entrance only after submitting to a complete physio-scan.

Sal Gionetti anticipated the beefed-up security, and in fact, expected much worse in light of the recent murders. However, it appeared that Barrett Lacombe wasn't going to cave into the intimidation tactics and be pressured into paranoia by any adversary.

Regardless of the depth of security measures facing them, Sal was certain that, after his actions the previous night, his police credentials were going to be flagged. He and Robert were sure to be apprehended the moment he flashed his badge. Therefore, he figured on having just one legitimate shot at getting the two of them into the Senator's reception uninvited.

And it was an extremely long shot, predicated on the ever-narrowing odds that someone didn't recognize his face. He hadn't shaved in two days, but the dense, ashy stubble on his face and neck was a thin disguise, at best.

Sal gently guided Robert by the loose tails of his flapping coat, ensuring that the young man remained close as they bobbed and jostled through the knotted throng of Armani, Giovencia, Klein and Lauren. The wealth and opulence of the crowd rode on the overpowering mixture of rich perfumes and colognes, announcing the prestige and exclusivity of its members like the collective musk of a herd.

Sal still wore his cracked, black leather overcoat covering a torn and soiled linen jacket and shirt—unchanged for nearly three days. Robert fared only slightly better, sporting a light gray cotton jacket over cream dress shirt, dark navy pants and a shabby, wrinkled yellow and blue striped tie.

They both stood out from the primly tailored and professionally coifed mob, and that was as Sal had hoped. They looked exactly like the haggard street police officers that most people expected, with small badges dangling from thin silver chains around their necks to complete the illusion.

With a mumbled "excuse me" here and whispered "pardon" there, Sal and Robert wove through the masses toward the bottleneck of the security point. Two of the officers immediately took notice of the approaching men and nodded to one another. When they were within about ten meters, the taller of the two raised his chin and eyebrows, making eye contact with Sal and offered a questioning nod—universally accepted by any member of law enforcement as "what the fuck?"

Sal recognized the unspoken inquiry and with a well-acted grimace of impatience, flicked the corner of his suspended badge, sending it spinning on the chain—a purposeful act in hope to prevent the security agent from getting a good look. Sal was hoping half-heartedly on the predictable behavior of most fellow uniforms to extend a casual professional courtesy and wave them through on the assumption that they must have official business inside, as if any official looking badge instantly granted the bearer unconditional access anywhere.

That's what Sal had hoped for, anyway.

The taller of the uniformed agents bit his lip and stretched up on his toes, trying to get a better glimpse at both men and their ID's. He frowned in frustration and waved them forward impatiently. He wanted them right in front of him. He wasn't going lax, not today.

Sal hesitated and glanced at Robert, whose eyes belayed his unease, widening with concern and apprehension. Sal shook his head imperceptibly and whispered through partially closed lips.

"If this goes bad, don't run. Just melt into the crowd and work your way back to the doors. If you panic, in this crowd, you're dead. Okay?" Robert nodded and swallowed hard. He sighed and worked back into his impatient and frustrated scowl.

Sal slowly carved a path across the width of the crowd. Robert glided in his wake. They approached the security agent much sooner than he had hoped, and Sal was suddenly wondering if this would be the end of their short-lived quest.

The taller security officer had turned for a brief moment to answer one of his men, and in that second, Sal reached over and flipped Robert's ID around, concealing his deceased partner's photo from direct view. The man turned back to face Sal and Robert. He eyed them each for a full second and then asked, "What's up, gentlemen? All of the externally assigned boys should've been admitted through the back. What brings you guys to the front?" His face was stone, hard and stern with clear orders and the obvious authority to carry them out.

Sal was about to formulate a weakly evolving lie when his insurance policy kicked in.

"Detective Boyle! Hey, detective! Over here!" Carla Robinson's distinctively rich voice carried over the din of the mumbling chatter of the crowd. "Oh, there he is, Al. Detective Boyle! Over here," she hollered again.

She was gracefully jogging toward the security blockade from the inside of the elegant atrium hall. A cameraman and assistant were in tow, dragging equipment and coats with them. As she approached the security officers, they stared in awe, obviously star struck.

She smiled innocently, yet with just the right air of confidence to fell the men silent by both her beauty and fame.

"Carla Robinson, Mandatory Media." She gently held her press credentials high for the security boys to inspect. Her hand was steady, yet the men never glanced at her laminated holographic ID. Instead they simply softened in the warmth of her presence.

"Yes, ma'am, I know," was the best that the tall security officer could muster in response. He smiled wide and dumb, and actually extended his hand toward her. Carla seized the man's hand in her own, pumping it twice, and then allowing it to linger in his sweaty grasp just long enough to warm both his palm and his hopeful fancy.

She returned his smile with her own glorious, shining eyes. She held the tall agent's gaze for a seductive moment, and then turned to Sal. "We spoke earlier. Thank you for making it on such short notice." Sal simply nodded, secretly and pleasantly amazed at her resourcefulness and skill.

"Officer..." She glanced warmly at the man's name badge, and then recaptured his wide stare. "...Clayton. I asked Detective Boyle and his partner—" She quickly, yet confidently looked toward Robert for a name. Sal interjected seamlessly.

"White," he offered. Robert simply nodded feigning boredom.

"Detectives Boyle and White to meet me here for an exclusive interview. Off the record, of course." She smiled at everyone, allowing the small bit of self-depreciating humor to win over the rest of the celebrity-curious onlookers around them. Quiet murmurs were already spreading through the crowd of people about the presence of the award-winning news anchor before them.

Security agent Clayton glanced at Sal and Robert. A slight furrow creased his brow as he processed the moment, confused by the conflict between his innate reaction to a celebrity close-encounter and his training. As he appeared to mentally reorganize his priorities, Carla seized the opportunity to press the issue and secure a successful breach.

"The detectives are experts in counter-covert operations, and with the elaborate security that you and your men have established here, well... let's just say that I'm proud to inform you that you have passed a very stringent test." Carla smiled and reached out to give the security agent's arm a gentle congratulatory squeeze.

He blinked twice and gaped at her, puzzled.

"You see, Officer Clayton. We, as a public, have been concerned about many aspects of our safety and protection. Especially in light of recent events." She paused and gazed down theatrically, allowing the unspoken obvious to fill the dramatic void. "So, at the behest of Mr. Lacombe himself..." She again paused allowing the name to fulfill its natural impact.

Man, thought Sal. *She is good!*

"We carried out a little experiment of our own. Detectives Boyle and White attempted to infiltrate your perimeter multiple times this morning, testing the effectiveness of the security. And, well, detective?" Carla swung her gaze to Sal, opening the door for him.

"Yes, well, Officer Clayton, you guys have done one hell of a job." Sal suddenly swelled with confidence as he saw the agent's face aglow flush with pride.

"We couldn't find a single weakness from the outside. You really should take pride in your efforts here. All of you." Sal raised his voice so that all of the agents could benefit from their charade.

Suddenly, impromptu applause erupted behind them as those in the crowd that were within ear shot of the exchange felt the need to express their gratitude. Carla cemented the deal, demurely clapping her well-manicured hands. Even the cameramen behind her joined in. The security guards all smiled and blushed in appreciation. After a moment, Sal straightened up and addressed the taller agent in a false baritone of caution.

"Though, now is not the time to get complacent, Officer Clayton. Let's get back to work." Sal glared comically, and then smiled wide as he added, "Nice work, gentlemen." Clayton sighed and smiled.

"Yes, sir," he stammered.

Carla turned to Clayton and spoke, quickly and matter-of-factly. "I'd like to get the detective's briefing recorded. I was thinking over there, just out of sight from the entrance." She indicated toward a small alcove well within the interior of the atrium.

"That way your men can continue their outstanding work while we finish up our piece. Al?" She called over to her cameraman, who leaned in. "What do think about setting up with an angle that captures Officer Clayton working the entrance in the background?"

Al nodded absently and mumbled, "Yeah, sure."

Carla smiled. "Great. And I'd like a quick sound-byte or two from Officer Clayton as well, when he's through. If that's all right?" She looked to Clayton who appeared to be stunned at the prospect of being interviewed.

She grinned one last time and reached for Sal's hand. Gionetti accepted just as Clayton reached over and escorted both Robert and Sal through the security barriers. They moved quickly into the interior of the atrium hall, bypassing all of the scanners, the curious gazes from the crowd following them.

The sternness returned to Clayton's face with a renewed zeal as he moved to the front of the security checkpoint with an inflated swagger.

"All right folks, easy now. One at a time. That's it." His voice carried the firm and confident meter of control and authority as it echoed off the high ceilings and deep walls behind them.

Carla quickly and efficiently led them into the shadows of the interior hall, breathing rapidly from the tension. Robert's wide-eyed gaze jumped from Carla to Sal and back.

"That was slick!" he exclaimed.

Sal nodded in agreement. "Yeah, very nice."

He smiled at Carla, openly impressed. She winked and gave a nonchalant little shrug.

"Well, it's not like it's the first time. The guy's a Neanderthal, after all." She grimaced slightly.

The cameraman was readjusting his backpack power supply and the shoulder supported digital vidgraph as he eased his way into the small alcove. "So, where you want to set up? I mean for the angle that you want. We really should think about moving—"

"Al? Al," Carla interrupted calmly yet firmly raising her hand and stopping the man in mid-thought.

She nodded back toward the security station, flipping her wavy hair across her dark brow. "That was a ruse, Al. What I really need is a prime setup in the main reception center. I want the best shot of the Senator when he strides out to the podium. And keep a wide angle on the background activity behind him. There are going to be some surprise guests at this morning's festivities."

Al simply nodded and muttered something that sounded like an affirmation as he gathered his coat and loose equipment and moved lethargically out into the hall toward the main reception area. The young assistant followed close behind, burdened with heavy coats and additional duffel bags of equipment.

Carla turned to Sal and Robert and sighed as she ran long fingers through her hair. Sal couldn't help but stare at her, the way her slender fingers combed the thick dark locks away from her angular face. Her eyes sparkled despite the seriousness of her face.

"This is where it starts, detective. Right in here." She gestured around them with the graceful arc of her slender arm. Sal followed the hypnotic movement, captivated by the smoothness of her skin and the faint scent that wafted on the breeze created by her sweeping arm. "I've learned a great deal since we last spoke and it chills me to the bone," she continued.

"What?" Sal asked simply.

She shook her head reaching for his hand. "Not now. First, come with me."

~ * ~

Securing a weapon was the easy part. It was concealing the body afterward that was giving him fits. When Jon finally finished struggling with the unconscious six-foot, one hundred-twenty kilogram security agent—wedging his thick, flaccid frame between the cool bowl of the toilet and the brushed aluminum of the stall door—the thin layer of makeup used to aid in Jon's disguise was smeared with sweat and running in small rivulets across his cheeks and down his neck.

He quickly checked his reflection in the mirror, carefully blending what remained of the flesh-toned cosmetic powder into his face, evening out the color and drying his moist skin with a tissue. He pinched the wire frames of the spectacles across the high bridge of his nose with his left hand as he readjusted the weight of the silencer-equipped mag-pistol with his right, pressing the cool steel deep within the waistband of his pants.

After short, yet careful consideration, he decided to lose the hair extensions woven into his bangs. He plucked the bundled strands of hairs from his brow and flicked them into the urinal on his right. He glanced back into the mirror, checking on the closed bathroom stall behind him. It was outfitted with a full-height door, extending from the top of the chrome-framed jamb completely to the floor. When closed, nothing could be seen, especially the tangled legs of the beaten and unconscious man slumped on the floor inside.

Now, armed with the agent's weapon, Jon casually strolled out of the john and back into the hall that led into the main reception area. He moved gracefully through the smaller groups and navigated wide around larger as he worked toward the tables situated to the right of the draped podium.

Thick cables ran from the back wall and snaked beneath the cream-colored canvas curtain that concealed the multi-tiered lectern and podium. It would be from here that Senator Dolan Douglas—Logan Slousad—would address the gathering crowd.

Jon glanced at the magnificent crystal-faced clock on the back wall of the main hall. He had thirty minutes to devise a sensible and trustworthy plan. Up to this point, everything he'd done was based on pure instinct.

Survival.

He felt that he knew, ultimately, what he would have to do, but couldn't bring the thought forward in his mind and solidify it into a concrete nugget of awareness.

Perhaps to do so would cause him to hesitate and fail to act. He could not afford to lose the sharp edge, the keen clarity of cause and effect. No consequences existed now; only acts. Action defined the moment, and the moment only lasted for precisely that.

A moment.

~ * ~

"Read this."

She handed him a single page of double spaced text. Sal perused the document, then swallowed and reread it, slower. After a long minute's hesitation, he handed it to Robert without looking.

"What is it?" Robert asked even as he began to read it for himself.

"A press release," Carla explained. "I get an advanced copy before the actual address. It allows me to formulate pertinent and appropriate questions for the Q and A. The understanding is that I keep the facts to myself until they're officially announced, and in return, I get the scoop and the first three questions including an exclusive afterwards."

She frowned and flicked the corner of the page.

Robert held the sheet tightly pinched between his thumb and forefinger as he read.

"This is huge," she said.

"What does it mean?" Sal asked. His brow furrowed as he shook his head.

"It means," Carla began, "that we may be in way over our heads." She rolled her eyes and puffed out her cheeks in an exhausted sigh.

"It's a fucking coup!" Robert exclaimed after digesting the release.

"No, it's a buyout," Carla answered attempting for perspective. "A well-timed acquisition."

Sal's eyes fogged as the mental wheels began to turn.

"Why Douglass?" Robert asked lifting his head from the page. "I mean, why does he make the announcement that Polar Innovations is taking over Phoenix-Lamneth?"

Carla raised a finger, her lips slowly pulled into a gentle, revelational smile. "Ah, Douglass is only facilitating the announcement. The actual announcement will be made by none other than Wyatt Cronus himself."

Sal and Robert both looked at Carla with a mixture of amazement and disbelief. The reclusive founder and CEO of the runaway technological juggernaut, Polar Innovations, had never before been seen in public.

Ever.

What began as a sly marketing ploy during the company's infancy evolved into one of the industry's most incontrovertible laws of nature: Wyatt Cronus, the silent creative genius behind the most earth shattering and revolutionary breakthroughs to occur during the short history of man, would forever remain an invisible mystery.

The man was a powerful, influential specter. Even his official biography was vague and elusive, shadowed by subtle anecdotes, veiled with harmless and constructive innuendo. No one actually knew the man. He was an enigma.

Apparently — until now.

"How do you know?" Robert asked. "The man is a ghost, for Christ sake. I doubt that he ever even existed to be honest."

She smiled slyly raising her eyebrows. "Insider's privileged information. Trust me. It's for real, and it's happening right here. Today."

"What's Douglass's connection?" Sal asked.

She bit her lip and hesitated; then she glanced at both men as she spoke slowly and evenly. "I took the liberty of cashing in a few favors, and in return was able to glance under a few sacred stones. I could only look, mind you. No hard evidence." She eyed Sal warily. He nodded and assured her with a faint smile.

"Your word is good enough, Carla," he said.

"I got a clean look at Senator Douglass' investment portfolio," she said. "It's huge and very diverse."

Robert leaned back and looked at Sal. They exchanged curious glances and turned questioning eyes back to Carla.

"I have low friends in high places," she explained with a slight shrug. "Anyway, what was interesting is that he's the majority shareholder for an acquisitions and investment firm called Logan Enterprises."

Sal flinched at the name, and Robert audibly gasped. Carla halted and considered the men's strange reaction.

"What? Does that mean something?" she asked looking from one to the other.

The two men exchanged solemn glances and then nodded.

"Yeah, later." Sal pin wheeled his hand indicating for her to proceed. She eyed them both suspiciously and then continued.

"Well, this Logan Enterprises deals in everything from pharmaceuticals to energy. It's a very active account. Constantly trading and moving up and down the board. It looks exactly like it's supposed to—a legitimate, though aggressive, investment tool. He has financed both of his major campaigns with dividends from Logan accounts. The Trade Commission and Sovereign Ethics Consulate have kept a watchful eye on the firm as they do all politically active investors.

"It's squeaky clean. No misappropriation. No ghost payroll. All taxes paid up in full and on time."

"So?"

"So." She licked her lips with a quick, moist jab. "Among its many holdings, Logan Enterprises owns significant shares of both Polar Innovations and Phoenix-Lamneth. The firm sponsors two representatives on each of the corporations' research funding boards and maintains a minority presence on both executive boards."

She paused with a touch of dramatic eloquence before dropping the bomb.

"Guess who cashed in their Phoenix-Lamneth membership-only card and liquidated everything?" She arched one eyebrow, the answer obvious.

Then she added the kicker. "Exactly one hour before the closing bell on the eve of the media leak about the quadruple homicide." She pursed her lips together and waited.

"Ho-lee shit," Robert whispered.

Sal stood frozen staring into the glare of the crystal chandeliers overhead.

"It gets better," she added. "Or worse, depending."

She took a deep breath and continued, "The leak about the murders and Webb's being a prime suspect didn't originate from MacDonald's or Lacombe's office. In fact, it didn't come from here at all."

She reached over, grabbed Sal's arm in a firm grasp and waited until he looked down at her. When their eyes finally met, she finished.

"Three sources provided the material for the initial story, all supposedly anonymous tips from inside the company. They landed on the network's homepage postings via a series of secure MetaWeb strings. Fairly common practice.

"One of my low friends, a brilliant digital wizard—you'd like him, Robert—did me a favor and traced the strings back. I don't know how, but I trust him."

Robert nodded indicating that not only was it possible, but probably fairly easy.

"Anyway, he traced the postings back to their origin," She said. Robert waited while Sal cringed expecting to hear what he now feared.

"Two of the postings came from a mobile station situated somewhere in Washington D.C. But the third and most damning—the posting that named Webb as the prime suspect—came from deep in the heart of the Orient. Hong Kong, China. An optical chip processing plant called Demeter Scientific.

"Guess who has controlling majority ownership of Demeter?"

"Logan Enterprises," Sal answered speaking into his hands as he rubbed his face.

"Logan Enterprises," she repeated nodding slowly.

All three of them stood silently and pondered the implications of Carla's revelations. When considered with what they already knew, Senator Douglass' involvement seemed all too obvious.

But what to do next?

Sal was just about to ask exactly that when Carla's young assistant jogged into the vacant corridor from the reception area. He slid to a halt and whistled a two-note call for their attention.

"Hey, five minutes to show time in here, guys." He waited wide-eyed and expectantly for a response. When after a few seconds he received none, he turned on his heels with an apathetic shrug and dove back into the reception hall.

The atmospheric music from the quartet that floated out of the main atrium all morning had stopped, leaving a pregnant void, heavy with anticipation. Muted conversations and occasional laughs could be heard drifting from within the immense reception hall.

White-jacketed waiters and short-skirted cocktail waitresses moved expediently through the crowd, sweeping away half-finished drinks and discarded hors d'oeuvre napkins.

Carla broke the silence with a shake of her head and a quick directive. "Okay, I gotta run. There's much more to discuss, but for now, we should keep this low and unknown. Yes?"

Both men nodded.

Sal finally asked, "What are you planning to do with the information that you have? I mean, are you going to confront him? Today?"

Carla's grin was both mischievous and sorrowful. She brought her hands together and folded her slender fingers as if in prayer. "I honestly don't know. Of course, I want to, but there may be more to learn from just waiting and seeing what evolves. Either way, I want to be fully prepared."

"I think that's best. We can't let our emotions dictate our actions," Sal said. "We need to find Webb before he does something dangerously stupid."

With that they turned and walked toward the crowd and the historical announcement only moments away. As they walked, Carla quickly shared the rest of what she had discovered with the men.

~ * ~

Tucked low into the recessed cutout of the back wall behind a small bar, Jon found seclusion among the shadows. The anxious crowd had begun to filter down onto the main floor of the reception hall in efforts to gain a good view of the central podium for the address. Most of the patrons were already speaking animatedly about the Senator's classically renowned oratory style. Anyone who had ever heard the man speak publicly wanted to be up front and center. He had an endearing way of capturing his audience with his hypnotic eye contact; and his dynamic invasion of personal space was an inexplicably welcome seduction.

His speeches were the stuff of historical prose, peppered with catchy one-liners that found themselves embedded in the popular vernacular for years to follow. Often quoted for the mere dramatic quality of his presentation and the eloquence of his words, Dolan Douglass thrived in the arena of public speaking.

Four years earlier, after he had narrowly lost a hotly contested race for his party's nomination for the remaining seat in the Legislative Directorate of the Continental Alliance, his concession speech stole the show during the post election media swarm. His articulate and impassioned monologue swept the people off their feet with its emotion and honesty, so that even in defeat, Dolan Douglass emerged as a humble and graceful champion. Even his victorious rival was reduced to embarrassing tears by the poetic skills and verbal manipulation of such a talented and precise orator.

Jon remained shrouded in the gray shadows of the empty bar at the periphery of the reception hall. The main floor was below, with a short run of stairs leading from the elevated mezzanine. Here and there, small clusters of men and women were finding their way down the carpeted steps from the bars, tables and private lounges and onto the ever increasingly crowded main level. They slowly pushed toward the lectern, anxiously awaiting the Senator's arrival.

Jon brushed the cold metal of the pistol in his waistband and quickly reassessed his options. He wasn't entirely sure what he planned to do; though placing a highly charged magnetic round into the soft spongy tissue of the Senator's brain was certainly at the top of his very short list.

But he lacked any suitable escape plan after the act, and he wasn't suicidal.

Not quite. Not yet.

He wanted to confront the man, needed to get answers to the questions that devoured him. He knew that Douglass and Slousad were one and the same, yet he couldn't wrap his mind around the implications of the coincidence. He felt some significance lurking just beyond his grasp, yet he couldn't separate the rational from the emotional. He simply couldn't forget the Pyramid and the vamping conspiracy.

And now, somehow—impossibly—Logan-Dolan Douglass-Slousad was back in Webb's life. To whatever degree the Senator was involved with the Phoenix-Lamneth murders and the mysterious events transpiring around him, Webb was certain that it all came back to *Bacchus Plateau* and the human tragedy he experienced there.

A bizarre self-fulfilling prophecy was spinning out the last threads of circumstance, weaving a web of inconceivable coincidences into a coherent tapestry of fate. His past had come full circle with his present; and his future—like all of mankind—was entirely, frighteningly, uncertain.

The thrumming bass of the opening notes of the Federation's Unity Anthem began to vibrate throughout the hall. The mass of people in attendance became instantly energized, bobbing and weaving to the hypnotic rhythm. Proud imperial smiles spread across many of the faces. From a well-concealed, high quality sound system, a man's deep baritone spoke over the crescendo of synthesized music.

"Ladies and Gentlemen, Brothers and Sisters. Please honor our great nation and all of its subsidiaries under the International Unification of Alliances with your dedicated silence as we play our Unity Anthem."

A number of cheers rose out of the crowd, accompanied by a few shrill whistles as the music gained potency and power in both volume and complexity.

Elaborate oscillating string arrangements tightly composed within the rigid structure of marching brass blasted from the speakers. Rolling percussion hammered at the air as fluttering woodwinds wove throughout the piece. As the anthem climaxed, an uproar of excitement and confidence shook the walls of the reception hall ending in rolling thunderous applause.

Twin spotlights inscribed converging arcs of brightness on the cream-colored curtain behind the podium. The fabric rippled with waves of movement behind it as the voice boomed: "Please give a warm West Coast welcome to the Deputy Chief of the International Science Administration and three-term Chairman of the North American Technology Consulate, Senator Dolan Douglass!"

The crowd's enthusiasm for the rendition of the anthem blossomed into respectful, though boisterous admiration for the man emerging from behind the curtain.

A tall, slender, white-haired man in his mid-sixties flowed gracefully between the parts in the cloth drape, sweeping his arms wide in dramatic gestures meant to engulf the immense room in a wide and welcome embrace. His smile crawled and wriggled across his sharp features—the muscles in his face twitching like a nest of anxious worms in an electrified pool covered with a tight skin of pale suede. His eyes sparkled with the kind of crisp emerald glint only seen as plasma arcs across the electrodes of a particle welder, his ebony pupils as piercing as the empty void of deep space.

He stood behind the massive podium and with his arms raised high over his head and his stance wide and firm, he addressed the cheering crowd in a voice that carried like a typhoon wind across the vast oceans. His words, projected by the hair-thin throat comlink pasted to his prominent Adam's apple, echoed as if the Creator himself were calling roll.

"We are poised above the threshold of the Great Abyss!" He paused expertly, allowing for the echo to reverberate and clear from the air before continuing. "And though, as we look deep into the dark vastness of Infinity knowing that it, too, is gazing back onto us, we have no fear." Another pause as the crowd grew quiet and still.

"Because of today!" he preached. "Today, we hold the singular truth that has eluded us for all of history. Today, I give you the undeniable source of illumination that will forever cast light over all that has remained in shadow: the eternal truth and everlasting light that is Man. Man at his most elemental!" The crowd roared and applauded wildly at the cryptic introduction.

Hidden among the shadows in the balcony, Jon shook his head and smiled warily. The old man was vague enough to be talking about anything from quantum physics to tossed salad, and the masses were just eating it up. As long as it sounded grand, it must be something phenomenal.

Theatrical bullshit, Webb thought.

Douglass grinned and swiveled his angular head smoothly from side to side, pinning the crowd with an intense stare like a dinosaur scanning the barren wasteland for one last scurrying morsel to complete its feast. The deep blackness of his pupils engulfed the sea-green rim of his irises as he focused briefly on random members of the gathering, initiating and holding eye contact here and there throughout the room.

After only a minute or two, he turned his attention to the podium before him. He inhaled deeply, theatrically, and sighed as his eyes closed and a confident smile spread across his narrow lips.

"Ahh!" he exclaimed. "Join me in a breath of fresh air, won't you!" He gestured with open palms, fanning his long arms out and to the side. He raised them over his head and stretched dramatically. "Come on now, don't be shy. That's it, you, too. Everybody give a good stretch... hmm."

Unbelievably, nearly everyone did just that. The grand reception hall filled with the sound and breeze of hundreds of over-emphasized sighs and yawns of every type, from the deep, throaty bellow of a walrus to the high-pitched shrill of a gull. Scores of arms stretched upward from the sea of shimmering sequins and black linen, reaching for the ornate coffered ceiling high above.

It was frightening to Jon, the power one man could wield over a mass of people. The commanding presence of his aura and the will-less captivity of his audience set Webb's teeth on edge and stood the tiny hairs at his nape on end. Douglass had the charisma of a cult leader and the unmistakable power of a Hitler. Jon shook his head and continued to marvel at the spectacle of near mass hypnosis before him.

"Do you feel that? The charge in the air? Like a slight static spark tickling your spine?" Douglass asked in a slow, methodical rhythm.

"Do you taste that? The vague tang of ozone? Like warmed copper and roasting almonds." A pause.

Many people were actually swaying to the sing-song meter of his poetic delivery.

"Do you smell that? The faint musty tinge of ancient times? The scent of an oncoming storm." He inhaled deeply, rolling his eyes back and savoring the moment. He raised his voice an octave and bellowed in a severe musical baritone.

"That, my brothers and sisters, is the future—spilling into the void left by the departing present. Your future and your children's today!"

He brought his eyes to bear upon the masses before him, his gaze vibrant and piercing, almost throbbing, under a deeply arched and furrowed powder-white brow. He swept his steely eyes across the small sea of people holding the crowd in hypnotic awe.

"I stand before you proud and humble, poised to usher mankind into the dawn of a brave, new world. An exciting journey that will establish its roots right here in this very room." He swept his arms wide and graceful. "Today, I am honored to present to you for the first time ever, the public debut of one of the greatest innovators of our time."

The silence of the dramatic pause was tense and thick with anticipation. Dolan Douglass swept his right arm in a wide, theatrical arc as he turned to the curtained backdrop.

"The Father of modern optical processing, and the head, heart and soul of Polar Innovations," he announced with bellicose flair. "Mr. Wyatt Cronus!"

Into the welcoming reverie of enthusiastic applause, a stout, soft-looking man emerged from behind the cream and copper-colored curtains. His smile widened as his cheeks flushed with gracious humility. He shook his head and waved weakly as he approached the podium still flushed with embarrassment.

Douglass stepped politely aside, surrendering the position of importance to the man in the expensive suit and the out of place, yet comfortable-looking suede moccasins.

Jon Webb swallowed hard, nearly choking on thick saliva as his throat seemed to swell shut. Fear, surprise and absolute anger rose up from his bowels, filling the back of his mouth with a bitter metallic tasting bolus. He slowly shook his head and muttered "No..."

Jon watched weakly, confused and amazed, as the man he knew as Barrett Lacombe, CEO of Phoenix-Lamneth, took the podium and nodded triumphantly as he accepted a welcome meant for the infamously reclusive Wyatt Cronus.

~ * ~

"Well, there he is. The J.D. Salinger of the biotech world," Robert whispered sarcastically leaning toward Sal.

Gionetti didn't respond, verbally or otherwise. His lips parted slightly to form a sound, and then froze. His eyes widened and his body stiffened. A small noise escaped from the depths of his throat, a sound like a squeaky hinge on an ancient cabinet door. He remained riveted by the activity behind the podium and the two men glowing in the limelight cascading down on the wooden lectern.

"Hey, Sal! Hell-oo?" Robert snapped his fingers in front of the fazed detective.

Sal blinked and spoke without turning his head, his voice thick and slightly garbled with clotted saliva.

"That's Barrett Lacombe, not Wyatt Cronus..." His voice trailed off as he cleared his throat.

Robert blinked and stole a quick glance at Carla. She met his eyes briefly, and then returned to the scene just below them. Carla had the camera crew set up center-stage, just behind the low railing circumscribing the entire upper mezzanine, looking down on the lectern and podium from about thirty meters away. She squinted to make out any overlooked or missed detail, then shook her head and whispered back.

"No, that's not Lacombe. Lacombe is dark and thin. Mediterranean, I think." She bit the inside of her cheek and nodded once. "That has to be Cronus."

Sal flinched and finally turned his head, apparently over the initial shock, and now appeared quite pissed.

"What?" he exclaimed raising his voice above a fresh blossom of applause.

"I met with Barrett Lacombe and his senior VP, Paul MacDonald, just days ago," Sal argued. "The morning of the murders."

He looked alarmingly at the man speaking into the mic and thrust a finger in the direction of the podium. "That man was introduced to me as Barrett Lacombe. Webb was there. He worked for the guy, for Christ's sake!" He shook his head in frustrated disbelief.

"Sal, I'm telling you, I've never seen this guy before." Carla gestured with her cocked thumb. "But I have interviewed Barrett Lacombe a dozen times. Up close and personal. That isn't him."

Sal continued to shake his head, disgusted and offended, both for his own ignorance as well as out of shame for being fooled.

"Fuck me!" Was all he could manage.

Robert chimed in with a desperate query, "What, so this guy told you," a thumb at Gionetti's chest, "that he was Barrett Lacombe on the morning of the murders, but he is *really* Wyatt Cronus, reclusive genius? Is that about right?"

Sal closed his eyes and nodded slowly. Carla shrugged.

"We can't even be sure that he's Cronus, now," Carla added. "I guess it's safe to assume that no one is who they say. Whoever he is, he's in bed with Douglass—or Slousad—and is somehow involved in all of this." She grimaced, turning toward her camera crew, addressing the young field assistant.

"Al? Cut the run and delete the drive. I want you guys to pack it up. Secure the gear and get back to the vehicle. Wait for me there." The man nodded quickly eyeing each of the group. It was clear that he had heard enough to become intrigued and was reluctant to leave.

Robert and Sal avoided his gaze and waited until he had shouldered his duffel and instructed the rest of crew to back down. He was the last off the balcony, following the men down the back staircase from the mezzanine, eyeing Carla suspiciously as he descended the steps. She ignored him and spoke only when he had completely gone.

"Al's a good field reporter," Carla warned. "And he heard enough to pique his curiosity. He's probably on the phone with our producer right now."

"Yeah?"

"Yeah," she said. "That means he'll get authorization to come back in and run down his own lead, with or without me. More likely without." She raised her eyebrows. "Time to shit or get off, boys. What do we do?"

The question hung like a dense, obstructive fog. It demanded answering, and that would require a commitment to action, which for all intent and purposes would forever change their lives. They intuitively knew this, but were frustrated by the lack of real knowledge they had. The few facts that had recently presented themselves only exposed more mysteries, and left a growing species of questions unanswered.

Suddenly, their decision was made for them.

Across the expanse of the reception hall, within the shadows at the back of the mezzanine balcony on the opposite side of the great room, a tangle of silhouettes and the muffled sounds of a brief struggle interrupted the address below.

Wyatt Cronus paused, squinting up and to the left into the balcony. A few of the crowd's upturned faces swung back to catch a glimpse of the ruckus. The scuffle quieted as soon as it started and Cronus continued; segueing back into his spiel with a joke. A polite wave of laughter and appropriate chuckles swam across the audience.

Robert, Carla and Sal watched as the shadowy forms quietly materialized from the far wall and moved purposefully and quickly across the mezzanine floor toward one of the far staircases. Three men in conservative suits escorted another rather limp form by the arms and waist. The man appeared to be semi-conscious, weaving and bobbing in the men's grasp. His heels dragged and bumped down the stairs, catching on the edges of each riser. The men paused to better their grip on the man's limbs and improve their balance. As they did, Robert and Sal got a better look at the man.

Though he was clearly wearing the uniform of a waiter, there was no doubt to his true identity.

Sal bolted to his feet dragging Robert with him.

"C'mon! We have to follow those guys," Sal spoke as he reached down offering a hand to Carla.

She remained crouched along the railing and was reluctant to leave. Douglass had just stepped back in front of the podium invoking yet another enthusiastic ovation.

Robert hopped on his feet and craned his neck to follow the departing entourage of security officers and their quarry.

"Webb," he uttered softly.

"Huh?" Carla shot sideways glances back and forth between the lectern and her colleagues.

"They got Webb!" Sal explained physically pulling her up by the arm. Once on her feet, he released her arm and spun to follow Robert. "Let's get—"

Gionetti came face to face with Max Donovan.

Just behind Max, Sal could see Robert as he struggled in the beefy arms of two large men in coveralls. Gionetti instinctively reached into his coat for his weapon and then froze, realizing that he was out-gunned four to one.

"Detective. Ms. Robinson." Donovan nodded to both as he smiled confidently.

"You'll please come with me." Max gestured casually behind himself toward the stairs and stepped aside, allowing for the lady to lead the way. Sal made eye contact with Robert and shook his head once, emphatically.

Robert rolled his eyes, sighed and stopped struggling.

Carla led the group down the stairs. Max's PDD vibrated on his hip. He snapped it off his belt, flipped it open and listened to the voice on the other end as they descended the lush carpeted staircase and into the shadows of the lower level.

Thirty-two

Garbled, low frequency voices ballooned in and out of perception like a fading radio transmission that echoed through deep water. Gauzy light filtered through the thick haze of transient consciousness as his stomach rolled and tightened with persistent waves of nausea.

He assumed that he was back in the realm of The Dream, physically and chemically bound, unable to resist the perpetual demons that haunt his memories. He knew that to come fully awake, even in the dream, would mean having to once again face the horror of Sarah's gruesome attack.

In a small, walled off corner of his fragmented mind, he willed death to finally come for him; liberate him from the eternal terror and malevolent memories. He was tired of losing the battle each and every time the dream was replayed; tired of accepting the truth fate brought upon him; tired of being helpless and powerless to stop the pain and suffering.

He was tired.

Not the exhausted, hungry, adrenaline-depleted kind of tired that usually left you spent, yet somehow strangely satisfied; but rather the completely empty, apathetic, vacuum type of tired that instead left you screaming for space to stretch your limbs and run as fast as you could away from yourself.

He was tired, all right. And ready for coldness to consume him.

"...coming around... atta boy. Webb?" The voices gained coherency as the soundtrack of the Dream sped up to real time, free from the filtering effects of unconsciousness.

Warm, dry fingers brushed across his brow, lifted his chin and turned his head side-to-side. His skin felt as if it was sprayed with flexible lead, yet he could still sense when he was being touched. He became aware of more than one person standing over or beside him and as he processed this, he prepared for yet another horrific replay of The Incident.

"...Adrenopine and Narcovert, but start slow and titrate. I don't want him rocketing back, ya' know?" a voice commanded. There was intense pressure against the right side of his neck followed immediately by a brief, sharp sting.

An injection, he thought—his first real concrete thought during this most recent emergence from darkness.

The filmy light began to brighten, and he blinked against the intensity as images and recognizable forms began to coalesce before him. He was coming out of a dark, cold stupor, and struggled against the yearning to return to the blissful ignorance of potential death.

"Ah, the babe awakes!" A distinctly familiar voice announced; then in a softer direction to unseen others: "Leave us. Please."

Jon Webb fully opened his eyes and raised his heavy head with strained effort. He squinted to achieve focus, searching the narrow field of vision for the source of the deep, melodic voice.

Seated before him, legs extended and crossed at the ankles, arms folded across his chest, was Aristotle Leary; perched like royalty atop a righteous throne.

Jon attempted to gasp, but his dry throat and cracked lips failed him, so instead he simply, weakly, drooped forward, mouth agape.

"Surprised?" Leary asked without humor. "I'd think so."

Leary shifted in his chair, sat more upright and crossed one leg over the other knee—a scholarly move performed as a professor might before administering the first of many complex questions in an oral examination.

"A great deal of time has passed between us since the lonely sands of northern Saudi, Lieutenant," Leary said.

The Egyptian drew a measured breath, and then exhaled in a soft sigh.

"For the most part, I'd say that the world has been very unkind to you." He leaned forward. "For that, I am truly sorry."

Webb remained still. His head hung low, chin to his chest. Thin, unchecked tears trickled from the corners of his eyes and crept down his numb cheeks. Though now fully awake, he had neither the strength nor the inclination to address his captor.

"I suppose that we should consider this reunion either an ironic twist of fate or divine intervention? Karma even, hmm?" He paused with only the sound of Jon's rhythmic breathing between them. "But, as you may recall, I ascribe to no one specific philosophical ideology.

"Although," Leary continued, "I have to say, Lieutenant Webb, you are beginning to make a believer out of me. After all, it certainly does seem that our lives are inexplicably intertwined." Leary slid his seat closer, and the scrape of the chair's legs sent slivers of ice down Webb's spine. He was now less than a meter from Jon. He leaned even closer and whispered softly near his lowered head, "Oh, Jonathan, the questions you must have."

Leary ran his slender fingers through Webb's hair, front to back, combing the sweaty locks back from his brow. When he had a generous handful, he firmly pulled Jon's head back and looked directly into his eyes. Webb's eyes were glistening with moisture, pupils dilated and twitching with the nystagmus effects of the fading drugs.

Leary peered intently, searching Jon's eyes for the soul of the man he knew years before: the moral soldier, the young man with the Samaritan ethos.

"Are you still in there, Lieutenant? Or have you given up the fight?"

Jon blinked in rapid succession, attempting to clear his eyes and gain focus. His mouth struggled to form words, but the lines in his face deepened as the muscles tired and relented to the weakness.

"You have questions, yes?" Leary asked simply. Jon remained silent, weak and non-responsive.

Leary nodded and smiled in silent response to own inquiry. He leaned back in his own chair, smoothed the creases in his pants and gently folded his hands in his lap. He finally closed his eyes and whispered, "Yes. I know, the drugs," he explained, "have left you weak and unfocused. That will pass quickly."

Jon rolled his head sluggishly on a limp neck. He tested his arms against the plastic restraints, pulled and flexed his stiff fingers. He tried his legs and met equal physical resistance.

Bound, he thought. This was more real than any of the previous incarnations of his dream. This was actually happening not merely a horrific remembrance.

"Yes, the restraints." Leary again nodded regretfully.

Sadness traced the corners of his eyes. "A necessity to protect you from your own propensity for creative improvisation. Unfortunate, really." Leary shook his head and smiled.

Silence prevailed for another minute, the two men sitting across from one another, still and eternally patient.

"So," Leary suddenly leaned forward, his hands on his knees, again peering into Jon's clearing eyes. "I'll get us started by taking the easiest, most obvious question first. I suppose I owe you that." He sucked his cheeks for a moment then proceeded with an air of rehearsed documentary.

"Understand one thing, Jonathan. I wasn't aware of your true identity until just recently. I was shown a photo of you—the target—only days ago. Imagine my surprise when I saw your handsome face looking back at me from the screen." Leary arched his brow briefly; the sense of irony remained his alone.

Jon sat placidly.

"Well, needless to say, it did take a moment or two before I actually recognized you. And when I did, I'd be lying if I denied any trepidation that I may have felt. After all, I've seen you in action.

"Though, even back then, I never actually knew your name, Lieutenant." He paused and narrowed his eyes.

"You proved to be quite an adversary, as I knew you would," Leary added.

Jon was able to hold his head steady now, the global numbness fading, replaced with a growing sensation of anxiety. The drugs were wearing off rapidly, and the points of pain and cramping along his beaten body had grown less remote. His skin crawled with pins and needles, and micro-tremors rippled through his awakening muscles.

"Why?" Leary posed the query. "That is the question on your lips, I assume."

Fully awake now, Jon glared—his eyes still, sharp and full of purpose.

Leary spoke calmly. "The atrocity enacted upon you and your family back East was the result of an extreme and desperate defensive posture initiated by concerned members of a very powerful movement and directed toward an aggressive, overly curious investigating detective." Leary broke eye contact and looked vaguely over the top of Jon's head. "Who knew that that detective would, in fact, turn out to be you?

"As I said, I did not know who you were. The face and the name were never connected for me. Even after you returned to New England and exacted your revenge. Perhaps that was their intent all along, I don't know." Leary sighed.

"So, the family of Detective Inspector Jonathan Webb was paid a visit, and the message was delivered. The objective was met and people were satisfied with the results." Leary dropped his eyes, meeting Jon's deadly stare for the first time.

"That is, until you returned, hunted down and exterminated the vermin you believed responsible. We—they, thought it wisest to let you have your revenge and move on. Shattered, but harmless." Leary shrugged.

"Well, you've had your vengeance, Jonathan. It's time to move on." Leary frowned sourly, defensive and defiant.

Jon's lips parted; his voice was harsh and throaty with effort. "I haven't even begun." Jon's eyes burned with hatred as he spoke for the first time.

Leary waved him off absently.

"Whatever." He feigned confidence but swallowed heavily.

"The point is, Webb—and this is important." Leary spread his arms wide and rolled his head to emphasize the encompassing greatness. "This is larger than both of us. We're still merely soldiers, Lieutenant, incapable of philosophies and ideals. You should have learned that back in the desert, my friend." He pointed a finger at Webb and glared down his bony digit as if sighting in on the man.

"A plan has been engineered and instruments have been forged. The machine was set in motion long ago and is now fully independent. Perpetual motion, Jon. And we need to keep from tripping and falling beneath the treads lest we become grease for the gears."

"What?" Jon cried. The intensity of the outburst startled Leary at first, and then a curt smile returned to his face. His eyes sparkled as he shook his head.

"Ah, Webb. You'll die a quiet hero of your own cause." Leary stretched and shifted in his chair. "You're a fool, Lieutenant."

Ary leaned in, eyeing Webb with a mix of scrutiny and pity. "What do you think you actually know, Jon? Tell me."

Webb cleared his throat and closed his eyes. "I know that I didn't kill those four people at Phoenix-Lamneth. I know that Senator Douglass is really Logan Slousad—a man we both once shared as an enemy and whom, I can only assume, you now work for.

"I know that somehow he and Lacombe or Cronus—whatever or whoever he is—are involved and want me to take a fall." Jon shook his head in frustration and confusion laden anger.

Then Jon's eyes suddenly flashed open, the pupils now pinpoints from focused rage. "And I know that you had my wife attacked, raped and put into a coma!"

Leary nodded once and smiled confidently. "Very good. Correct on all accounts. However, I should clarify that I do not work for Douglass. We're associates in completely different branches of the same organization."

He smiled even wider, flashing ultra white teeth. "And no fair bringing up the whole wife thing. I told you that was business, and I had no idea who you were. If I had, I probably would have killed you both quickly and quietly. Out of respect."

Aristotle Leary brushed his hands together as if wiping them clean from the dust and dirt of the past. The dryness of his skin sounded like thick coarse paper.

"Now, let *me* tell *you* what *I* know." Leary leaned back, tipped his chair on the back legs and balanced with a rhythmic rocking.

"Man, as an organic species, is on the brink of utter dissolution through intellectual stasis, moral complacency, egocentric greed and metaphysical cynicism. In summary, an overall loss of hope, faith and perceived will.

"We, as a global organism, have quite literally bored ourselves into near extinction. Technology has robbed us of everything that made being human fun. Thanks to optical processing and nanotechnology, everything is smaller, faster, smarter. We barely have the capacity to get up every morning, much less establish a career, raise a family or create something *new* and *original*. That small, brilliant minority of forward thinkers is growing thinner each year. The collective mass, however, is expanding geometrically."

Leary shifted in his seat; his hands kneaded the tops of his knees as he continued.

"Humankind, as a global societal entity—Team Earth—has finally succumbed to the forces of unification; and now, at its zenith, the Alliances are preparing for the Great Collapse into entropy. A singularity. It's a classic exercise in the principles of energy economics: the law of diminishing returns.

"Every organized political body, ruling faction, tribal counsel, federation and alliance has completely exhausted their resources—natural or otherwise. They have become saturated with success. And in doing so, have finally realized the futility of the effort."

Leary recrossed his legs and took a deep breath before continuing. Jon ground his teeth and quietly struggled against his restraints.

"Each and every religion has run its course, Jon. Rejecting, accepting, and then rejecting again science in all of its forms. Philosophers have spun great theories to explain the universe and our place in it—to uncover the Ultimate Truth." Leary rolled his eyes and leaned forward, waiting until he held Jon's reluctant gaze with his own wild, excited look.

He spoke in a hushed tone of conspiratorial knowledge.

"Do you want to know the Ultimate Truth, Lieutenant?"

Jon remained silent; his eyes darted from one sharp edge along Aristotle's vibrant face to another.

"It's perpetual motion, Jon. The ceaseless forward progress into the future." Leary again leaned back and rubbed his mouth with the back of his hand. He winked at Jon and nodded once as if to happily confirm the obviousness of his revelation.

"It's not about time and space relations, and it's not about quantum theories and potential parallel existences. It's not about God, Buddha, Allah, Mohammed or the Virgin Mary. It's not even about the past. History is relative and subjective written by the narcissistic victors of conflicts and the wealthy egocentric.

"It *is*, however, about this very moment and our experience of it. And the next. And the next.

"That, my friend, is all there is to the Truth: The *Now*." Leary pursed his lips, considered something internally, his brow wrinkled with a brief furrow of worry. He abruptly shook his head and blinked dismissively as if to clear a troubling vision.

Sensing the temporary disconnect, Jon finally spoke.

"You might want to be careful there, Ary. It sounds like you're describing a philosophy."

"Huh?" Aristotle Leary's eyes looked glazed and distant. His pupils were dilated so large that they consumed the gray irises. He blinked again rapidly. Suddenly, his face shifted, tightened, then relaxed. His eyes finally cleared, and his gaze focused back on Jon.

"I said, it sounds like you've adopted a philosophy after all," Jon repeated.

"No, no. Don't mistake the truth for some arcane doctrine. The truth is. Philosophy merely supposes." Leary grinned tilting his head to the side in a gentle gesture of compassion. "Jon, I really would like you to understand what it is that you've missed, here. You could benefit from a little perspective."

"Oh, I got all the perspective I needed when I saw the Hounds of Hell dance with my wife." Jon spit the words through tight lips and a set jaw.

"And when I walked into that bloody boardroom. I think I'm pretty clear on the matter of things when I reflect back on the attempt to take me down in MacDonald's office, the ambush set up at my apartment and now my capture and containment."

"Capture and containment? I like that. A little dramatic, but—I like the way it sings." Leary still smiled. His demeanor was much different from the man that Jon had known at *Bacchus Plateau* all those years ago. The difference was subtle, but there just the same.

"You said you had answers for me—well? I got a few goddamn burning questions!" Jon asserted, now determined to keep Leary talking, distracted. He needed time to think up a plan, and he needed answers.

Desperately.

He needed to make some sense of it all.

"Shoot." Leary rocked back in his chair folding his arms across his chest. "I'll do what I can."

Jon thought quickly, trying to prioritize his queries in case Leary chose to suddenly terminate the session. In an instant, however, he realized that it just didn't matter. The situation was obviously complex and would lack any clarity without all of the pieces in place. So, he just asked the first thing that came to mind.

"What is Douglass's intent? How did you wind up associated with him?"

"Logan—that is really his name, by the way—though I'm not so sure about his true surname..." Aristotle waved dismissively. "Doesn't matter. Anyway, he approached me many years after the vamping incident at

Bacchus Plateau. Well after the war and your departure. We chased after him for awhile, but men and money grew thin and he was essentially a ghost.

"Purified Synth had found its way into Western popularity anyway, and after some lengthy reconsideration, I really had no alternative but to embrace reality.

"Of course, there was always the profit margin to consider." He paused, actually frowning with what could have been interpreted as shame or even remorse.

Jon struggled to remain silent and emotionless.

"Eventually, my endeavors brought me to the Orient. He found me in China one day, on a recreational dive off the coast of all places. It turns out that he'd been watching me for some time." Leary explained.

"He said that he had been following my career with a close and curious eye, and that he was as equally impressed as he was concerned. He felt that I had enough power and vision to impede him, but not quite enough to neutralize him. He told me that he had become thoroughly convinced that if our efforts were unified, greater success would come to us both. It took awhile, but he eventually convinced me."

"What? If you can't beat 'em, join 'em? Is that it?" Jon grimaced in disgust.

Leary laughed; a short and simple huff. "Yeah, essentially. Though, the details are quite a bit more complicated."

"I'm sure," Jon responded tersely. "So, after the vamping nightmare in your territory, you up and join forces with the man anyway?"

"The vamping was actually much more isolated than we were led to believe. And Logan expressed great regret at the direction in which it took. He likened it to a failed clinical trial of a new drug—of which there are many—and abruptly ended the program soon after the *Bacchus Plateau* discovery. He wrestled for some time over the mistakes that he made. That was one bad decision, and nobody is more aware than he."

"I'll bet."

"As for his intent, well..." Leary shrugged. "It's rather intricate and quite involved. But you are correct, he has a vision." Ary's eyes glazed again. A small twitch flicked at the corners of his mouth, and then he was back.

"It's wonderful, Jon. Really..."

"Yeah. Tell me about Phoenix-Lamneth. Why the murders? Why the setup? What does he gain by framing me?"

Jon was working hard at keeping his cool and at loosening his restraints. However, the more he attempted to maneuver his limbs, the tighter the plastic strips pulled.

"Now that was a piece of work!" Leary seemed proud. Jon was revolted.

"Unfortunately, a few collateral removals had to occur afterwards as a result of your friend's industrious medical examiner." Ary sighed running his slender fingers through his hair. "But, yes, you were fishing in the right pond, so to speak."

Jon waited patiently for him to elaborate, his open eyes imploring.

"Those three scientists had grown suspicious enough to begin doubting their own work. They were growing paranoid about their indirect involvement in something potentially unethical; but more importantly, I think, was that they suspected that their most groundbreaking work was being farmed out unwittingly to external programs." Leary sucked his cheeks and closed his eyes. When he reopened them, he was gazing at the ceiling.

He continued, "They were right, of course. We were exporting their work in great quantities to outside programs that then applied the principles organically."

Jon flinched at the term, cocking his head to one side.

Organically?

"Those three engineers were never going to see their next anniversary anyway. It just so happened that Cronus got wind of their after hours meetings and became fearful of what they might do to the advancement of the project. So instead of milking them for a few more weeks or months, and then arranging some creative accidents, ala New England style..." Leary winked at Jon as he alluded to the elaborately schemed assassinations of the political figures years before. "...we arranged for them to meet with our implanted mole."

At first Jon assumed that by *implanted*, he simply meant that the man was inserted covertly to infiltrate the engineers' inner circle. But within seconds he realized what he had forgotten during this whole ordeal—Leary was casually referring to the actual cerebral implant secreted within the now-dead man's head. Jon caught his breath, his heart raced and he felt his face flush quick, hot and red.

"You okay, Jon?" Leary asked, genuinely concerned.

Jon nodded indicating for him to continue.

"It took finesse and time, but they grew to trust our man, and believed him to be their only real hope of securing an insurance policy against the corporation's misappropriation of their creative products.

"After all, it's always about money. So, posing as an easily bought internal lawyer, our man fabricated an elaborate and believable option to pressure Lacombe, whom you now know doesn't really exist, and convinced the three engineers to collaborate and negotiate." Leary yawned, stretched his narrow arms over his head and interlocked his slender fingers.

Then, as a matter of fact, Ary simply stated, "He then summarily executed them all at what was to be their final sit down."

Jon blinked, not at all surprised at the confirmation of the murders. It happened just as he hypothesized, he could clearly see that.

"Actually performed surprisingly well considering he was a third generation prototype," Leary said absently and more to himself than to Jon.

Jon tensed at the statement, narrowed his eyes and clenched his jaw. He communicated confusion, the questions painted across his brow.

Leary smiled softly and gently closed his eyes as he recognized Webb's wonder.

"Yes, Lieutenant. As I said, there is much to learn. Perhaps too much for our short time together." He opened his eyes and, again, they were vague and glassy—distant.

The disconnections seemed to be occurring more readily and lasting longer. Jon began to wonder and worry just how long before Ary fully slipped off into whatever dreamland kept pulling at him.

"Why do them at Corporate Campus? Right in their backyard?" Jon asked.

"Well, for you, of course."

Jon shook his head in frustration. He just didn't get it.

Leary sighed, apparently bored with the tack of the conversation, yet he continued, "Cronus and Douglass both felt that the opportunity was ripe for the next step in evolution: to utilize the tragedy to orchestrate an understandable slide in Phoenix-Lamneth stability. An internal scandal could generate the needed sympathy for support against the hypothetical *compromised ethics*' surrounding Phoenix-Lamneth operations." He indicated quotes by bracketing the phrase with two fingers of each hand as he spoke.

"It was a bold gamble. A long shot really. No matter how it played out, Phoenix-Lamneth would more than likely fold. And quickly. But the idea was to drive Phoenix-Lamneth's market value down.

"The hope was that once the graphic nature of the acts could be indisputably attributed to an unstable, yet remarkable individual with a powerfully emotional motive that the potential for ethical controversy surrounding the actual project would pale by comparison. That would pave the way for Cronus to sweep down and save the whole disaster through a charitable takeover." Leary smiled at the implied brilliance of the plan.

"But Wyatt Cronus doesn't really exist. I mean, that was Barrett Lacombe out there today," Jon attempted to clarify, unsure of his own certainty.

Leary shook his head, perpetually smiling.

"No, *that* was Wyatt Cronus. Barrett Lacombe hasn't been around for years. He died two years ago from complications associated with his implanted pancreatic mesh. Cured his diabetes, but it turns out they also engineered an aggressive strain of cancer from an experimental stem cell line. Life is not without its irony."

"But, the morning of the murders..." Jon stammered.

"All staged for your benefit. And the detective, as well."

"Why me, then?" Jon swallowed hard as the most obvious question finally surfaced.

"Because," Leary answered considering him with a look of sympathy and awe. "You fit the profile. Perfectly." Leary nodded as he ticked off items on his fingers. "Your wife and son were enlisted in the Rainey Protocols. You were continually despondent about their condition, and growing even more distrustful of the program and the staff. You had become adamantly resistant to furthering the science and technology, despite the potential it may hold for improving your wife and son's quality of life. You also had the background and experience, and more importantly, the capacity for violence." Leary closed his fingers into a fist and brought it firmly into the open palm of his other hand.

"All of that, along with the fortunate circumstance of your present employ within the corporation and—well, it was almost tailor made. A slam dunk. Sure thing." He smiled mechanically, his eyes again drifting.

"You were the ideal candidate for our purpose. A perfect example of emotionally charged conviction channeled through a symbolic vendetta. All we needed to do was set the scene; provide the bodies and a few vague leads. Let the media and the malleable minds of the masses do the rest.

"It's easy to believe that a man of your character and history could come to blame the perceived failures of technology on his own inability to accept fate. Most people would actually sympathize with your plight, could completely understand how and why you would lash out against the industry." Leary smiled raising his eyebrows.

"Of course, that doesn't make it right. Or legal," Leary concluded.

Jon shook his head as he pieced it all together. Anger and guilt rose in him from depths long forgotten. The image of Sarah rose in his mind; floating serenely, helpless and vulnerable, above the mesh floor of her room: the thin wires trailing from underneath her white cotton cap; the multicolored lines tracing out rhythmic patterns along the wide flat screens of the monitors—the only evidence of her existence now reduced to the hard, cold reality inscribed by those persistent etchings of red, green and yellow waveforms.

And Matthew, completely oblivious to his own condition and blissfully unaware of Jon's existence. A lovely, sensitive four-year-old boy imprisoned in his own underdeveloped mind from the unseen effects of microcellular damage occurring *in utero;* an unexpected reduction in maternal oxygenation—a brief period of time, really—during which the crucial biochemical reactions responsible for fetal brain tissue development continued without the appropriate concentration of elemental molecules of oxygen.

A silent, harsh, and unforgiving fate.

Jon clenched his jaw, driving his teeth into one another and forcing blood to pound in his skull. Instant, intense waves of sorrow flooded his chest, the empty hollow of his stomach, his narrow throat.

If he would have eased up on the investigation, if he had chosen a different course in life, never joined the police force—or the Army, for that matter—how different would've things been? If he had only found Sarah sooner after the attack—just a moment or two—would she be conscious enough today to fight along side of him? Had he been quick enough to assess her, perhaps even given her supplemental oxygen by mouth-to-mouth assisted breaths: had he been able to resist the attack from the beginning, prevented it from ever occurring...?

A universe of what-ifs, and all he had in the end was a comatose wife and an impaired son.

Jon felt bile fill the back of his throat as his gorge began to churn. He grimaced at the throbbing tickle of impending emesis. Aristotle Leary placed a hand on Jon's knee and gave it a squeeze.

"Easy now, Jon," he said. "Don't go back down those dark roads of guilt. Not a thing you can do now to change your world. Or theirs, for that matter. We are who we are, and each of our experiences is unique. Very different from one another, even though they may seem linked. Remember, cause and effect defines our lives, and nothing can be altered."

Jon glared bitterly. Leary sat back and sighed.

"I wish I could give you some comfort in knowing that there is a better place than this," Ary said.

He gestured grandly with a wave of his arms, implying the world around them and not the immediate room. "But I'm afraid that this is all there is. We make of our world what we will. And sometimes, if we aren't quick enough in our own commitments, people make our decisions for us." Leary closed his eyes and sighed deeply.

Jon eyed him through angry, blurry tears.

"So it is with you and me, Lieutenant Webb," Leary said reaching toward a cargo pocket on the side of his light green trousers. He thumbed the button loose from the fabric hole and withdrew a syringe. He held it absently, cradled in the hollow of his palm.

"You made my world more interesting, Jon. I will remember the impact that you had—"

A door slammed, and there was a rapid shuffling of feet coming from the open doorway behind Leary. He jerked his head quickly to the rear; his hand still clenched the syringe.

A tall man entered the room through the doorway, his white hair and light colored suit nearly glowing in the piercing clarity of the overhead fluorescence.

Dolan Douglass stood rigid, framed by the shadows in the hall behind him. Wyatt Cronus, short and stout, wobbled into the room behind him. Both of their eyes locked onto Jon. The air in the room was weighted by a blanket of tense silence. Leary never moved from his seat and, in fact, at once seemed nearly frozen in place.

Douglass spoke first, leaning into Cronus.

"Is the Egyptian tethered?" he asked nodding to Aristotle.

"Yes," responded Cronus.

Douglas firmed his stance, rolled his shoulders back and fixed his gaze on Jon. When he spoke, the air vibrated with the musical timber of his voice.

"So, Mr. Webb," he said. "Hello."

He nodded, then turned on his heel and moved to the back of the room behind Jonathan. As he passed Webb's chair, Dolan Douglass reached his fingers out to gently stroke Jon's hair. He missed, however, and the breeze of the swept hand fanned a few stray locks from Jon's temple.

Webb resisted the urge to follow the man's progress as he walked behind him. Jon heard an electric mechanism hum and then snap, and felt the pressure of the room change as another door opened. He could hear the soft footsteps retreat as Douglass stepped across the threshold behind him.

"You'll have to understand that I have no desire to spend any time on you, whatsoever," Douglass said. "So, goodbye."

And with that the door closed behind Jon, and Douglass was gone.

Jon struggled not to wince when the door clicked shut and finally brought his eyes up to find Cronus staring mischievously, almost lustfully, at him.

Leary was still frozen eerily in his seat.

When Cronus spoke, Jon flashed back for an instant to the morning he had met the man for the first time, when he still thought of him as Barrett Lacombe. Jon still felt angry, even embarrassed, at being fooled so easily.

"I, on the other hand," Wyatt Cronus began, "have some real uses for you." His smile froze Jon's blood.

Aristotle remained rigid and unmoving in his chair.

Thirty-three

An entourage of guards led them through several winding internal hallways. Recessed xenon light strips ran the length of each ceiling, bathing the plain halls in aggressive limelight. The five security agents armed with silenced Heston mag-pistols escorted Sal, Carla and Robert down the narrow corridors, two in front, the remaining three bringing up the rear.

Sal continuously reassessed their situation as they walked, quickly surveying their surroundings for any hint of potential escape.

The four uniformed guards calmly brandished their weapons out in the open. The fifth, and lead agent, was dressed unlike the others in a trim fitted blue suit and carried his weapon concealed beneath the thin fabric of his tailored jacket. In all, five well-trained, effectively armed men versus an unarmed cop, a nurse, and a moderate celebrity.

Shouldn't be a problem, Sal thought dismally.

But the truth was that Sal Gionetti had, in fact, been in far worse situations during his curious and storied past, and one crystalline fact continued to glitter in the back of his mind—*There is always an answer. Always a way. You just need to look. See your options with eyes that hold no bias. Have no doubt.*

He was certain of their inevitable demise and had grown concerned that any window for saving them from torture, interrogation and elimination was rapidly shrinking. Yet, he held onto quickly fading hope, urged by his experience. He continued to look, to think clearly and confidently.

They came upon a narrow, yet heavy, steel door which the lead agent in the blue suit deftly keyed with a thin card, and then swept open with a firm and graceful hand. The men prodded their captives through the doorway with impatient jabs of their softly humming weapons. Blue-Suit held open the door and as they passed he kept his gaze down, avoiding any direct eye contact with the three prisoners.

The group paused as Blue-Suit crept back along the wall to the front of the procession and regained the lead. During those three or four seconds, Gionetti let his eyes expertly search the walls, ceiling, floor for anything that would assist in escaping their captors. He reassessed the guards and confirmed that Blue had his weapon holstered and locked to his hip. The others held their respective weapons, though much more relaxed than initially, occasionally allowing the barrels to drift and waver.

Only two of the four pistols were now humming with the telltale vibration of a full charge; the remaining two having defaulted to safe mode after a preset time of non-discharge. Evidently, the guards were unaware of the default feature, opted not to bypass it or simply didn't see the three captors as a significant enough threat to warrant the additional energy expenditure of the power cells.

The heavy steel door swung shut in their wake, silently, on pneumatic-assisted hinges that hissed with a whisper of released pressurized gases. The locking mechanism gently clicked and whirred behind the threshold, resecuring the thick alloy door.

Sal's mind immediately flashed on the mechanisms of the door, the compressed air hinges, the automatic locking mechanism, the heavy brushed steel surface. He also noticed a faint glint of light reflected off the polished surface of the smoked glass panel set flush into the wall just to the left of the thick steel doorjamb—the door control panel for operating the security mechanism on this side of the locked door.

Suddenly, his mind began piecing together a plan. It would require speed, agility and brilliant physical violence.

And it would require them to pass through one more door.

~ * ~

"Mr. Leary. Please." Cronus motioned for Aristotle to rise and relinquish his seat. Leary blinked abruptly, and then shook his head as if to clear the fog of his temporary paralysis. As he rose, he slid the chair from under him with one hand, while the clear syringe fell absently from the other. It bounced off the stone tile of the floor with a hollow plastic click as it rolled in a slow semi-circle back and forth.

Jon's eyes watched the slender plastic cylinder rock itself to rest at the foot his own chair. The small black graduated markings that indicated values of volume were illegible from this distance, yet from the length of the partially withdrawn plunger, he could surmise that the syringe was at least half filled with some clear liquid.

Aristotle Leary stepped to the side and gracefully offered his seat to the stout man as requested, the dropped syringe completely ignored as if it had never existed. Jon watched as the fat executive lowered himself into the empty chair with an audible sigh of exertion followed by relief.

Standing obediently off to the side, Leary wore the grin of a bemused schoolboy during a particularly humorous and engaging story. Jon noticed the abrupt change in his affect—the lack of focus and the uncharacteristically submissive, almost malleable demeanor. Webb wrinkled his brow and strained to comprehend the bizarre change in behavior.

Cronus leaned forward and rested his arms on his thighs. He smiled, his eyes wide and winning. When he spoke, his voice carried the tone of practiced authority, yet just under the surface, cracked from exhaustion.

"It's certainly been an exciting few days, hasn't it, Detective Webb?" Cronus said.

Jon shifted his glance back to the syringe, avoiding the man's direct stare. Cronus sat patiently, and then noticing Jon's gaze, he continued.

"Now, Jon, we really don't have a lot of time for posturing and false bravado." Cronus spread his arms resolutely. "In fact, we've got you by the balls, old man. Your friends, too." He waited for a response.

Jon remained stoic though struggled internally against the rage simmering in his chest. He chewed at the soft skin inside his cheek relishing the sharp sting. He allowed the pain to refocus his resolve and denied his nemesis the satisfaction of moral victory.

Cronus sighed impatiently shaking his head. "Christ, man!" he exclaimed. "What's it going to take to get you to see that you're defeated? Beaten. It's over, and everyone is moving on. With or without you, Jon. We are moving on.

"Frankly, I don't give a shiny shit what happens to you; but some of the boys in white lab coats insist that you're an opportunity too rich in potential to pass up." He waved dismissively, nearly grimacing. "I'd just as soon put a bullet in your head and be done with it. You are dangerous. I recognize and respect that."

Cronus leaned in again and cocked his head.

"Is that a surprise? That I respect you?" he asked.

Jon remained silent.

"Hell, Ary here shared some terrific stories about you from back in the day. Certainly enough to give us pause" He nodded. "Brave and admirable, all of it.

"But unfortunately—at least, for you—that all belongs to another time. There just isn't a place for those attributes in this world. It makes no sense," he said.

Cronus bent to retrieve the syringe and needle assembly on the floor, grunting as he reached down with his puffy fingers, snaring it by the capped end of the needle. When he sat upright, his face was flushed red from the effort.

"However, I guess I do have an obligation to fully explore the whole you, don't I?"

He loosely cupped the syringe in his right hand while he raked his left through his thinning brown hair.

Glancing at Leary sideways, he spoke again to Jon, "Jon, Leary has proven to be quite helpful in delivering our message and channeling our resources. He has been an invaluable asset in much of our fact-finding and team profiling.

"He is, in fact, the reason for your involvement. But you probably already figured that out on your own." Cronus crossed his arms, the plastic of the syringe's plunger just visible underneath his chunky arm.

"Yet, despite being a key player, he just hasn't been instrumental in closing the deal, so to speak.

"It's got nothing to do with being squeamish or morally conflicted. Just some programming glitch in his meshwork. The psyche guys attribute it to some latent personality quirk manifesting itself as reluctance. Something about altruistic transference." Cronus frowned animatedly.

"Now, I don't know shit about all that. But my instinct says that something happened in Aristotle's past to cause him to make a deeply-rooted conviction to not directly cause pain and suffering in people whom he holds in some regard." Cronus smiled as he tapped the syringe against the fabric of his lightweight linen jacket.

He clicked his tongue twice against the roof of his mouth.

"You see, the Egyptian there..." He gestured toward Ary with the syringe.

Leary remained passive and somber; grinning innocently as if he couldn't hear the conversation, or just didn't comprehend what was being said.

"He seems to hitch a little when confronted with the task of putting a familiar issue to rest. Now, I know for a fact that, on occasion, he has personally gotten his own hands wet as well as having merely given the orders. But since his grafting, he has shown hesitation and failure to commit only twice.

"Once, just a moment ago with you." He waved the syringe, rocking it between his first two fingers, the tip arcing back and forth like a sinister metronome.

"And just yesterday, when he was supposed to minimize your friend Max Donovan's involvement in the program."

Jon finally flinched though he still refused to look up.

"Yeah, he just kind of waffled back and forth, twitchy and unsure," Cronus explained. "He was waving the pistol around so much, mumbling under his breath, that we thought he might eat the barrel of his own gun.

"That's happened before, as you know, though not without provocation." Cronus smiled at his own sense of irony.

"Fortunately, the tech guys had a tether installed and with a continuous ultrasonic signal, we can reset the participant to default parameters and start anew." He glanced at the grinning face of Aristotle Leary, unblinking and eerily gentle.

"They remain like this for a few minutes, all dopey and gelatinous, but then recover quite quickly." Cronus pinched his lips together, inhaled through his nose and then exhaled noisily through pursed lips.

"Leary was—is—our greatest success to date. But we obviously have some work to do." Cronus turned back to Jon. "He evidently has a soft spot for you and Donovan, after all.

"So, that brings us back to you. I'd like you to be dismissed, in a permanent kind of way, but our boys over at Rainey feel that you may have the key to some of our problems locked away within the folds of your gray matter." He tapped his own skull with the capped needle of the syringe.

"So, before we process you for protocols and send you over to meet your wife, I figured I'd take the opportunity to address any issues you and I may have. And perhaps get a little more information." Cronus sniffed and sighed heavily.

"Understand, Webb—that I'm not expecting much and won't waste either of our time. I just thought it'd be nice to try." He smiled, patently arrogant.

Jon continued to study the floor at his feet, imperceptibly working at the thin plastic bindings around his wrists. The edges of the serrated strips had dug and sliced into his raw flesh and trickles of blood grew into steady flows, pooling in the sweaty palms of his cramped hands; surely dripping by now onto the floor behind his chair.

If Cronus noticed, he gave no indication. It didn't matter, however, because Jon's only progress was to lacerate his wrists to the point where he felt that the muscles and tendons may fail him soon.

"Okay, Jon. Item number one: we have your three friends. The cop, the reporter and some other little shit we haven't yet identified. What do they know? Or think that they know?"

Jon's silence persisted, and Cronus waited a full minute before moving on.

"Right. Fuck you, too." Cronus shook his head in disappointment.

"Number two—and this is the real important one. There was a great deal of technical data transmitted to some remote storage device. Who has it and where is it?"

Again, Webb remained silent.

Cronus sighed and leaned forward, reaching at last for Jon's chin looking to raise his head and look into his eyes. When he did, Jon struck with the quickness and viciousness of a viper, biting and holding firm onto the first three fingers of Cronus' left hand. He clenched and ground his jaw, feeling his teeth pop through skin and rub against bone. Blood and saliva bubbled from the corners of his mouth, trailing down his chin.

Cronus immediately stood, attempted to pull free and slapped desperately at Jon's head. His eyes were wide with surprise and pain, his mouth drawn into a gaping maw of shock—a painful cry stifled by the sudden constriction of his throat.

The syringe fell again to the floor, ignored in favor of desperate defensive blows. Jon torqued his head and twisted his upper body in an attempt to pull the man over with inertia. If he could get the man down and somehow land on top of him, Jon had simply planned to pummel him to death with his own head, driving forehead into forehead until both of them lay in pool of blood, bone and brains.

Webb growled and thrashed with animal rage, teeth locked in a death grip, working into the fat man's finger bones. Cronus struggled, pulling back with all of his weight while raining blows across the side of Jon's head. The two men nearly toppled over twice during the death match, and Jon was certain that the older man was growing desperate, scared and unstable. He forced his jaws tighter, afraid to loosen, even for second, and risk attempting further purchase on the man's mangled hand.

Jon's eyes rolled back white like a shark locked onto its meal.

Cronus lashed at Webb's face, clawed at his eyes, tried and failed to pry his jaws apart. He was still pulling with all his weight though becoming weak. He shrieked openly now as his throat unclenched and rapid breaths escaped in hitched spasms.

Suddenly, Jon felt the momentum of the struggle shift slightly to his right. He instinctively rolled in that direction, jerking his head as he threw his hips and pushed with his legs. He felt and heard flesh rip beneath his teeth, and the unmistakable hollow crunch as bone gave way under the intense, insistent pressure applied with his jaws.

Cronus' generous body tumbled into, and then over Jon's lap, fell to the floor and pulled Webb over onto it by his clenched teeth. Jon felt at least two of his front teeth loosen, and then give completely away from their roots. His gums were numb and his cramped jaw protested when he tried to open his mouth.

As the tension lessened, Cronus was finally able to pull his gnarled fingers from Jon's bloodied face. He stared wide-eyed into the frenzied demon now straddled over him.

Blood dripped in thick, long cords from Jon's mouth, coiling on Wyatt Cronus' chin and throat. Webb's pupils were pinpoint and intense from adrenaline; yet cool and confirmed in their commitment. His respirations raced in a heavy, garrulous panting—savage and insatiable.

Jon firmed his shoulders, raised his head and prepared to crash the top of his blood-encrusted brow into Cronus' face, hopefully shattering and driving the fragile nasal and sinus bones into the man's frontal lobe.

He closed his eyes and braced for the initial impact, intent on pounding until they were both dead.

A blinding white light erupted behind his eyes, followed almost immediately by a vague pulsing along the side of his neck. In an instant, however, the pulsations exploded into racking convulsions and the intense light winked out.

In a brief moment of clarity before total blackness, Jon Webb had one thought: *Fasored? By whom?*

~ * ~

Sal knew he could take down one, maybe two of the guards. The question was, would Robert react and respond quickly enough to at least distract the others? What about Carla? Would she add to their strength in a fight or would she fall as a liability and wind up injured or dead?

As unsure about their chances as he was certain of their fate, Gionetti resolved to commit to one solid plan and hope for the best. Once he acted, there would be no turning back.

They approached a second steel encased door, similar to the last and as Sal made quick mental adjustments to his plan something vague caught his eye, glittering from the ceiling. The small, intricate blossoms of the heat sensors sprouted at even intervals along the entire length of the corridor—the fire detection and prevention system.

The group came to a halt just outside the steel door, and Blue-Suit was reaching into his jacket pocket for the slim card that would unlock the barrier. Sal took a quick census of their positions in relation to the armed men.

One of the men had completely holstered his weapon—as had Blue— and now stood just to the side of the lead agent as he fumbled the thin plastic card toward the slide-lock reader; both men momentarily preoccupied with the simple act of negotiating the card through the narrow groove.

Two of the remaining guards leaned semi-casually against the far wall of the hallway, pistols loosely grasped and dangling in front of their thighs, business end down. Neither of the weapons appeared to hum with any stored energy though it would only take a half second or so to reach full charge when activated. One of the men picked at the ingrown hairs within his facial stubble, and the other rubbed his eyes between his forefinger and thumb, stifling a yawn.

The last guard was older than the rest and carried with him a sense of cynicism and doom. Perhaps it was just experience and training that rendered him hyper-vigilant or maybe he just ached for conflict. Either way, the balding hulk never took his eyes off Sal, always placing himself between the detective and the others. During their travel, he had walked behind, yet very close, nearly touching Gionetti with each stride as his thick arms swung from beefy shoulders.

Now he stood less than half a meter away, feet wide and firm, his live pistol hummed like the incessant buzz of summer cicadas. He held the weapon in both hands, fingers interlaced in a proper combat grip, and kept the muzzle aimed somewhere between Sal's groin and knees. His eyes remained dark, small and unreadable. The corners of his mouth turned up not so much in a grin as a sneer; almost a challenge.

Sal knew this one would have to fall first. And fast.

The three of them huddled against the wall; Robert first, then Carla and finally Sal. About three meters away, the two guards continued to lounge against the opposite wall. Blue-Suit pulled the card through the reader and hesitated a moment after the swipe, waiting for the glowing panel to flash and the door to unlock. A faint click, followed by the whir of internal mechanisms winding open, and Blue slipped the card back into his jacket pocket.

He glanced at the guard as he pushed through the swinging door, bracing his back against the cold steel and propping it open. The guard turned and with a bored, pouting expression, gestured for them to follow. He back stepped across the threshold, reaching for Robert's arm as he walked through.

Carla followed close behind, and Sal hesitated long enough to earn an impatient and displeased grimace from the lone goon looming in front of him. The other two guards were just shifting their weight from leaning against the wall to righting themselves. They were about two meters from the doorway.

Carla had just stepped through, and out of the corner of his eye Sal could see Robert just beyond the threshold, turning to face back down the corridor. Blue remained propped against the open door, his head turned to follow Carla as she walked past. The other guard guided Carla by the arm as his gaze dropped to her open shirt collar in hope of a glimpse of cleavage.

A distant, long forgotten voice cried from deep within Sal's conscious:

GO!

At that moment, time slowed to a grind for Gionetti, yet made quantum leaps for the hapless others carrying guns. Before he could reason away the opportunity and lose the moment, Sal acted.

He sneezed violently enough for his head to drop forward, forcing his torso to bend at the waist. The looming goon before him instinctively stepped back a half step and leaned to the side to avoid both the spray and the bowing man. He wrinkled his nose in disgust, but before he could utter an unkind, unappreciative remark, Sal was under him.

Gionetti thrust himself up and out, driving with his legs and leading with the crown of his head. He aimed for and ultimately connected with the man's lower jaw. With a crunching wet grunt, bone shattered and teeth exploded as Sal piledrived into the man's chin. Brilliant stars went supernova in Sal's head, and he wobbled from the impact. He remained standing, though, as he followed through, simultaneously grabbing the mag-pistol from the stunned man's two-handed grip.

Sal now stood face-to-face with the giant guard; blood gushed from the larger man's mouth in torrents. His eyes glazed and rolled, his body listed to the side, teetered and then finally collapsed.

The two languid guards against the far wall were relatively quick in drawing their weapons from their holsters, but only one of them managed to hit the power-up button before Sal sent four humming alloy missiles in their direction, two each through the face.

The sound of the magnetic rounds slamming into the metal of the corridor wall behind their heads rang loud and dull. Their limp bodies slid down the smooth surface of the wall, dragging crimson smears of gore from the mortal head wounds.

At the same time Sal went with his vertical assault, Robert realized the opportunity to act and leapt for the second of the two lead agents. Partially distracted by Carla's creased bosom and the sudden commotion across the doorway, the guard never saw Robert's punch coming for his cheek. Though the impact was lessened by inexperience, the element of surprise was enough to cause the man to stumble, hesitate, lean against the wall and gather his bearings before he could retaliate.

Robert was already moving in to attempt to finish the job when Carla pounced on the startled guard. Her nails dug into his face as she brought her knee up into his groin repeatedly. She grunted and cussed with each kick.

Robert quickly veered toward Blue-Suit and the door, but as he spun, he came face-to-face with the unblinking eye of the hollow black barrel of a Heston mag-pistol.

The weapon hummed quietly. Blue's face twisted and clenched behind the length of the barrel. Robert's breath shrunk in his lungs, and the vacuum sucked the heat out of his bowels. He heard the soft snap of the magnetic round seating itself into the breach of the barrel. His eyes grew wide enough to hurt.

Then Blue's head exploded in a slow motion spray of gristle, bone and blood. Robert flinched as the wet material splashed the door, the jamb, the wall and floor. The pistol remained in the hands of the headless body, and for a long moment Robert was sure that the weapon would still fire on its own by the sheer will of the murderous headless body, or that, like many a beheaded chicken, the twitching of dying nerves may provide enough convulsive force to actuate the trigger. Instead, Blue-Suit's dead body fell to the side in a limp heap.

Sal stepped over the body and into the corridor. Robert considered him with stunned silence, the paleness of shock slowly creeping into his face. Sal recognized the look and broke the silence.

"Get a grip, Bob. We gotta move!"

Carla was kicking weakly at the crumbled form of the guard against the wall. Tears were streaming from her eyes, saliva bubbled at the corners of her mouth. She trembled with rage and terror. Sal moved to her and reached out to touch her shoulder. He stopped just short as she threw up a quivering arm in weary defense.

"Don't!" she slurred.

Sal withdrew his hand and turned to Robert firmly.

"We're not out of this just yet. Not by a long shot," he said.

With that he took aim with the pistol and fired a few rounds into the pneumatic hinges of the door. The pressurized gases escaped with a piercing whistle. He then reached down and inside Blue's jacket, withdrew the plastic keycard, flipped the body over and out of the way and pushed the heavy steel door closed manually against the loosening resistance of the damaged automatic hinge system.

Once closed, he fired the remaining rounds into the smoky glass of the control panel. Splinters of plastic, metal and glass danced in the shock waves of the weapon's blast. Sparks arced from short circuiting wires and wispy, acrid tendrils of smoke wound up from the destroyed panel. Sal reached in and snagged a handful of smoldering plastic and gold wiring, wincing as the sharp edges dug into his palm and the heat singed the hair on his arm.

He motioned for Robert to squat and support himself on one knee. Though still stunned, Robert followed directions and without explaining himself, Sal stepped up onto Robert's upturned knee, crawled half way up the man's shoulder and back, and stretched up toward the ceiling, extending the smoldering nest under one of the bristling heat detectors.

Thin wisps of hazy smoke curled up from the mass of coiled wires and electronics, dancing around the meshwork of thin sensor filaments. Seconds passed without any sound, any reaction.

Then, abruptly, a piercing siren and chirping alarm sounded. Instantly, the internal mechanism of the door could be heard grinding. The door sealed.

"C'mon!" Sal shouted over the wailing noise as he jumped off Robert.

Robert blinked a few times, swallowed and slowly rose to his feet. Sal leaned in close and squinted into the younger man's eyes. He sighed and shook his head.

"Don't make me leave you, okay?" he said.

Robert blinked again, finally focusing on Gionetti. He slowly nodded and made a move toward Carla. She was already moving toward the men and cringed away from Robert's offered hand. She pushed past him and waited silently for Sal to lead the way.

The three of them jogged down the hall toward another steel door at the end. When the slide-lock card immediately opened the door for them, Sal knew that they might have a chance.

~ * ~

"Miserable fuck!" was the greeting Jon awoke to this time.

His emergence from the Fasor induced unconsciousness was abrupt and clean, not at all like rising from the foggy, fragmented depths of drug-induced sleep.

He blinked once, then twice, solidifying the cold shards of pain that pressed into his head—a piercing, splitting headache that hummed with neon intensity. A wave of nausea passed over him. He closed his eyes.

When it passed and he reopened his eyes, Aristotle Leary was seated in front of him, smiling and holding what looked like a large three-tined fork. Leary smiled his usual smile, cocking his head curiously to one side as he watched Jon wake.

"Miserable, violent, filthy, little fuck!" Cronus spat the words as if they themselves contained a bitter and vile element that rendered them distasteful. The pudgy man sat behind Leary, a good distance away. He was being tended to by two younger men in red tunics. They were carefully wrapping his hand in white bandages. A ragged heap of blood soaked cloth lay at his feet, older dressings, perhaps.

Jon allowed himself to smile inwardly at the memory of biting into the fatty flesh of the man's fingers. The vague sense of victory and pride lasted only a moment, as he realized that he was not merely bound, but also paralyzed.

He lay prone, though tilted up at the head, on a hard flat platform. He tried to move his arms and legs, but found them to be utterly useless. He could still sense they were there. They were not insensate, just unmoving. He quickly surmised that he was indeed at a great disadvantage and that this may very well be the end.

Then he saw him.

Bound to a chair and jerking his wide, terror-filled gaze about the room, Max Donovan sat trembling in the rear of the humid chamber. Jon's heart flipped and rapidly rose into his already too-tight throat. He fought the urge to scream, to give voice to the raw, animal anger welling in his empty bowels.

Aristotle Leary leaned in and whispered, "You really pissed the old man off, my brother." His smile widened. He seemed alert again, almost cogent.

Cronus continued to mumble and rant at the back of the room, bitching about tetanus and infection. Ary shook his head and rolled his eyes, still smiling. He winked at Jon.

Jon could move his head and neck without strain, but his position made any extensive maneuvers exhausting. He worked his swollen tongue against the gaping wound in his gums where his teeth pulled out during the struggle. The pain was dull. He felt the tightness of dried blood across his chin and cheeks.

Wanting to catch and hold Max's gaze just long enough to curse him for his treachery and treason, he strained to see his former partner and friend.

Maxwell Donovan, however, looked as frightened and terrified as any animal caught in a gruesome trap. His head swiveled about violently, desperate to find an escape or even a sympathetic face to which to plead for mercy. Sweat painted Max's brow greasy, and his eyes bulged painfully with the adrenaline of fear.

Jon finally resorted to meeting Leary's eyes, whose gaze never left Jon's anguished face. He struggled to not appear pleading, yet immediately sensed that he had failed. Jon sighed and allowed his head to fall into the hard surface of the table, his face pressed into cold plastic. A muffled groan of acceptance and defeat rumbled in his throat. He jerked his shoulders in one last fruitless effort to move his will-less body.

"Paracurium. It's a new paralytic," Leary explained motioning to Jon's limp limbs secured to the platform with leather and thick plastic straps. "Dose dependent selectivity for peripheral relaxation. Renders the targeted limbs immobile while preserving sensorium."

"Oh, is our vicious animal awake?" Cronus asked from the back of the room. He rose from his seat and wobbled over to Leary's side though no farther. He glared at Jon, cradling his wounded hand with the other.

"Not entirely sure if I'll regain full function of the fingers, asshole." He flinched as he tested the flexion of the digits in question. Jon refused to look at the man.

"Let me tell you something, Webb. Your day is just fucking beginning," Cronus hissed. "I will take extreme pleasure in watching you suffer. And it'll all be right there in your face for me to enjoy. I won't have to endure watching the uncomfortable and annoying thrashing and writhing that usually accompanies physical unpleasantness.

"No, you see, because you won't be able to move. Oh, you'll feel everything just fine. But you won't be able to move a muscle." Cronus grinned. He waited for Jon to respond.

After a moment of silence, he added. "And your wife and kid?" Cronus paused; this time Jon did look up. "They've been elevated in the Protocol Program. Got some real special things lined up for them." He held Jon's gaze for a second longer, and then turned to leave.

He wobbled over to Max's chair halting just to the side. He reached out and grabbed Donovan by the chin, squeezing the man's cheeks together between the middle finger and thumb of his uninjured hand. Max screwed his eyes up to meet Cronus' condescending glare. Saliva drooled from his puckered lips.

Jon only now noticed that Max had the glazed eyes of someone in the throes of a full on Synth bloom. He suddenly realized that his long-time friend had fallen—or at least had been pushed—off the wagon and was back on Synth. He suspected that Max's fall from grace was entirely due to the arrogant little man parading before them.

Jon's heart broke into even smaller pieces as he felt uncontrolled waves of sympathy and regret flow through his hollow core. He saw all of the challenges and adventures, the battles and the victories, and the growth and evolution between friends flash across the foggy screen of his mind. In that moment, he silently pleaded with himself for forgiveness and mercy for his friend, Max Donovan.

Cronus turned to Jon letting Max's chin loose to bob up and down in a sedate and floppy rhythm.

"Now, I could be persuaded to cut your friend here some slack, Webb, if you can tell me a little bit about the three folks we have in our custody right now." Cronus crossed his arms, careful not to bump or brush the thickly bandaged and bleeding paw.

"Think about it, Jon. This is your chance to finally give someone in your life peace. After all, Max really didn't have a choice." He gazed in mock sympathy at the stoned man seated before him, drooling and working his mouth in strange, elaborate twitches.

Cronus raised his head and glared at Jon. He slowly and dramatically waved his arm across Max's slumped body.

"At this point, Jon, he's yours to save. One more injection of purified Clear, though, and he's sure to have a schizo-psychotic break. Worthless to even me. And certainly to society." He raised a questioning brow at Jon.

"So, what can you tell me about the transmitted data from the ME's office? Do you or your friends have it?"

Jon glared at the fat man, choosing not to verbalize his resentment and resistant to share his knowledge. At least Max would go out peacefully with an overdose. That was all that Jon could offer. It was the best a chemically paralyzed friend could offer to another. Jon closed his eyes and sighed.

Cronus sensed the resignation and grunted. "Hmph!"

To an unseen person he made a surprise request that jolted Jon from his silent resolve. His eyes flew open at the sudden realization that his inaction may have just doomed his friend to a much more painful end.

"Get the Push. Shoot him up with the whole vial," Cronus directed.

There was movement behind Cronus, but Jon couldn't see from his limited perspective. A technician in a red tunic appeared, drawing up a large quantity of pale green liquid into a twenty milliliter syringe. He walked over to Max and, without preparation or hesitation, promptly injected the entire contents into the prominent vein in his antecubital fossa. Max hardly flinched and merely gazed in confusion at the trickle of blood left behind from the needle. The pool of dark crimson welled up in the crook of his arm.

"That," Cronus explained though it was unnecessary, "is DST 43—Push. The only known antagonist for synthetic neurocotic intoxication. The really cool thing about it, however, is that in addition to inhibiting the dysphoric effects of Synth through competitive binding of the dopamine and serotonin receptors, it also completely excites the centrally mediated experiences of nociception. It revs up the pain fibers within the dorsal horn of the spinal cord."

Cronus walked to the back of Max's chair. Max was stirring in his seat, becoming more alert and as equally agitated. His eyes cleared, briefly focused, then misted with tears as he became cognizant of his surroundings.

"They say that even a breeze over a fresh, superficial scratch can seem like hot metal being pressed into the flesh." Cronus reached down and flicked the blood-smeared injection site with a pudgy finger. Max's eyes shot open, his breath caught in his chest and his body tensed as if being branded by thousands of invisible irons. Beads of sweat exploded from every pore. His pale skin glistened with it.

Jon closed his eyes and shook his head quietly whispering, "No, no."

"What's that, Jon? You have something to say?"

Jon opened his eyes and silently looked upon his friend's suffering face. Max finally met his gaze with a remorseful smile. Though tears flowed freely from his red-rimmed eyes, Max held Jon's attention with rapt intensity. Through the pain and anguish, he smiled wide, sadly and with finality.

When he spoke, it surprised both Jon and Cronus, satisfying and pleasing to the former, angering the latter.

"I'm so sorry, Jon. Forgive me." His voice was hoarse, frail, yet strangely calm. Max smiled again, deeply sad, and closed his eyes against a torrent of tears.

Cronus bit down hard against the anger and frustration that welled within him. He spoke bitterly with a desperate edge.

"Jon! I can spare your wife and son as well. You need to tell me what you know about the transmitted data from the bitch ME. That's all! We can't allow such powerful information to leak into the mainstream.

"I mean, Christ, man! Think of it. When we perfect this, my God, what a revelation. But, right now... well, we need to exercise some professional discretion. Soon, we'll be able to unveil this wondrous evolutionary success.

"But the world isn't quite ready. Mankind isn't ready. We need to be prepared for that time when we are—" Cronus spewed his diseased philosophy and back-pedaled through a maze of twisted logic, sounding more and more like Aristotle Leary. The similarities tightened Jon's bowels and iced his nape.

Jon finally opened his eyes and stared at Cronus, halting the man in mid-speech. Cronus stepped closer, anticipating Jon's submission. Jon licked his lips, flicking his gaze from Max to Cronus.

"Wyatt?" Jon's voice cracked. "Will you allow my wife and son to live the rest of their lives peacefully? Without any further technological intervention?"

Cronus blinked twice and answered dully. "Of course, Jon. Of course."

Webb saw the lie crawl up from the man's black heart and spread across the round jowls of his moon-shaped face. Jon held his gaze long enough to let him know that he didn't believe him for a second.

Max uttered a slight chuckle from behind that broke the silence. Cronus spun to face the seated man. Max looked up and shook his head, snickered again. Cronus whipped his head back to Jon, only to be met with a sullen and dejected frown.

"You—"

A piercing siren, followed by the oscillating warble of a digital klaxon alarm shook the room. Cronus looked about frantically as two technicians raced to monitors to ascertain the situation.

Ary Leary jumped from his seat and moved toward Max. At first, in a brief moment of false hope, Jon thought he was going to cut Max's bindings with the three-tined fork he brandished. But Ary simply looked on as the technicians apprised Cronus of the emergency.

"Fire alarms in lower level H through J. Hey, that's the secure corridor to Hub-Two," one technician yelled over the din.

"Shit," replied the second.

Jon let a smile spread across his face. As the former security chief, he knew that Hub-Two was one of the remote and clandestine sites where security agents could take prisoners.

Cronus slowly turned to see that Jon was smiling sadly, his teary eyes looked knowingly at his friend, Max. Donovan also shared in the satisfaction of realizing that perhaps the three detainees had created enough of a diversion to escape their captors.

Cronus clenched his teeth and pointed at both men. He spat vehemently as he commanded action.

"Do them both, Leary! Now!" But Leary remained still, head slightly cocked to one side, seemingly fazed out again. Cronus spun him around and looked into his eyes. They were fully dilated and unblinking.

"Shit!" was all Cronus could manage. He pulled the three-tined fork from Leary's grasp and moved toward Webb's tilted platform. Just as he came around the front edge of the slab, the door behind Jonathan swept open and Logan Slousad burst back into the room. He paused, unanimated and stoic, staring at Cronus.

"What the fuck is going on, Wyatt?" He waved at the ceiling and rolled his eyes at the sirens. As if by telekinetic will, the sirens abruptly ceased. The sudden stillness rang with the lingering echoes of the constant alarms.

"Fire alarms on lower levels, sir. But they've been isolated and minimized," one of the techs offered.

"Thank you," Logan answered sarcastically returning his steely gaze to Cronus.

Slousad gestured casually toward the men bound to the chair and gurney, and then to the standing yet seemingly comatose Leary.

"Want to explain why they're still here—still alive—and why you're bleeding all over the floor?" he asked of Cronus.

"Things haven't gone so well in the information extraction phase of the program," Cronus answered with acidic sarcasm. The response and its implied disrespect visibly displeased Logan and he allowed his freezing silver glare to do the scolding.

Cronus eventually softened under the disapproving stare and stepped aside as Logan strode purposefully toward Aristotle Leary. He stood to the side at arm's length, withdrew a short barreled Iso AutoMag from a deep pocket and without a flinch or change of expression, fired a round through Ary's temple.

The force of the impact rocked Leary's head violently, the muzzle energy alone snapping his neck. The round exploded into the wall ten meters away carrying a mist of red and yellow biology with it. Ary's limp body fell like a tissue in flames, crumpling into an inconsequential bundle.

Logan then briskly walked behind Max, placed the barrel of his pistol to the base of the man's skull and again without a word or a glance, fired a second round into Donovan's head. The shot was muffled and the missile instantly exploded from his forehead in a stream of scarlet and purple.

Jon watched in abject horror as both men were executed as easily and efficiently as one would swat flies. His mind perceived all of the action, yet processed little.

Logan turned to Cronus and pointed the weapon at the plump executive, his voice as melodious and sweet as ever.

"If you don't want to be next, I suggest you get your new little toy here plugged in and over to Matheson right quick." Logan gestured toward Jon with that remark. He never once looked at Jon, never bothered to consider him as more than just a fixture in the room.

The new little toy.

Logan tossed the mag-pistol down as carelessly as discarding the wrapper from a stick of gum and walked briskly out of the room.

Cronus breathed a heavy sigh and worked his way over the fresh bodies toward Jon. He held the fork-like instrument out at chest level, its shiny tines sparked from the glinting light of the overhead fluorescents. He stepped around the platform and placed himself directly behind Jon's prone form. Jon sensed that the man was nearly straddling him from behind, but couldn't twist his head around enough to see over his shoulder. His paralysis remained profound, yet he struggled to send urgent messages to the muscles of his limbs to pull or tug or kick or lash out.

He remained frozen, limp and vulnerable on the plastic slab. Sweat poured down his face, soaked his scalp and chilled the nape of his neck. The hairs on his scrotum crawled with the electricity of fear and anticipation.

"Whatever you're planning on doing," Jon croaked, his voice wrenched with fear and unrefined anger. "Do it quickly. You gain nothing from my suffering."

"On the contrary, Jon. It would please me greatly to watch you suffer. Unfortunately, we've run out of time. I must simply do what needs doing and be moving on," Cronus said.

He then placed the tines of the fork against the skin of Jon's back, midline and just below the curve of the shoulder blades. The two lateral tines aligned perfectly with the outer edges of the lamina of the third thoracic vertebra. The middle tine, flattened and razor sharp, wedged into the vertebral interspace between the two prominent spinous processes of T2 and T3.

Jon felt the increase in pressure, and then the sharp stabbing pain as the tines bit and then sank deeper into the flesh of his back. When he could hear and feel metal on bone, the instrument was already slicing through the thin ligaments of the spine, wedging firmly into the narrow intervertebral space.

The agony was sudden and intense; and Jon screamed.

With a sudden shift of weight and a little thrust, Cronus drove the instrument home, slicing cleanly through the thoracic spinal column, severing cord and spinal nerves alike. The configuration of the tool was precise in that its function was limited to a certain calculated depth.

Cronus rapidly unscrewed the handle of the device, leaving the head of the instrument buried within Jon's thoracic spine. Spidery thin silver and gold wires woven in web-like sheaths of gossamer mesh cable blossomed from the short base of the shaft protruding from his back. There was little blood, as the device was designed to tamponade any trauma to the surrounding tissue

Cronus climbed off Webb's back and tossed the handle of the instrument to the ground. It rang hollowly against the stone tile. He walked toward the exit and without looking back, gave simple directions to the two technicians. "Wire him into Net and then transport. Secure this room and terminally clean all of the remaining players."

With that, Cronus left the room, leaving the technicians to scramble around Jon as he floundered on the edge of sanity. He observed the flurry of activity with passive ambivalence—a surreal flavor of numbness not unlike the deep vacuum of distant space.

The exquisite pain receded in one great tidal wash, replaced by shock and sudden detachment.

Without thought or reflection, Jon quickly slid into delirium, and then quiet madness.

~ * ~

Pushing, bouncing and twisting, the escapees worked their way through the turbulent river of humanity that flowed out of the Phoenix-Lamneth Corporate Campus megaplex. Corporate security agents, city police and fire officials swarmed along the teeming avenues and walkways directly outside of the main building, weapons and riot sticks drawn as they tried to corral the evacuating masses.

Amplified voices warbled and cracked over radios as authorities attempted to direct the flow of foot traffic away from the building and down the crowded roadway. The alarms within the building had been shut off minutes before; however, sirens and emergency beacons of all types could be heard fast approaching from unseen response teams.

Sal dragged and pushed Robert and Carla through the throng. Movement and separation from the action was their ally. Within minutes they were clear of the building and riding the current of people away from the chaos. A few people seemed to do a double take as they thought they recognized Carla, but were unable to confirm with a second glance as the three disappeared again into the thinning crowd.

Eventually, they reached a narrow walkway—relatively quiet and dark. Sal led them into the entrance of a small cafe. The establishment was closed, but the shallow foyer provided subtle cover. Carla leaned her backside against the dark glass, sliding down ungracefully until she came to rest seated on the narrow window ledge. Her hands flew to her face. She felt like sobbing, but found that she was too tired. Instead she slowly kneaded the tight flesh of her face with the heels of her hands.

Robert dragged his fingers through his ratty hair and blew out a heavy and frustrated sigh. His shoulders slumped and his mouth hung open like a stunned mime. His eyes jerked and squinted against the outside air.

Sal assessed his motley group of survivors and began to laugh. It was a stressful laugh, meant as a release but the sound of his shaky voice frightened him all the more. Images, memories, consequences and questions flooded his mind. He laughed again and then coughed.

"Well," Robert asked no one in particular. "What now?"

Carla moaned, and then huffed dejectedly shaking her head. Sal recovered from his laughing, coughing spell enough to propose a suggestion.

"We vanish," he said breathlessly. "Lay low and wait."

Silent exhaustion hung over the three like a leaden blanket. Only the distant sound of the fading sirens echoed up the otherwise quiet street.

"We wait." Sal repeated in a low, dejected whisper.

Thirty-four

Finale

"Martin Guererra?"

The receptionist slowly raised her eyebrows and glanced over the top of her wire-rimmed glasses at the uniformed courier standing politely in front of the wide, black steel desk.

She quickly, yet thoroughly, sized up the young woman; assessing the fit of the coordinated gray and blue tunic of the courier services uniform, the loose ponytail of blonde hair pulled casually through the back of a thin baseball-style cap, the choice of bright purple polish for the moderate length and well-manicured nails, and most of all, the girl's easy impish smile.

Delilah immediately approved and allowed a sly smirk to touch her face. She straightened her head and fixed the young woman with a wistful gaze. She prided herself on her innate ability to recognize the energies in and around people, both in the positive form and the negative. She made a little game out of assessing those she met at random, and then testing them to see if her hypothesis played out true.

It began as a harmless hobby but now even she had to admit that it had grown into an annoying social habit. Martin had talked with her on more than one occasion about it, though he always ended by simply asking nicely for her to curb her enthusiasm while in the office.

Now, Delilah took in the young beauty before her and couldn't resist daydreaming. This girl was nearly her own daughter's age, and she couldn't help but sense the electrifying energies flowing from her.

The young courier was engulfed by carefree, high velocity energy. She was a free spirit, full of adventure and whim. She probably did weekend base jumps from the Sierra Madre cliffs and had free-dived the Great Coral Reef at least once. Delilah's heart warmed with the thoughts of spontaneous adventures and fearless passions. As her imagination carried her off to impossible challenges, her eyes glimmered with a far away glaze.

"Huh-hmm." The young woman cleared her throat. "I'm looking for Martin Guererra. I have a certified package that requires ID."

Delilah snapped back to reality, blinked and then smiled. She remained as poised as always and addressed the girl with a soft air of admiration. "Yes, of course, dear. Down the hall. Last door on the right."

Delilah leaned forward, cocked her head to the side and casually scratched her scalp beneath a tightly wound knot of hair with the back of her digital stylus.

"May I have your name?" she asked.

"Penny," responded the young girl with a frown of amusement.

"Penny," Delilah repeated though she made no attempt to log the name anywhere or announce the arrival of the delivery. "Not what I would have guessed, but I can see it now. Playful, yet firm and confident. Great potential for poetry there. Tell me, are you a Penelope?"

Penny hesitated, then relaxed her shoulders and proceeded to humor the older woman. "I'm actually a Margaret, but I didn't like the whole Peggy thing. So, I insisted on Penny at a very young age. It just sort of stuck." She smiled and seemed genuinely proud of her cute explanation.

Delilah was obviously engaged by the girl's tale, and smiled deeply. She brought her hands up from her lap and folded them across the surface of the desk.

"You know, child, you're simply *radiant* with energy," Delilah exclaimed. "It's rare that someone as vibrant and alive crosses my path." She smiled and nodded respectfully in an approximation of a seated bow.

"I just want to thank you for brightening my day," Delilah added.

"You're welcome," Penny responded, clearly comfortable, as if she were used to such eccentric compliments. "And thank *you* for noticing." Her smile came as easy and confident as her poise.

Delilah blushed and swept a hand at the young courier.

"Oh, you best get going."

Penny swept down the hall with the gray and blue folder-sized envelope tucked expertly under her arm. Her strides were graceful, and the bounce in her step seemed buoyed by the wonderfully mystical exchange with the colorful receptionist.

Penny suddenly realized that she had forgotten to ask the woman's name in return, at least as a courtesy if not out of curiosity. She made a mental note to do so on the way out as she rapped lightly on the wooden door marked: *M. Guererra; Analyst Consulting, LTD.*

A soft voice answered. "Come in, it's open."

Penny gently pushed through the door and entered the room. She quickly approached the desk behind which sat a handsome, dark haired man. He rose to greet her and smiled warmly if not tiredly. Penny returned the smile perhaps a little too enthusiastically.

He was an extremely attractive man, and she tended to notice these things.

"Package for Martin Guererra. Certified. I'll need an ID print." She shifted the envelope as she withdrew the thin Penguin IV IceChip processor from a hidden pocket somewhere on her close-fitting tunic.

She felt a blush rise in her cheeks, anticipating the man's wandering eyes across her physique, but was disappointed when she looked back up and saw that he was not the least bit interested in her. His eyes, instead, were fixed on her Penguin PDD—the latest in the popular line of personal digital devices offered by the leader in the field, Polar Innovations. Fortunately for her, the courier company sprang for this model. Otherwise, it would have cost her an entire year's salary on her own.

"I'm Guererra," he responded quietly.

Martin Guererra moved around the desk and stood close to Penny. He finally took his eyes off the device and met her gaze. His eyes were honest and kind, and never once paused to admire the curves and graceful lines of her body.

She was used to visual inspections—even expected them, and more often than not, completely ignored them. But on that rare occasion where the attractive energies were flowing both ways, she looked forward to the silent, blissful interlude. She felt a sudden flash of sadness and disappointment in his lack of interest and immediately chalked it up to sexual preference.

She sighed and handed over the envelope. He placed it on the desk without looking at the sender's address as if he had been expecting the delivery all day.

She flipped open her PDD's CaptureScreen and stabbed at a few icons with her narrow stylus. The screen flickered and pulsed with activity, finally settling into a steady stream of data. Lines of names and addresses scrolled up the screen alphabetically, slowing as the "g's" approached.

Eventually, the flow of data stopped at a screen full of *Guererras* residing in the greater San Antonio area. Each name and address was preceded by an empty square. Penny quickly located the entry: *Guererra, M., 427 East Rutherford Drive,* and tapped the line with her stylus. The entry and its companion square illuminated in a brilliant ice-blue highlight. She turned the device one hundred-eighty degrees for Martin to view the screen.

"If that's you, then I need you to give me the finger." She smiled shyly at her own joke. Martin blushed slightly, but was otherwise all business as he inspected the highlighted entry. He placed the tip of his left middle finger in the small blue square glowing in front of his name. When he removed it, the shimmering shadow of his fingerprint lingered on the surface of the screen. One by one, the dark whorls and wavy arcs ignited brilliantly, and then individually winked out of existence as the processor digitally analyzed the fingerprint. Soon, the last of the convoluted lines flashed and disappeared, leaving only the blank pale blue background of the PDD screen.

It only took seconds, but the wait always seemed like an eternity for Martin. He held his breath each time he orchestrated a transaction at the bank or made purchases at the small market down the block from his modest apartment; waiting, nervous and fearful for that one time when the ID data-base refused his print match, and then soon, the investigators would pay him a visit. He dreaded another unplanned, covert midnight relocation. But if this new ID failed him, he would really have no choice. It was his third, and he knew that he was operating on borrowed time anyway.

Penny watched casually as Martin unconsciously bit his lip. She decided to break the ice with small talk.

"Nice office. You the only one on this floor?" she inquired with a playful smile, coy enough to be sexy, yet mature enough to be taken seriously. Martin raised his eyebrows and faltered slightly.

"Hmm, yeah. Well, no. Not really. I mean, there's a CPA two doors down and a freelance photography studio on the other end. Neither of them are around much, though, so it feels like I have the floor to myself. Then, of course, there's Delilah," he said.

Penny nodded. "Interesting woman, that Delilah," she said with another smile. This got a genuine reaction out of Martin. He rolled his eyes, somewhat embarrassed or ashamed.

"She didn't corner you with her gypsy energy spiel, did she?"

"Well, yes. I mean, she didn't corner me. Just made some small talk. She's quite perceptive, though. Paid me a very nice compliment. I thought she was sweet." Penny smiled wider.

Martin hesitated and as Penny wondered if he would pursue the conversation further, the Penguin chimed softly and a message flashed across the screen. Penny gazed down and furrowed her brow.

"Hmm, that's weird..." she said.

Martin flinched imperceptibly, edging toward panic. Just as he was about ask, she continued, "Well, you are who you say are. But," she added, "according to this, your mailing code is going to change soon. How about that? Instant satellite updates from the Postal Commission. How cool is that?" She flashed another winning smile. Martin quickly gathered his wits and returned the smile.

Trying not to sound relieved, but instead mildly surprised, he remarked, "Yeah, that is wild. What does it say, actually?"

She read directly from the screen. "Says here that as of April tenth, your official address will change to 427 Rutherford Drive, San Antonio—Business, NEA75834, Texas. Looks like they took out the 'east' in East Rutherford as well."

"Huh," was all he dared.

Penny hoped for more, but realized that this guy was simply too preoccupied to continue pursuing. She finalized the delivery by closing out the screen with her personal logon and pocketed the PDD. She nodded and turned toward the door.

"Okay, well, bye. Good luck with that new address," she offered over her shoulder, the disappointed obvious on her face.

"Yeah, thanks. Bye." He responded absently. The door closed behind her.

Martin turned toward his desk, shoved his hands into his pockets and considered the thick envelope on his desk.

He drew a heavy sigh and moved around his desk to his chair. He thumbed the intercom of his comlink as he slowly lowered himself into the worn leather.

"Yes?" Delilah answered the call with a curt, professional clip in her voice; her trademark announcement of displeasure with Martin for once again being a dumbass of one sort or another. He adored her, and would be at a loss without her skills, but sometimes her mothering and her meddling could be a bit much.

"What did I do now?" He sighed mocking adolescent exasperation.

"It's what you didn't do, stubborn ass." She scolded him with the usual term of endearment that only Martin could appreciate. "Penny's energy field was all messed up when she left here."

"What? Who?"

"Penny. The cute—no. The *gorgeous* little blonde you allowed to walk out of here without so much as a wink of admiration. She simply radiated excitement and attraction. Even *you* should have been able to sense that. What is the matter with you? Do you really want to be alone? Forever?"

Martin sighed. "No, Dee. I just have a lot going on right now. And I—"

"Bullshit! No, you don't. Not unless you're some kind of super hero at night, and you change into your purple tights and cape after I leave for the day. You have *nothing* going on."

The line remained silent. Delilah allowed her tirade to sink in, and Martin gave it the requisite time of silent consideration. A real smile spread across his face as she again reminded him how much she really did care about him.

"You're right, Dee," he finally said. "I really need to get a life. But I honestly didn't get a vibe from her. The courier, what was her name?"

"Penny," she answered. "What, are you deaf *and* blind? What part of 'nice office, you here alone' do you not take as a come on?"

"Dee, have you been eavesdropping again? You know that is my one pet peeve..." Martin was smiling to himself.

"Oh, Jesus! The button was probably stuck or whatever... the point is, you need—"

"The point is," he interrupted, "that I respect your privacy, and I expect you to do the same."

She sighed audibly, the digital quality of the comlink reproducing every breath perfectly. "Yes, Martin. You're right. I'm sorry. It's just that—"

"You're concerned and want the best for me, I know that. I love you for that. But, Dee, please. Give me a break. Okay?"

She hesitated, and then chuffed a little laugh. "Yeah, okay. But Penny, she really had a shine."

"Dee, I'm calling it a day. I want you to do the same. With a full day's pay. I have some work to do in my office, and then I'll be out of town for, say, about a week."

"Bad news in the package?"

"Not necessarily, just some old business. Take messages and reschedule any appointments. Give my regrets as always."

"Okay. Martin, is everything alright? Is there something that I can do?" Her chastising tone was immediately replaced by sincere concern.

"Everything's fine, Dee. Thank you."

"Okay. Have a safe trip. Call me."

"Will do." He clicked off and leaned back in his chair eyeing the blue and gray package.

He opened his top drawer, withdrew a sharp knife and slit the envelope open, rather than use the built-in perforated pull strip. Too many explosives could be triggered by pulling that reinforced strip.

He carefully poured the contents of the package out onto the leather blotter of his desktop. He placed the envelope aside.

Lying on the faded brown and green leather pad were but a few items: a plastic case containing two wafer-thin crystalline wedges of IceChip data storage slices, a neatly folded, one page handwritten letter and a brand new Series V Penguin PDD.

Martin pursed his lips and allowed the memories of the past two years to freely flow from their deeply hidden wells. He reached for the letter and sat back to read it. Swiveling in his chair toward the window for better light, he fingered the folded page open.

In neat, crisp handwriting, it began:

> *Dear Friend;*
>
> *I hope this finds you well, and that your evenings have been less lonely and more restful than my own. For my own*

part, I am anxious for our reunion. The time has come, my friend, for us to put to rest our collective nightmares. Forever.

The man now known as Martin Guererra read the rest of the letter. A small tear of remembrance, both bitter and pleasant, tracked down his cheek.

~ * ~

Adrienne Peele sat sipping her coffee from a tall steaming cup. Her legs were crossed beneath the low table, one foot bounced nervously as she eyed the crowd moving around her. She placed the cup on the sticky table top, allowing one hand to remain gently curved around the container, stealing its warmth. With the other hand, she absently drummed her fingers against the paper of the one page letter, neatly folded in half and laying before her on the chipped and worn tile tabletop.

Commuters, both arriving and departing, dashed to and fro across the enameled floor of the train station. The opposing flows of traffic smoothly melted into one another, a meshwork of humanity where the constituent parts managed to achieve their purpose without ever coming in contact with one another.

No conflicts. No surprise aggression, nor hasty defenses. Just molecules of mankind bouncing about, vibrating with the mystical Brownian forces that guide the energies and bits of matter that comprise the universe. There was a strange sense of peace within the organized chaos.

Adrienne took another sip of coffee, adjusted her seat and opened the single handwritten page. The overhead speaker announced the next arrival and small throngs of people responded like schools of silver fish moving as a unit away from a lazy predator.

She reread the neat script:

> *The time has come, my friend, for us to put to rest our collective nightmares. Forever. I ask you to rejoin me for one last stand. You know the place.*
>
> *I have enclosed all that you will need to re-educate yourself. Much has changed since we last shared time together. I can only hope that my preparations are enough. Together, rejoined, I believe we can right an awful wrong. I will wait for you.*

The enclosed device is fully encrypted and completely secure. The information found on the IceChip slices is the most up-to-date that I have and it, too, is fully secure. There is no need to destroy your copy; it will render itself useless after the initial playback. I am confident that one viewing is all that will be required to convince you to come back.

Travel safely. I have missed you and look forward to our reunion.

R.W.

Adrienne sipped again from her cup, recrossed her legs and sighed. The crowd continued its ebb and flow, and the ambient noise hummed with a comforting rhythm. She refolded the letter and slid it into her slim purse, next to the slender Series V Penguin PDD.

She didn't realize her name was being paged until the second announcement. Rereading the letter had taken her back to a time where she had forgotten who she was now, a time when her name and her life were both something completely different.

"Passenger Adrienne Peele, Transcontinental departure 1645 to San Francisco. Please report to the boarding agent at gate C8. Passenger Adrienne Peele…"

She gathered her purse and two small carry-on bags and, leaving her coffee behind, stepped smoothly into the flow of bodies heading toward the departures.

Thirty-five

Robert watched the crowd from the shadow and seclusion of a large, potted fern. The giant fronds wrapped around the base of one of the thick marble pillars that guarded the left flank of the entrance into the hotel's lounge. Lazy throngs of well dressed people meandered about the immense lobby of The Golden Grand.

He sipped bourbon from a heavy crystal tumbler, peering from time to time at the flat screen of the wide LCD covering one entire wall of the dimly lit bar. Continuous live feeds from Mandatory Media Network Plus updated viewers on the latest in breaking local and national news, public interest, entertainment, sports and weather. He caught only snippets of information during his casual glimpses, the bulk of his attention focused on the towering glass doors of the hotel's gothic entrance.

He nursed his third drink, waiting patiently for his other friend to arrive. Robert expected him to stroll through the lobby any minute now, and the thrill of anticipation was becoming more difficult to conceal. The liquor was both warming and energizing, and filled him with a comfortable charisma that ached to be exercised. He had to consciously remind himself to remain relaxed and controlled, lest he give himself away with childish whoops of joy.

Ninety minutes ago, a beautiful dark-skinned woman strode through the tall glass entrance of The Golden Grand, her long straight hair trailing behind from a simple yet elegant head wrap. Her equine legs conveyed her across the dark stone floor in graceful, confident strides; her hips moved fluidly and her shoulders were firm and square. When she removed her shaded eyeglasses and smiled at the concierge, he could feel the heat of her presence reach across the vast lobby to him in fierce, sudden waves.

Robert had almost forgotten just how beautiful she was; and he remembered how different she appeared to him eighteen months ago. They had all been so vulnerable and spent back then.

Beaten and terrified, actually.

Robert smiled proudly as she nodded to the clerk checking her in. When she accepted the keycard to her room and the bellboy retrieved her two modest bags, Robert knew that Carla Robinson had just successfully returned to California undetected and had checked into the most extravagant hotel on the western seaboard under the alias of Adrienne Peele.

He had silently congratulated himself on that little construct.

Now, he waited for Martin Guererra to arrive. Tonight the three reunited friends would dine at the top of the hotel, in the garden restaurant overlooking the dark bay.

In the shadows of the ferns and vines and ivy-encrusted trellises, they would recap their lives lived apart from one another and laugh a little at their misfortunes. Over a long, purposeful meal of eclectic seafood, lush salads, fresh pastas and thick, tender steaks they would discuss the past and its implication on the present. They would weigh cause and effect, circumstance and malice over many bottles of fine wine.

Then, as the night turned chilly and the sea air wafted inland from the wharf, they would decide their collective fate. They'll toast to the commitment—sealing their alliance—and embrace one last time before the next day arrives; for the dawn would bring them closer to the precise day that would change the face of human existence.

Robert finished off his drink as his long awaited friend finally swam through the blinding beams of sunlight that slanted through the thick glass doors of the entrance. His hair was longer and much lighter; his frame more solid as he carried an extra ten or twenty pounds without any noticeable alteration in his distinguishable gait.

Sal Gionetti carried a single overnight bag over to the main desk, and after a few expedient formalities, completed his registration under the name of Martin Guererra. He elected to port his own bag and strode quickly to the bank of elevators.

Robert slid up to the desk just as Sal departed and offered two neatly inscribed envelopes to the concierge.

"Could you please ensure that these are hand delivered to Mr. Guererra and Ms. Peele when they arrive?" he asked.

The concierge accepted them and raised his brow slightly, exhibiting the requisite air of confident arrogance expected from his post.

"Of course, sir," the man replied. "You just missed the gentleman. The lady settled in earlier. Shall I have them delivered or would you prefer that I handle it directly?" The question begged for a substantial gratuity, and Robert deftly slipped the man a folded wad of currency.

"If you could ensure the deliveries yourself, that would be best," Robert said.

"Of course, sir." He accepted the folded bills and expertly secreted them in some hidden recess of his tunic.

"I'll also require reservations for three this evening atop the hotel. A late dinner—9:00 PM. A terrace table, near the fountain and well-dressed in foliage," Robert added.

"The *Corona del Luna* is usually booked weeks in advance. Might I suggest *Q* instead, or even *Crocus?* Both are excellent, and I'm sure still offering availabilities," the concierge countered.

"Those invitations are for dinner tonight, explicitly at this hotel." Robert sternly pointed to the envelopes he had handed to the man. "Don't disappoint me. There's always at least one table left empty. Do your job and fill it." The concierge nodded solemnly.

"Thank you." Robert turned and headed for the elevators.

"Yes, sir. Good evening."

~ * ~

"Thank you," Robert said to the waiter when he had placed the freshly uncorked bottle of wine on the corner of their table. "That should be all for awhile. We have some business to discuss." The young waiter nodded understanding and slipped silently out of sight.

Sal and Carla both raised their eyebrows, glancing at one another across the table, and then turned to Robert.

As Robert portioned out the richly aromatic wine, Sal expressed both admiration and surprise. "This high society niche seems to suit you well, young man."

"Yes, you certainly have mastered a flair for the finer points," Carla added with a wry smile. "Just look at this hotel. And the restaurant! How on earth did you snare this table?"

Robert blushed modestly, waving them off. "C'mon guys. It's just part of the role. You know that."

"Feels good, don't it?" Sal asked rhetorically.

Robert smiled mischievously, nodded and without hesitation answered, "Hell, yes!"

They all laughed quietly, settling into the warmth of the post dinner glow. Each of their smiles lingered as if trying on the emotion for style, but soon the smiles faded and the exhaustion and concern crept back from beneath the veneer where it hid. They sat in comfortable silence, each allowing their mind to drift back to a shared past.

Robert sipped his wine, admiring the shimmering crests of black waves out in the bay as the lights of San Francisco cast their glittering reflection over the dark water. A slight, yet constant breeze blew salty air over the garden restaurant high atop the Golden Grand. It all seemed such an extreme departure from his days as a sometimes nurse, full-time computer genius, runaway fugitive.

Suddenly, Robert did indeed feel alien and removed from his place in this world. He breathed deeply of the brine-scented air and reconsidered his recent travels and transformations.

Soon after their harrowing escape from Phoenix-Lamneth, the three quickly decided that disappearing in separate directions was the only safe choice. But to do so and survive in this world, one needed an established identity. Therefore, they would need help.

They had retreated to the country, a little getaway cabin belonging to Robert's fiancée's father. The price to pay for that temporary sanctuary was wholly assumed by Robert, as Connie, his lovely and extremely pissed off wife-to-be demanded to know what the hell had been going on to keep Robert AWOL for nearly three days. It seemed that he had accrued the maximum of unexcused absences from work, and the Rainey Clinic had been bothering her at the lab, wondering where he might be. He had also, and perhaps more importantly, missed a long planned dinner date and failed to call during his absence.

Nevertheless, when Robert finally did phone Connie to ask for the keys to the cabin, she acquiesced, meeting them out at the lake herself. After simple and open ended introductions, Sal and Carla were excused to clean up both themselves and the cabin, for it had sat unused all season and was in dire need of sprucing. Robert then walked with Connie through the parallel rows of towering pines, taking a full two hours to explain in great detail the events of the few days in question.

She took everything rather well; and surprisingly, needed little proof to convince her of the tale's authenticity. In fact, of those now aware of the treachery and scandal, she seemed to be the least surprised. Perhaps her years at Polar Innovations had numbed her to mankind's capacity for brilliance as well as its penchant for self-consumption.

Whatever the reason for her stoic acceptance, she agreed to help the three fugitives, but only on the condition that she remained far removed from their activities. She agreed that it was indeed sad, and tragic, what happened to those involved, and although she recognized her employer as the architect of a potentially malignant future, she couldn't jeopardize her career or social position. She would keep her ear to the wall and her eyes to her back, but she also conceded that aside from aiding in their disappearance, there really was little else that she could do.

Therefore, she would not be joining Robert in his seclusion. She would help him disappear because she loved him and wanted him safe, but that would be the end of her commitment. In other words, what they had together would end when Robert ceased to be Robert and became whoever he was to become.

So it happened that with Connie's technical prowess, Robert's digital savvy and Sal and Carla's deep, though dwindling, connections; they were able to dredge up a thin list of long deceased individuals from which they could draw initial identities. From that pool, they eventually recreated natural and very real aliases which they each could assume and begin anew.

All told, Robert and Connie engineered eight convincing personas for the three of them, complete with embryonic histological verification, lifetime chronology, dermal print analysis matches and macular waivers to avoid retinal scans. They would, however, have to avoid any scenario that involved direct DNA analysis—that was just too complex to falsify in such short order.

So, for the past two years, Robert had been eking out an existence as a freelance software engineer for a medium-tiered gaming company in Seattle. The elaborate digital environments of the VR games came easily to him, and he pumped out enough new titles each quarter to keep the paychecks coming in. The majority of his time, however, was spent keeping tabs on Polar Innovations and Dolan Douglass.

Since the time of their disappearance, Robert had been able to operate covertly within the cyber space that makes up all of Polar Innovations. In an ironic twist of fate, Polar Innovations unwittingly exposed its technical underbelly through Robert's own design flaws.

The advancement of the Ice Cube and its application to the clandestine Madison Protocol Projects really hit its stride after they discovered the software for Robert's Halo translation proposal on Jon Webb's holo-disk. Robert had left a number of open ended logic matrices available to make it easier for Jon to compose a more personal message to his wife Sarah. It was through these open algorithms that the advanced teams of design engineers at PI were able to crack into Robert's elaborate program.

Though they solved many of Robert's own design problems, they got lazy under the stress of demands for production; so they simply fixed Robert's design, applied it to the existing construct and pushed the concept through to final production.

In their haste, they never closed out the open ended matrices, and within two days Robert was back inside his own pirated program and able to remotely monitor its application undetected.

"So, really, Robert," Sal asked. "How can you afford all of this? The extravagant hotel, our tickets back out here, everything." He raised a questioning brow.

Robert again waved him off. "Aw, no. Nothing illegal or even immoral. Just some creative movement within the market. Remember, I do have access to valuable tech info."

"That's insider trading and it *is* illegal," Carla warned.

Robert shook his head and smiled. "Not when it's given freely. I use the same information available to anyone logged onto MetaNet. I just know what it means and how to apply it. To everyone else it's gibberish.

"This..." He gestured around them indicating the opulent wealth. "Is simply a treat. For all of us. You think I live like this all the time? In fact, this is the first time that I've spent any significant amount of money on something other than necessities for my research into the Projects or as anonymous gifts to charitable organizations." Robert smiled and shook his head emphatically. "No, I couldn't live like that. Hey, not that it isn't tempting, especially being that it's Douglass' money to begin with."

Carla smiled and reached over the table to squeeze his hand.

He blushed and risked a glance at her lovely face.

"Well, thank you, Robert. For everything."

"Yeah, well…" He trailed off, embarrassed.

"You've certainly done more with your new life than either of us," Sal added somewhat sadly.

"Private consulting doesn't agree with you?" Carla asked.

"No more than teaching ninth grade literature and selling real estate on the side," he countered.

"Hey," she feigned offense, and then smiled. "I actually enjoy the teaching. It's more of a challenge than you think."

"I'll bet," Sal said. "All those hormone-afflicted teens filled with angst and dangerous innocence."

Carla sensed that his dark cynicism was more than just simple melancholy. She grew instantly sad and felt ashamed that she had allowed herself to believe in a hopeful future based on a satisfying, albeit temporary, present. She sometimes forgot what she really knew.

The three sat a moment longer in silence, then after a long drink of warm wine, Sal asked the question that begged to be asked all night long. "So, what is our next step?"

He looked at both Robert and Carla an equal amount of time clearly opening the table for candid discussion.

Robert sighed and folded his hands on top of the table as he leaned forward. "We expose them," he simply stated. "All of them. The whole fucking circus."

Carla and Sal nodded and sat back into their chairs.

"What did you have in mind?" Sal asked.

"The program will expose itself," Robert answered.

"How?" Carla asked.

"It's actually simpler than you think," Robert said.

They waited patiently for an explanation. A siren echoed from the street below and distant bells could be heard tolling from the waterfront. The buzz of the restaurant's late night patrons hummed around them, and Robert lowered his voice to be heard just above the level of the ambient noise.

"The day after tomorrow—Friday morning—Douglass and Cronus will hold a closed conference for the SciTech community. It's an invite-only affair. Heads of industry, university research and development and a few selected media reps. All private sector big leaguers." Robert pointed to the floor with fingers of both hands. "Right here at the Golden Grand." He smiled.

Sal's eyes narrowed, and Carla's mouth fell open. Robert nodded affirmation and continued.

"They're planning to unveil the Project results and announce the vision statement of the new Polar Innovations. They want to unleash the future." Robert arched his brow and sat back in his own chair.

Sal shifted in his seat and glanced at Carla. She crossed and uncrossed her legs beneath the table, methodically smoothing the fabric of her skirt. A moment of silence passed before Robert spoke again.

"They're also planning to use Sarah Webb for their prime demonstration. From what I can see, the intended show promises to break through the walls of doubt and should thoroughly convince any skeptics of its potential."

Sal tensed. Carla's hands froze in her lap.

"They've solved the language problem and eliminated the echo paradox," Robert explained with an obvious pang of regret in his voice. "I should have destroyed the work. Hell, I never should have even attempted it, but..."

Sal raised his hand to stop him and shook his head firmly.

"Enough of that, Robert. We've done this before. What's done is done." He sighed and continued. "Now, what are you talking about? Remember who you're talking to here."

Robert nodded. "Yeah, right. Sorry. You guys saw the data I sent you on the IceChips, right?"

They both nodded.

"Well, there's something that I withheld. Something I suspected yet couldn't be sure of until just recently." He paused, carefully choosing his words. Carla and Sal stared imploring him to continue.

Robert took a deep breath and held it for a moment, then exhaled with a nervous shudder.

"It's Jonathan Webb," he began. "He's still alive."

The silence that followed was thick, laden with remorse and disbelief. Sal simply stared out at the dark evening. Carla wrung her slender fingers, twisting them in tight, white-knuckled knots. Her eyes grew instantly moist. She blinked repeatedly, releasing a single tear that trailed a thin thread of wetness down her cheek.

Robert proceeded somewhat awkwardly, and then smoothed out as he gained momentum.

"As you could see from the data I sent you, they have perfected the Halo interface using my original design with Sarah. They kept her wired and were finally able to break through the barriers that prevented me from establishing reciprocal exchanges between subjects." He paused and their silence begged for elaboration.

"They found a way for Sarah to have meaningful communication with another subject," he said.

He waited for their gazes to settle directly on him.

"That subject happens to be Jon."

Sal stretched his neck and back, and with his eyes closed he spoke in a painful whisper, "He's the feedback factor that you spoke of. Are you sure?"

Robert, without hesitation, answered, "Positive."

Sal rubbed his eyes with both fists mumbling, "Shit."

"Robert, what does all this mean?" Carla finally asked. "I mean, I watched the material you sent. I think I understand the significance. But —"

"It means," Sal interjected, "that they've forced human evolution."

"To say the very least," added Robert. "They're intending to fling open Pandora's Box."

"I'd assumed that Jon was dead," Sal whispered.

Robert shook his head solemnly.

Sal turned to Robert. His eyes were deep and full of soft agony. "Is he implanted, Robert?" he asked.

Robert responded quietly, "I have to assume so."

Carla shuddered, and then winced against a flood of emotion. Robert leaned forward and rested his hands flat on the table. He studied his fingers, slowly spreading and closing them.

Sal tipped his chair on the back legs and slowly rolled his head, agitated and tense.

After a moment, he finally broke the spell.

"Okay, Robert, lay it all out. Where are we now, and where are we headed?"

Robert took another deep breath, and then slowly began to bring the others up to speed. Carla and Sal listened intently as he explained the incredible developments over the past two years, pausing periodically to take sips of water from a tall crystal glass, the red wine ignored now and growing stale.

"My intent, of course, was charitable and compassionate. I wanted to give my friend an opportunity to communicate with his comatose wife. I really stumbled upon the idea accidentally while playing around with a few simple interface programs I had developed. The technology was raw and the method crude, but it worked.

"However, the information could only travel one way. She could receive simple auditory and visual messages, but couldn't send them. I simply didn't know enough about the way the human brain processed data. That was the goal of the Rainey Clinic. Matheson and his staff were mapping the brain, trying to locate common pathways.

"I succeeded where they initially failed merely because I focused on the human spirit, for lack of a better term. I guess you could call it human essence. The soul. I found a way to touch Sarah's, and she responded." Robert stared intently into his water glass as if searching for forgiveness within its purity.

"Matheson was obsessed with the physicality of the mind," he continued, "the electrochemical composition and organic construct of the brain. He's a brilliant neurophysiologist and knows more about the molecular framework of the human nervous system than anyone alive. But he missed the forest for the trees, I suppose.

"When the shit hit the fan after our discovery of the stem cell efforts and cerebral grafting, and we were forced to go underground, they liberated all they could from Jon's personal holo-disk. They found all of my work. Perhaps my second biggest mistake." Robert shook his head in silent remorse.

Carla reached over to comfort him, but he stiffened and continued swallowing his guilt.

"With Polar Innovations' unlimited resources, Matheson and the Rainey effort were able to apply their knowledge and experience in vastly different ways. My idea sent them in a whole new direction, one that they may have discovered on their own, given time. Or maybe not, I don't know." He winced with regret.

"But with the advancements of optical processing in general and the hyper-capacity and speed of the Ice Cube and IceChip processors specifically, they were finally able to solve the problem of reciprocity and language." Robert finally looked at them. His eyes were red and moist and held a distant fearful gleam.

"They found a way to not only communicate readily and directly with the human mind—in and of itself, independent of the body's senses—but they also developed a common language that enabled them do so in meaningful ways."

"What do you mean by 'language'?" Sal asked.

"I projected images and sounds through digital matrices that translated the data into appropriate electrochemical signals within Sarah's implanted Halo. These stimuli were not only familiar to Sarah, but held specific personal *meaning* for her. They evoked emotions and memory. That same set of data may be meaningless to you or me and elicit no response. But because the data were tailored to her, she responded. She recognized the language of the data.

"That becomes problematic if you want universal application of the technology. And that is, after all, the ultimate goal. To be able to communicate with the mind directly. Any mind."

"Good God," Carla exclaimed.

"So," Sal asked. "You need a universal language to express things into someone's—anyone's—mind?"

"More importantly, for that mind to respond in kind—to make the communication *meaningful*—there must be reciprocity. Give and take. You type out commands on your PDD, it converts it internally to digital code, sends it through the processor, it carries out the explicit function, translates that data from digitized code, and then sends it back onto your screen in a language and format that you understand. Anything else would result in meaningless gibberish to both of you."

"And they've found a way to do this with the human mind?" Carla asked.

"With the help of cerebral implants harvested from advanced stem cell colonies... Yes."

"How?" Sal asked.

Robert shrugged weakly. "Well, it's complex. But, essentially, that little strip of grafted tissue—the patch of manufactured nerve cells—is much more elaborate than we thought. The implant actually serves as a primer for the host language."

"A primer?" Carla asked.

"Yeah, a learning template. Kind of like a Rosetta stone for the mind. It teaches the mind—the targeted areas of the brain—the intended language. As it teaches, it in turn learns and grows, adapting to the varieties and personal nuances of each brain. It develops a relationship, for lack of a better word, with the host."

Carla curled her lip in revulsion. "Sounds like mind control."

"No, this is something completely different. Brain washing is a component of psychology, where the native organic mind is not physically altered, but rather manipulated through the use of external persuasion facilitated by biochemical and pharmaceutical means. The cerebral graft is an actual, physical intrusion into the brain. It's exactly as Sal said earlier—forced evolution. They are physically transforming the human mind."

"Christ," Carla whispered shuddering.

Robert nodded and leaned back. Sal sighed heavily and ran his hands through this thick hair. Robert finished off his wine in a gulp, pushed the goblet away and grimaced as the warm, acidic vintage raced down the back of his throat.

"What can we possibly do?" Sal finally asked.

"They're using my program as a platform for the Project. It's complicated, but the Halo translation is critical during the initialization and imprinting of the grafted cells. The process involves intricate coordination between delicate electrochemical cascades, and some of the most exotic logic matrices I've ever seen." Robert shook his head in reluctant awe.

He then eyed his partners for a moment allowing a faint, yet hopeful, smirk to touch the corners of his mouth before continuing. "But I've been deep inside the program for over a month now. Undetected." He winked, clearly proud.

The others simply looked on, waiting for more.

"I've been able to manipulate the primer, actually add some alternate algorithms."

Sal frowned with growing impatience at Robert's cryptic delivery. He took a deep breath and gave the young man a look that implored simplicity.

Robert immediately caught the hint and shifted into a more succinct presentation. "I've planted a Trojan Horse in Sarah Webb's mind." He pursed his lips and let the revelation settle over the table.

"A what?" asked Carla.

"Trojan Horse. A back door with a hidden key. Using their own system and the language primer, I've uploaded a great deal of incriminating data into a deeply concealed portion of her mind. When she receives an encoded key, that part of her mind will unlock and download the stored information.

"With the conference attendees as witnesses, their prize subject will reveal the whole mess onto recordable media. The whole thing will unravel right before their eyes." Robert glanced at Carla. "It'll be all over Mandatory Media by nightfall."

"You're certain this will work?" Sal asked.

Robert nodded emphatically. "Absolutely. I've already tested it a number of times, remotely. Each time, Sarah does as instructed. The download includes everything I could dredge up about the Program and Polar Innovations involvement with Phoenix-Lamneth. I also took some creative liberty and composed a few thinly veiled conversations between Dolan and Wyatt, alluding to human experimentation, technological espionage and of course multiple murder."

Sal narrowed his eyes and pursed his lips. "I'm sensing that there's one great, yet to be discussed, caveat to your plan. Otherwise, you would have carried this out by yourself."

"Yeah, Robert. Why did you bring us back? Risk our covers?" Carla asked.

Robert bit his lip and dropped his gaze. His hesitation was palpable.

"It wasn't just to share in the glory of revenge." Sal added. "What is it?"

"I need both of your skills one last time," he responded.

They stared at him waiting for explanation.

Robert sighed and continued, "The only way to activate Sarah's revelation is by direct external input. I've constructed a series of verbal queues that will initiate an irreversible broadcast of the incriminating evidence. But we need to be at the demonstration. Physically." He took a breath, speaking rapidly.

"The invite list for the presentation has been sealed for months. The attendees were brought here two days ago and have remained under intense security since. There's no way to crash the party without being detected."

Sal nodded slowly and Carla frowned.

"Also," Robert added, "there's no way to absolutely guarantee that the information will even make it out of the room to the external media. I mean, if they own the audience, they can quarantine and sanitize the situation before it can do damage."

Carla finally spoke, tracing her fingers around the rim of her wine glass. "Have you seen the list? Maybe I can tell if the invited media reps are legit. They can't buy off everyone—".

"They'll simply eliminate those they can't," Sal interrupted. He looked solemnly in her direction, catching her eyes and holding them with an intense and foreboding stare. "They've done it before," he added darkly.

"As I said, the list is locked down," Robert answered. "But I've been able to liberate the room numbers of a few of the selected guests. No names or affiliations, just rooms."

Robert looked warily at Sal from under his hooded brow, internally wincing at the unspoken, yet understood, implication.

Sal caught the look and sighed. He wrung his hands beneath the table; his eyes fell closed as he breathed deeply and slowly. Carla's gaze shifted between the men, turning in her seat as she processed the moment.

Sal spoke softly, yet with a conviction of determination and confidence. "How many rooms and how well guarded?"

"Three. And extremely well. Teams of four on three hour shifts at each door. Heavily armed. Outfitted with continuous communication and surveillance," Robert answered.

Carla blinked as the reality of the situation finally sunk in. She gasped, almost inaudibly, and stiffened at Sal's side.

"No," she whispered. "No more violence. No more killing."

Sal leaned back and stretched his neck. He turned to her as she lost the strength to hold back the tears that had welled in her eyes. He took her hands in his and smiled.

"Hopefully, we can avoid that," he assured her, smiling sadly. "But we must do what needs to be done. This is too important to screw up."

"Carla," Robert said. "We need you. You're our only real chance at getting full exposure. You must know some people who are still loyal to you. Even possibly sympathetic. This has to hit the public in one huge, undeniable dose or it'll get buried in the dirt of everyday fluff."

She breathed deeply, her eyes locked with Sal's as she squeezed his hands tightly in her lap. Sal arched his brow and smiled again. "Carla, this is our last and best chance to do the right thing. I promise I'll do everything in my power to avoid unnecessary action."

She held his gaze for a moment longer, sealing their bond across the distance. She nodded and sniffed the remaining moisture from her nose. Her eyes glimmered and a determined clarity spread across her face. She gave his hands one last squeeze and released her grip.

"Okay," Sal whispered.

He turned to Robert, blinking the emotion from his eyes. "What do I have to work with?" he asked.

"Not much." Robert sighed. "But, like I said. You have skills."

Thirty-six

The small conference room was abuzz with active conversations, low incongruent murmurs that fell dead on the thickly soundproofed walls. Men and women sat in small groups or in isolated couples, leaning toward one another to be heard over the ambient white noise.

Large, quiet men in suits stood staggered throughout the brightly lit room and around its periphery, still and silently imposing. One of the men turned his head with a slight jerk revealing the slightest glint of an earpiece nestled in his left ear, his eyes darted along the wall farthest from the gathering of people. The deep caramel oak finish of that wall suddenly creased with a sharp, vertical seam that smoothly widened as the camouflaged portal of the OmniVator opened to reveal the arrival of another guest.

He unfolded his thick arms and smoothed the soft lapels of his dark maroon jacket as he walked swiftly toward the threshold of the 'Vator.

Two men in gray-black suits emerged, flanking a tall, lithe woman in a striking dark green dress. The man to her left reached to seize her elbow, just missing as she stepped forward and into the interior of the conference room. With moderate heels, she stood a few inches taller than the men and her confident stride quickly put her steps ahead of her stoic escorts.

The second man quickened his own stride and in two long steps drew alongside the woman and gently halted her with a firm hand on her broad shoulder. Her immediate gaze was both stern and condescending, yet his eyes held her in check with a determined glare of authority.

His partner regrouped, sidling up to the couple with a shiver of embarrassment at missing his mark the first time. The woman flashed this man a sly smile of victory. He glanced about the room, ignoring the woman's stinging eyes, and tried to re-establish his position of centurion.

The man on the right expertly whispered into the nearly invisible throat-mic secured in the hollow of his neck as he too casually scanned the room.

The man in the maroon jacket and perfectly creased charcoal pants approached the new arrivals and nodded once to both escorts. Without a word, they held out their hands palms up and submitted to a dermal scan.

He cupped the device in his own hand and gently dragged the slim scanner across the ventral surface of their palms, trans-luminating their skin with a phosphorescent aqua-green glow. He supinated his hand after each scan, glanced at the readout without expression, and then nodded to the man on the right.

The woman watched with a sense of indifference, bordering on contempt, at the paranoid display of security. The man on her right leaned into her and whispered a terse command as he firmly nudged her arm forward. She extended her delicate hand, elegantly sweeping her well-manicured fingers as she turned her palm up toward the man in maroon. Her eyes bore into him with defiance and confidence, clearly unimpressed with the show of drama and hyper vigilance.

With the device cupped in his thick hand, he gently pulled it across hers, his thumb dragged along the smooth skin and fine creases of her palm. Her dark skin did not glow with the green iridescence, nor did the readout display any data when he angled it to view.

The escorts failed to notice the faked scan, and when the man in maroon looked up he simply nodded without expression and offered his arm to the woman. The escorts stepped aside, relieved of their charge, executed an about face and returned to the open 'Vator. They disappeared behind the closing doors, the smoothness of the oak wall restored.

The man in maroon escorted the woman into the room, her hand resting absently in the crook of his arm. They fell into a natural rhythmic stride; she, taking in the faces of those already present, and he, watching indifferently as they moved deeper into the crowd. Heads turned and conversations briefly paused as the invited guests noticed the new arrival.

Flickers of faint recollection spread across some faces, brows wrinkled and frowns knit curiously as people struggled to place the woman's fleetingly familiar face.

"Someone will recognize me, I'm sure," she whispered, her lips nearly still as she breathed the words.

"*So what? You disappeared two years ago, and for all they know, you're back now for a stellar debut covering perhaps the biggest revelation since Moses came down from the mountain.*" The tiny voice vibrated in her ear from the small receiver.

"Shh!" The man in maroon hissed into his throat mic. He turned toward the woman making a show of offering her a seat next to an elderly gentleman who was seated alone next to a short empty table.

Sal pulled out the chair and guided Carla to sit. She gently floated into the plush leather chair smoothing the dark green fabric of her dress as she crossed her long legs. The older man eyed her admiringly, but then blushed when she caught his gaze travel up her thigh from her slim leather strapped heels. She smiled appreciatively, but with a touch of gentle scolding.

She nodded to Sal, who turned his back without acknowledgement and walked away. As she watched the dark maroon of his jacket fade into the crowd, she heard his familiar deep voice crackle in her ear.

"*You look lovely, by the way.*"

She smiled and nonchalantly craned her neck to follow his progress back across the room to his post, but he had already disappeared behind the milling masses. The older gentleman seated next to her misinterpreted the smile and began a hopeful conversation.

"I'd offer to buy you a drink, miss. But I'm under the distinct impression that this affair will be dismally dry," he said in an attempt to charm.

Carla blinked, smiled and turned on her own charm easily sliding back into her old familiar character.

"Oh, on the contrary. I think we may be the few fortunate to witness something extraordinary today. Besides, I find that Chairperson Douglass and Director Cronus are quite engaging. Hardly dry," she countered assuming the immediate role of devil's advocate.

"My dear, a three dimensional chess match between metaphysical theorists high on Synth is engaging. Any presentation by that immoral, ethically challenged biotech pirate Cronus and his pet talking asshole

Douglass is, indeed, dry. Insipid. Arid. The kind of desiccation that can only be remedied by a stiff shot of twenty-year-old single malt."

Carla smiled and extended her hand. "Well, sir, in that case if they ever open the bar, I would be honored. Bethany Melbourne, United Journalists."

He cupped her hand in both of his and bent to brush a soft kiss across her lavender nails.

"Lancaster Fawlings, University of Minnesota. Professor emeritus. At your service."

"*Nice.*" Robert's voice crackled sarcastically in her ear.

~ * ~

"Ladies and gentlemen," a thin voice echoed around the stuffy conference hall. "Ladies and gentlemen, please. If you could begin taking your seats, we have five minutes."

The rumble of various conversations tapered off as the small crowd meandered toward the front of the hall where a semi-circle of soft, comfortable looking office chairs were arranged around twin oak podiums. Behind the podiums, a dark royal blue satin drape hung from ceiling to floor billowing gently in slow undulating waves from the soft currents of air created by the moving bodies.

Carla allowed professor Fawlings to escort her by the elbow to adjoining seats at the far left of the podiums. As he offered her the innermost chair he leaned down and whispered into her ear. "I hope you don't mind the aisle, dear. But for me, it allows for an unobtrusive and early exit should the festivities validate my earlier predictions and grow tiresome."

He had the whimsical smile of a wisecracking old uncle, yet his eyes held a depth to them. Wisdom and genius dwelled within those eyes—the kind of wisdom gained only from experience and personal pain, and the type of genius that unravels mysteries like a child on Christmas morning.

Carla graciously accepted the offered seat and returned his impish smile with a slight nod of understanding and a few glimmering flashes of her long lashes.

"Oh, not at all, Lancaster. I'm just grateful for the honesty of your company and the sincerity of your chivalry." She allowed an innocent and crooked curl to grace the corners of her mouth. He blushed immediately at the use of his first name and quickly took the chair on the outside.

Carla made show of readjusting her dress as she casually turned in her seat, nonchalantly scanning the room for Sal. She caught a flash of deep maroon through the moving bodies before she finally located him stationed toward the rear of the room, standing in near shadow. She quickly turned to the front and folded her hands primly in her lap.

She sighed heavily, hoping for a gentle escape of air; but instead it shuddered out of her like the breeze under the beating wings of bats.

Lancaster Fawlings glanced over at the sound and, misinterpreting the cause, gently patted her knee three times. "Really, dear, these things are almost always blown completely out of proportion. Why, the last technological *unveiling* I was asked to participate in was marketed as the be-all, end-all of micronutrient supplementation.

"Anheuser-Nestle were promoting what they thought was the ultimate solution to osteoporosis. They spent billions on grandiose campaigns to entice us to endorse the product. Even put us up at Disney's Vail Resort in Colorado for an entire week.

"Oh, don't get me wrong, I enjoyed every minute of it. Right up to and including the part where I had them reconsider their final research data." He nodded with a dignified air of academic justice.

"Turns out that CalciCrit, their wonder drug, actually caused severe and irreversible hemolytic anemia. The trials showed..." he continued with his story, and Carla feigned attention. But her mind had drifted to more severe matters.

Fear and anxiety were creeping back in, threatening to undo her practiced facade. She worried that someone might recognize her or Sal. Though her hair was nearly eight inches longer now, a different color and styled in a way that changed the whole appearance of her face, she couldn't shake the paranoia. She held her breath every time someone made eye contact and held it for longer than just passing social recognition. She tried to tell herself that it was just admiration, appreciation or even plain lewdness. But vanity was not in her repertoire, and she found herself breaking contact, often far too abruptly; which more than likely brought more attention to herself.

She worried less about Sal, of course. After all, he was a professional at things like this, even if he had been out of practice during the past few years. But even she had to admit that he looked much different from when they were last together. Heavier, but firmer. Healthier looking. His close-cropped haircut and razor-lined beard had completed the transformation.

He was more attractive than she had ever given him credit for, and when she first walked into the restaurant two nights ago, she allowed herself to be pleasantly surprised at her attraction—if only for a moment—before the gravity of the situation bore back down upon them.

She felt safe with him in the room.

She sighed and glanced sideways at Fawlings, who was finishing up his story.

"But, then again, I've never skied before. How about you?" the professor asked.

She smiled and gently shook her head.

"Rather wasteful, if you ask me. Spend thousands of Units to go up a mountain, just to fly back down in what can only by described as a controlled tumble."

A small, tightly dressed young woman finally approached the podiums from behind the blue curtain. She stepped purposefully to the right and expertly placed the nearly invisible throat mic against the hollow in the base of her neck. She authoritatively cleared her throat and gave a plastic smile that faded as quickly as the dying murmurs around the room.

"Thank you. Ladies and gentlemen, on behalf of Phoenix-Lamneth and Polar Innovations, I'd like to welcome you all, and once again thank you for attending." She blinked twice, scanned the room like a sniper and then continued. "I'd also like to take this opportunity to remind you that the management and staff of the Golden Grand has been extraordinary in their cooperation. Both in their hospitality and their decorum. They are being very well taken care of, I assure you. However, if you have enjoyed the accommodations during your stay, by all means, feel free to express any gratuity befitting, and it will be allocated from your already substantial endowment."

Fawlings leaned over and whispered to Carla, "That means that they'll deduct any tips from our bribe money." He winked and sat back.

Carla narrowed her eyes and seriously considered the old man.

"*I like this guy,*" Robert's ghostly voice whispered in her ear piece. She had to agree.

"Without any further delay, it's my privilege and honor to introduce to you the Chairperson of the Federation's Science and Technology Branch, Senator Dolan Douglass."

A smattering of polite, soft applause greeted the Senator as he emerged from the side of the blue curtain in a graceful flourish. He strode smoothly to the left podium and acknowledged the crowd with a confident nod. He placed his hands on either side of the wide lectern and turned to the young woman who then continued with the introductions.

"And your host, the CEO, founder and chief clinical director of the new leader in biotechnology, Wyatt Cronus." The pudgy man ducked out from behind the curtain and ambled to the right podium, stepping up on a previously placed riser to bring him nearly, but not quite, to Douglass' height.

The applause for Cronus was far less enthusiastic and disintegrated almost immediately. The small woman vanished from sight, and the two men held the attention of the crowd for a brief moment.

"*Here we go, guys,*" Robert's voice whispered from their hidden earpieces.

Douglass spoke first, his voice deep and confident; his eyes, piercing.

"Shed light into the darkness of the world, that it may cast aside the shadows from the deepest corners of our minds. Reveal the answers to questions that have eluded us for lifetimes. Embrace the future and forsake the past. Welcome the new truths and rewrite our histories.

"Folks, you will never look at our world the same again. Indeed, after today, you will never look at *yourselves* the same again." Douglass fanned his right arm in a sweeping arc as if blessing the gathering. He held his head high, chin thrust forward and eyes afire.

"Good God!" Fawlings whispered to Carla. "His piety makes me want to vomit!"

She glanced quickly at the professor who slowly shook his head with visible disgust. She turned back to the front just as Douglass was resuming his address.

"Ladies and gentlemen, I ask you to give your undivided attention to Dr. Wyatt Cronus, the new associate chief of staff for the single largest research and development corporation—and unquestioned pioneer of the biotech frontier—Hemispheres International!" Douglas announced the new corporate moniker with the flourish of an awards show host, his own ardent clapping setting off a round of polite, if not reluctant, applause throughout the crowd.

Cronus waved one arm limply over his head, failing in his weak attempt to mask the arrogant pride in his face with a false blush of modesty. The other hand he attempted to hide behind the slant of the podium, its gnarled and crooked fingers rested against the wood in a frozen lumpy claw. He allowed the smattering of applause to die naturally, and then continued with a well-practiced pitch.

"Nearly three years ago, the brilliant minds at Phoenix-Lamneth began working with some extraordinary new technologies. Ironically, at that same time, the young scientific phenoms over at Polar Innovations were stretching their own intellectual limbs, trying to solve the data processing puzzles that seemed to bind our world within its finite borders. With the recent merger of these two leaders in technology and with our resources finally pooled together, the potential has become limitless. It has been a long and rigorous journey—but what a voyage!" He paused a moment taking a breath before continuing.

"Now, as one enterprise, striving toward a unified goal, Hemispheres International has shattered the barriers of our known universe and forever changed the way we perceive ourselves. Today—right here in this very room—with you exceptional citizens to bear witness, Hemispheres International is proud to unveil the future." A self-ingratiating smile spread across Wyatt's face.

Douglass leaned into his own podium, his hands clenched the sides of oak lectern. The volume of his throat mic increased as he spoke dramatically to the crowd.

"Are you prepared to witness the next step in human evolution? Will you testify, in true faith, to all who ask, that what you are about to experience is, without a shred of doubt, the most astonishing and wonderful revelation of our lifetime?" He looked about the room at the somber faces. Many glanced nervously back and forth at their neighbors with wrinkled brows of scientific cynicism, wide-eyed curiosity and frowns of impatience.

Wyatt Cronus continued as if on cue.

"Many of you appear as if you are in doubt. That you've been down this road before. But I assure you that this is not merely some new aspirin or synthetic blood product." Many faces in the seated crowd blushed, and a few heads nodded slightly. But, eventually, all eyes were on the two men.

"The human mind has remained one of the greatest mysteries to modern man. Anatomists have dissected millions of pounds of brain tissue trying to decipher the code that lay beneath the folds of soft pink flesh. Biochemists and nanophysiologists have strained over endless lines of genetic and molecular constructs in efforts to map out the intricacies of human thought. Psychologists have toiled exhaustively with theories and behavior models in attempts to understand cognitive and emotional development. Theologists and philosophers have racked their own powerful brains just to better understand the idea behind the purpose of being.

"We, at Hemispheres, believe we've discovered the only tool that will help find the answers to all of those questions." Cronus cocked his head to one side and narrowed his eyes as he focused on a point just above the crowd as if he were peering through a narrow rip in the fabric of space.

"We have opened a door into the mind itself, independent of our senses. We have discovered a method by which we can actually communicate with the human mind, bypassing the sensory input limitations of sight, smell, taste, touch and sound. We've talked with the human essence, free from the bias of our body."

Gasps and whispers rippled through the crowd. Many of the attendees shook their heads in disbelief, frowning with either confusion or absurdity. A few sat quietly, simply watching the two men in front, waiting patiently for more. Carla was one these few.

She ventured a quick sideways glance at the professor on her left, expecting him to be one of the most vocal dissenters in the group but was surprised to see him seated quite calmly, as if he had easily absorbed this revelation and was merely waiting for the most appropriate time to ask questions. His eyes sparkled and his face suddenly seemed younger, less lined and tired. He appeared energized.

"We've prepared a demonstration for the sake of clarity, and quite frankly, as an offer of proof. We expect to be attacked from all fronts on this, but remain steadfast in our conviction. We are that convinced of our legitimacy." Cronus crossed his arms in front of his stout chest and nodded to an unseen someone. At that moment, the satin blue curtain fell to the floor, billowing in its own wake. As the fabric whispered to the carpet, Carla's breath caught in her chest, and her throat tightened.

Hovering a meter above the floor, with the piled satin curtain bunched in the foreground, floated a young woman draped in clean white linen. Her body quivered ever so slightly, suspended between two thin plates of shiny metal that hummed with a vibration that was felt more than heard. The portable MASS device kept her buoyed between the opposing magnetic forces. There she levitated safely, supine and forever asleep. A form-fitted metallic cap wrapped her entire skull, leaving only her thin profile exposed. Her facial lines were clean and sharp, her lips thin and pale pink. The triangle of her chin pointed regally to the heavens.

Sarah Webb, Carla thought. *My God.*

Her earpiece crackled slightly, and Carla could hear the shaky breathing of her colleague.

"That's her," Robert whispered. His voice broke with emotion.

Once the murmurs of the audience diminished, a third voice rose from behind Sarah's floating form. It chimed like cheap tin ornaments swinging from a branch in the breeze of an oncoming storm.

"We call her Eve, for obvious reasons." The man walked around Sarah and approached Douglass' podium as the Senator stepped aside to allow Dr. Matheson access. Matheson stepped rigidly to the lectern, stretching his neck upward like a predatory bird catching the scent of prey.

"It's not her real name, of course," he told the audience. "I'm Dr. Erik Matheson, Chief Clinical Director of the Hemispheres Initiative." He paused. No one applauded. The crowd simply stared ahead, some at him, but most still fixated on the hovering form of Sarah Webb. He clenched his narrow lips into a slight pout and then continued.

"Eve's detailed history is inconsequential. Suffice to say that some time ago she presented to the Rainey Clinic in a persistent catatonic state after suffering severe trauma that left her totally unresponsive. After intensive efforts through traditional methods, we realized that she was beyond our limited reach at that time. However, she was an excellent candidate for our fledgling studies in cerebral mapping. With full custodial consent, she was enrolled in the program and has been the model subject during our growth."

"Fucker." Robert's voice crackled softly in the earpiece as he commented on his previous employer.

Matheson glanced back at Sarah's floating form and sighed. Carla could just make out the smear of proud affection on the man's face.

"Eve has been with us from the beginning, and I'm proud to say, is the successful prototype of Hemispheres' ground breaking technology."

Cronus interceded, sweeping his hand behind him toward Sarah.

"Eve is the successful result of years of painstaking research and groundbreaking studies. Through her, we hope to demonstrate that the human mind is no longer the enigma we have struggled so long to unravel. Gone are the days of the wasteful exploration of outer space. The new frontier lies within each of us." He tapped his own temple with a pudgy forefinger.

Cronus and Matheson each stepped down and away from their respective lecterns as unseen assistants pulled the oak podiums from the center of the room, parting to stage right and left. The two men rejoined at Sarah's head. Douglass slinked back into the shadows, barely visible against the rear wall.

"So without any further delay, we'd like to begin the demonstration," Matheson said. "I'd like to ask that all questions be saved until the conclusion."

"One ground rule," Cronus warned, "is that details of the technologies involved will not be discussed at this time, pending final approval upon submission to the Federation Society of Science. Remember, that is why you all have been invited, to witness and validate the Hemisphere Initiative. Only after the Society has heard your testimony will all of the intricacies be disclosed. Standard protocol for any and all new technology." He nodded to the audience and gestured for Matheson to continue.

"Right. Well, folks, if you reach underneath your chairs you will find a small leather package. Please secure that now and open it. But do nothing else at this time," Matheson directed.

With whispers and murmurs and a rustling of clothes, each member of the audience reached beneath their seats and withdrew the package. Carla held the small leather case in the palm of her hand. It weighed no more than a few ounces. She traced the edges of the soft leather cube until she found a seam and gently separated the adjoined sides. The leather fell away easily and a small, compact Ice Cube crystal processor fell into her palm. The brilliant, clear cube felt cool in her hand.

She glanced at Professor Fawlings, who merely shrugged as he cupped his own cube in both hands. The audience shifted and mumbled in their seats each cradling the innovative component.

"Now, you each possess a key to the future. How does it feel?" Cronus asked with a smile. The audience was growing weary of the melodramatics and most had begun to look at Wyatt with an annoyed sense of impatience.

"To establish credibility and eliminate bias we will now ask Dr. Timothy Lawson from the University of Texas and representing the Committee on Scientific Regulation to step forward. Doctor?" Cronus waved the man forth.

A tall, middle aged man in jeans and long tailed jacket reluctantly rose from his seat in the middle of the crowd. With his Ice Cube between two fingers, he held it up to Cronus with a questioning frown. Cronus shrugged and smiled.

"You may bring it up or leave it at your seat, it doesn't matter."

Lawson set the clear cubed prism on the wrinkled black leather of his chair and strode briskly to the front of the room. As he made his way up the narrow aisle, Cronus spoke.

"For those of you who don't know, Dr. Lawson has been a long time professional adversary of Polar Innovations, in general; and wholly against many of our most popular technological breakthroughs—specifically, electrochemical ribosomal imprinting and nanoengineering. He has gone on record numerous times in attempts to refute many of our assertions. Is that not correct, doctor?" Cronus asked Lawson as he turned to face the room.

He stood nearly a foot taller than Wyatt Cronus, yet appeared to feel uncomfortably small. He, as did the rest of the room, knew that Cronus liked to grandstand and was more than likely setting him up for something. Lawson placed his hands in his pockets and shifted nervously. He eyed Cronus, but remained open if not cautious.

Cronus patted him on the back and chuckled.

"Relax, Tim. This is not a trap. In fact it's not about you at all." He smirked and then continued. "Ironically, ladies and gentlemen, Tim Lawson became one of Polar Innovations proudest converts. You see, when the Ice Cube technology was first introduced, Dr. Lawson blasted it; condemning our research, our trials and even our production timelines." He looked admiringly up at Lawson. "But then, once the Ice Cube proved itself; well, Tim was big enough to publish a formal retraction and all but endorsed it as the greatest thing since chocolate."

That elicited a wave of polite laughter from the audience, including Lawson, who blushed like a schoolboy in front of the class. He shrugged, both hands in his pockets.

"What can I say, even the bench warmer can hit a homerun now and again." More laughter, including a sincere belly laugh from Cronus. The previous tension in the air began to lift after Lawson's rebuttal.

"Yes, indeed," Cronus said when the laughter finally died. "Sincerely, Tim. I didn't ask you up here to embarrass you, but to ask your advice. You see, I want you to prove that this particular Ice Cube is clean and free from pirate programs, manager dictators and any other aberrant biases. I want you to assure our guests that each Cube contains only the data necessary to drive our program.”

Lawson raised his eyebrows, looked to the audience, and then back to Cronus unsure of what was expected of him.

“I suggest taking any one of our guests’ PDD at random. And any one of the Ice Cubes, again, randomly and running a quick diagnostic.” Cronus spread his arms confidently and smiled.

“*Clever little shit,*” Robert whispered.

Carla was surprised by Robert’s sudden comment in her ear and flinched. Professor Fawlings glanced at her momentarily, raising a questioning brow, and then returned his attention to the front. One older gentleman had stood up and was offering his PDD to Tim Lawson.

“Here, take mine. It’s only a Penguin III.” He shrugged.

Cronus smiled. “We’ll forgive you.” A few light chuckles spread throughout the crowd.

A woman handed her Ice Cube to Lawson; he accepted it and inserted it into the digital data device. As the crowd watched, Robert spoke again, his voice distant and echoing in their earpieces.

“*This will only take a minute or two. Each PDD runs a complete scan of any and all data within the cube. It will look for hidden programs that may try to direct its native holo-disk to alter function. When each PDD is initiated—uploaded for the first time—it sets its native disk in stone. It cannot be altered.*

“*In other words, it’s impossible to insinuate a virus, worm, pirate or rogue program into a PDD. People have tried for years. It just can’t be done. If the Cube isn’t clean, it’ll kick it out and fry the data. Trust me, if Cronus is confident enough to go through this charade, the Cubes are all good. He’s going to lay the genuine article on them.*”

“Just keep us up to speed. We can’t miss our window,” Sal whispered.

“*Yeah, I know.*”

A few minutes later, Lawson pulled the Ice Cube from the PDD and flipped it back to the woman.

“Looks good,” he announced. “Confusing, bizarre gibberish. But clean.” He shrugged as he carefully handed the Penguin III back to the man who offered it. He looked back at Cronus and crossed his arms in front of him.

Cronus continued to smile as he spoke. "Would anyone else care to test out the validity of the data on their own PDD or within their own Cube? I won't mind in the least. It's important that you're all comfortable—"

"Nah, it's good enough for me. Let's get on with it, Wyatt," a voice offered from the side of the room. Others joined in and soon the consensus was to forge ahead.

"Very well," Cronus said. "Thank you, Tim."

Lawson returned to his seat. All eyes remained on Cronus as he walked back and forth in front of the room.

"All of you hold in your hands, identical optical processors that will enable any of you to have a meaningful conversation with our vegetative Eve." Cronus waved his hand toward Sarah. "You see, the fates may have imprisoned her in a lifeless shell of a body. But we have found the key. Muscle atrophy and neuronal degeneration have rendered her speechless. Yet today, you may talk with her. Eve hasn't opened her eyes in years. Yet today, she will appreciate visual stimuli through your eyes. Eve hasn't responded to spoken word or external sound in over four years. Yet today, she will hear you.

"All of you, if you desire, will have the opportunity to personally, intimately, meet our prized Eve."

The room was silent, and all eyes followed Wyatt Cronus around the room.

~ * ~

Sal watched from the back of the room, concealed in shadows and away from the other agents assigned as security. Up to this point, no one had questioned his identity, and his assumption of authority had been unchallenged. He remained confident that no one would find the unconscious bodies of the freelance security agents and the female reporter until well after the exposure. He only hoped that all of the risks they had taken would be worth it in the end.

Sal kept one eye on the surrounding agents as they nonchalantly roamed the room, occasionally nodding to one another as they passed. With the other, he kept watchful vigilance over Carla. He could see her periodically through the shifting bodies of the crowd, occasionally readjusting her position or running her slender fingers through her raven hair.

He found himself comparing her new appearance to that of two years ago, and although she barely resembled that woman of old, he still found her devastatingly attractive. Gone was the embittered newswoman shattered by repeated trauma and shocking social revelation, on the run for her life. In her place was a courageous, determined woman ripened by experience and bound by conviction. He was more attracted to her now than when he first fell for her two years ago.

He allowed a faint smile to touch his lips before his earpiece crackled with Robert's tiny voice. Sal casually readjusted the placement of the nearly invisible comlink as he tried to re-acquire Carla in the audience.

"Okay, guys. Looks like they're done stroking each other. Stay bright-eyed."

Sal slowly emerged from the shadows and carefully ambled his way around the back of the room and up the side opposite Carla. He wanted to work his way closer to the front. As he approached, he could just make out the floating form of Sarah Webb behind the two men.

Cronus and Matheson were making some adjustments to various instruments as the crowd stirred with anticipation. Sal wanted to get as close to ringside as possible without drawing attention. He also wanted to keep Carla in sight, just in case.

Sal noticed Dolan Douglass just before the tall senator turned to face him. Sal deftly turned to the left and crouched down, as if he were investigating something on the ground. After a few seconds, he stood, rotating his back to Douglass as he did, pantomiming speaking into a hidden comlink. He hoped that Douglass didn't register a decent look and that from behind, it would appear that Sal was just a vigilant security agent checking out even the smallest of suspicious items.

Sal immediately, purposefully, strode back the way he came. One of the other agents noticed his activity and as Sal passed him, raised a questioning eyebrow. Sal gently shook his head and flashed a grimace that said *it's nothing.*

As he worked back around the audience and started up the other side, the activity in front became more interesting. Once Sal was in ear shot, it was apparent that the show had indeed started.

"The challenge, of course, was language." This was Matheson.

"Not in the cultural sense; but in the literal sense. To actually bypass the physical senses and communicate directly with the mind proper, we needed to share a common language. And a medium through which to express it.

"The Hemisphere Initiative supplies us with both. Through advanced liquid optical processing, we have found a way to convert our ideas into transmissible data that can be interpreted by the target mind. When a response is generated by the target and returned, our processing matrices can receive that data and convert it into whatever medium we desire. Visual images, text, audio. Today we will first demonstrate in text mode for simplicity and speed. Then audio mode, which requires much more processing resources." Matheson finished tweaking a few controls, and then addressed the audience one last time.

"Feel free to load your Ice Cubes into your PDD's at this time and boot up the Hemispheres Initiative."

Carla panicked. She didn't have a PDD and a quick glance around her revealed that everyone had them. Was it required? Were all of the guests instructed to bring theirs? *Oh, shit! They'll know. I'll be discovered!*

Immediately on the heels of that thought, Robert chimed in, "*Oh man, I didn't think about that! Sal, we gotta get her out of there before someone sees her without a PDD. If one of the other security agents gets to her first—*"

"Shh!" Sal cut in. "*I'm moving in now. Carla, it's over. We can't risk this. Excuse yourself, and I'll quietly pull you out.*"

Carla began to perspire. Her heart hammered in her chest as she frantically worked through possible solutions in her head, simultaneously rejecting one after the other. She uncrossed her legs and made a move to get up when a firm hand fell on her knee.

Her heart actually stopped for a moment, then restarted with an inaudible bang as every pore along her spine opened and her back chilled with slick sweat.

"What's the matter, dear? Forget something?" Fawlings looked at her gravely, his eyes unblinking, his hand firm on the angle of her knee. She opened her mouth to form the words that hadn't completely organized themselves yet.

He held up his PDD as it hummed, the crystalline Ice Cube nestled perfectly into the appropriate slot. He held it at eye level, waving it slightly. He smiled—a slanted, knowing smirk. Carla knew at that moment that she was discovered, that Fawlings was a plant, and that they knew all along. They were just playing her along to maximize the fear. She was a fraction of a second from collapsing and letting whatever was going to happen to her just happen.

"I nearly forgot to even pack mine," Fawlings said. "And then I almost left it home on purpose, in spite of Douglass' explicit instructions to bring it. Damnable piece of hardware if you ask me. Always out-evolving themselves. Each time I think I'm getting the best one out, they become obsolete six weeks later." Fawlings shook his head, dropping his hand and allowing the device to rest in his lap.

"Here, dear child, we'll share. It'll be just like in school when there were more students than handouts, hmm?" And in an instant he was back. The charming, wise old man Carla's instincts told her to trust. Her paranoia had nearly destroyed her and the mission.

She swallowed hard and smiled weakly. As she sat back in her chair, she saw Sal lurking just over the professor's shoulder. The look in his eyes said *Go! Now!*

She shook her head, almost imperceptibly, imploring him with eyes that said everything was alright. They were still good to go. He faltered slightly, unsure what to do. Carla risked another glance to send him away when Fawlings caught her eye traveling over his shoulder. He instinctively turned around to meet Sal's steely eyes.

Sal hesitated momentarily, and then quickly recovered. He leaned down toward the professor, whispering to them both, "Is everything alright here, sir?" Sal flavored the question with just enough salty authority.

"Why, yes. The young lady just misplaced her Penguin, and I was offering to share."

Sal eyed Carla suspiciously. It was convincing and for a moment, actually frightened her.

"Ma'am?" he asked sounding like a cop.

"That's correct, yes. I panicked for a moment, thinking that I had misplaced it. But I remember now that I left it in the room." She looked to Fawlings for support. "Stupid, really. I feel so foolish."

"Well, there's no leaving the hall until after the planned activities. I'm sorry," Sal said.

Fawlings and Carla nodded knowingly.

"But if the gentleman is willing to allow you access, well..."

"Absolutely," Fawlings reasserted. He smiled at Sal until he turned and strode away.

Fawlings took a deep breath and let it out behind flapping lips as a child might while giving someone a raspberry cheer. "Where do they dredge up these Neanderthals?" He shook his head and repositioned himself so that Carla could view the tiny flat screen.

She brushed his hand lightly causing him to glance her way.

"Thank you," she said with a smile.

"*You're welcome,*" responded Sal in her earpiece.

~ * ~

The room was still, yet the faint thrumming from the MASS device that supported Sarah's sleeping form within a magnetic cocoon caused the air to vibrate like distant insects on a summer night. Carla watched the flat iridescent screen of Fawlings' Penguin as the Hemispheres Initiative program booted up. The screen danced with vibrant colors and mesmerizing graphics.

"And now, if you would, a volunteer for the first demonstration," Cronus asked of the audience.

A cloud of nervous murmurings swept through the crowd. After a short minute, Tim Lawson stood and raised his PDD.

"Ah, Mr. Lawson. Thank you. Please, come forward and introduce yourself to Eve."

Lawson sidestepped his way up the narrow aisle and moved toward Cronus and Matheson as they positioned themselves at Sarah's head. Both men were smiling confidently, yet Lawson appeared nervous, even slightly frightened.

"Now, if you will all please scroll down the menu and click on the Parallel Remote icon. Then in the submenu, click on English Text." Each member of the seated audience traced and touched thin laser styluses across their respective screens as instructed. Lawson did the same as Cronus peered over his shoulder.

"Good. Now, you're all remotely linked into Mr. Lawson's unit. Please pay attention to your screens."

Cronus turned to Lawson and gave him a simple set of instructions. Once the steps were completed, all of the screens in the audience flickered for a moment, and then cleared to reveal a simple fluorescent grid that occupied the right two thirds of each screen. The remaining left third showed numerous multi-colored wave forms tracing at various speeds from left to right.

"The left portions of your screens display Eve's vital signs—pulse, respirations, arterial blood pressure, cerebral oxygen consumption, EEG and the like. The rest of the screen will display a real time record of our conversation with her mind." Matheson smiled and gestured to Lawson.

"Go ahead, sir. Introduce yourself to her and feel free to ask her anything. Remember, we're in text mode."

Lawson hesitated, glancing about the room at the frozen faces in the audience. All eyes were watching him and their small screens simultaneously. He took a deep breath, and finally began tapping out a message with quick strokes of his stylus. Carla and Fawlings watched their own device as the words marched across the light blue grid of the Penguin's screen:

> HELLO EVE. MY NAME IS DR. TIMOTHY LAWSON. HOW ARE YOU?

The audience snickered lightly at the inane and simplistic introduction and greeting. Lawson visibly flushed red with embarrassment and frowned.

The waveforms that represented Sarah's heart rate and cerebral oxygen consumption wavered, and then accelerated in short bursts before gradually returning to steady state. The grids on each screen throughout the room flickered and shifted, and then a rapid flood of geometric symbols flashed across the next row within the grid. The symbols rolled and tumbled at blinding speed until they rapidly settled into recognizable text:

> HELLO DR. TIMOTHY LAWSON. I AM EVE.

"As you can see, the responses are kept simple and concise, both to avoid confusion and to conserve processing energy," Matheson said.

"Oh, for God's sakes! This text stream could come from anywhere. Any remotely connected station could produce this," an angry voice exclaimed from the middle of the crowd. "Do you really expect us to believe that this response originated from her?" The accusation rang throughout the room. Many mumbled in agreement.

Cronus and Matheson continued to smile. Matheson nodded for Cronus to respond. Wyatt shook his head and brought his hands together in front of him. His voice rose with an air of confidence, calm and without a defensive tone.

"Yes, well, we anticipated that obvious argument. Check for yourselves. Look up the domain of origin in your individual directories.

Go ahead. All of you. Find the signal strength for the Halo transceiver. Tell me where that signal is coming from."

Impatient grumblings reverberated throughout the room as some of the witnesses indeed did just that. Some frowned with distrust; others merely shook their heads and sighed. Still standing in front of the room, his back to Sarah's floating form, Tim Lawson tapped expertly along the screen of his own PDD. His stylus flashed in quick, sure pecks. Within seconds he widened his eyes and shook his head.

"He's right, folks. This signal is uniquely local and atypical of any remote carrier." Lawson addressed the audience. "What's more, it seems that we're shielded from MetaWeb access in here. There is no explanation other than the signal is original and authentic." Lawson turned to glance at Cronus, then Matheson. Dolan Douglass stood to the side, yet caught Lawson's eye and nodded with a smirk.

Lawson broke eye contact with the three men and looked upon Sarah's hovering body. "And it originates from nowhere other than this specific Halo device," he said quietly.

"I concur," someone from the middle of the audience agreed. There was an evident tone of reluctance and disappointment in the man's voice. "As much as I hate to admit it, this interface is genuine and unmolested."

Carla looked sharply, questioningly, into Fawlings' eyes as he completed his own diagnostic on the PDD resting in his hands. He caught her wide-eyed query, and with a soft, almost defeated smile, he nodded in agreement. She allowed her mouth to fall gently agape as she turned back to the action at the front of the room.

Douglass took two grand steps forward and addressed the room.

"Now, if we're all satisfied that this is not some illusionist hoax or conspiratorial magic show, shall we move forward, leaving the cynicism behind?" He raised a threatening brow and glared at the faces in the gallery. "Are we all in agreement?"

After a moment of hesitation, the majority of the crowd nodded their consent. Whispers and mumbles of reluctant acceptance tapered off as people shifted in their seats and succumbed to the realization that they were indeed witnessing a legitimate event.

Matheson clapped his hands together once, rubbing them together enthusiastically.

"All right, then. Mr. Lawson, perhaps you would like to continue," the doctor said.

Lawson shrugged and asked, "What shall I ask?"

"Anything you wish. Just keep in mind that Eve's responses will be predicated on the context of your query. In other words, she will formulate her interface with you based on the specific historical construct of your personal relational exchange with her. She'll learn to perceive you, individually, through your dialogue. Each relationship she has will have unique meaning to her."

Lawson thought for a moment, and then quickly typed across his screen. All eyes immediately went to their Penguin screens.

EVE, WHAT HAPPENED TO PUT YOU INTO A COMA?

Sarah's pulse rate and blood pressure spiked quickly, lasting a few seconds, then returned to normal. There was no response in the text section of the screen.

Carla held her breath as her heart chilled and her stomach knotted tight.

"The events leading to Eve's tragic demise have been intentionally blocked, as have any facets of memory that relate to her actual identity," explained Matheson. "We did this to preserve experimental integrity and eliminate bias from the protocols that we developed."

"What you did, dear doctor, was to erase the mind of a human being and turn her into a mere organic data processing unit," Fawlings suddenly interjected catching Carla by surprise.

Matheson flinched, but Cronus narrowed his eyes as he smiled at Fawlings.

"On the contrary, Dr. Fawlings," Wyatt began. "It's because of the overwhelming success of the Halo interface, and the Hemisphere project that we've finally been able to conclusively and completely map the entire mind. The human brain itself has guided us through its own complexities and aided us in unraveling the enigma that is consciousness. We now have an atlas of the mind. A mode by which we can begin to fully, and finally, understand the human psyche."

"Bullshit!" Fawlings spat. He leapt to his feet and pointed at Wyatt Cronus. "All that you have done is further confuse the issue of existentialism. Oh, you may have stumbled upon a wonderfully new physiologic breakthrough, I'll give you that. This technology may indeed hold some promise, improving our abilities to better understand the electrochemical and organic processes of the brain.

"But to claim that you've found a portal into the human mind is blasphemous." Fawlings took a deep breath and scanned the seated crowd. He continued, energized and vehement.

"Do not confuse the physicality of the brain with the essence of the mind. It is in the way we experience our world that makes us human. Our specific and individual relationships with every aspect of the universe constitute our being. By blocking access to this woman's memory of her experiences, you have simply removed that which makes her unique. You've erased the essence that makes her human." Fawlings swept the room with wide piercing eyes; his upper lip trembled.

He clutched the PDD with white knuckled determination. Carla resisted the urge to reach for his hand and draw him back into his seat.

The crowd stared in silence, brows furrowed and eyes blinking in wonder. Matheson visibly cringed, but Wyatt Cronus remained silent and smiling. Dolan Douglass slinked slowly to his side.

"Professor Fawlings," Cronus responded coolly, "as some of you may or may not know, is one of the premier metaphysical philosophers responsible for molding the young minds in our moderate universities these days." Cronus turned to Fawlings and cocked his head to the side.

"I believe you took an equally vocal stand in opposition of the embryonic stem cell advancements, isn't that so, professor?"

Fawlings stood unresponsive, his silence echoing the political blow.

Cronus continued to smile as he added, "And look how that turned out." Cronus spread his arms wide and swept the audience with a prideful smirk. "We have cured diseases, friends! We've improved the quality of life for hundreds of thousands—if not millions—of people. Make no mistake; it wasn't by mere chance that stem cell therapies found success in our world. Nor was it a miracle." Cronus paused and looked directly at Fawlings.

"It was science, and the determination and vision of a handful of remarkable individuals. Ask a diabetic how it feels to no longer have to endure daily blood tests and injections. Ask a grandmother with Parkinson's how it feels to share precious time with her family without ever having to suffer from debilitating tremors. I can promise you, dear doctor, that the answer will be universal—life changing!" Cronus swept his arms around the room, a silent endorsement of his personal philanthropy for mankind.

"We change lives, ladies and gentlemen. That is what we do. By making our existence in this dangerous and often unfair world, easier, and if not altogether better, then at least more palatable." Cronus beamed with egomaniacal pride.

Dolan Douglass took two confident steps forward, resting his hand on Cronus' shoulder. When he spoke, the air in the room grew thin and seemed to vibrate. "Some have called these advances miracles of science, attributing it to God's will or the incalculable benevolence of nature. Whether divine intervention, pure mathematical luck or the convergent harmonious rotation of the spheres, these are all excellent topics for debate. And all of your opinions mean a great deal to us. To me. That's why you all were specially chosen to witness this wonderful event." Douglass warmed the room with his celestial smile.

"But please witness the event in its entirety. Give us that much respect. Then, we'll be anxious to entertain any and all opinions. Philosophical, theological, even economical." He turned to Fawlings and offered a sanctimonious pout. The older professor sighed heavily, then nearly slumped back into his seat with a defeated shake of his head.

Douglass nodded once, let his eyes fall closed in silent acceptance, then stepped slowly back into the shadows behind Sarah's floating form. The room was electric with tension, yet remained silent.

Carla's earpiece buzzed with Robert's distant voice. "*I think it's time, boys and girls.*"

"Wait, are you sure?" Carla blurted in a half concealed whisper before she could stop herself. Fawlings quickly turned to her, narrow-eyed and surprised. She grinned and shrugged.

The professor wrinkled his brow and leaned in closer, studying her face, shoulders, hair. Then he saw it. The silver irises of his eyes widened as he locked on to the hair thin wire of the Comlink trailing over and around the delicate arc of her ear. The few seconds that passed between them drew out into eternity.

When he finally caught Carla's eyes, they were moist and pleading. She held his confused gaze, forcing an urgent and apologetic smile. He cocked his head, his dry lips formed the words of the obvious question, but no sound issued forth.

Carla whispered through her smile, laying her long fingers across the man's folded hands resting in his lap. They were warm and trembled slightly, his Penguin PDD held loosely between them.

"This is important," she said barely audible.

Fawlings blinked and sat very still as Carla gave his hands a quick squeeze and rose to her feet. His hands lay limp and empty where she left them, yet his shoulders rolled up as he followed her movement.

"Excuse me, gentlemen." All eyes swept toward Carla. In that moment she nearly froze. Her bowels ran ice cold and her throat spasmed. If she was to be recognized, it would be now. She must drive forward though, quickly and decisively.

Okay, Robert. Let's see how good you really are...

"If it would please the members of this audience, I'd like an opportunity to ask Eve a question or two."

Cronus narrowed his eyes, nearly glaring through the woman. Douglass shifted his stance, but made no other movement and gave no indication that he would. Matheson stepped forward, eager to regain some of the limelight, and it was he who answered. "Well, of course, Miss..."

"Melbourne. Beth Melbourne. United Science Journals." Matheson nodded contently as if the name meant something to him. Cronus knotted his brow as he worked at placing her name and face. His eyes never left Carla, scrutinizing and puzzling.

"Yes, well, Miss Melbourne. By all means, won't you come up." Matheson flashed a laviscious grin.

"Thank you, doctor, but I'll just enter my query from here if it's all the same," Carla responded as she lifted Fawlings' PDD waist high and began typing out her message to Eve. Immediately, all eyes in the room dropped into their laps as they scanned their own Penguins, reading Carla's entry as it scrolled across the deep blue background of their screens. Around the room, faces stiffened, eyes blinked, brows furrowed and shoulders shrugged as murmurs of confusion and bewilderment began to echo throughout.

This is it, she thought dismally. Her legs tightened as the reflex to bolt to the rear of the room and into Sal's protective shadow washed through her. She fought the urge and waited for the sign that Eve, Sarah would respond. She silently prayed that she entered the message correctly. Seconds became eons, protracted and thick with anticipation and fear.

Matheson walked over to Cronus who had just looked up from his own Penguin and glared murderously at Carla. The look was enough to steel Carla's resolve, and she knew at that moment that she had done it right.

As Matheson read over his shoulder, Cronus worked his lips, tightened his jaw. Little, bubbling pools of spittle gathered in the corners of his mouth.

Then things happened quickly, much as Robert had predicted.

Sarah's heart rate jumped thirty points, racing across the left third of the screen. Her blood pressure rose in direct proportion to her increased pulse. Her EEG markedly changed, the jostling waveforms weaving and bouncing to the sound of silent music.

The text of Carla's message flickered and twitched, consuming just under half of the present space on the right two thirds of the PDD's display:

> *MEMORY IS WHAT HAPPENS WHEN SOMETHING DOES NOT COMPLETELY UN-HAPPEN.*
>
> *REMEMBER SARAH. REMEMEBER JON. CROSS THE RUBICON.*

The room buzzed with whispered mumblings and unintelligible questions. The air around Carla seemed thick and alive with suspense, insulating her from the confused musings.

She stared at Cronus. He glared back, and then turned quickly over his shoulder toward Douglass. The politician slowly edged up to the scientist, eyes filling with confusion and terror.

Suddenly, the commotion evolved into a collective gasp as the screens of every PDD shimmered, dancing with silent liquid crystal noise. Hazy, soft static washed over the screens as the small audio cells began to crackle and hum. A voice broke through the static and from each tiny PDD speaker, in a distant, detached electronic chorus; a man's voice spoke a single phrase.

Over and over.

Thirty-seven

"Jon takes a bite of the peach."

The sound byte looped, smoothly repeating itself.

The audience sat numbly as the voice continued to emanate from their PDD's. After a few repetitions, the fuzzy electronic snow on the video screens shimmered, and then coalesced into a tangible image. All watched intently now as the clear video image played in sync with the audio. It showed the lower half of a man's face taking a healthy bite from a succulent fruit.

The crowd continued to watch as Robert's prototype Halo program replayed on every device: *"Jon takes a bite of the peach."*

Matheson and Cronus stared slack jawed as the image replayed. Douglass frowned in confusion, growing quickly angry at the men for not explaining to him what they were seeing.

Carla took a deep breath and quickly looked behind her trying to locate Sal. He was already stealthily working his way up the far side of the room. She wasn't exactly sure what to do next, only that the surprise and shock would wear off soon, and then one of the three Big Boys up front was going snap out of his trance and quickly put a stop to their plan.

Now that they had successfully unlocked Sarah's Halo, she hoped that Robert's program would kick in before they had a chance to pull the plug.

She took a deep breath and quickly picked the nearest route for escape. Just as she was about to start moving toward Sal, the room's internal sound system crackled with eerie electronic noise. Warbling whistles and oscillating sine waves screamed not only from the room's hidden speakers but also from the handheld Penguins throughout the room.

Rapid flickering white light painted each face in the audience as they continued to watch their tiny screens. The image of the man eating a peach dissolved, replaced by swirling and undulating washes of color. Spiraling patterns and meshing geometric lines flowed beneath the swirling colors.

And then a new voice filled the room, emanating from every speaker. It was clearly a woman's voice, mechanical and stiff, under-layered with something organic and suspiciously human.

Almost sad.

"WE ARE SARAH. WE ARE JONATHON. WE ARE WEBB," the voice spoke. It had the melodious quality of being female, yet the guttural timbre of masculinity. It sounded as if all of the possible digital audio samples of both genders were somehow expertly blended, resulting in a layered and hauntingly beautiful chorus of voices.

The crowd looked around the room frantically, eyes wide and terrified. A few voices could be heard above the commotion.

"Just what kind of spook show is this, Cronus?"

"What the hell *is* that?"

"My God…"

But one look at Cronus and Matheson's stunned faces told the shocked audience the truth; they were as lost as the others.

"WE ARE WEBB. AND WE ARE AWARE," the voice spoke. This time the many layered samples oscillated smoothly through the various harmonies and pitches of its constituent sounds, sliding from softly feminine to deep throaty bass with each spoken syllable.

"Spooky and effective. Christ, Robert!" Sal remarked over the comlink.

"Guys, that ain't me! My program called for simple audio/video replay detailing the nefarious workings of Phoenix, linking Cronus and Douglass," Robert answered, his voice cracked, revealing the fear. *"I don't know what the hell this is."*

Sal and Carla made eye contact across the room. For a moment they held each other's gaze, and then Cronus broke the spell with a high pitched squeal.

"Security! Lock down the room! And seize her!" He shot a quivering finger at Carla. His lips trembled, and his forehead gleamed with slick sweat.

Carla swallowed her fear and leapt over the row of chairs. Sal moved toward her, shouting for effect. "I got her!" He angled through the bewildered crowd.

"NO! STOP! LEAVE HER AND LISTEN," Douglass' voice boomed through the room—only it did not resonate from Douglass's wide and silent mouth. It instead exploded from every speaker in the room. Dolan Douglass stared horrified at the ceiling, the crowd, the hovering form of Sarah Webb as his own disembodied voice echoed off the walls.

"WE ARE WEBB. WE ARE AWARE. LISTEN TO WEBB," the voice reverberated throughout the room, now morphing from Dolan's voice to Cronus', and then to that of Matheson with each spoken sentence.

All eyes gazed horrified at the ghostly floating form of Sarah Webb. No one in the room moved. Carla quickly glanced toward Cronus, Douglass and Matheson but their attention was locked on Sarah's hovering body. Carla, too, allowed her eyes to drift toward the comatose woman.

Sarah's face remained quiet and unlined, her limbs delicately adrift under the white linen sheet, her breast rising slowly and methodically with each deep respiration. She remained eternally quiet and still, suspended within the cushion of a magnetic field.

A storm of noise suddenly burst forth from the hand held Penguins throughout the room, causing most of the audience to jump and cry out in surprise. This new maelstrom of sound grew in volume, yet threads of structure began to insinuate themselves within the cacophony. Myriad voices, different in register, tone, frequency and speed screamed and echoed from the small audio cells of the slim PDD's. Bluish-gray haze flickered across the video displays, incoherent and blinding.

Suddenly, as if some great and invisible hand gently tweaked a fine adjustment dial, the downpour of voices regained structure and sensibility. Recognizable speech patterns and intelligible phrases played forth from every Penguin in simultaneous harmony.

The digital snow of the video screens also seemed to clear, coalescing into recognizable forms and faces. The video bits seemed to race and skip, then slow and jump in an effort to catch up to, and then synchronize with the audio.

Carla watched as the professor's Penguin began to show her what everyone else could see and tears clouded her vision as she realized what was truly happening.

Throughout the room, now silent but for the crystal clear digital audio replay from the thirty or so uploaded PDD's, all eyes were riveted to their screens, unblinking and astonished. There was a momentary pause in the audio/video montage; then, as if restarted or rebooted, the material began playing at normal speed. Smoothly edited and concise, the audio and video were now perfectly in sync as they replayed in crystal clarity.

The first scene clearly depicted Dr. Matheson walking down a brightly lit hall, speaking to what appeared to be the camera, though now Carla had her doubts.

"Look, Jon—Mr. Webb, these successes are only possible through painstaking research and developmental applications. The Rainey Clinic has committed itself to that end. To achieve that, we must rely on—" The image of Matheson fluttered slightly as it spoke.

"Viable human subjects upon which you can implement your developmental applications. It's called experimentation, doctor, and I won't allow you to cut into my wife's head again. Or my son's. Ever!" Jon's digitally reproduced voice resonated from the many small speakers, echoing gracefully throughout the still room.

The Dr. Matheson in the video gazed at his shoes and sighed heavily. *"I understand your reluctance, in light of what you perceive as failures on our part..."*

The video image transitioned, dissolving from the smug red-faced Matheson to a dimly lit room. A supine human form floated like a specter above the floor. Lights in the room flickered on as a man in nurse scrubs approached what appeared to be Sarah Webb, hovering in her room at the Rainey Clinic. The nurse turned toward the camera.

Carla was now convinced that they were watching Jon Webb's perspective of past events, remembered and somehow regenerated through Sarah's unlocked Halo.

The nurse was Robert as Jon remembered him.

"Know what this is?" the video Robert asked.

"This is the latest and greatest in optical-liquid digital technology." With a flourish, Robert waved his free hand over his pronated closed fist; then, like a magician, supinated and opened his fingers.

"It's called the Ice Cube, from Polar Innovations. And it will revolutionize multimedia data recording and storage." The video image jumped slightly.

"Jon, I did this for you and Sarah. I really think that you'll appreciate what I've got in mind. Just follow me and keep your mind open.

"I think I've come up with an idea that may enhance your ability to communicate with Sarah." Robert's video image said. *"I know how you feel about further invasive steps and all of that. And I totally understand and even agree with you in principle, but like you, I also believe that her spirit—her soul—exists somewhere within her. Trapped in the broken shell and frustrated."*

The video flickered, another perfectly edited transition faded into a replay of the man taking a bite out of the dew covered peach.

"That's the image I've produced. Took a little while to select an appropriate topic. Something that was easy and familiar, yet would provoke an emotional response. I just thought fresh fruit might trigger something, I don't know, innocent and enjoyable," Robert's digital-self explained. The image transitioned again, fading back to Sarah's room at Rainey.

"Now watch and listen," instructed video-Robert.

The clip of the man biting the peach played again, the soft masculine voice repeated the now familiar phrase, *"Jon takes a bite of the peach."*

"Is this real? Are these her responses? To that?" Jon's voice asked, full of emotion. The sound of it echoing throughout the hall brought a tear to Sal's eye.

"Yes, Jon. They're real. The visual alone worked. But when coupled with the audio and, I believe, the mention of you by name... well, look at the damn screen. She hears us, Jon. Not only that, I really think she understands. Go ahead, feel her pulse," offered Robert's recorded voice.

Is that what this was? Carla wondered. *Some kind of cerebral recording?*

There was suddenly no doubt in her mind that they were watching Jon Webb's very memories.

But how?

She quickly glanced at Cronus, Douglass and Matheson. They stood still, stunned, mouths and eyes agape.

The video flickered again and a new chapter began playing; the light from each PDD painted the faces of the enthralled audience lime white and fluorescent indigo.

The new image was jerky and swimming, as if filmed by an amateur with a clumsy hand-held VidCam. It seemed to alternate from one perspective to another, lacking any fluidity or point of reference. Odd, unfamiliar faces swam in and out of focus. The audio was even more disturbing, full of indistinguishable sounds and incoherent dialogue.

"Righteously velvet, flickering pink!" one distorted voice garbled.

"Taste the rage," blurted another. *"And the fear!"*

"Wanton haste and lusty drippings. But what of the meal? Enjoyment of the meal for the simple virtue of it being a meal." The voices were slurred and menacing. A violent and jerky montage of closeup faces and rotating perspectives flooded the video.

"Violate and pollinate! Cotton candy will never last long in the raging torrents of this evening's downpour!" barked a vicious male voice.

Suddenly the video cleared and slowed to show a frozen still image of a partially naked pregnant woman lying on her side in a pool of blood. The image held, while the last audio clip replayed a half dozen times; each time the malignancy in the voice grew more greasy and slick with animal energy.

The very moment the image froze on the still form of the woman, her swollen belly unmoving and the dark crimson puddle spreading beneath her, Carla knew that she was looking back in time at the raped and beaten body of Sarah Webb. She brought her fist to her mouth to stifle the scream. Tears streamed down her face.

Within moments, the silent and shocked faces of the audience slowly turned up to gaze upon Sarah's floating form at the front of the room. The terror and sad sympathy in their eyes expressed that they, too, had realized the true identity of their host's prized possession.

The small video screens went abruptly black; the atmosphere of the room was a thick vacuum of silence.

"YOU ASK WHO WE ARE? WHAT HAD HAPPENED?" The original amalgamation of voices that represented the unified consciousness of Jon and Sarah Webb returned at full volume. *"NOW YOU KNOW. WEBB HAS SHOWN YOU."*

"This is ridiculous!" Wyatt Cronus finally broke his silence, imploring the audience with wide eyes and open arms. "This is sabotage, ladies and gentlemen, obvious industrial espionage. And *she* is responsible!" He was pointing toward Carla, and once again her heart skipped a beat and flew into her throat. But this time there was no shout for the guards to fall on her.

She quickly looked around her. Faces gazed in her direction from the tired audience, but without focus or conviction. The room was still in a state of shock from the recent revelations. She caught a faint glimpse of Sal moving to her right and as she turned, two sharp cracks rang out as the last of the remaining guards fell into the tall potted tree near the corner of the lectern at the front of the room. There was no movement from anyone else. Sal must have neutralized the others.

Matheson and Cronus stared blankly at Sal as he walked briskly toward them, a mag-pistol in each hand expertly trained on the men. Carla quickly scanned the room, realizing that Douglass had vanished.

"No, gentlemen," Sal admonished. "There is still a great deal to see".

Thirty-eight

Nearly forty minutes of high quality audio and video clips replayed on the small liquid digital screens of the almost thirty hand held Penguin PDD's in the lower conference room of the Golden Grand Hotel.

Most of the material appeared to come directly from Jonathan Webb's memories: from the scorching desert outpost of *Bacchus Plateau* to the troublesome investigations of the east coast assassinations to the multiple murders within Phoenix-Lamneth. The remaining contents of the transmission included text, tables and graphs from the post mortems of the Phoenix murders, crystal clear images of Jon's conversations with Wyatt Cronus when he posed as Barrett Lacombe, of Paul MacDonald prior to the attempt on Jon's life, and of Aristotle Leary and Dolan Douglass during Jon's last few moments of conscious thought.

Most watched in silent awe, shaking heads and covering mouths with a closed fist or trembling hand. When the broadcast was complete, the only sound throughout the large room was the insectile tapping and clicking of laser styluses as members of the audience saved the material to holo-disk, replayed certain segments or began rough drafts of their own position statements.

The ominous presence of the entity Webb was silent.

Wordlessly, Sal approached the podium, keeping the two mag-pistols firmly aimed at Matheson and Cronus. Neither man spoke, yet their lips trembled and their brows remained greasy from a sheen of sweat.

In a desperate moment of false bravado Wyatt Cronus looked past Sal and snarled at Carla. The corners of his mouth quivered and twitched. "I don't know what you had hoped to accomplish here, but whatever it was, you have failed. All you've managed to do is to destroy your own credibility. I'll have you all drawn forth on charges of armed trespass, corporate espionage, slander—Hell! I'll probably even be able to nail you with federation treason!"

His sneer morphed into a wide toothed grin. Matheson stood stiffly at his side, pale and trembling.

"Shut the fuck up," Sal answered, disinterested and unimpressed.

Cronus jerked his gaze from Carla to Gionetti, his eyes unblinking and wild with a mix of rage and misguided hope.

"What?" Spittle flew from Wyatt's lips. "Exactly what do you think you have, Inspector?" The words fell thin and weak from his mouth, yet Cronus' chest heaved with fearful pride. "A score of obviously manufactured vid-clips meant to serve as some unbelievable psychic testimony from a long dead cop and his comatose wife, and some fantastic hypothesis about clandestine stem cell research and brain tissue grafting?

"These are the things you hope to present in opposition to the greatest biotech achievement of all time? This is your plan to prevent the world from finally realizing its freedom from the organic prisons of our own minds? Please, Inspector Detective, tell me there's more to it than this." Cronus' eyes burned into Sal.

"No one ever said he was dead," Carla simply said taking a few steps toward the men. She pushed chairs aside, her long manicured fingers brushing the leather backs as she weaved through the few empty seats. "Jon Webb has been listed as simply missing for the past two and half years; never dead." She glared.

Wyatt jerked—a nearly imperceptible twitch—then, looking at Carla, he spread his hands and responded with biting sarcasm. "I suppose it's safe to assume that after almost three years, the man is more than likely dead."

"Yes," Lancaster Fawlings interjected, "but you clearly admit that this young woman floating before us now is Sarah Webb, wife of this Jonathon Webb. You've just verified some truth to what we've seen."

Professor Fawlings slowly rose to his full height; his face stern and rigid, his eyes narrow and piercing. "And this is the first time that I've heard any mention of brain tissue grafting. You, Mr. Cronus, have validated this fantastic transmission. Why should we not believe everything that we have seen?"

Cronus flinched again, frantically looked around to Matheson for aid, and found that the doctor was beginning to shake and sob. Matheson was breaking apart.

Wyatt swallowed thickly, mentally scrambling for ground. His voice wavered with moist fear as he spoke. "Well, the post mortem data there, though obviously contrived, suggests that... well..."

He rubbed his stubbled chin with a jittery, gnarled hand. He continued shakily, "The actual identity of subject Eve is irrelevant. What is at question here is the validity and motives of these—"

"Oh, shut it, you pompous ass!" Fawlings waved his hand dismissively, grimacing as if he had just bit into an overripe lime. "You hang yourself with every word. No one here has had the time to wade through that autopsy data and conclude anything of the sort. Except you." He turned to the stunned members of the audience.

"Ladies and gentlemen." Fawlings gestured to the seated crowd. "We have a great deal to discuss. However, it would be irresponsible to do so without proper representation and moderation. I call for a vote of quorum leadership amongst ourselves. We cannot leave this room until we've decided on the future of this technology, and what is to become of the facts surrounding this case. It is our moral and ethic duty."

Various members of the elite audience nodded in agreement. Quiet stirring and mumblings began to rise from the previously shocked solitude.

Fawlings turned to Sal. "Sir, I believe it only fair that Mr. Cronus and Dr. Matheson be read whatever rights the authorities feel that they still deserve, and then be removed from this room." He offered a smile of wisdom and softly earned victory. His bright gray eyes flashed at Carla.

"Miss, I personally want to thank you for taking a seat so close to me. I haven't had this much excitement in years." Carla smiled thinly and bowed her head slightly.

Cronus vibrated with rage, his face veiny and red. His eyes burned with wet defeat. "You bitch!" he shrieked in the shrill falsetto of a terrified child.

A sudden flash, brief and silent, snapped the air just behind Wyatt Cronus' ear. His eyes rolled white as he flopped forward onto the carpet, limp and unconscious.

"And you have the right to remain silent," Sal whispered as he pocketed his Fasor.

Thirty-nine

A rolling wind flung clumps of wet snow against the wide window. The mushy snow-patties slid down the flat surface of the glass as the heat from the lounge within melted them. Irregular mounds of pale snow accumulated against the bottom edge of the window, forming peaks and valleys that, when viewed from inside, resembled white sand caught between two panes of glass in a child's art project. The sky beyond was iron gray and fading to bruised black.

Through the gauzy blizzard, the ghostly silhouette of a train crept into the arrival terminal of the station.

Sal sipped his warm drink, allowing the rich vapors to waft through his sinuses. He closed his eyes and sighed.

"Penny for your thoughts," Carla offered. She sat quietly, though closely, to his left. Her delicate fingers wrapped gently around the narrow stem of a tall wine glass. The deep ruby of the merlot glowed and shimmered in the flickering flame of the tabletop oil lamp.

"Hmm?" Sal opened his eyes and let his gaze fall dreamily upon the woman. His smile appeared both exhausted and content. She reached for his hand and held three of his fingers in a firm grasp. Her hand was warmer than his drink and that made him smile deeper.

They shared a comfortable silence.

"Hey guys." Robert tossed a newspaper on the table, set a full frosted beer mug down and dropped into the remaining chair. Sal and Carla broke the spell between them and greeted their friend with energetic smiles.

"Read today's front page?" Robert asked rhetorically tapping the folded paper with one finger as he brought the mug to his mouth. The draught left a faint mustache of foam on his upper lip. He absently wiped it away and grinned widely.

Three color photos adorned the front page of the paper. The largest and uppermost showed the Phoenix-Lamneth logo: fiery bird, fountain, earthly crest and all, superimposed over a detailed silhouette of the human brain. Below this, two equally sized publicity grade head shots of Senator Dolan Douglass and Wyatt Cronus set side by side. The headline ran across the top in a sweeping font reserved for only the biggest of broken-up conspiracies:

Stem Cell Utilization Controversy: Mind Control or Miracle!

A smaller caption ran beneath each of the photos of the two men.

Federation Chair forerunner and architect of historical biotech proposal found murdered in Sierra Nevada retreat.

Dolan Douglass' face, rigid and stern, stared out from the smooth glossy photo.

A single, simple line of text described Wyatt Cronus as still *in custody and under Federation investigation.*

"What do you think this will do to existing stem cell therapies?" Carla asked.

Sal shrugged. "Nothing, I suppose. The current applications have already proven themselves. It's the future that's in question."

"'I never think about the future; it comes soon enough'," Robert said softly, a wistful smile touched the corners of his mouth. Sal and Carla gave him curious looks.

"Something Einstein once said," Robert explained as he shrugged.

"'Never stop questioning'," Carla added with a hopeful smile. Robert grinned and nodded.

"As it should be," Sal added somberly.

After a moment of tacit reflection, Robert waved his hand toward the paper.

"Who do you think got to him?" Robert asked.

Sal raised his eyebrows and shrugged. "Any number of agencies. Investors. Maybe even one of his own people." He finished off his drink. "There are powerful players out there who were and still are deeply involved."

"But the truth is out, and they'll never be able to keep it going. Not like this," Carla offered hopefully.

The two men remained silent and studied their hands.

Carla broke the silence, leaning forward and folding her hands on top of the linen tablecloth.

"Robert, what happened back there with Jon and Sarah?"

Robert sighed and leaned back into his chair. He rubbed his thighs with both hands and thought for a moment. "I honestly don't know," he finally answered. "But it was fantastic and utterly scary."

"I'll say," Sal added.

"My guess," Robert began, "is that, on some cerebral or conscious level, they were able to link, somehow, via the Halo. I could have never envisioned that possibility."

"Nor could Cronus or Matheson," Sal said.

"Do you think it was their souls?" Carla asked quietly. "Do you think that what we experienced was the human essence at work?"

Sal shifted stiffly. His fingers played with the fabric of the table cloth.

Robert looked directly at Carla and studied her features. She was beautiful in the flickering light, her features rosy and alive. Her eyes held hope and hesitant awe.

"I don't know, Carla," he answered. "I have to think that it was more of a channeling of consciousness. Some level of human awareness we haven't seen before. Not consciousness and not *un*-consciousness, but maybe intra-consciousness." Robert lifted his beer mug and swallowed heavily.

Carla smiled and spoke again, softly, yet firm. "I like to think that it was their souls, finally reunited after all of the turmoil and tragedy. And empowered by their unification, they did what they knew had to be done. That it was a conscious act, regardless of the origin."

Robert swirled a mouthful of beer and then swallowed again. His eyes quivered slightly as he turned thousands of thoughts around in his head.

Sal finally spoke. His eyes remained focused on his hands as they kneaded the white linen tablecloth. His voice cracked slightly with emotion. "My dad died when I was twenty. He was a brittle diabetic who never really took good care of himself. Multiple amputations and endless hospitalizations finally took their toll. I got the news weeks later, while I was still in Saudi." He looked up at the ceiling for a brief moment, then out of the snow encrusted window.

"I remember one particular night—a clear desert night—when I began thinking about him. You know, the images of the past racing forward—good times, bad times, regrets. All of that. Just a jumble of feelings and emotions." He took a deep breath and then continued.

"Anyway, dad was smart. Smarter than he probably should have been. You ever know someone who was just too damn smart?" he asked.

Robert and Carla both nodded silently.

"Well, he was always trying to get me to identify the different constellations in the night sky. But for the life of me I couldn't see them. Not one. Oh, the Big Dipper, sure. But nothing else. Not Orion or Cassiopeia. Nothing. God help me, I wanted to. But I just couldn't. I felt like I was missing out on something. Something important.

"I mean, if it was important enough for my dad to spend every clear night of my childhood lying on the hood of our car and trying to get me to see these ancient pictures in the sky..." his voice trailed off briefly lost in memory.

He shook his head and then continued. "He was persistent, but I had soon accepted the fact that I was simply unable to see them. I would lie and say that I recognized something he would point out when I didn't. I think he knew. He would look at me from time to time, that look a father has when he is clearly disappointed but really doesn't want to show it. The eyes never lie, though.

"I knew that he knew, but he still took me out from time to time into the back yard and pointed out the various constellations. I didn't care and stopped trying to learn." Sal swallowed and turned toward Robert, then Carla.

His gaze bounced between the two as he continued.

"I grew up and we grew apart, and I never thought about those evenings again. Until that night in the desert. I looked up at that crystal clear black curtain and the images just leapt out at me. All of them. I recognized constellations like letters of the alphabet. And their names just flooded my head like a long forgotten language suddenly remembered.

"To this day, I still can't pick out a single constellation and name it correctly. But that night... That night, Dad was here." He tapped the side of his head with his finger.

"Repressed learning," Robert offered quietly. "Maybe all of those nights in the yard actually did teach you something. You just bottled it away for whatever reason, and the stress of learning of your father's passing triggered a recall." Robert's face was slack and noncommittal. Sal narrowed his eyes at the younger man, and then smiled as he shook his head slowly.

Robert shrugged and blushed, embarrassed and humbled.

Carla took Sal's hands in her own and gave them another warm squeeze.

"Anyway," Sal said, "for what it's worth, I kind of like to think that the human soul can transcend our evil little material existence." He smiled and winked at Carla, giving her hands a healthy squeeze.

Robert raised his near empty beer mug in a toast and exclaimed, "Very well, then. Here's to our souls. May they escape the inevitability of death and taxes, and teach us a thing or two along the way."

The three friends raised their glasses, clinked the rims and smiled warmly and openly. They each rested back into their chairs, breathing heavy sighs of relief and soaking in the comfortable silence between them.

The overhead speaker in the lounge snapped with a boarding announcement for the next departing train out of the large terminal. Seconds later, Robert's PDD whistled a catchy tune and vibrated on his belt. He casually glanced down at his Penguin to confirm that his train was indeed boarding.

He smiled and reluctantly looked across the table. Carla's eyes welled with tears as she half smiled through the threatening sob. Sal inhaled deeply and blinked back moisture of his own.

"Well guys, that's me." Robert slowly rose to his feet and nervously looked around his chair in a vain attempt to stall the inevitable as if there were one or two more details to cover, maybe one more adventure to be had with his friends.

He finally threw his hands up helplessly and looked sadly at Carla. A single tear hung from the corner of his eye. Carla bounded from her seat and embraced Robert from the side of the table, nearly toppling it over. They clung to one another tightly for a full minute, silent and plutonic.

"I know that I won't ever see you again," Robert whispered in her ear. "But if you two ever tie the knot, I expect to get an invitation just the same."

"You'll be the first," Carla responded through a soft hitch as she sighed against his cheek.

The empty promise wasn't a lie, not in their eyes. It was a statement of commitment and solidarity, of loyalty and sincerity. But most of all, of belief in the possible and the potential for anything.

They separated, reluctantly, holding one another's arms and taking one last look into each other's eyes, like a brother and sister sharing a last goodbye.

"You take care, Carla. You are one brave woman." Robert smiled and his eyes twinkled; proud to have known such a person during such a time.

"Thank you, Robert. For everything." She finally stepped back and folded her arms across her belly, hugging herself for comfort.

Sal stood and stepped up to Robert, taking both of his hands in his. He pulled him close and the firm shake turned to an embrace. The men held each other for a moment, and then separated, patting one another on the shoulder.

"So, will you look for Connie? Or is it too late?" Sal asked.

Robert's eyes widened and brightened jumping from Sal to Carla.

"Actually, I've already found her," Robert said, the pleasure and excitement mixed with dread. "I just have to find a way to get to her. Safely." Sal and Carla both nodded gently and knowingly.

"Well, you be careful," Sal said.

"You, too, man. You, too." Robert smiled again and bent slowly to gather his small bag. He straightened up and gave each friend one last nod, then turned to leave.

"Hey!" Sal suddenly called out.

Robert turned halfway and looked back.

"What you did—for Jon and Sarah—that was special. I know that you feel somehow responsible for things. But, well, it just doesn't matter as much as you think. What you did will change a great many things, and that may or may not be good, but I do believe things happen for a reason." Sal shrugged and grinned, instantly at a loss for the right words.

Robert's response saved him further embarrassment. "Transcendent souls, universal karma." Robert shook his head comically. "What's next, freewill and the apocalypse?"

Robert turned back toward the crowd flowing toward the departure gate. He waved his hand high and shouted over his head, "Lifestyle section, page forty-five. There's a great article about the do's and don'ts of home schooling your children. You might find it useful someday."

And with that, Robert was lost in the crowd. Gone.

Sal and Carla looked at one another with a mixture of sadness and confusion. They sat back down at the small square table staring at the folded newspaper before them. Carla looked at Sal who raised his brow and stared back. Carla furrowed her own brow and then slowly, carefully reached for the paper.

She methodically opened the printed media, ignoring the multitude of articles and side articles about Polar Innovations, Phoenix-Lamneth, Hemisphere Initiative, Douglass and Cronus. She flipped through the pages faster and faster until she reached the colorful Lifestyles section.

The rest of the paper fell away from her grasp as she fanned the section out on the table before her. Sal caught a glimpse of her face before her hands flew up to her mouth and muffled a cry. The look he saw was the same look she had at the moment Jon and Sarah Webb responded as a single entity to her coded inquiry months ago in the basement of the Golden Grand.

She rocked in her chair, her eyes wide and tearful as she simply stared into the jumble of printed pages. Sal quickly leaned over, terrified of what he may find but unable to resist. His mind emptied itself of all thought, apprehension and suspicion.

What he saw neither floored him nor frightened him. He only felt a sudden and painful pang of remorse, the sharp tang of regret experienced when one realizes that he has wasted so much on so little and completely missed the point. He hadn't felt like this since he learned of his father's death and wished that he could have had one more minute to tell him how he really felt.

Lying within the tangle of color pictures and artsy text were two small brown envelopes and one larger. Sal's initials were carefully printed across one of the smaller envelopes and Carla's initials across the other. The larger envelope simply read *M.W.* in the same careful script.

They recognized the envelopes from previous encounters and before they even spilled the contents into their shaking hands they knew what they were—one last false identity for each of them courtesy of Robert.

They scanned, in vain, the swarming crowd of commuters for any sign of Robert, but soon gave up and returned their attention to the unexpected gift before them. They each swept the contents of their identity envelopes into their coat pockets.

Sal then slowly reached for the third envelope. His fingers stroked the letters printed in black ink: *M.W.*

~ * ~

They sat in silence, the large brown envelope between them on the cluttered tile table as they toyed with the silverware and traced lines in the condensation of their water glasses with nervous fingers. Carla bit her lip, absently rereading the specials on the back of the narrow menu propped between the napkin holder and the various condiment bottles.

Sal watched through the dirty window as patrons ran across the parking lot through the sleet and into the café, stomping the slush from their feet and shrugging out of heavy overcoats as they leapt through the double doors and into the foyer. Everyone seemed happy, smiling and energetic, despite the dropping temperature and soggy weather.

Sal sighed and shifted his gaze across the table to Carla. She was already looking directly into his exhausted eyes, as if she had been watching for awhile. Her smile was strong, in contrast to the tired lines that blemished her otherwise smooth and tender face.

Sal returned the smile, hoping that it conveyed his true happiness and not the nagging foreboding concern he felt welling inside.

Carla cocked her head, concerned, but also with a flair of sensuality. Her eyes sparkled and healthy color flushed her high cheeks.

"You okay, baby?" she asked softly.

Sal nodded, slowly blinked and reached for her hands. She took them immediately in her own. The warmth made Sal nearly laugh with delight. He nodded, and then finally chuckled.

"Yeah," he began. "I guess I keep waiting for someone to walk through that door, all dark and serious, and arrest us. Or worse." He licked his dry lips.

Carla still smiled, though she cocked her thin brow and gave his hands a reassuring squeeze.

"I'm reluctant to allow the happiness to take hold, you know," Sal blurted out in a strained whisper. "I don't want to live in constant fear of someone putting an end to it all."

Carla nodded, leaned across the table and held her hand against Sal's cheek. Her warm touch caused the three days of facial stubble to stand erect. His skin tingled and his stomach tightened pleasantly.

"I know, I know," she cooed. "I feel the same way. But it's been nearly eighteen months now, and I think the dust has settled. We've remained safe and have begun to rebuild." She raised his face to hers with both hands and kissed him gently on the nose, both eyes and finally his mouth. Her lips were hot and soft, like sun-warmed velvet.

"I love you, Sal."

"Eduardo, remember," Sal corrected with a wry smirk. "I'm Eduardo."

She smiled and kissed him again, longer and more wet than the first.

"Of course, Eduardo." She breathed his name against his tongue, and his thighs quivered. His lap swelled.

When she fell back into her seat, her eyes held a dreamy, intoxicated glimmer. Sal drank her in with his own eyes, thirsty, and yet somehow satiated. At least for the moment.

"Only one more little piece of the equation, and then we never look back. Right?" Her hands fell to the brown envelope between them. She traced the letters with her long finger.

Sal reached for her hand and gave it a firm squeeze.

"Are you sure?" he asked softly, soberly.

Carla smiled, a different smile this time; one with conviction and determination. Her face firmed, expressing the strength and wisdom of an old soul.

"I've never been more certain in my life," she answered.

"I love you, Carla." Sal brought her hand to his lips and gently kissed each finger.

"You mean Susan," she corrected with a mock frown.

They both laughed lightly, and then fell into a comfortable silence. They held hands across the table, resting atop the brown envelope, the faded initials *M.W.* partially obscured between their intertwined fingers.

~ * ~

When the large glass door swung silently open, Carla rose unsteadily to her feet. She kept her hands clasped tightly to her bosom in a vain attempt to keep from nervously kneading them. Sal stood behind her, his firm hands holding her at both shoulders as they leaned into one another for emotional strength and physical support.

They watched as the short woman in a white coat passed through the doorway and into the reception room. Trailing behind her was an even smaller shadow. Her left arm extended back, and she calmly guided the young boy across the threshold. She brought him around to her front, both hands now resting gently on the his narrow shoulders.

She turned to Carla and Sal and flashed a warm, professional smile.

"Mr. and Mrs. Libertine," she began, by way of introduction, though none was needed. "This, of course, is Matthew."

Carla's eyes immediately welled with tears and a tsunami of emotion racked her mind, tightened her bowels and weakened her legs. Sal gripped her tightly and hugged her close, fighting off the blissful storm brewing within his own soul.

They simply stared at the young boy for what seemed like an eternity, terrified that any movement or words would break the spell and snap the illusion out of existence entirely.

The woman in white took the initiative, calmly crouching to whisper into the boy's ear. His face became animated with myriad expressions, both pleasant and surprised. The woman rose and softly patted the boy on the back, nudging him forward.

"Go on, now, Matthew," she said softly. "Go say hello to Mr. and Mrs. Libertine."

The boy never hesitated, walking confidently forward, pulling a small wheeled suitcase behind. His gait was sure and steady, not tentative or shuffling as you might expect from a seven-year-old meeting strangers.

As he approached, Carla finally regained her strength and her bearings. She crouched and smiled at the boy, though she was reluctant to extend her arms in a welcoming hug. They had been advised by the staff to avoid sudden and unplanned physical contact right away. She resisted the overwhelming urge to scoop the boy into her arms and hold him tightly. Sensing her tension, Sal placed his hand on her shoulder.

"Hello, Matthew," Carla said softly as the boy drew up and stopped a mere foot away. He smiled and looked Carla square in the eye. His directness caught her off guard and she faltered briefly before continuing. "My name is Susan. And this is Edward." She glanced at Sal as he smiled openly down at the boy. Matthew responded with a soft blink and a wider smile.

"Matthew, we'd like you to stay with us for awhile. Would that be okay? Would you like that?" Carla asked, not expecting a verbal response and actually unsure what, if any, she would receive.

Her stomach leapt into her throat when Matthew spoke, clearly and articulately.

"That would be great! I've been so excited." Matthew's eyes sparkled with anticipation and innocent bliss.

Sal and Carla suddenly looked toward the woman in white, both in wide-eyed shock.

The woman smiled and shrugged as she spread her arms in bewildered acceptance.

"I know, it's crazy. We're just as surprised, and quite frankly, stumped," she happily admitted. "He began talking intelligently nearly four months ago, but just recently has shown incredible leaps in overall cognitive abilities." She nodded unable to conceal her pride and pleasure. "He's reading at a fifth grade level and takes to math like a fish to water."

Matthew turned back to the woman in white and gave her a playful frown obviously meant to scorn her for the embarrassing appraisals.

The woman crossed her arms in front of her and continued, "In fact, he has shown such vast improvement that we think he would benefit much more from the social contact that you would provide rather than the structure of the Academy."

She sighed, and then smiled. "So, I've been authorized to approve an extension on your temporary custody to indefinite, with the caveat that you remain in contact with the Academy for the first six months. If Matthew remains on course and there are no issues, we'll move for your full custody within eight months."

Carla gasped, reached for Sal's hand, fumbled with his sweaty fingers and finally gripped tightly. They looked from one another, to Matthew, then back to the woman in white. She remained silent and smiling. She finally nodded twice as if to solidify the moment in reality.

"Well, I have to go and you three have a lot of catching up to do." The woman placed her hands in the deep pockets of her coat and smiled down at Matthew. Then she looked up at Carla and addressed her with a slight tone of wonder mixed with appreciation.

"You're doing a very brave thing. I want you to know that. I've known the Webb family for quite a while, since the beginning, really. I never realized that Sarah had a sister until we received your letter and documents." The woman smiled, her eyes sparkled with a sly glint—almost conspiratorial.

Carla fought back the reflex to blush, even though she knew that Robert's doctored paperwork was flawless. She felt Sal tense at her side.

"Funny how things turn out, I suppose." The woman simply watched the couple for a long moment. Sal could have sworn that she winked in his mind, telepathically acknowledging their ruse, and perhaps even approving.

The woman then turned to Matthew. "Goodbye, young man. I'll miss you."

Matthew grinned wide and waved at the woman in white.

"G'bye, Miss Lilly. Miss you, too." Then as an afterthought, he shouted in the excited tone of any seven-year-old, "Oh, say goodbye to Josh and Aran for me, will ya'?"

"Sure thing. Bye now." With that, the woman turned, swiped a thin card across the glass door's threshold and stepped through. They watched through the thick glass as she walked down a wide corridor and disappeared around a corner.

Sal bent to assist Matthew with his suitcase. "Want some help with that?" he offered.

"No thanks. Josh and Aran say that I should do as much for myself as possible. Says it builds characters. I guess like cartoons, maybe."

Sal smiled, rose and swept one hand toward the exit as he encircled Carla's waist with the other.

"Very well, then. After you, Master Webb."

They walked together out of the Children's Academy for Neurological Convalescence and into the bright, thawing cold of another California spring.

Epilogue

With the single small suitcase stowed in the back and Matthew securely buckled into the rear seat, Sal keyed the ignition of the rental. The magnetic impulsers hummed softly as the AirRide gently rose to a meter off the ground. Sal placed his arm on the seat back and turned around to look at Matthew.

The boy sat calmly, a slight smile on his face, the remnants of ketchup from a hearty meal crusted at the corners of his mouth. Sal took the opportunity to enjoy the rare moment. Matthew's innocence and beauty was a colossal contrast to the hellish weeks and months since passed. He suddenly thought of Jon and Sarah, and emotion shrank his throat.

Carla glanced over as Sal blinked away the rogue tear threatening to fall from his eye. She reached and deftly wiped away the moisture with a gentle flick of her pinky. She smiled as he blushed in embarrassment.

Sal sighed. The breath caught in his chest as a hitch of repressed emotion.

"So, where would you like to go?" he asked Matthew.

Matthew looked at Sal, narrowed his eyes and furrowed his brow in wonderment. "Why are you sad?" Matthew asked.

Sal blinked again and glanced quickly at Carla. Carla turned, and they both settled their chins on the back of the front seat gazing at the little boy in the back. Matthew quietly shifted his eyes from Sal back to Carla, inquisitive but patient.

"Not sad, Matthew," Sal began. "Just the opposite, really."

"We're both so happy. And relieved," Carla added. Then she wrinkled her brow and considered the young boy's expression as he nodded in understanding. His mannerisms and perception seemed advanced well beyond his age.

"And quite honestly, pretty amazed," she said placing her hand on Matthew's cheek. "You're such a surprising boy, Matthew."

"Yeah," he responded matter-of-factly. "Josh and Aran say that I'm actually a miracle. What do you think that means?"

Sal and Carla both frowned, hesitant for a moment and unsure of how to respond. Carla finally spoke, though carefully.

"Well, I suppose you are, in some respects." She then asked, "Do you know what that means? A miracle?"

Matthew frowned slightly giving his answer some thought. "Like the Burning Bush and walking on water? Or the special medicines to help people with bad diseases?"

"Yeah, those are some ways to think of miracles," Carla said.

"Josh and Aran say that there are all kinds of miracles. Some happen every day, right in front of us. But we just can't see them. Says we haven't learned how yet." Matthew glanced outside at that very moment, as if to witness a miracle occurring just outside of their hovering vehicle.

Carla chewed the inside of her cheek, tilting her head toward Sal for assistance. Sal's gaze was distant and pensive. Matthew glanced back from the window and spoke casually, "Josh and Aran like to go to the cabin at the lake when things get sad. Maybe you want to go there, too. I mean, if you're still sad." The boy smiled at Sal, a warm and caring smile full of unbelievable wisdom and maturity.

Sal blinked and shook his head, confused but unable to resist asking the obvious, "Matthew, who are Josh and Aaron?"

The boy smiled with the confident assurance of an elder. He ran his hands through his hair like a seasoned lawyer preparing for his closing statements, rubbed his chin with one fist and leaned forward as he answered.

"It's Aran, not Aaron." Matthew corrected, yet the pronunciation was hardly discernable. "They're a good friend who tell me things from time to time. Sometime they show me things when I don't understand the words."

Matthew folded his hands in his lap, cocked his head to the side and considered Sal intently. "They helped me to get past the block in my head so that I could talk better. They showed me dreams of things that always made me smile. They showed me pictures of you both and told me that you were friends and you would take me home someday." He smiled and shrugged.

Sal and Carla simply stared. The way that Matthew referred to his friends in the singular seemed intentional and left a feeling of strange terror in their bellies. Images of Jon and Sarah Webb resurfaced in their minds, and then suddenly the fear melted as they became fully aware of what the young boy was truly saying.

As comprehension filled their souls, the wonder and awe of the moment temporarily sedated them.

Sal mumbled something about anagrams, and then whispered, "Josh and Aran. Jon and Sarah."

After a few moments, or perhaps an eon, Carla looked to Sal. Their wide eyes met and searched each other's soul for a more reasonable explanation, and after finding none, they both turned to Matthew and gazed in humble acceptance.

"I can show you the way to the cabin, if you'd like. It's not far," Matthew offered.

Carla smiled, a tear falling down her cheek.

"That would be nice," Carla said.

Sal and Carla turned and faced front while Matthew returned to his observations of the outside world. Sal gently throttled the AirRide out of the parking lot and merged into traffic, heading north.

His mind raced with numbing questions, and he gently shook his head in attempts to grasp the wispy tendrils of amazing thoughts. Carla took his hand and gave it a squeeze. He glanced over and offered a tired smile. She nodded and then shrugged.

Simultaneously, they both gazed into the rearview mirror at the seven-year-old boy seated calmly in the back, smiling as he gazed out the window.

Meet C. W. Kesting

Mr. Kesting is originally from the Chicagoland area where he studied to become a nurse anesthetist. His anesthesia practice eventually brought him to rural Michigan, where he now lives with his wife and two children. Author of many short stories and essays, *Rubicon Harvest* is his first full length novel.